The Unlit Lamp

And Selected Stories

by Elisabeth Sanxay Holding

Introduction by Judith Rose Ardron

Stark House Press • Eureka California

THE UNLIT LAMP / SELECTED STORIES

Published by Stark House Press
1315 H Street
Eureka, CA 95501, USA
griffinskye3@sbcglobal.net
www.starkhousepress.com

THE UNLIT LAMP
Originally published and copyright © 1922 by
E. P. Dutton & Company, New York.

SELECTED STORIES
"Hanging's Too Good for Him" (Munsey's, Sept 1922)
"A Hesitating Cinderella" (Munsey's, July 1923)
"Like a Leopard" (Munsey's, Nov 1922)
"The Aforementioned Infant" (Munsey's, March 1923)
"Old Dog Tray" (Munsey's, May 1923)
"The Married Man" (Munsey's, Dec 1921)

ISBN: 978-1-944520-69-4

Book design by Mark Shepard, SHEPGRAPHICS.COM

First Stark House Press Edition: December 2018

FIRST EDITION

THE UNLIT LAMP

Claudine has been raised in a liberal, accepting family, and is used to getting her way. When she decides to marry Gilbert Vincelle, her mother is shocked. He just isn't right for her. Her mother sees him as a pompous, obstinate youth, humorless and hidebound. But Claudine is adamant. After the wedding, she quickly realizes her mistake. But her family is just as adamant—Claudine has made her choice, and now must adapt to her new husband. Which she does by withdrawing into herself, stifling her creative and carefree nature, and accommodating her stodgy new husband.

As the years go by, Claudine has three wonderful children, and pours all her energy and love into them instead. There is Bertie, the youngest, careless and flippant; Edna, the accepting middle child; and Andrée, her first born, her favorite…and headstrong, so like herself. But when Andrée falls in love with the wrong man, Claudine is quick to forget her own experiences, and does everything in her power to discourage her young daughter. After all, how could Andrée do this to her … and how will Claudine live without her?

The Unlit Lamp is an emotionally charged social drama from 1922, filled with the issues that burned so bright during the Roaring 20s as changing morals began to break down the traditional family structures of the past.

Also included are six stories from *Munsey* magazines of the 1920s, each one an incisive delight, filled with the contrary-but-well-meaning characters that Elisabeth Sanxay Holding portrays so well.

Elisabeth Sanxay Holding

I'm writing about someone I hardly met – my grandmother. I grew up with her daughters – my mother and my aunt – her darling girls. From them, I learned some of her myth as a mother and of her strength and struggles as a woman. She came from a dynasty of strong women who were independents spirits in a world that had rigid ideas of a woman's role and place in the economic order. From the depths of the Depression, she took responsibility for the economic survival of her family and harnessed her art, her craft, a questing mind and a social conscience to that goal. She was a free thinker; she loved to swim, at ease in the open sea.

When going through some family papers, I found two large cardboard boxes stacked high with lined foolscap sheets. Her small, close, uniform and intense writing covers sheet after sheet, ink now fading. These are her manuscripts. Hundreds of thousands of words, crafted by hand, bring her strength of will, her drive to produce into the room. What did it take to sustain that determination over those furlongs of faded foolscap? I want to put on record how hard won her achievements must have been.

She was a conscientious worker and craftswoman. She took her craft seriously, relying on deliberate thought, planning and hard work. She set herself the discipline of sitting down to write every morning. In the first seven months of 1928, she completely re-wrote a 90,000 word novel and wrote a 60,000 word serial and eleven short stories. Her day was organized into a routine that she strictly adhered to, not pausing for a cigarette or coffee until the appointed hour. Her daughters knew not to disturb her when she was working.

This was no hobby – it was an all consuming effort. She could not find peace without knowing she could provide for her mother, herself and her girls' future. The family fortunes were unpredictable, plagued by insecurity and lurching from the sale of one story to another. She experienced the misery of her writing getting stuck, while being tormented by a sense of haste to get working before she became penniless again. The Wall Street crash and the Depression left her penniless, unable to sell any work. Her family went without. Her sense of honour meant she agonized over the inevitable debts that accrued.

It was a wearing way to live. Her health was not good. In 1923, at the age of 34, she had pneumonia and was tormented by how she could continue to provide for her two little girls. By the time she was 39, she was experiencing extreme fatigue; her energy and confidence were low and she had trouble sleeping. Fatigue and depression continued to plague her but she strove to overcome all this by sheer force of will and strength of spirit driven by her fierce loyalty to her daughters. In spite of her ill health, her last novel was published in 1953, just two years before she died at the age of 65.

She rarely had the luxury of working without these financial pressures, of experiencing a sense of satisfaction from what she produced, of standing back and working on the big canvas of her novels. In her lifetime, she never reaped the benefits of great rewards or the critical acclaim that her work eventually came to attract. But her spirit and strength of character lives on in our family – six grandchildren, eight great grandchildren and four great great grandchildren. There is something of her in all of us. We are proud to celebrate this internationally esteemed writer as our own. I would wish for her to know that her work is still valued and enjoyed well into the 21st century. It's still out there engaging people's minds and intelligence. I would want her to rest reassured that her labour still bears fruit in her legacy to us, her family, and to her readers.

Judith Rose Ardron
Sheffield, England
October 2012

The Unlit Lamp

A Study of Inter-Actions

Elisabeth Sanxay Holding

BOOK ONE
THE BRIDE

CHAPTER ONE

A DANCE ON STATEN ISLAND IN 1890

"Good Lord!" said young Vincelle, turning up the collar of his overcoat. "I didn't know we were going to the ends of the earth."

"It's worth it," said his friend.

They sat in total darkness while the hired hack dragged them up the hills of Staten Island; it was a bitter night, and Vincelle wasn't prepared for it. He shivered and pulled the rug higher over his knees. He was taking a little more than his share of that rug, but Pendleton, feeling himself more or less responsible for the cold, made no complaint. It was he who had persuaded Vincelle to make the arduous trip from Brooklyn to Staten Island, to attend a dance, and to see the prettiest girl there was to see. And Vincelle was a fellow accustomed only to cities, to warm, well-lighted houses and theatres and swift transitions in street cars and hansom cabs; he was, moreover, not adaptable and not compliant.

He looked out of the window with a sort of dismay; nothing but bare trees against a sinister night sky; now and then a lighted house in a big garden. The horse went steadfastly forward, with a monotonous jerking of his head; outside on the box loomed the swathed and shapeless figure of the coachman, who didn't appear to be driving, but to be waiting to get somewhere.

"Is it much farther?" asked Vincelle, in an ominous voice.

"It's not really far from the ferry," said his friend. "Only being uphill all the way makes it seem longer."

"I'm numb with cold ... Why the devil wasn't I satisfied with the pretty girls in Brooklyn?"

"It's worth it, I tell you!" Pendleton assured him, earnestly. "I've never had such good times in my life as I've had at the Masons'. Informal, but a good tone, you know. Charming people!"

Vincelle didn't answer at all. He made up his mind to be very critical; he felt that the Masons needed to be almost superhumanly charming to compensate for so much discomfort.

They began the ascent of an outrageous hill, and the cheerful Pendleton, looking out of his window, announced that they were "practically there—

the house is at the top of this hill." He turned down the collar of his coat and gave his silk hat a careful rub with his sleeve; he began to stir about under the rug. But Vincelle made no preparations whatever; he intended to look cold and uncomfortable; it was not for him to please, but to be pleased. The carriage entered a gravel driveway with a sudden burst of speed, and drew up under a porte cochère. Lights were shining from the long windows curtained in white, and the sound of their wheels had brought a man-servant to the door.

For a moment Vincelle lingered while Pendleton made his arrangement with the driver, and then they entered the house together. And it astonished Vincelle. It was so extraordinarily full of light and colour; on either side of the hall were open doors, showing big rooms brightly carpeted, with blazing fires and flowers everywhere. From some distant region he heard voices, laughter, footsteps. The man-servant ushered them into a smaller room, carpeted in red, and lined with book shelves, where on little table before the hearth stood a huge punch bowl; he proffered, and they accepted; then he led them up the fine stairway to a bedroom which was hospitably ready for them with a roaring fire. He returned with a jug of hot water.

"Dinner in half an hour, gentlemen," he said, and went away.

No use denying that Vincelle was impressed. Certainly they didn't do things in this way at home. Jugs of hot water, instead of a chilly and possibly very distant bathroom, wood fires instead of hot-air registers and gas logs, flowers in February, instead of potted palms and rubber plants. Moreover, this idea of leaving it to a servant to welcome guests impressed him by its casualness; his mother always received visitors with ceremony, as soon as they crossed the threshold. He recognized here something exotic and rather disturbing; he got up and went over to the bureau, where he could critically regard himself, for he had decided that, after all, he would try to please.

He was a handsome fellow, very dark; he had heavy features and a sullen and obstinate mouth; he was not very tall, but stalwart and powerful. He was twenty-five and though he looked even younger, owing perhaps to that tragic sulkiness, he had a thoroughly adult and responsible air. He was no fop, like Pendleton; there was sobriety and decorum in the cut of his coat; he was even then every inch the business man. Evening dress did not become his thick-set figure, but he was naturally not aware of that.

"Do they have a gong—or send after you when dinner's ready?" he asked, still intent upon his image.

"They do not! You're supposed to know, and if you're late, they don't wait for you. Come on! You're lovely enough!" said Pendleton. He surveyed his friend good-humouredly; it didn't disturb him that Vincelle was handsome and he was not, or that Vincelle had money and was almost sure to make more. The Masons wouldn't care about that. He was consoled by certain advantages of his own; he was lively, cheerful, witty in a very mild way; everyone liked him; he was, in an innocuous sense, a "ladies' man," master of the utterly lost art of polite flirtation. He was tall, slender, elegant, with a long, sharp nose and a bulging forehead; his hair and eyebrows were so light as to look almost white; he had wrinkles about his little blue eyes; it is of no significance to say that he was twenty-seven, because he was ageless, and would be in no way different ten or twenty years later.

"Come *on!*" he said, again.

In great decorum, conscious of their immaculate appearance and their value as eligible and admirable young men, they descended the stairs and entered the drawing-room. The subtle air of excitement which Vincelle had felt upon entering the house was intensified here, the same abundance of light and flowers, and a big fire. But with the addition now of an agreeable babel of voices.

Pendleton led him forward to a stout lady in black silk, with an august, kindly face and a very high colour.

"Mrs. Mason," he said, "may I present—"

"This must be Mr. Vincelle," she said, cheerfully, and held out her hand. "You're just in time. We're about to have dinner."

And she took the arm of a young man in spectacles and led the way into the dining-room, followed by all the others, without order or ceremony. She was not the aristocratic person the young man had expected, but she was dignified, and that sufficed for a mother. No more introducing was done, and he sat down between two girls who talked to him immediately and agreeably. But he couldn't respond; he was a little out of his element; he was accustomed to formality, ceremony, an air of sobriety, and it didn't agree with him to be plunged suddenly into the midst of a dozen strange people, without, one might say, his passport. If people didn't know who he was, then where was his prestige?

He looked about him. There were certainly a dozen people, all of them young, with the exception of the hostess, and a queer, bearded man who was unaccountably dressed in a rough grey suit and who likewise had the effrontery to wear run-down morocco slippers. That was bad; that was odd and eccentric, and everything he objected to most strongly. But the two girls beside him addressed him as "Professor," and if he were a professor, that explained it, though without justifying it. His glance left this unpleasant object, and sought for his friend, and found him opposite, lost in conversation with a girl. That must be *the* girl, of course! He stared at her, entranced. Pendleton hadn't exaggerated in the least. She was charming, fascinating! Mentally he made use of the adjective which probably four out of every five of the young lady's admirers used. He called her "fairylike."

As a matter of fact, she wasn't quite pretty, but no male person had discovered that. She destroyed judgment. She was a little, slight thing, rather pale, with reddish hair that stood out like an aureole of fine copper threads. She had warm brown eyes, the kindly eyes of her mother; small, pretty features. But her charm and her distinction lay in her wonderful animation. One could, he thought, look at her for hours, and never tire of her gestures, of the change of expression on her mobile face. She was witty, too; or it seemed wit to him, her dear little grimaces and her jolly, good-natured banter. No, he didn't blame Pendleton in the least; she *was* worth the trip. Her dress satisfied his exacting requirements too; it was white, much beruffled, cut a little low in the neck, with short sleeves, and it had a train. It was the dress of a young lady, for in these days there really weren't any girls.

She raised her eyes and met this new young man's glance, and smiled at him—a hostess's smile, friendly, but a little impersonal. He was gratified to see that she didn't appear at all serious with Pendleton; she was, he thought, somewhat mocking. And from that hour, he decided to consider his friend's well-known worship as a thing of no consequence, simply one of Pendleton's innumerable little loves—a sort of joke....

It was an excellent dinner; he couldn't remember a better, and it was surprisingly abundant. He was accustomed to frugality, and more or less austerity. His mother had finer linen, more silver, more magnificence, but never had she had on her table a feast like this, such honest, unpretentious excellence in food. There was one wine served throughout the meal, which was not according to his standard of elegance, but it was a good wine, beyond denial.

When the meal was finished, the ladies rose and fluttered away.

"Not much time, you know!" said Mrs. Mason, warningly, as she left. "It's after eight!"

The professor then produced a box of cigars and a decanter and they lingered for a time in the warm room, very content. But the sound of carriage wheels interrupted them; they threw their cigars into the fire and went into the big room across the hall, where Mrs. Mason was waiting. A succession of bundled-up forms went past and up the stairs, descending in due time as more young ladies; the room began to fill. Pendleton was busy taking his friend about and introducing him here and there, not leaving him until his card was quite filled and he had secured two dances with Miss Mason herself.

What was it about this particular dance which made it different from all the other dances he had attended? Why did he have such a surpassingly enjoyable evening that he looked back upon it with a smile all his life?

There were pretty, lively girls, a floor like glass, good music, a matchless supper; but there was nothing unusual in that. No, there was some quite special quality about it; a charming festivity, a revel wholly youthful and innocent and happy. He held the adorable Claudine in his arms for two waltzes; he had very little to say to her, but he was by nature taciturn; he listened instead. He was lost....

The carriages began coming back and the dance guests to take their leave. He watched one group after another of bright faces vanish, then at length the front door closed upon the last one, and Mrs. Mason, with a sigh that was half laughter, sank into a chair.

"Mercy!" she said. "I'm getting too old for this, children!"

There were only the house guests left now, and the family, standing about the big room. There were himself and Pendleton, the lovely Claudine and her mother, and five other persons, whom he was beginning to be able to place now; there were a daughter and her husband, there were two bosom friends of Claudine's, and the incomprehensible young man in spectacles.

"It's after two o'clock," said Mrs. Mason. "There's a little sort of breakfast laid out in the dining-room for you young people, if you're hungry again. But don't be long over it, and don't disturb your father as you come upstairs. Good-night, all of you!"

She rose heavily.

"And, Lance, you'll put out the lights and lock up?" she added.

The young man in spectacles nodded.

"Mother," said Claudine, "it was lovely! It's so dear of you!"

Her mother looked at her for a moment with a faint smile.

"You're only young once!" she said.

Trite words, certainly, and none of her hearers felt their force. Her other daughter kissed her warmly, her son-in-law escorted her to the foot of the stairs, and her stout, black-clad figure was seen ascending, wearily, a little bent.

She puzzled Vincelle; she had no elegance; he felt sure that his mother would call her "ordinary." Yet there was about her a dignity, an authority, he had never seen surpassed. And her way of entertaining you had a sort of vigour and originality about it; he felt that she didn't care much what other people did, or what was correct, but was concerned only with comfort, gaiety, and this unostentatious, invincible dignity of hers.

"Come on!" said Claudine, and they all followed her across the hall.

A new mood had settled upon them; they weren't conscious of being tired, but they were, all of them, subdued, inclined to a pleasant seriousness. The room was shadowy, except for a hanging gas lamp above the table, and the glow of the fire. They sat about the table, hungry in spite of the hearty supper they had consumed a few hours ago, and the young man in spectacles began to talk in an unaccountable and eccentric fashion about Pre-historic Man, and drew a picture of him, cowering and shivering on such nights as this.

"A life of incessant fear," he said. "Imagine that. Never to know security. Never to see any possibility of safety. No chance of old age."

Vincelle listened, but he felt vaguely that Pre-historic Man was rather blasphemous and Darwinian and free-thinking. It was also displeasing to observe that Claudine was interested.

"It's safety that's made us develop, isn't it, Lance?" she asked.

He shook his head.

"It's safety that's making us decline," he said. "It's making us soft and weak and dull."

"But if we weren't secure, we couldn't have any art," said Claudine.

"Art!" said the young man, with a harsh laugh. "Art! The opium dreams of drugged, idle people!"

The married sister interposed, laughing.

"Don't be so serious, Lance! Claudine, dear, you're not attending to us!"

For Claudine was sitting at the head of the table, dispensing tea and coffee. The sparkling brightness had gone from her face, she looked pale and a little weary, but lovelier than ever. Vincelle was now disposed to admire her more seriously; she had poise and dignity, and she could talk in a way to startle him. She had something to say even on the topic of Pre-historic Man; she had ideas which *he* couldn't have had.

"Life lost its meaning," Lance went on, "when it ceased to be a struggle."

"For Heaven's sake, when did it cease to be a struggle?" said Pendleton. "They forgot to tell me. I thought it was still pretty hard to get a foothold."

Lance ignored him.

"Man waged a magnificent and heroic struggle with Nature," he said, "but was defeated."

"But was it really so heroic, Lance? It was an involuntary struggle, it hadn't any aim. It seems to me that now, when we're conscious, and can really try to improve—"

"We don't. We can't. It's too late. We're in the final stage of evolution. We went the wrong way."

"Lance is a paleontologist," murmured the girl next to Vincelle. "He's wonderful, isn't he? But so gloomy!"

Vincelle had no idea what a paleontologist was, but he didn't like them. He felt horribly out of it. He couldn't be learned, and he wouldn't be funny, like Pendleton. He was quite aware that he wasn't making any sort of impression here. Claudine must have become conscious of his dissatisfaction—perhaps he showed it—for she suddenly addressed him.

"What do you think, Mr. Vincelle? Do you think we're a miserable, doomed remnant?"

He flushed.

"I've never given it much thought," he said. "I've been busy keeping up with business."

His poor little remark sounded so sulky and infantile that even he was confused.

"And politics," he added, in an attempt to sound broader-minded.

Lance drew out his watch.

"I'm going to lock up now," he said. "Five minutes before the lights go out!"

There was a chorus of good-nights.

"Don't forget that Father's asleep!" warned the married sister, as Claudine and her two bosom friends went chattering up the stairs. Pendleton and Vincelle followed them and turned down the hall to their own room. Pendleton began flinging off his clothes, but Vincelle sat motionless in an armchair before the fire.

"Who is that fellow they call Lance?" he asked.

"Oh! Him? He's a cousin. The Professor's protégé. He lives with them, you know. Nice chap; a little bit crazy. But then the old man is too. Both scientists, you know. Professor's a botanist. Come to bed, old boy, and get that light out, will you?"

Tall and lanky in his night shirt, Pendleton stretched tremendously.

"Come to bed!" he said, again. "Come and get your beauty sleep, my boy. Your face is your fortune, you know."

Vincelle answered him with a sudden burst of anger.

"Oh, yes, but I'm not quite a fool, you know. A fellow can't hold a position in a business like mine without some trace of brains. I may not know much about Science, but I know a damn lot about the Art of Making Money. And I'm not a boor, either," he added. "Hitherto I've always managed to hold my own in any sort of social gathering. I've been considered worthy of a word now and then...."

A loud, artificial snore from his friend cut him short. He turned out the light and undressed in the firelight. But he felt his face burn in the dark with a resentment he was not able to analyze.

CHAPTER TWO

A VINCELLE IN HIS NATURAL HABITAT

He waked the next morning to a marvelous peace. Pendleton was still sleeping beside him, and there was no other sound but his quiet breathing. Vincelle felt very wide awake; he got up instantly, and he was glad to believe, from the silence, that it was still very early and that he would be able to get home before eleven. He had forgotten to wind his watch the night before and it had stopped, but he fancied that he could sense the time. He went over to one of the windows and pulled up the shade with a rattle; it wasn't his nature to consider the sleep of friends. It was a bright, frosty morning, very clear; before him lay a neat back garden, and behind it a stable. Not a sign of life. He drew on his socks, always the first step of his routine, and suddenly a disturbing thought assailed him. He went over to Pendleton and shook him and shook him until he opened his eyes. Pendleton swore at him.

"Look here!" said young Vincelle. "Where do I shave?"

"Don't shave!" said Pendleton. "Go to sleep again like a Christian."

"No. I told Mother I'd try to get home in time to take her to church."

Pendleton pulled out his watch from under his pillow. "Ah!" he shouted, exultantly. "Half past eleven already, my son! Foiled!"

Vincelle frowned.

"I haven't missed in years," he said. "Poor old lady! She counts on it."

"Now perhaps you'll shut up and let me go to sleep again."

"Where can I shave? Is there a bathroom?"

"Ring the bell," said Pendleton. "And someone'll bring you hot water."

But when he was dressed in the clothes he had brought with him in his bag, he hesitated to go down alone in this strange house. He strolled about the room, smoking, until Pendleton was ready, and they descended together. There wasn't a soul to be seen.

"They've all gone to church," said Pendleton.

This struck Vincelle as grossly inhospitable, someone should have been there to attend to him. But a nice little servant brought them an excellent breakfast in the dining room and after it they sat comfortably in front of the fire, enjoying cigars from an open box on the sideboard.

"As soon as they come back, we'll go," said Pendleton. And they did so. Mrs. Mason offered them the use of the family omnibus in which they had returned from church, but Pendleton said they'd rather walk. She did not invite them to stop for dinner, which Vincelle considered impolite. If she didn't want them, why couldn't she simply invite them in a half-hearted, unacceptable manner?

"I must thank you for a most enjoyable time," he said ceremoniously.

She smiled and held out her hand.

"Come again!" she said.

Claudine, too, gave him her hand, but her glance and her smile were lamentably devoid of significance. Evidently he wasn't, for her, a special person; he was nothing but a young man who had come down for a dance. They set out down the hill, and he was able now to gain an idea of the place at his leisure. It was a big wooden house with a cupola on top; it had no pretension to beauty or architectural style, it was in fact, quite hideous and ungainly, made of grey clapboards with a slate roof; square, except that on one side a little greenhouse was built out from the veranda. The garden, too, although large, was not like the gardens of other people: there was no fountain, no nicely set out shrubs. There was a beautiful old box hedge enclosing it, but inside it looked irregular and untidy.

Pendleton was talking cheerfully.

"What do you think of her?" he asked.

"Very attractive," said Vincelle.

"Did you ever see anyone like her?" he pursued.

Vincelle admitted that he hadn't.

"I don't mind telling you I'm pretty hard hit," said Pendleton.

This was something his friend had very much wished not to hear.

"What about *her*?" he asked, briefly.

Pendleton groaned.

"She's such a little flirt!" he said. "Of course, I'm not in a position to marry now, anyway. I'm not making enough to keep myself. And by the time I can ask her ... with all these fellows hanging round her all the time ... Lord!"

Vincelle considered this frankness unmanly and indecorous. Never would he have admitted a liking for a young lady until he was certain that she returned it.

They crossed on the ferry, standing outside in the fine, cold air, on the deck of the ark-shaped old boat. They reached New York and just caught the Wall Street ferry and at last disembarked in the familiar air of Brooklyn. They both lived in the august Columbia Heights district, Pendleton in a house which was respectable, but no more, and Vincelle in a fine one, on a corner, with a garden quite twenty feet wide. He respected this garden, because it represented extra property and also because it kept them aloof from all neighbors; through the high iron fence could be seen its winter desolation, a complete and woeful barrenness. At the best of times it was hardly an oasis, nothing grew in it, and nothing was intended to grow in it, except a wretched ancient wistaria, two bushes of Japanese holly and a tall shrub, dry and dead. The common use of the garden was as a place in which the house plants could stand, the rubber trees and palms and orange trees in tubs. Every Spring old Mrs. Vincelle bought a number of potted geraniums and had them planted in a certain bed where they blossomed, mangily, for a month or two.

He bade his friend good-bye here and ran up the brown stone steps, opened the door with his latch key, and entered into a chill vault, dark, muffled, dismal. He hung up coat and hat on a gigantic piece of furniture which towered up to the ceiling and which was at once a hat rack, a pier-glass, a bureau with six drawers and a low table with a marble top. Then he ran up the thickly carpeted stairs to a bedroom on the floor above where he knew he would find his mother.

Sure enough, there she was, sitting in her rocking chair, with folded hands, looking out on to the quiet street, a fragile little old lady of sixty with a contemptuous, wizened little face and melancholy brown eyes. She was dressed in her Sunday dress of black silk with a white lace vest, she wore her best earrings, her diamond brooch, and a fine wool shawl bundled about her narrow shoulders.

"Well!" she said with a smile.

Her son approached and kissed her reverently.

"I was very sorry, Mother, to miss taking you to church," he said, "but I didn't wake up until eleven. It was three o'clock when we got to bed."

She raised her eyebrows.

"Did they dance on Sunday morning? Well, I dare say no one thinks of such things any longer. However, it didn't matter, Gilbert. I had a touch of rheumatism, I shouldn't have gone anyway."

"Pshaw!" he said solicitously. "Your shoulder again, Mother?"

"It doesn't matter. Sit down, Gilbert, and tell me all about it."

He sat down opposite her, smoothing his sleek black head.

"Oh! The usual thing!" he said.

"Are they nice people?"

"Oh, yes, nice enough. The father's a professor."

"That may mean anything," said the old lady. "I've known some professors who were very nice people and some who were impossible. Did you see that girl that Ashley is so enthusiastic about?"

"Yes, I saw her."

"Mrs. Pendleton tells me he's head over heels in love with her."

"Oh, well, you know what Ashley is. He's always in love."

"Is she as pretty as he imagines?"

"I don't know what he imagines," said her son, a little peevishly. "She's a very attractive girl. Look here, Mother, I haven't had any dinner."

"Mercy me," cried the old lady. "And it's nearly four o'clock! Why didn't you stay in Staten Island? Our dinner's over and done with hours ago. Ring the bell, Gilbert!"

He did so and it was promptly answered by a woman servant.

"Fetch Miss Dorothy," she said.

She had risen in her agitation regarding her son's shocking hunger and began pottering about the room, frowning, lifting up little articles from the bureau and the table with trembling old hands. It was a fine, big room with a Turkish rug on the floor and an assemblage of solid walnut furniture. It was crowded with knickknacks, photographs, a hundred and one mementoes of her past life. It hadn't the look of a bedroom, for the bureau was hidden behind a screen and the bed was a folding one, displaying nothing but an immense bevelled mirror set in a broad frame of polished wood. Her son had never, even in childhood, seen the least trace of disorder in this room.

"Pshaw!" said the old lady, "she's asleep again, I suppose. The older she grows the lazier she gets. She's forever creeping upstairs and going to sleep.... All nonsense.... Here am I so troubled with insomnia that I don't get five hours rest out of the night and I don't think anyone's even seen me taking a nap.... Well, Dorothy!"

A woman stood smiling in the doorway, a stout, grey-haired woman with a tousled, guilty air, a cousin, who earned her bitter bread as a companion for various relatives. She was always spoken of as staying with Aunt This and Cousin That; after two or three months she was sent away, with a sort of rage engendered by her submission, her poverty and her stupidness, and then when the memory had worn off, she was recalled. Her usefulness was never admitted, but always exploited.

"Why, Gilbert!" she said, with an air of pleased surprise. "I didn't hear you come in!"

"I don't think you'd hear a sound if the house was on fire!" said the old lady, tartly. "It's dangerous, the way you sleep. We could all be murdered in our beds, and it wouldn't disturb you."

"Why, Cousin Selina, I wasn't asleep I was writing letters!"

"Well, now perhaps you'll be able to attend to this poor boy. He hasn't had any dinner. And I'd calculated on his having a hearty meal there, so I hadn't planned for a very big supper. And Katie's out. Run down to the kitchen and see if you and Mary can't fix up something nice for him. And tell Mary supper at five instead of six."

Miss Dorothy looked terrified. She knew so well the very meagre resources of this household where there was never quite enough of anything, where each egg was mentally numbered.

"I'll do my best," she said, doubtfully, and vanished.

"Now run upstairs and get ready!" said the old lady.

There were three big, unoccupied bedrooms on her floor, but it had seemed to her, and to Gilbert, more fitting for a bachelor to live on the floor above. He had a very large room there, furnished with austere majesty, an ugly and uncomfortable room which he accepted as he accepted everything else in the life his mother had arranged for him. There was a black dressing-room attached, furnished with a marble wash basin and two big clothes presses: it was supposed to belong to his room and the one next, jointly, but as Miss Dorothy now occupied that adjoining room, the second door was well bolted.

He sat down in a large, high-backed rocking chair with a tapestry seat, one of the many pieces of furniture sent upstairs in disgrace after long service. He began, absent-mindedly, to rock and to think—about Claudine. His thoughts were all distressful and clouded; he felt himself irresistibly attracted by that gay little creature, and he resented it. He resented everything about that dance, the casualness, the cheerfulness; his own home seemed to him admirably correct and majestic. He felt quite unaccountably insulted. These people had treated him in cavalier fashion....

He was naturally inclined to sulkiness. It was his refuge from an incomprehensible world. And perhaps his great capacity for being offended came from an equally pathetic source, perhaps it was a sort of protest made by his youth and his manhood against his bondage. He wasn't aware of the bondage: he believed that his relations with his mother were ideal and that he "humoured" her in a respectful way. But as a matter of fact, he was less free, he was more under her dominion, than even Miss Dorothy. It would scarcely be an exaggeration to say that he was hypnotized. He had been led to believe that he was happy; the poor, sullen lonely creature. He never laughed: he very seldom smiled; he hadn't a spark of humour or gaiety in him. Pendleton privately considered him "heavy," and heavy he was. It hadn't prevented him from making a few conquests though. His handsome face, his invincible innocence and possibly his money and his well-known ability in business had won two or three little hearts; but though he had been flattered, he hadn't been much touched. He had never before in his life experienced anything like this; this was positively uncomfortable. He was obsessed and annoyed by the memory of Miss Mason of Staten Island. Her sparkling face, her liquid voice, the surprising novelty of her had completely captured him. The idea of a girl as pretty and popular and charming as she being able to talk with a—what was it—a paleontologist in so grave a way....

Summoned by Miss Dorothy he descended through the silent house to the dining-room in the basement, always used when the family was alone, and attacked the dismal feast set before him. He was silent because he was silent by nature, having nothing to communicate, and the two women were silent, for what in Heaven's name had they to say to him or to each other? Meals in that household were perfunctory and ascetic; the old lady didn't like to waste money on food, it needn't be either appetizing or nourishing so long as it was according to tradition, and decent. They finished, and all went solemnly up-stairs again; the little old lady first, noiseless over the thick carpet, incredibly slight and unsubstantial, then her son, the staircase creaking under his heavy tread, the quiet darkness reverberating with his loud, masculine cough, and last of all Miss Dorothy.

They went into the back drawing-room and sat down in the chairs they invariably occupied. The old lady closed her eyes, for that nap she always took, and always denied. Miss Dorothy, owing to the fact of its being Sunday, couldn't take up her fancy work, which was then one of her strongest claims to gentility and gave her at least a semblance of elegant uselessness, and she too closed her eyes, not to sleep, but to continue in her weary and muddled brain her intricate calculations, "planning" she called it. She had to plan for a new black skirt. Could she manage with that alpaca Cousin Selina had given her and if not could she possibly spare the money to buy a new one? She hadn't a salary; simply, when she left to stay with the next relative, Cousin Selina would give her something in an envelope and it might be enough or it might be very little. She had no occupation for her thoughts but her planning; poor soul. She hadn't a single interest in life.

As for Gilbert, he being a man, had to read the Sunday newspapers and to smoke. He had an arm-chair and a foot-stool and a smoking stand, placed ready for him, in a good light. But his peace was gone. He was sunk in black depression.

CHAPTER THREE

GILBERT GOES A-WOOING

"Well ..." said the old lady. "She's very—*peculiar*."
There was no word her son could have disliked more; he frowned.
"Why?" he demanded. "In what way? How is she 'peculiar'?"
"She's been brought up," the old lady began, and stopped. "After all, you're the one to be suited, Gilbert. You're marrying her, not I. If you've got it into your head that she's the only woman on earth to make you happy, very well. Marry her. And I only hope you *will* be happy."
"Yes," he said, "that's likely, if you're going to quarrel with her."
"Gilbert," said the old lady, "I've never quarreled with anyone in my life."
True enough, he was obliged to admit it. He saw that he had used a

wrong word. She didn't quarrel, she didn't argue. But she conquered. And when she disapproved of people, she changed them. He had never tried to understand her methods, but he had seen the results. He supposed it was force of character and that it must be admirable and beneficent.

"You needn't worry about that, my boy," she went on. "I've never yet had a word of disagreement with any of my sons- or daughters-in-law."

"I know it, Mother. But living under the same roof ... and she's been brought up very differently."

"Yes; just as I said," the old lady observed. "Very peculiar.... However, if you've made up your mind, my boy, there's no use talking about it. I'll do my best, as I always have done and always expect to do."

Her son believed this; he had never doubted that she was a perfectly noble, perfectly wise and magnificent woman and he worshipped her. There was an inscrutable and malicious smile on her shrunken lips; the changeless, infinitely remote smile of god-like amusement at earth's follies which one sees on the face of a bronze Buddha. She had a majesty beyond the need of charm or of fashion. She belonged to an old Brooklyn family which had become aristocratic by reason of having lived in the same place for four generations, and she had married into a similar one. She had always been rich and immeasurably secure, living isolated in the big house on "The Heights" like the somewhat ferocious monarch of a desert isle, an obscure and uncomfortable existence in which nothing was accomplished and nothing enjoyed. She disdained society as frivolous; and all luxury was to her abomination. She made, she said, a "proper use" of her money.

Her chief claims to moral excellence were these: that she had borne six children, and that she had lived for sixty years; and above all because of her marvelous lack of sensibility, an imperviousness which no actual image of Buddha could have surpassed. She had looked on at suffering, anguish, despair, unmoved, and that was fortitude; she had witnessed birth, death, without a gleam of curiosity or speculation, and that was common sense. She had been "just" toward her little children with all the blindness proper to that virtue.

"It makes no difference why you do things," she always said. "A thing's *right*, or it's *wrong*. I don't want to hear your reasons."

He recognized the old familiar attitude now, the old air of saying— "Very well; go your own way, and learn by bitter experience!" Within herself he felt she was saying— "You'll have to reap what you sow. You'll make your bed and you'll have to lie in it." And so on.

"You don't approve of my marrying her then, do you?" he asked.

"You're twenty-five years old," said his mother, "You're old enough to decide for yourself."

He felt more irritated than his ideas of filial piety allowed. He drank his coffee slowly and reminded himself that his mother was a widow and that all her other children had married and left her. His thoughts were readily distracted that day, though, and goodwill very easy to him. He sat back, lighted a cigar and looked about him, at the dismal basement dining-room, used for all the family meals, with its barred windows through which one could see the feet of passersby, and the horrible walnut buffet and sideboard and the massive square table, and the twelve chairs, three invalided and permanently in corners, the faded carpet that had once been upstairs, the immense crayon picture of a lion's head, the general economical hideousness of this room which proclaimed the old lady's genial idea that anything was good enough for the inmates of the house, and the owner. He had never liked the room, but he fancied it this morning as it *might* be—a Paradise, with the charm, the youth, the mysterious strangeness of a young wife in it.

Here, without question, the young wife would have to come, because Gilbert could not and would not consider leaving his mother alone. And to be candid, dared not. He owed everything to his mother, he said. Hadn't she made sacrifices to give her children every advantage, lessons of various sorts, and unstinted moral advice? She talked candidly of moulding their characters, and that is just what she had done. She had moulded them in her own image, supreme and devastating blasphemy. They were all of them like fainter copies of her own sharply written character. This man sitting across the breakfast table from her now was literally made by her. By nature credulous and imitative, he had lent himself perfectly to her manipulations; he thought exactly as she had taught him to think; he disagreed with her in some points, because she had taught him that a man must in certain respects disagree with women; he knew things, he had had experiences unknown to her, but she had caused him to believe, sadly, that a man must so conduct himself. She had taught him that, as a man, he must disappoint his mother. She despised him a little, but she certainly, undeniably loved him.

She looked at him, stalwart black-avised fellow, with his heavy brows and his obstinate mouth. Wasn't he *manly*, she thought!

"Ah, well!" she said with a sigh. "No doubt it's all for the best, Gilbert."

He finished his breakfast in manly silence,—which no decent woman dare trouble—and getting up, went round the table to his mother, dutifully to kiss her good-bye.

"I'm sorry you didn't—take to her, Mother," he said, a little grieved.

"Well," she answered. "*You're* marrying her, Gilbert, not *I*."

"If she'll have me," he said. "I haven't asked her yet, you know."

He had long ago promised his mother never to propose marriage to any woman without telling her first. And it was in loyalty to this promise that he had lured Miss Mason from Staten Island to Brooklyn under pretense of showing her a wonderful picture on exhibition in a department store—a Dutch peasant sweeping her cottage, and the motes in the sunbeam were reputed marvelously life-like. It was a quite natural thing, after gazing at this picture for fifteen awkward minutes, to suggest a call on his mother living so near. The old lady had heard more than one mention from her son of this Miss Mason from Staten Island, and she knew, and Miss Mason knew, that this was a visit of inspection.

After it was over, and the beloved young lady had left the house on his arm, he had, of course, to take her back to Staten Island. And never had she been so nice to him, so kind, so gracious, never had he felt so encouraged. The next evening was her birthday, and he had been invited to the little dance by her mother.

"Why don't you come to supper?" Miss Mason had suggested. And they had both turned red and become silent, a little startled and alarmed. Because they knew, both of these, that this would be the time....

"She may refuse me," he said, and with a glance his mother saw all the anguish he was trying to hide.

"I don't think she will!" said she with a most detestable smile, which fully expressed her opinion of Miss Mason and her matrimonial hopes. "I don't think there's much fear of *that!*"

But Gilbert knew better, and he spent a day of black misery in his office. As the afternoon wore on he became sure that she would refuse him. She had such a lot of fellows hanging around—and all of them had those qualities which he lacked, those fascinating social graces.... He so silent, so unready, a clumsy dancer, a man interested in nothing but business—and the Republican party. He dreaded, he shrank from asking her, and yet he was feverishly impatient to do so before those other fellows had a chance.

Never was there a lover more humble than he. And he liked to be humble; he liked to think how a great, powerful fellow like himself could be brought low by a slip of a girl. It was a wonderful example, he thought, of the Power of Love. Well, who knows....?

He had been seeing a great deal of Miss Mason during the past three months. He had gone with Pendleton to make their party call in due form and he had found her on that occasion more friendly and more intimate. It was a Sunday afternoon, and she was alone with Lance. Her mother and father, she said, had gone out for a walk in the Silver Lake woods—which Vincelle thought a very peculiar thing for an elderly couple to do, above all, on a Sunday afternoon, when respectable people were best invisible. There were a good many things about this family which he could not approve of; Lance was one of these. That thin sunburnt young man in spectacles with his gloomy face and didactic air jarred upon him beyond reason. He had observed too, that Lance had been reading to his cousin, in cosy intimacy, before the fire in the library.

But Claudine had been remarkably kind to him, and gentle and friendly. Moreover, Lance had had the decency to remove himself and his big book. Pendleton, of course, monopolized the talk, with his flippant nonsense, but Gilbert felt that that did him no harm. He felt that he, sitting in silence, with only a word now and then, a sensible word, mind you, appeared more manly, and he was right! He touched the heart of the lively young lady; she felt suddenly rather sorry for him, and because he was stupid she fancied him more honest than others. She quite cordially invited him, to come again.

He did, and this time alone. He didn't even mention the fact to Pendleton, and when Pendleton learned of it he took it amiss.

"I introduced you there," he said, "I didn't think you'd go behind my back that way, Vincelle."

"I was invited," said Gilbert, "and I went. I didn't know the family was your private property. I didn't know I had to account to you for every—"

"Damn unfriendly, *I* call it!" said Pendleton.

Gilbert smiled scornfully.

If their friendship had been a more genuine one, this would have caused a serious quarrel; but it was a forced sort of friendship, simply brought about by propinquity. They had grown up together, gone to the same school, the same dancing school, they moved in the same set. They had no respect for each other; Gilbert despised the other's frivolity and lack of money-making ability, and Pendleton looked upon Gilbert as a surly and ungenerous young boor. After their brief disagreement about Miss Mason they went on as usual, except that they were wary about the Staten Island visits. They went down there at different times, never again together, and each took what advantage he could get.

The unhappy Gilbert had suffered much, and perhaps learned a little. He had been dreadfully humiliated. Once Claudine had asked him to ride with her and he had been forced to admit that he didn't ride. Her astonished face....! And he hadn't read any of those books she knew so affectionately.

He had, when younger and slimmer, played tennis, but of late years since he had become so engrossed in business, his great recreation had been poker. As for books, he liked reading as much as the next man, provided they were entertaining books. And he liked music, too; not operas, but not trashy stuff, either; he liked Schubert's *Serenade*, and *Traumerei*, and things like that.... He hadn't Pendleton's talent for picking up information, for knowing something about everything, but when he heard Pendleton talking so glibly, he consoled himself by remembering that he had had an education *exactly* like his, of precisely the same length and the same price.

So Pendleton couldn't really know any more than he did, no matter how he talked.

The free, careless air of that household had encouraged him. In other families where there were marriageable daughters, he had had an uncomfortable feeling of eligibility, he had felt that everything he did was important and significant, and that he must be careful. Here it was obvious that no one cared. He could come and be welcome, or he could stay away. He had begun to bring flowers and candy, which Claudine received with pretty appreciation. But other people brought flowers and candy, also, and were as nicely thanked.

He made an effort to study her to learn if she really was a flirt, as Pendleton said. But he couldn't decide. She reigned like a queen over a court of admirers, but without undue coquetry. She was, in spite of her gaiety and liveliness, a serious girl. She read marvelous books. She played astounding music; she was a great companion to her father on his botanical walks and she collected "specimens," dried and pressed in a book. Weeds, they looked like to Gilbert, but he was willing to admit their value. He had never imagined anyone so happy as she, so interested and delighted with life. She was a fine horsewoman, she skated and danced beautifully; she took long, long walks in the country, and enjoyed them wholeheartedly; she went to the opera, to concerts, she read, she practised her music, she painted in water-colours, she had any number of friends and all sorts of informal society, she hadn't a dull or idle moment in her existence.

He saw no evidences of domesticity in her, but that didn't trouble him. It wasn't an era of domesticity. A wife, in his class, was an ornament and a diversion. Domestic science was an unknown term to both of them. Claudine had escaped the thorough training of her two elder sisters; her mother had conscientiously taught them to cook, to sew, and to superintend a household, just as she herself had been taught, but with this youngest and brightest child, she had lost heart. She was growing older; she was tired. And moreover, it seemed to her that the time for all that had passed. No one would ever expect Claudine to cook or to sew.

"Let her enjoy herself while she can," her mother said to herself. "Youth is over so soon."

She would make a charming hostess, let that suffice. Gilbert asked no more. He was completely dazzled.

His feelings would be incomprehensible to a later generation. They were such polite, respectful feelings! He never thought of Claudine and himself as a woman and a man. She was a young lady, and he was a gentleman, and even in his most secret soul he respected her. He wanted to marry her and he let it go at that. He didn't even analyze her charms.

He was a man of invincible honesty. He wasn't clear-sighted; he had no self-knowledge, but neither had he any subtlety. He loved Claudine: he longed to give her everything he had. He felt himself unworthy and inferior beside her purity, her innocence, her lovely young spirit. He had tried to the best of his ability to set before her whatever advantages there might be in marrying him, but not through conceit, only to persuade her.

He had brought with him on one occasion an old magazine, to show her an article in it— "The Old Vincelles of Brooklyn." It had been written by a sort of Miss Dorothy, a humble and admiring relation, and it was a narrative of that singularly unillustrious family, beginning with the Huguenot who had come first to American shores, and mentioning with solemn veneration a long line of lawyers, ministers, and business men, all respectable, serious, and thrifty. Not a vagary, not a passion, among them.

He showed her this not from pride—although he was proud of it—but merely as an added inducement, in the same spirit he had talked to her of his "business prospects," and his remarkable progress. It was as if he said, "Here is all I have, beloved girl, won't it compensate for what I am?" And now he rested his case. He had nothing further to offer. His inarticulate and unhappy wooing was at an end. He was going to ask her, quite simply, if she would have him.

He arrived at the house in the June twilight. The house was still unlighted, the windows were open, the curtains fluttering gently in a little breeze. There was a magical fragrance from the garden: it was in all ways a magical evening. He never quite forgot it.

He dismissed the carriage at the gate and walked along the drive, the gravel crunching under his deliberate tread, the perfumed breeze blowing against his miserable and sullen face. Because, under his serious and pompous demeanor, he was after all, very young; almost a boy. And his whole heart was set on this, his whole heart! Claudine was the one woman on earth for him.

If she only knew the power she held in her little hands, he reflected!

CHAPTER FOUR

CLAUDINE'S PECULIAR MOTHER

I

No one could have known this better. She was in her room, standing before the mirror, looking with critical attention at her image. She was at her loveliest and well she knew it. She was in white, with a pale green sash about her twenty inch waist. Her red hair was curled over her forehead in a low bang, below which her brown eyes were marvelously bright and alluring. Her face was radiant with happiness, but there lay over it a faint shadow, a sort of tenderness.

This was to be the day. She knew it. She had read his determination in his face the day before. And it was all coming out just as she had wished it to come. Ever since her school days that had been her dream—to be proposed to by a dark, handsome man in evening dress, at a dance. There had been other proposals but none of them just right; there had been other men to whom her fancy had strayed, but never like this. She felt for this silent and stalwart young fellow a pity, a compassion that bordered on pain. She didn't like to let him out of her sight. She longed so to make him happy. He seemed so lonely, so helpless, so neglected, so pitiably in need of a comrade. Since she had seen his horrible home and his chilly old mother, she had loved him more, felt more sorry for him than ever. Oh, no doubt about it, he was the man!

The sense of impending change was upon her. This room would never look the same to her again, her own face would never have quite this look again; after this evening everything would be *different*. She was lively and high-spirited, but she was in no way frivolous. She wouldn't make a promise unless she meant to keep it. This was the most important step in her life, and she had considered it well. She had studied her man; she felt that she knew him. She was well aware that he wasn't clever, and that he wasn't very good-natured, but she was so accustomed to good-nature, to kindness, tolerance, that she did not know their value. Let him be a little cross if he wished, the dear old bear! She would wheedle away his ill-humour with her own gaiety. She would be the light of his life, she would bring youth and happiness into his monotonous existence. She could be more to him than to any other man.

Divine and naïve idea of a young girl, innocently conscious of her own immeasurable value!

II

It had been a beautiful day for her, a day of profound significance. She had been waked up by her mother coming into her bedroom to kiss her and wish her "many happy returns." Half asleep she had watched the stout figure moving about the room, pulling up the shades to let in the light of the summer morning, picking up the clothes she had left carelessly about, folding bits of ribbon, straightening the articles on her bureau with that silent and inexhaustible kindness she counted upon as she did upon the very sun.

"Well!" said her mother at last, with her benevolent smile, "are you never going to look at your little presents, chickabiddy?"

Then she had sat up, her short heavy braid over one shoulder, and began opening the packages always found on birthday mornings at one's bedside. The gifts had brought tears to her eyes. The love in them, the unspeakably dear intimacy! Her mother had embroidered a dozen linen handkerchiefs, and an exquisite sachet case for them; her father had presented her with the bottle of Cherry Blossom perfume he had bought every year since she was a child—and which she didn't like—and a big box of chocolates with a ten dollar gold piece on top. Lance gave her a book of verse. Then there was a photograph in a silver frame of her eldest sister with her three babies; there were six pairs of French gloves from one brother and a beautiful edition of "Ingoldsby Legends" from the other, and from the sister who had married only a year ago a combing jacket, trimmed with pale green ribbons. She had so well remembered Claudine's tastes!

"Oh, Mother!" she had said, with a sob, "you're all so good and dear! I wish ...?"

"What *do* you wish, Goosie?"

But she didn't quite know. Perhaps she wished to clutch at Time and hold him here forever.

She had got up and dressed and gone into the garden before breakfast to look at the flowers, and to pick a very few. The roses were just beginning; they were so lovely that she almost wept again. The buds were drooping in a sort of enchanted drowsiness, some yellow, some so faintly pink, some a dark and wonderful red; she touched with her finger the waxy satin petals, she bent over them to inhale the fragrance of them, that heavenly fragrance warmed with the sun. She went about from one bed to the other, to see what new thing had come up, what was flourishing, what was disappointing. Her father was a notable gardener; she hadn't his skill, but she had his love for growing things. She enjoyed the garden perhaps more than he did, for she had not his anxieties about it. She sauntered over the wide lawn that ran all down the hillside, the sun warm on her bare head, her white dress trailing over the grass, and as she went she reflected, with a little fleeting melancholy in her happiness, Nineteen! Nineteen such wonderful years in this garden!

But the years to come she thought, would be far more wonderful.

III

The Masons were quite unabashed in their family celebrations—Mrs. Mason had a perfectly clear conception of the value of these ceremonies in holding together a family, and she made the most of them, in her calm way. It was a revelation to young Vincelle; he thought it somewhat childish and absurd and not quite the thing. The table that night was set with unusual magnificence with a lace cloth and four silver candelabra, and at the end a wonderful cake was brought, frosted with pink and white and green, and bearing twenty candles, one for good luck. He was the only guest and he felt embarrassed.

After the dinner the dance, the same sort of dance that had been on the occasion of his first visit, but without that unique flavor. He felt a little chilled, a little aloof, dreading unspeakably what lay before him. Never had Claudine seemed so distant, never had she seemed so much a stranger. He began to grow certain that he had no chance at all. Perhaps it would be better if she did refuse him, and he could go home again....

Young men invited to dances at Mrs. Mason's house in those days were expected to dance, and Gilbert had not much time for reflection. He went dutifully waltzing about the ball-room with one young lady after the other, and once or twice went out upon the veranda with a partner. Actually a moonlight night; he couldn't have devised a better setting....

The moment came. He stood out there with Claudine, on the lawn, in the moonlight. She had suddenly grown quiet: he could see her face plainly, and it was grave, serious, almost sad. She looked more than ever like a spirit, in her white dress with her slim bare neck and arms.

The breeze blew the end of her silvery scarf against his face, and brought to his nostrils the faint scent of the perfume she used—some innocent, old-fashioned thing of her mother's. He took her by the arm and led her under the shadow of a row of horse chestnuts.

Poor devil! He had no fit words. God knows what he faltered out.... But she didn't care. Tears came to her eyes; indeed they were both very close to weeping. She reached out and touched his hot trembling hand, and they clung to each other, mute, with their pitiful young love, their hearts aching with the beauty of the matchless night and the supreme moment, unique in their lives, never again to be recaptured.

"Don't tell anyone to-night!" she whispered, and for these few hours it was their secret.

IV

The very next day the trouble began. His mother received the news of his acceptance with a smile of satirical amusement.

"You're old enough to know what you're doing," she said. "And so is *she*."

"Claudine's only nineteen," said her son, answering her tone rather than her words.

"*Is* she?" said his mother. "I shouldn't have thought so. She seems very sophisticated…. But I suppose that's her upbringing."

Pursuant to Claudine's instructions he had taken an afternoon off from the office so that he could go down to Staten Island, and see her father. This ordeal didn't particularly distress him: he felt that as a son-in-law he was faultless. He had practically no past; nothing that could be troublesome, anyway, and financially he was ready and anxious for the most minute investigation.

The Professor received him with kindliness. He said "Well, young man!" offered him a cigar and said that as Claudine had made up her mind, what were they to do? He asked him a few questions, and then sent him off to Claudine. But, as he left the library, he met Mrs. Mason in the hall. And her look astonished him. Her bland face wore no smile for him: on the contrary, she gave him a glance so cold, severe and merciless that he winced.

When he learned the truth he was still more taken aback. She objected! Claudine was tearful and dejected. She said they'd had a dreadful time that morning.

"Father says I'm to decide for myself, and that neither he nor Mother ought to interfere. But Mother said—Oh, Gilbert, I can't understand Mother! It's not a bit like her! … She said she'd never consent to her dying day."

"But why?" cried the affronted and amazed young man.

"She thinks—we're not suited to each other."

"Rubbish!" he said, scornfully. That was a woman's objection for you! Nothing against him financially, morally or physically, but some absurd feminine notion of suitability. He was a little relieved.

"I suppose the truth of it is, she doesn't want to lose you, Claudine. I don't blame her."

"Oh, no!" said Claudine, "it can't be that, because—" she stopped short with a sudden blush.

"Because what?"

"Because—I know it isn't that…. Oh, Gilbert, do try to—win her affection!"

"I don't see why I should!" he answered. "Upon my word I don't see why I should humble myself—"

"She's my mother, Gilbert, and I love her."

"Yes, of course, my sweet girl! But, after all, if you're going to marry me, I come first, don't I? If you really love me—" She began to cry.

"You *know* I do! Only—you can't imagine how dear and wonderful Mother's always been."

He said he could have a talk with her and he did. It was not a pleasant talk. This benevolent matronly creature, whom he had always taken for granted as a part of Claudine's background, had suddenly come alive as a woman, as a difficult and unmanageable feminine creature.

She said:

"I should prefer not to discuss this matter with you, Mr. Vincelle."

"But why?" he protested. "If you have any objection to me, isn't it only fair to tell me what it is? To let me defend myself?"

She shook her head.

"No," she said. "I couldn't put it into words…. I am positive that you cannot make Claudine happy."

"Why do you think I can't make her happy, Mrs. Mason?"

"It isn't in you," she said frankly. "You are not suited to each other."

"Well, I believe a woman can adapt herself to any man, if she really cares for him."

"Claudine's not adaptable. It would be necessary for *you* to make concessions—to be very tolerant and wise. And I don't think you would be."

He smiled indulgently.

"I think I understand her," he said. "And I'm used to feminine ways, you know. My mother—"

She shook her head.

"It won't do!" she said, with emphasis. "I shall never consent to it."

This was the most outrageous affront imaginable. If she had objected to him for any other reason, because of his morals, his religion, his social standing, his financial position, he could have endured it, because he could have argued and proved her absolutely wrong. But just simply to dislike him….

Of course, he knew how perverse, unreasonable and provoking women were, a man must take that into consideration. But that a mature woman should be so idiotic as to insult an eligible suitor for her daughter's hand was a thing unheard of. He despised her; she had no common sense; she had no regard for her child's welfare….

He asked Claudine if she would marry him without her mother's consent.

"As long as your father agrees, and there's no valid objection," he said. "You wouldn't jilt me because your mother's taken some sort of—" he checked the words on his lips and said, very moderately— "taken a dislike to me, would you!"

But he could get nothing sensible from her; only that she really did love him, and that her mother was so dear and wonderful, and that there was no hurry, anyway, was there!

He refused to stay for dinner; he went home in a state of sullen rage, and he carried his intolerable hurt to the person whom he fancied best appreciated his worth. He got cold comfort.

"There's as good fish in the sea as ever came out of it," said his mother. "They're very peculiar people. They'd never suit *you*."

"I don't want to marry the family," he said sharply. "Claudine's not responsible for her mother."

"Her mother's responsible for her, though. She's brought her up according to her own ideas. If you take my advice, you'll put the whole thing out of your head."

He went up to his own room, with a most unpleasant fancy that all these women knew things about him which he didn't know; that they were all, his own mother included, ruled by motives not to be comprehended by him. He was very unhappy. If it were only a matter of Claudine and himself! When he had the dear little thing in his arms, she was his, she loved him, she forgot everyone else; if they were married, it would always be so. He did understand her; he knew he could make her happy if they were alone.

If they had a little house somewhere, by themselves.... He began to dream impossible rustic dreams; he saw them in a vine-covered cottage, such as he had certainly never seen; he fancied Claudine running down the path to meet him when he came home, flinging her arms about him, her bright sweet face uplifted, her curly hair blowing ... oh, he was frightfully unhappy!

He didn't know whether he ought to go down to Staten Island again, or not. But Claudine wrote to him, and told him to come. Her mother didn't the least mind their seeing each other. So he went, sulky and reluctant, and was very well received. Mrs. Mason was quite natural and pleasant, and treated him just as she treated everyone else; and Claudine was heavenly. She found a chance to slip out into the garden with him, and as soon as they were alone, she kissed him, quite of her own accord.

"You see," she said. "Poor mother thinks that if we see each other often enough, we'll quarrel, or something of the sort. So if we just wait long enough, and she sees that we *don't*, she'll realize that she's wrong; and it will be all right."

"How long will it take?" he asked, gloomily. "Five years?"

"Oh, mercy, no! Only be patient."

"I can't be! I don't want to wait! I love you so! I don't want to waste years—"

"They won't be wasted, Gilbert. They'll be the happiest time of our lives. You're happy now, aren't you, this very moment?"

"Not so very. I want you for my own, Claudine."

"I am your own. I love you and love you, darling Gilbert."

Impossible to argue with her innocence; he resigned himself to get what joy he could from these stolen moments. And he knew that no matter how long he had to wait, no matter what humiliation and unpleasantness he had to endure, Claudine was worth it.

Suddenly, without the slightest pretense of reason, Mrs. Mason gave in, she no longer objected.

"Marry him if you want to, chickabiddy," she said.

They were all astonished and a little uneasy. A change had come over that incomprehensible woman. Her color was as ruddy, her activity as great, she was as kind, as pleasant, as competent as ever. But an immense moral apathy had seized her, she no longer interfered, no longer gave advice. Let her husband smoke fifteen cigars a day, let her child marry whom she would, she seemed indifferent. She had become strangely and terribly remote. She seemed to have a grim secret of her own, a knowledge of some event in comparison with which all these things were of no importance.

No one realized what shadow had fallen upon her. They were willing to accept her change of heart as a whim. But she who was about to be exiled forever had come to see the futility of resistance. She saw her own death coming toward her; she could bear to watch it. And she saw so clearly too that when she was no longer standing in the highway, the others would still go on, and that cry after her child as she might, no sound would ever again reach her.

Gilbert and Claudine were married that autumn in a little church on Staten Island. Old Mrs. Vincelle was brought there, like a Buddha carried in a procession, and there were a certain number of Brooklyn *haute bourgeoisie*. But it was a Mason wedding, and Mrs. Mason dominated it. She gave a marvelous breakfast after it in the house on the hill, and hers was the last face they saw as they drove away. She had come out into the road, to look after them, a stout, dignified figure in black silk waving her hand, and smiling after her youngest child....

CHAPTER FIVE

CLAUDINE LEARNS TO ADAPT HERSELF

Before she had been in that house an hour she knew that she could never be happy there. She wasn't ready when the dinner gong sounded, but Gilbert hadn't waited. Lateness upset his mother, he said. She had tried to hurry then, but she was an inveterate dawdler, and it was some time before she was quite dressed. She came downstairs with the sprightly air proper to a bride just returned from her honeymoon, but it was a forced and desperate sprightliness. She felt all the helplessness and terror of a deserted child among strangers as she descended the dark old staircase, padded so thickly with carpet that it was like walking in a bog.

On the newel post was a standing lamp in which burned a gas jet turned very low, in a shade of red, green and blue glass. She turned along the narrow hall, past the open door of the front parlour, feebly illuminated, the middle parlour, the obscure and neglected back parlour, all dark, still, and bitterly unfamiliar to her. She reached the steep flight of stairs leading to the basement, and began going down in utter darkness and silence. The door at the foot of the flight was closed; she fumbled for the handle in an absurd panic and stumbled forward as it burst open.

They were sitting at the table in there, Gilbert at the head, his mother at the foot, and they were taking their soup, evidently determined to begin right with the child, to show her, pleasantly but inexorably, that she would never, never be waited for. She sat down at the place laid for her, facing the door, and the servant brought her a plate of soup.

"*Well!*" said old Mrs. Vincelle.

Her tone was tart, but good-humoured, and she smiled at her daughter-in-law.

"We're old fashioned here," she said. "Meals served on the minute. That's the way I was brought up. And Mr. Vincelle was very strict; if one of the boys was late for a meal, he had to sit at one side of the room till we'd all finished and then eat by himself."

"I know.... I'm sorry," said Claudine. "But I couldn't find things, this first evening."

Gilbert looked at her indulgently for an instant, and then turned his attention to the roast chickens that had been set before him. He rather prided himself upon his carving, he felt sure that Claudine would observe and admire his dexterity. He had had, in fact, ever since they had arrived that afternoon, an air of showing off, as much as to say—here you can see me in my own kingdom, at my ease, my natural self. He had consciously tried to impress her; he had given a great many orders to the servants, and had found fault. But he had not produced the impression he intended; Claudine saw him suddenly as a little boy, pampered, spoiled, but led by the nose. His mother ruled him absolutely.

In a way she was pleased to find that in spite of his sturdiness and his impatient masculinity he was certainly very human, but on the other hand, it frightened her. She so greatly needed to respect him, to look up to him, to see in him a great spiritual authority. She had left the security and peace of her girlhood to follow him, and he must lead.

Why did he look so young and sulky to-night? He caught her looking at him and he smiled again, tenderly, but with a sort of constraint. It never occurred to her that he too was suffering from a great disappointment. He had believed, poor devil, that with Claudine he would have a new life; and lo, it was nothing but the old life with a new person in it. She was overshadowed; she had suddenly lost importance; she had quite ceased to be that rare and precious creature he had adored, and had become a sort of phantom.

"You're not eating!" said the old lady, suddenly. "Don't tell me you don't like chicken!"

For she too had her disappointment. She had arranged a dinner really sumptuous according to her very frugal mind, and no one appreciated it!

"Oh, yes, I do like it, very much!" said Claudine, hastily. "Only ... I think I must be a little tired. It was so stuffy in the train."

"You mustn't take notions about your food," said the old lady. "A young married woman owes it to other people to keep up her health and strength. You must *eat*, whether you *feel* like it or not."

"Yes, I know!" said Claudine, pleasantly.

She was mortally afraid of bursting into tears. All their meals hitherto had been eaten in hotels, or trains, or boats, where there was plenty to divert her, to make her forget that thing which had been gnawing at her heart all the time these last two weeks, but now in the quiet room, with these two quiet people intent upon their food, there was nothing to help her. It rushed upon her like a flood—that terrible homesickness.... On this mild September night they would be sitting in the lofty dining-room, with the windows open on the dear old garden. She could imagine them in the light of the suspended lamp, her mother, her father, Lance, perhaps other familiar friends' faces, the neat and smiling Selma waiting upon them; she could imagine their talk, casual, cheerful, full of family jokes, with the scholarly leaven introduced by her father and Lance.... And at every pause would be heard the sounds from the dark garden, the trees stirring, that branch of the big grape-vine tapping against the window....

Gilbert and his mother were talking, in a disconnected and perfunctory way. She asked questions about the honeymoon; he gave her the names of hotels, details of the accommodation they had secured; she had a little gossip for him of old friends. When they stopped talking, there came to her ears utterly unfamiliar sounds—a carriage rattling by over the cobblestones, a footstep ringing on the pavement overhead, passing the barred window, mournful whistles from the river.

After the roast came the pudding, a vanilla blanc mange, made in a ring, the centre filled with strawberry jam, and cream poured over it all. And this demolished, they all rose; Gilbert gave his arm to his mother and they started up the stairs, followed by the disconsolate bride. She felt more than ever like a forlorn child, following these two people so much older and solider, so much more positive and self-assured than she. Her life was to be nothing but a wretched struggle to please them....

They entered the austere front parlour where a flicker of gas revealed the shrouded furniture, the huge, gold-framed pictures on the walls, the grand piano; they passed through this to the second parlour, and in here the dutiful son made a light and settled his mother in her favourite chair. The younger woman sat down near her, with an uncertain smile and her husband drew out his cigar case.

"Do you ladies object?" he asked facetiously.

"Go along with you, Gilbert!" cried the old lady, "I do declare I've missed the smell of smoke since you've been away."

She leaned back in her chair and regarded him with complacency as he blew out great clouds of smoke.

"Nice to be *home*, Claudine?" he asked.

"Oh, yes!" said the little liar.

He hadn't much more to say; he was a silent fellow at all times and tonight he was tired and a bit out of sorts. All this travelling about had unsettled him; of course it had to be done, but he was glad it was over. They would be much happier now, being settled down. To tell the truth, the honeymoon had not been quite the rapture he had imagined. Claudine had been—he reflected: well, Claudine had been too damned polite. She had pretended to like everything; she hadn't been quite human. No matter what went wrong, she had kept on smiling.... With undeniable relief he allowed his mind to drift back to Business.

The old lady dozed, her two withered hands lying on the arms of the chair. There wasn't a sign of life in the room. Claudine got up and crossed the room to an immense walnut secretary and tried to read the titles of the books on the shelves with eyes dimmed by absurd tears. Hopeless volumes of sermons, forgotten and tedious poems. But she kept on looking at them, with a false interest, only that she might keep her face turned away.

Gilbert was touched by her lost young figure in that silent room.

"After all, it's pretty dull for her here," he thought, and he wanted very much to make her happy, but didn't know how. He had expected that somehow she would light up, transform, enliven this household; he hadn't quite realized that he would be literally expected to do what all young lovers so gallantly promise—to make her happy. He couldn't help thinking of Mrs. Mason's words.

He wanted to get up and put his arm about her, but he was afraid of his mother's ridicule. And blind instinct suggested to him the one thing that could solace her pain, that at once dried her tears and made eager her leaden heart.

"Play something for us, won't you, Claudine?"

"Do you really want me to?" she cried.

He got up and went into the front parlour, where he turned up the gas and opened the piano. Then he seated himself nearby, with a pleased smile.

"Now!" said he.

She ran her strong little fingers over the keyboard in ecstasy. The piano was out of tune and very stiff, but it was music anyway. She hesitated a moment; she considered her audience, and fate inspired her to play *Traumerei*. This was one of the few pieces they both knew and, like very many others, they were delighted to hear what they knew.

"Brava!" said the old lady.

"I always did like that thing," said Gilbert dreamily.

Her heart warmed to them, poor darlings who knew so little beauty! She felt that in this way she could reach them, could make them understand her. She went on, a tranquil flow of undisturbing harmony, melodies which she believed they would recognize and like. She played to them with profound earnestness, as anxious as a siren to charm the careless sailors.

Gilbert sat lost in admiration. This was beyond question a proper wife, a young, charmingly dressed creature who played the piano soothingly in the evening. He thought she had never looked lovelier, so straight, so slender, in her beruffled blue dress, her curly head thrown back. What greater charm could a woman have than a lulling art like this, to dispel the cares of the harsh masculine world? His heart swelled with proud affection; he was passionately anxious to cherish and protect this exquisite young creature so miraculously thrust into his dull existence.

She stopped playing; let her hands rest on the keys, and waited, perhaps to be urged to continue. But her hearers seemed to take it for granted that the playing was ended.

"Brava!" said the old lady again. "I hadn't any idea you were such a musician, Claudine. Very pretty!"

And Gilbert said:

"You have a fine touch, Claudine."

She knew that he couldn't have distinguished a good touch from a poor one, but she was not annoyed. She felt very kindly toward them both, because they had listened willingly to her music, and because she had been able to play and to solace herself. She got up and closed the piano, and Gilbert bent over her, to kiss her warm cheek.

"Wonderful little woman!" he said. "I'm a lucky dog!"

She was very happy. Here was a way out; she would practise her music faithfully, perfect herself, become absorbed in it, and there would be no tedious hours. She could become a really fine musician, the wonder and delight of a little circle.

She followed Gilbert back into the second parlour, lost in her dream. But to the others the music, a pleasant little interlude, was over, and the rest of the long evening stretched before them. The old lady began to crochet, and Gilbert took up his newspaper.

"Like to see the Woman's Page, Claudine?" he asked.

Now Claudine had a lamentable dislike for newspapers. She never read them; she wasn't well-informed. No one in her house showed much interest in current events, they envisaged human life as an immense and absorbing history, and the present as one small day of it. Her father was a sort of benevolent Anarchist who couldn't endure the thought of restraint laid upon evolution; her mother was blandly indifferent to anything outside her own family; Lance lived in pre-historic ages. Nevertheless, she accepted the Woman's Page, read the fashion hints, a little article on the care of house plants. Then she put the thing down and sat doing nothing

"Don't you do fancy work?" asked the old lady.

"Yes, sometimes," said Claudine. "But ..."

She rose.

"I think I'll go to bed now," she said. "I'm so tired."'

Gilbert looked up from his paper and the old lady stared at her, affronted and amazed.

"It's only half past nine!" she said tartly. "I should think you could wait till eleven, like the rest of us. I dare say you're not any more tired than anybody else."

"Never mind, Mother, if she's tired ..." Gilbert began, but Claudine had sat down again with flaming cheeks.

"No!" she said. "I'll wait!"

This was her first rebuke and she felt it a most unmerited one. It was the first time she had ever heard of a fixed, arbitrary bed hour for adult people. It had occurred to her a natural thing to go to bed when you were sleepy. Sometimes at home, the day after a dance, she had gone to bed directly after dinner, with a book to divert the few waking minutes, and at other times she had sat up almost till morning reading or finishing some enthralling bit of sewing. She felt a great anger toward Gilbert, with his half-hearted protest. There he sat reading his silly paper, page by page, every word … what did he expect her to *do?*

The old lady glanced up suddenly.

"Come, child!" she said. "Don't sit there and brood! Gilbert, get her the 'Pigs in Clover'!"

"She won't like it," he answered, deep in his paper.

"Rubbish! It's something to pass the time and that's all the young folks care for in these days. Get it for her!"

So from inside the secretaire Gilbert brought out a round box with a glass cover inside which were marbles to be rolled through certain partitioned alleys, and finally, if one were skilful, into a sort of little house. He kissed Claudine as he gave it to her, an apologetic, almost a guilty kiss, but she had no smile for him. She sat with the thing in her hands, twisting it this way and that, letting the little balls roll as they would through the alleys, and ready at the least word, the least gesture, to burst into outrageous and most bitter laughter.

One of the marbles suddenly rolled into the pen, and, unaccountably, with this feeble satisfaction, the storm within her subsided. She remembered having read somewhere that lunatics were given games and diversions like this to quiet them. She wished that she could tell that to her father … she wished that her father could see her, rolling marbles about in a glass-covered box.

Gilbert was gently shaking her.

"Sleepy-head!" he said. "It's after eleven! You've been dozing!"

Both he and the old lady were greatly entertained. Their dazed victim went upstairs, quite well aware that now, when at last she could get into bed, she would lie awake for hours.

CHAPTER SIX

THE KEYNOTE

She waked up in the dark, terrified by a great banging at the door. She thought the house was on fire, that someone was ill, that thieves had broken in. She shook Gilbert fiercely. But he didn't stir.

Barefooted she rushed across the floor and unfastened the door.

"What is it!" she cried.

"It's seven o'clock, ma'am," said a meek voice.

"Seven o'clock!" she repeated.

"Yes, ma'am, I always call Mr. Gilbert at seven."

"Oh, I see!" she said. "I didn't know...."

She closed the door and went back to the bed where Gilbert still slept.

"Wake up!" she said, severely.

Still he didn't move. She clutched his big shoulders and tried to shake him, but he only groaned.

"Oh, do wake up!" she cried, in a sort of desperation.

"All right!" he murmured, but his eyes remained closed.

She was on the point of tears! She would really have liked to hurt him. She seized his hair and pulled it vigorously, and at once he sat up, dazed and resentful.

"Look here!" he said. "That's no way."

"It's seven o'clock!" she said coldly. "I should think, if you're so sleepy in the mornings, you'd go to bed earlier."

She herself was very weary and depressed. She had, as she had expected, lain awake a long, long time, unhappy in the darkness of that unfamiliar room, with the shutters all closed, and no sight of the sky to console her. At home she had always kept her windows unobscured so that lying in bed she could watch the moon, the, stars, the clouds, the sky whether clear, stormy or ominous. The very shapes of the furniture had distressed her, she had tried to make them out in their corners, as she had listened to the muffled, unfamiliar city noises.

She wasn't at her best in the morning; that was a recognized fact at home, and she was always carefully let alone. But Gilbert put her to shame. When at last he was roused, he was marvelously cheerful; he got up whistling, and set about dressing in leisurely fashion, talking a great deal. He was very much pleased at occupying the majestic room on the second floor, it gave solidity to his new importance as a married man. He thought his mother had arranged it very tastefully, he pointed out to Claudine the new velvet lambrequin on the mantelpiece and the pincushion the old lady had made for them. He picked it up from the bureau and looked at it with affectionate eyes—a tremendous long blue sausage covered with pleated silk and lace.

"Wonderful, at her age, isn't it?"

Claudine obliged herself to say "yes," but unkind thoughts possessed her as to the value of such work at any period of life. She sat listlessly combing her hair, trying to hurry, so that she shouldn't again be late, but quite sick with longing for a breath of air, a glimpse of sunshine.

"I really can't get dressed in the dark!" she said, irritably. "Couldn't we have one of the shutters opened, Gilbert?"

"No," he said. "Not possibly. The people across the street could look in."

"Then light the gas," she said. "I can't do my hair in the dark."

He was a little shocked at this extravagant idea, however he did it, and kissed her, because she looked so pretty with her hair about her shoulders.

They descended the stairs together and entered the basement dining-room, where the old lady was pottering about among her rubber plants and ferns. She took her seat at once at the foot of the table behind the coffee urn and the process of breakfasting began, a meal astounding and repulsive to the bride. Such coffee! And no cream, no fresh fruit; prunes, oatmeal, ham and eggs, poorly cooked, poorly served.

"You're moping!" said the old lady, suddenly.

Claudine looked up with a faint smile.

"I'm never very lively the first thing."

"Nonsense! A young married woman can't give way to all sorts of moods and fancies. It's her duty to be bright and smiling and start her husband off cheerful."

Gilbert frowned.

"Never mind, Mother!" he said. "Claudine's got her own way of being cheerful, and it suits me. I understand the little woman, don't I?"

Claudine was delighted, she would have liked to jump up and rush to him and kiss him. Their eyes met in a friendly and beautiful understanding. This was what she loved in him, for which she had married him, this solid loyalty, this sympathy. She was no longer unhappy.

"Now!" he said, cheerfully. "Let's see the news!" and picked up the newspaper. He read an item aloud now and then, not because it could by any possibility interest the two women dutifully lingering over their coffee, but because it interested him. He smoked a cigar leisurely, and then it was time to go.

Claudine went upstairs with him into the front hall, she took down his tremendous overcoat from the rack and laughingly let her arms sink with its weight.

"Mercy!" she said. "How *can* you bear it, Gilbert?"

"It's nothing compared to my winter one," he said in his schoolboy way, and suddenly lifted her up, kissed her warmly, and set her down again.

"Good-bye, sweetheart! Be happy—and don't quarrel with the Old Lady!"

Then he ran down the stairs again to take leave of his mother, and left by the basement door. From the front parlour window Claudine saw him walking off in the cool September morning, big, stalwart, determined ... *going out*.... Envy possessed her. Oh, didn't she wish *she* could walk out of the house like that, away from the old lady, and forget it all!

She didn't quite know how to proceed; she didn't know just what her share in the housekeeping was to be or what diversions and duties would fill these days. But she was already aware that she needn't ask, that old Mrs. Vincelle would certainly inform her as to what was expected of her.

She went up the dark, thickly carpeted stairs to the floor above. It was perfectly still and silent, and in order, swept and dusted, all trace of activity vanished. She looked in at all the open doors with infantile curiosity, all alike, thick, dark carpets on the floor, lace curtains at the windows, shades pulled half way down, marble mantelpieces covered with fringed velvet lambrequins, small tables on which were photographs in silver frames, huge bureaus, huge arm chairs, huge rocking chairs, with lace antimacassars, and inevitably a horsehair sofa furnished for naps by a folded "Afghan" of bright coloured stripes. Her bedroom—their bedroom, was no different from the others; there was nothing intimate or friendly about it. Whenever she went into her own room at home, a hundred things at once suggested themselves to her, letters to write, a bit of sewing to be done, a book to read. Here there was nothing whatever; she couldn't imagine anything to do here. She very unnecessarily "tidied" the bureau top, and looked at her own reflection in the mirror. Mrs. Gilbert Vincelle—a young married woman.... Romantic and interesting creature....

She wandered downstairs again; the chambermaid was dusting the second parlour, scene of last evening's bitter ennui, but the front parlour was empty, and she ventured in, drawn irresistibly by the piano. She opened it, half afraid to disturb the musty silence of the house; she ran up a scale, and it sounded monstrous. But the touch of the keys restored her courage; she began to play, and as usual lost herself in her playing. She had not yet unpacked her music; she had to draw upon her memory, fragments, entrancing bits, which she played over and over.

She was interrupted by the voice of the old lady, raised shrilly to penetrate the music.

"I've ordered Willie for eleven," she was saying.

Claudine stopped, a little dazed from the harmonies.

"Ordered Willie?" she repeated, stupidly.

"The carriage. We'll just have nice time to get your wedding presents put away first. Aline has them all unpacked in the back parlour."

It was an imposing array, and it raised Claudine's spirits. She stood surveying all the silver, the cut glass, the fine china, the linen, the clocks, vases, lamps. She looked at them all over again.

"Isn't this lovely. Don't you really think this is the prettiest?" she kept asking her mother-in-law, and the old lady replied with grim indulgence.

"But this isn't going to get your things put away," she said, at last. "Now, let's see.... The linen you can put up in the linen cupboard; I'll have a shelf cleared for you. We'll take the cut glass down into the dining-room. As for the silver—well, if I were you, I'd put it in the safe deposit this day and hour, but of course you won't. The young folks are all for display these days. So we'll take it into the dining-room with the rest."

And thus was all her glittering new wealth disposed of. It gave her an unpleasant feeling of childishness; her things were all superfluous, toys to be made room for among the regular, adult, useful things. No tea would be poured from her silver pot, no dinner served with her array of intriguing dishes, of flat and perforated and curved silver; in whatever room her clocks went, they were unnecessary second clocks. She arranged a great many ornaments in her bedroom, where they were quite incongruous; she even put in there a china umbrella stand because there was already one in the hall.

It was high time now to dress; she found some satisfaction in getting into a new grey broadcloth costume which she felt gave her quite a new dignity. She observed that she was rather pale and that, too, pleased her. She looked like a woman of experience, a mysterious and perhaps somewhat disillusioned creature. The old lady, in a black mantle and a small jet bonnet with a widow's veil, was waiting for her in the hall, they descended the steps and got into the little closed carriage and went rattling off over the streets of Brooklyn. A most uninspired city, Claudine reflected, calm, quiet, self-sufficing, an absolutely Vincelle place. They went first to the butcher, who came hurrying out to receive the order, for old Mrs. Vincelle rarely set foot in a shop, then to the fruiterer's, then the grocer's. She inspected nothing; the only question she permitted herself was "Are the oranges good to-day, Frank?" and yet she prided herself upon her old-fashioned virtue in going to market in person every day and she believed herself a match for any tradesman.

Then, without further instruction, the old coachman turned the heads of the two fat horses, and they went trotting off to Prospect Park, for the invariable daily drive along the same route to the same spot. It was a beautiful morning and Claudine was happy. From time to time the old lady inclined her head to the occupants of other carriages and then Claudine would feel the charm, the interest of her new position as a young married woman. She was conscious of her youth, her slight, delicate figure, her new tailor-made costume, all the touching dignity of a bride.

They reached the consecrated turning point, they turned and drove home again. The old lady talked a little, she pointed out a house now and then, or gave a word of explanation of some regal old dowager driving past. She was affable, she was almost kind, and in her heart she was a little proud of this pretty young creature—an acquisition of her son's and therefore the property of the family. And what a blow to Brooklyn, that Gilbert should have passed over all its maidens, and taken a wife from Staten Island!

They reached home at one, and lunch was at half past one, the nastiest sort of lunch, wafer-thin slices of dry cold mutton, all sorts of little warmed-over concoctions. Claudine made up her mind to change all this as soon as possible.

After the meal they went upstairs and the old lady lay down on the horse-hair sofa in her bedroom and drew the gay colored "Afghan" over herself.

"You might as well rest, Claudine," she said. "No one will be coming to call this afternoon. They'll give you a day or two to settle down."

And she resolutely closed her eyes.

Claudine hesitated.

"Would it disturb you if I played the piano?" she asked.

"Yes, it would!" said the old lady, affronted. "I dare say you can wait."

Once again that dread feeling of despair came over Claudine. She didn't *know what to do!* Her clothes were all quite new and perfect, there was nothing about them to alter or to mend. She looked in vain for something to read, but it was a house almost destitute of books. She wandered about, looked out of the windows, but there was nothing to see except a quiet street, lined with brownstone houses, and one solitary nursemaid with a perambulator. She would have liked to go into the kitchen. She had, in fact, expected to play the role of young mistress of a big house, but she dismissed the idea. Her mother-in-law would never, never allow that.

She unpacked her music and mapped out a course of study for herself—an alluring course of exercises and immensely difficult pieces, which she intended to attack with new patience and energy.

"Goodness knows I'll have time enough!" she reflected, ruefully. "I'll set aside two definite hours every day, and not let anything distract me. This afternoon I'll run over the things I've picked out."

At three o'clock she heard the old lady creaking about in her room, and music in hand she flew downstairs. Never had her fingers been so nimble, so sure, never had she worked with such complete satisfaction. Here was a field for definite accomplishment, a little living stream running beneath the stagnant lake which was to be her existence. She was expected—she was required, to be utterly passive, she was not to do anything, she was simply to *be*. To be a Good Wife. That was to fill the universe, that was to comprise everything. She was very willing to be a good wife, but she couldn't help thinking that there could still be a certain amount of time left impossible to fill with wifeliness.

Now Claudine was not the material of which artists of the first rank are made. She loved music, as she loved literature, and flowers, and many other things. She had, to a certain extent, that quality known as temperament, a sensitive and ardent soul. But she had very little patience, and she was neither thorough-going nor resolute. It is possible, even probable, however, that under the pressure of her ennui and with the spur of her enforced insignificance she might have developed her talent into something remarkably good, for she had a talent. But it was not to be.

She completed an hour of Czerny's *Finger Dexterity*, then she opened her

Liszt Album and attacked a terrific piece which needed all her intelligence. She frowned; she played over and over again a superhuman run.

The old lady's voice interrupted her.

"Mercy *on* us child! How long is this going to keep up? Your husband will be home before you know it and you haven't changed your dress."

Claudine looked round with a distrait smile.

"I will—in half a minute.... This piano needs tuning badly. And more than tuning. It needs—"

"It'll do very well as it is, I dare say!" said the old lady, briefly.

"But it isn't good to practise on a piano—"

"Practise! What do you want with practising? You play very nicely."

"Oh, but not nearly well enough! I'm going to keep on with my lessons."

"What!" cried the old lady. "Lessons! A young married woman fiddling about with piano lessons!"

Claudine was surprised at this sudden hostility.

"Yes; why not?"

"Haven't you anything better than that to do with your time?"

"What else *should* I do?"

"I never heard such rubbish in my life! A married woman taking lessons! What do you think you're going to do? Give concerts?"

Claudine was not skilled in quarreling. She had always been quite free to follow her inclinations, and her inclinations had never been harmful or ridiculous. She was accustomed to dignified independence, no one in her household had the least desire to interfere with any of the others, and she could not understand such interference. She felt herself growing very angry with this meddlesome and tyrannical old person, but she made a gallant effort to answer nicely.

"It's only that I'm very fond of music," she began.

"You'd better be fond of your husband, that's my advice! Piano lessons! ... Very well, young woman! There'll be no practising on *my* piano! It's there to be *played* on and not fiddled on and banged on."

Claudine actually turned pale.

"But you surely can't mind my practising ...?" she cried.

"I do. All the neighbours'll hear you. A married woman strumming and jigging away like a school girl.... Piece of nonsense!"

Anger got the better of Claudine.

"I never heard of anything so unreasonable and so ridiculous!" she said. "I don't intend to give it up."

"Women that can't give up their childish nonsense have no business to get married. Now then!"

She walked over and closed the piano and handed Czerny and Liszt to her daughter-in-law.

"You put all this nonsense out of your head!" she said. "And run upstairs and put on a nice fresh dress and see if you can't tidy that wild looking head of hair before Gilbert gets home."

But when Gilbert got home he was not welcomed by the smiling and charming young wife he had a right to expect. Instead he found Claudine locked in the bedroom, her eyes red with weeping, and in a state of terrible excitement.

"Gilbert!" she cried. "Your mother says she won't let me practise on her piano!"

He was astounded and a little frightened. So they were at it already!

"Well ..." he said. "I don't know.... It'll probably blow over, if you'll use tact and patience.... Anyway, it's a small matter."

"It's *not!* It's not! My music is all I have left!"

"Hold on, Claudine! That's rather strong!"

"I didn't mean to hurt you, Gilbert dear. Of course, you come first, only you're away most of the time.... And you don't know what it means to me. The idea of her being so domineering and cruel!"

"Claudine," he said, very gravely. "I hoped this would never happen. Especially as you're so fond of your own people.... I thought you'd understand how I felt about—Mother. I *know* she's unreasonable sometimes—but remember that she's old, and I'm all she has left."

As an argument this seemed remarkably weak to Claudine, but the tone, the very pitiful inconsequence of the poor chap, touched her to the heart. She began to weep in his arms, bitterly, forlornly, knowing herself defeated, pitying herself and pitying him still more.

He kissed her and smoothed her disordered hair, perplexed and unhappy. He was very tender and kind to her; he bathed her eyes with cold water, he took the pins out of her hair and released the complicated structure. Her sobs ceased; she grew calm and tranquil again, and when the gong sounded for dinner, she came downstairs on her husband's arm, smiling, nicely dressed, the very model of a bride.

But that night, when they were alone in the bedroom again, she returned to the subject.

"Gilbert!" she said. "Let me get a piano of my own!"

"I couldn't, dear. Mother would never consent to that. No, darling, better put the idea out of your head for the time being. You'll find lots of new things to interest you."

"But won't you speak to her, Gilbert? Won't you *help* me? Gilbert, if it's something I want so very, very much, don't you *care?*"

"Of course I care!" he protested. "I want you to be happy. But ... after all, it's Mother's house, and she has to be consulted."

"Then let's live by ourselves, Gilbert!"

"We can't move to-night!" he said laughing, and turning out the gas, got into bed.

But Claudine could not sleep. She had a dreadful feeling of being trapped, of being a captive, helpless, weak, insignificant.

CHAPTER SEVEN

THE HEDGE WHICH GREW SO FAST

I

In order to escape she had told the old lady a deliberate lie. She had said she was going shopping with Mrs. Martinsburgh, because Mrs. Martinsburgh was a highly approved of young married woman considered to be a good influence for the peculiar young Mrs. Vincelle. Whereas she was really going to meet Lance. She had written to him to meet her in a certain respectable restaurant where ladies on shopping tours often went to lunch.

It was a risk; she was quite likely to be seen there and her outrageous escapade reported to the old lady, but she was desperate. She had to see him. She went upstairs and secured a table, self-conscious and wretched at being there alone. She dared not look about the room for fear of seeing a familiar face, she dared not tell the waiter she was expecting someone. She pretended to study the menu, taking a long time to order, hoping and hoping that Lance would come. But he was late as he always was. Her lunch was set before her and she felt obliged to begin eating it. The room was full, she expected every moment that someone else would be put at her table. She had laid her muff and hand bag on the chair beside her as a futile protection, and sipped her chocolate with an engrossed air.

By raising her eyes, she could see her own reflection in one of the mirrors which lined the room; she was paler, thinner, more elegant but—what was it that had gone from her face? She fingered her veil with a delicate little gesture, and glanced down again to her hands, adorned with rings. She wondered if Lance would find her changed?

And just at this moment she heard his voice, his calm, serious voice, always so low that it was difficult for strangers to understand him.

"Hello, Claudine!" he said. "Am I late? How are you?"

He sat down beside her and looked at her seriously through his spectacles.

"Well!" he said. "You've changed.... What on earth did you want to see me for?"

The recollection of her suffering rushed over her. Her eyes filled with tears. "I had to talk to someone," she said. "And there was nobody else."

"But—" he began, and stopped. This was a matter for caution, she who had a husband, a mother, a father, brothers and sisters, and yet could find no one but himself to confide in.

Five years before, when he was a boy of twenty, he had come to live with his uncle, Doctor Mason. He was a youth of strongly scientific tendency, too poor to study, and the doctor had offered to keep him. His mother was a garrulous, vulgar woman, with a bitter tongue, well able to make life a burden for her household. Her husband, the doctor's younger brother, endured her with English fatalism; he was an ineffectual sort of chap, anyway, who like so many of his countrymen had turned to farming in the hope of finding in it a refuge from competition and struggle. He had a wretched, stony, hillside farm in Sullivan County, which produced next to nothing; the family were kept alive only by the exertions of his relentless wife and the boundless charity of his brother. Lance, amazingly christened Launcelot—had lived in calm, unceasing opposition to both parents. He would be a paleontologist, and he would not devote himself to money-making. If he did make anything through that work, his parents could have it, if he didn't they would have to do without.

He was the most unimpressionable, unsusceptible young man ever born. Nothing moved him, nothing troubled him. He was a pleasant housemate, for he was never impatient or cross, but he remained marvelously aloof. He sat at the doctor's feet, worshipping his scientific knowledge, grateful to him for the opportunities he had given him, the years in college, the quiet and peace for independent study, he was grateful to his aunt, too, for her kindly care of him. But he would have been delighted to go to the ends of the earth on an expedition, and it wouldn't have cost him a pang to bid them farewell forever.

The only soul with whom he was really human was Claudine. They had been like brother and sister, only at once more friendly and more formal than brothers and sisters usually are. And Claudine was quite conscious of something not at all brotherly in Lance's regard. She had had too many suitors to be deceived. She had very carefully maintained a nice balance. She knew that he thought she didn't know, and she was artful about it. She thoroughly respected Lance, he was the most candid, unbiased, truly independent person she had ever known, and he was kind, consistently and invariably kind, without effort, simply because it was his impulse to be so.

It was upon his candour, his intelligence, his kindness, that she counted now.

"Oh, Lance!" she said. "I'm so unhappy!"

"What's the trouble?"

The waiter was hovering near.

"You'd better order something," she murmured.

"I'm not hungry!"

"But you must, Lance! Please! It would look so queer."

"A glass of milk," he said, "and a piece of apple pie, then!"

The waiter was astounded and offended at this plebeian order; he had, nevertheless, to go and fetch it and they were able to talk again.

"What makes you unhappy, Claudine?" he asked.

"I suppose I ought to bear it, and say nothing, but I can't any longer. Lance....! I want to leave Gilbert!"

This time she had certainly shaken his scientific calm.

"What!" he said. "After three months!"

"I wish I could tell you.... But I could never make anyone understand. It's just—unendurable."

"Isn't he—decent to you?"

"It's not altogether Gilbert's fault. He tries to be kind. He thinks he is. But it's the whole life. Oh, Lance, it's so horrible! It's like being buried alive...." She had to stop, to struggle with her tears. "I've tried. I've really tried my best. But I can't stand it. I want to go home and live with Father and Mother. Oh, Lance, do you think it would be wrong?"

He regarded her thoughtfully.

"Do you mean as a general principle?" he asked. "Do you mean—do I think it's wrong for a woman to leave her husband?"

"I suppose I do mean that."

"It's hard for me to say," he went on, frowning. "I can't say I've ever thought much about the modern system of marriage. I suppose it's the best—or at least, the most expedient system for our present stage of development. But I haven't considered exactly what it is. Is marriage popularly considered indissoluble? No, there's divorce. No! ... I suppose it's an arrangement for the convenience of both the parties to the contract. In that case—"

"But I never thought about divorce!" she cried. "I only wanted to get away. Can that possibly be wrong?"

Lance was never greatly concerned about ethical problems, certainly not about the relations between men and women. It didn't seem a matter of much importance to him. He envisaged the human race as gradually progressing, adopting now this expedient now that; marriage he had looked upon as a rather silly but necessary part of modern existence. As for woman's revolt, feminism, and so on, he merely smiled at it all. He knew too much about Pre-Historic Woman.

He bent his mind to the problem as to whether the sanctity of marriage was a help or a hindrance to civilization.

"I can't see that there's anything wrong in it, Claudine," he said.

"Then you think—" she began. "But oh, I don't know what Father and Mother would say. Everyone but you would think I was wicked—and that my life was ruined.... Just because I want to be myself!"

He glanced up in surprise at her tone, and saw her eyes fastened on him, swimming in tears, the most beautiful eyes he had ever seen. It came to him with a sort of shock that this was Claudine's specific case, and not a general problem; that it was not women who wished to leave their husbands, but Claudine who wished to leave Gilbert. He saw that she was a lovely and innocent young thing, unhappy and desperate; he saw suddenly what this might lead to. She would be cast adrift, blamed, gossiped about, always under a sort of cloud. Her position in her own home would be an equivocal one, an unending embarrassment and distress. Hers was not a strong spirit; she couldn't go forward unsupported. A terrible pain seized him, he turned his eyes away because he couldn't bear to look at her. And the most intolerable part of his pain was his certainty that she could grow out of her pain; that what she now found unbearable she could one day regard with indifference. She suffered cruelly; she thought her fate was a lamentable and wretched one, and it was really nothing; a trifle, a few moments in her history.

"What would be the sense of my going on?" she asked him. "I don't make Gilbert happy, and I'm—dreadfully unhappy myself."

"It isn't important—to be happy," said Lance. "The question is, are you useful?"

"No! No, I'm not!"

He pushed away his plate with a nervous gesture.

"You want to know what I think," he said. "Well, I think you'd better go back to your husband."

II

She went home, to dress for a euchre party which was to be given in her honour. She felt numb and cold, ready to die of despair. Everyone was against her. No one understood, no one cared, what she suffered. She had appealed in vain to all the people who loved her, and they had all said—
"Continue to suffer. It is best for you."

She had gone to her father for his support in the piano battle.

"Buy me a piano of my own, Father!" she had entreated. "Send it to me as a present. Then the disagreeable old thing *can't* object."

"But, my dear!" said her father. "When in Rome—you know! If I were you, I should avoid conflicts. There's no use exasperating your mother-in-law. The wisest course is to conciliate."

She had gone to her mother, to pour out all her misery at living under the domination of a strange woman, at not being mistress in her husband's house. But her mother had no comfort to give.

"I don't see what's to be done, chickabiddy," she said. "You can't expect Gilbert to leave his mother alone at her age. It can't be cured, so it must be endured."

Gilbert was still more hopeless. When he saw her dejected, weary, full of nervous excitement and irritability after her long day of emptiness, his remedy was the theatre; and when even that didn't enliven her, he too became irritable. He was beginning to lose patience with her, he was willing now to admit that she was peculiar. And he felt that he was justified....

Justified in doing things which she never mentioned to anyone. They had had quarrels, the very memory of which appalled her. She remembered coarse words he had used, brutal expressions, sneers, gibes. He was always very sorry, always apologized, he said he had the devil's own temper; but Claudine could not forget them. She was neither quick to anger nor quick to forgive. When her temper was aroused, she was cold and contemptuous and often childishly indignant, but she was never fierce, never cruel. She could not understand or forgive his absolute loss of dignity.

And she could not understand what he called his weakness! She remembered the first time he had revealed it as one remembers a nightmare, the very thought of it brought back the incredulous horror she had felt. He hadn't come home to dinner that night, he had sent a telegram, "Detained on business. Will not be home till late," and Claudine and the old lady had sat down at the table alone, in that sort of hostile intimacy which had grown upon them. After dinner they had gone up to sit in the old lady's room where it would be cosier for two lone women, the old lady with a book and Claudine with the fancy-work she had taken to in desperation.

Just before bed-time Gilbert came in, flushed, jolly, anxious to talk. He had sat down and entertained them with a long account of the dinner he had attended, and the speeches he had heard.

"Best thing for business," he said. "You get to know just the men you need to know. It was an impromptu thing, but wonderfully well done."

And he told them everything he had had to eat.

"And by the way," he said, "They had some oyster pâtés that were the best things of their kind I've ever eaten, bar none. I spoke to the waiter, and he packed me a couple in a box and I brought them home. They're downstairs with my overcoat. Will you get them, Claudine?"

She did so, and he opened the box and took the pâtés out.

"Just try this!" he said, offering one to Claudine.

"I couldn't eat it now, thank you, Gilbert," she said. "Tomorrow I'd enjoy—"

"No! Nonsense! Eat it now! I want you to!"

She shook her head, smiling.

"To oblige me!" said Gilbert in a grieved voice.

The idea of gracefully yielding, of doing something *she didn't want to do*, never occurred to Claudine.

"No, thank you!" she said, more firmly.

"I insist!" said Gilbert.

That made her laugh, she thought he was rather funny, anyway, with his excessive garrulousness and his oyster pâtés. She was about to answer him with a good-humoured joke, when she saw his face suddenly change, and grow convulsed with rage. She hardly heard what he said, she was so startled. He jumped to his feet and addressed her in a furious trembling voice, and suddenly took the pâtés, on their little frilled paper plates, and threw them on the carpet and stamped on them.

His mother got up and came near to him.

"Gilbert! Gilbert!" she whispered, patting his shoulder. "You'd better get to bed, my boy!"

He threw a savage glance at Claudine and walked unsteadily away. The old lady bent over her cherished carpet, regarding the damage with distress.

"Dear! Dear!" she said. "*I* don't know...."

She never looked at Claudine, standing behind her, wringing her hands, her teeth chattering with a sort of nervous chill.

"I don't know!" she said again. "I suppose I'd better leave it so until the morning. Then in the daylight, perhaps...."

As she straightened herself she met the eyes of her daughter-in-law.

"What are you doing here?" she asked.

"Let me stay with you!" cried Claudine.

The old lady looked at her with frigid contempt. "You go to Gilbert!" she said. "Your place is with your husband."

"No!" cried Claudine, desperately. "I can't!"

"You go!" said the old lady. "Quick! I'll have none of this under my roof."

And she went so far as to take her by the arm and hurry her out of the room. But there was no cause to be worried about any further scene; Gilbert had gone to sleep, fully dressed, on the bed.

III

And the next morning he regarded it all as a great joke. He complained ruefully of a headache, but he was proud of it. He burst out laughing when his mother mentioned her damaged carpet, and to Claudine's surprise, the old lady was wonderfully indulgent. He told Claudine not to mind, it wouldn't happen again; but it did, more than once. Only on special occasions, though, as he pointed out to her; he was no drunkard. He was simply a good fellow; and he felt that she ought to appreciate his social qualities. He was sincerely aggrieved at her attitude, her scorn, her cold aversion. He told her she was straitlaced and puritanical; he thought she was shocked because he could not imagine that she was disgusted. She didn't find him devilish; she found him repulsive. It was not a question of forgiveness; she felt for him a profound distaste and aversion which she never again overcame. It was not even that she had ceased to love him; she had simply discovered that she never had loved him. She was not by nature affectionate or indulgent; she was fastidious, always a little apart from life, never quite human. She was a dutiful egoist.

She looked back over these three months of married life with a sort of cold wonder. The long, long days, the tedious drives, the dull calls on dull people, the unpleasant meals, the stuffy dismalness of the house! She thought that the Vincelle friends were the most unspeakably tiresome people in the world. To go with her mother-in-law and sit in their augustly gloomy parlours for the required fifteen minutes, or to receive them in like fashion at home, to sit at their dinner tables, or to see them sitting at hers, was an infliction almost beyond her endurance. Except at dinners, she saw nothing but women; they had euchre-parties, receptions, luncheons, once in a while a matinée party. A harem world of pampered women, interested in nothing, women whose husbands were pleased to see them expensively dressed, wearing jewels, who required them to be ladylike; but didn't expect them to be seductive. They were all good, all complacent, and they seemed to Claudine years and years older and more mature than herself. She made no friends. Vincelle heard that one of the young married women did china painting, and that aroused a spark of interest in her. She approached the alleged artist, young Mrs. Ryder.

"Oh, yes! I love it!" the artist told her. "Of course I don't have much time; but I positively made up my mind *not* to drop it after I married. It's such a mistake, don't you think, to get into a rut? I believe a man thinks ever so much more of his wife if she has some interests of her own."

Claudine's heart sank; then it was, after all, nothing but another harem accomplishment, a trick to secure attention.

"Of course I don't have much time," the other went on. "There's so much to do, isn't there?"

"What *do* you do?" Claudine asked, with earnestness. "I wish you'd tell me what you do all day?"

"Oh ... so *many* things!" murmured the other, taken aback. "There's the house-keeping, of course—and social duties ... and with a man in the house there are each a lot of little things...."

Now it must be admitted that Claudine was not a lover of her kind. She had no special interest in humanity; she was not ready to see the simple human qualities in those about her. She was an aloof, eager soul, greedy for activity, for gaiety, and for something more than that. She wanted food for thought; she was not very original, she needed perpetual stimulation, a constant flow of external impressions. She did not wish to meditate, she wished to observe.

She was baffled at every turn. She tried to discover what it was that enabled the old lady to pass the time so tranquilly without impatience or weariness. After a few orders to the servants and her marketing, she had nothing to do. Other old ladies came in during the afternoons to talk with her; often there were old ladies from the country spending a few days with her, they talked of other old ladies known to them with a sort of good-humoured indifference.... Perhaps that was the key to it—a profound and cynical indifference, nothing mattered; one endured and existed, and life consisted not in accomplishment, but in a perfectly passive Duty.

The old lady said Claudine was excitable, and even went so far as to call her frivolous. And yet the only part of Claudine's life which either she or her son took with any seriousness were these horrible little frivolities, the euchre club, the dinner parties, the calls. Her social duties....

"What in the world makes you so restless, child?" the old lady asked her one afternoon. Claudine had come into her room and was wandering about looking at the photographs, asking idle questions.

"I don't know what to do with myself!" she answered suddenly.

"Do? Why, what under the sun do you *want* to do?"

"I don't know.... But it seems.... Oh, it seems such a waste of time!"

"I must say you have very queer notions for a young married woman, Claudine. I've never heard of anyone else with such notions. You have your home, and your friends. And there's the euchre club, and Gilbert takes you to the theatre every mortal week. What more do you want?"

This Claudine was unable to answer. The old lady regarded her severely.

"I only hope," she went on, "that the time will never come when you'll look back on these days as the happiest time of your life.... I remember when I was a young married woman—" she sighed. "I can tell you, I hadn't much time to worry about what to do, with my five children."

"I wish I had five children," said Claudine.

The old lady looked at her again.

"Humph!" she said.

IV

She was ready now for the euchre, she cast a last glance in the mirror and gathered up her little possessions, handkerchiefs, gloves, cardcase, and muff. A composed and mature figure she looked, in her grey broadcloth dress with a trailing skirt and well-boned bodice, slender, dignified in spite of her smallness. A lady—a young married woman, a finished product. She was supposed to have done with adventure, romance and excitement, she was presumed to have settled down.

She smiled frigidly.

"We'll see!" she said. "Just wait! They're all against me—even Lance. But I won't give in! If I can't get away, then I'll change all this! I won't have a life like this. I won't! I won't!"

CHAPTER EIGHT

A YEAR LATER

I

The old lady was going upstairs to the store-room on one of her periodical rummaging excursions, conducted for mysterious purposes of her own. She looked through trunks, bags, and boxes, and emerged from the dark little room quite exhausted, but without bringing anything with her. As she passed the big bedroom she looked in at the open door and smiled to herself, with grim satisfaction. There sat Claudine by the window, her head leaning against the back of a venerable rocking chair, her eyes fixed dreamily on the ceiling. She had been sitting there quite three-quarters of an hour, and perfectly content in her idleness. Not a trace of restlessness, of mutiny, about her, the sparkle too had gone from her glance, she had a new, half melancholy charm....

The old lady admitted that Claudine had at last "settled down." She was still peculiar. Perhaps more peculiar than ever, but that was a matter beyond hope of remedy. It was her bringing up. She had queer notions about sitting alone, and she very obviously discouraged conversation, she read pretentious and quite immoral books, but as she never said or did anything improper, Gilbert and his mother were agreed to overlook these unpleasant eccentricities. Naturally, they remonstrated with her at every opportunity, but in a despairing way.

She was conquered, and she was happy. Not one of the hopes of her girlhood had been fulfilled; she had seen no foreign countries; she had met no remarkable people; she was denied the active and interesting life she had expected. But she was able to smile at these lost hopes. She was happy.

She had lost the best and dearest friend of her life, her mother. She was obliged to live without a confidant, without sympathy or encouragement. In losing her mother she had irrevocably lost her girlhood, and been cast adrift on a strange sea. But she had resigned herself even to that bitter loss.

She was well aware that she had missed the beauty and romance of the love between a man and a woman. She certainly didn't love Gilbert, she didn't even like him; she was in fear of coming to hate him. But even that she endured with tranquil indifference, as she endured her fettered existence, her hostile mother-in-law, her wearisome social duties.

Because she had Andrée. She wanted nothing more. Andrée was enough to fill heaven and earth for her. Her love for Andrée, her hope for her, the watchful care of her, gave her utter and complete satisfaction.

It had come as an astounding revelation. She had looked forward to the coming of a baby with despair and revolt; it would be, she thought, another link in the chain slowly forging to bind her to slavery. She didn't feel old enough or wise enough for a baby. She looked upon the whole thing as a horrible indignity put upon her by merciless Nature, and she even hoped that she might die.

She took it for granted that it would be a son, because everyone else required a son from her. Another Gilbert, she thought, a pompous and obstinate creature whom she could never hope to influence, and who would soon learn to disapprove of her. She looked forward to its birth with dread and terror, she imagined the wretched tedium of being obliged to carry it about, to nurse it, to be perpetually tied to it, the broken nights, the distasteful duties.

And to think that it was Andrée who had come, after all! This son, who was to have been named Andrew, after Gilbert's father, had been miraculously transformed into that wonderful little dark-haired baby, that tiny, plaintive little creature whose first cry had almost broken her heart.

She had lain with the little bundle beside her, and from time to time reached out a weak hand to turn down a corner of the blanket and look at its sleeping face. The *queer* little thing! The pathos, the marvelous appeal of its weakness, its aloofness, the charm of its doll-like completeness! She never tired of looking at it, she never wanted it out of her arms. Its fierce and despairing cries pierced her soundest sleep; its faintest stir aroused her.

She occupied the big room on the third floor, so that the baby shouldn't disturb Gilbert, and after the nurse went, she was alone with the baby. Miss Dorothy had eagerly offered to take charge of it at night, but Claudine wouldn't listen to that. She had a little bassinet beside her, where the baby was supposed to sleep, but at the least sound, she would take it into the bed, to lie close to her, while she comforted its inexplicable little woes, whispered to it, sang to it, stroked its downy, restless little head.

She passed hours of mystic happiness alone with it in the big silent room, where a night-light burned dimly. They would lie looking at each other; she would gaze into its solemn unfathomable eyes, trying to impress her image upon it, trying to reach it. It would fall asleep clutching her finger, and she would weep with joy and terror, afraid of everything, haunted by spectres of croup, whooping-cough, of accidents, of all the cruel chances of life.

Gilbert had very much objected to the name Andrée. But Claudine was so ill and weak, and so determined, that he had submitted to it. He thought it was a charming and wonderful baby, and that it would undoubtedly be a comfort to him in his old age. He boasted about it to his business friends; he said it was the greatest thing in life. But he saw only the promise in it; he was impatient for it to develop, to become responsive and human. But Claudine loved it at each moment; she dreaded its changing. Every day she thought, "This is the very sweetest age! I wish she would stay like this forever!"

It was now two months old, and on this day was taking its first airing, in the arms of a highly recommended nurse-maid. The old lady had a prejudice against perambulators; she thought it all nonsense anyhow to take babies out into the street, but as Dr. Perceval was newfangled and insistent, she made no objection to a daily outing, provided it was carried. Perambulators were against nature; babies were meant to be carried, she said.

Claudine took little interest in this discussion. As long as they did nothing actually harmful, she didn't care. Her only concern was to protect it, to keep it near her; matters of hygiene she considered a little unreal.

She heard the sound of heavy and deliberate footsteps ascending the stairs, and she rushed out into the hall.

"Be careful, Katie!" she called. "Go very slowly, and be sure you don't catch your foot!"

She watched with frowning anxiety the progress of the nurse and the bundle in her arms, and the instant they reached the hall, she snatched the baby.

"She's asleep!" said the nurse, warningly, but in vain, because the wicked mother had kissed it until it was awake and crying and had to be rocked. It was the first separation, it had been out of the house nearly an hour. Who was to blame her for her rapture at getting it back alive and well?

And it looked so queer and darling in a little lace bonnet, with muslin strings tied under its querulous face, and a coat with capes encasing its helpless arms.

"Oh, Andrée!" she cried. "My heart's darling! I don't think I can ever let you go again!"

II

A year later there was another little girl, and after that, the requisite son. They were delightful, pretty, healthy babies, and she loved them passionately. But they were not like Andrée. There could never be anything in the world like Andrée. She concealed her fanatic worship of her first-born; she was a wonderful mother to them all, patient, gentle, wise. She took an unfailing delight in them; she gave her life to them joyfully; she was flattered and enchanted by the solemn loyalty of little Edna and the teasing affection of her small son. But the look of understanding in Andrée's eyes was immeasurably dearer to her; the clasp of Andrée's hand, a kiss from her, were the very consummation of her life.

BOOK TWO
THE BREATH OF LIFE

CHAPTER ONE

AFTER TWENTY YEARS

I

"Lord! I'll be glad when this is over!" said Andrée. "And this is Father's idea of a holiday! The poor thing actually said he envied us!"

Her younger sister was engaged in drawing on her stockings.

"Come on, Andrée!" she said. "We'll be late for lunch and Mother does hate that so.... No: I suppose this *would* be a treat for poor Father, after being shut up in a hot office all the time."

"I'd like to see him stand it for *one week!*" said Andrée, grimly. "Just for one week, that's all!"

"And then, of course, it's cheap," said the sensible Edna. "I suppose he has to think of that, poor thing, with Bertie going to college and you and your awful Mr. MacGregor. We must be a tremendous expense."

"I don't want to be!" cried Andrée. "And I wouldn't be, either, if he wasn't so darned obstinate. I've told him and told him that I could easily earn enough to pay for my lessons by teaching. Mr. MacGregor says I'm thoroughly qualified, and that he'd help me to get pupils. But no! Father pretends to be so advanced, and says he wants us to be able to earn our own livings, and then when we can, he stops it. He and Mother are both hoping and praying I'll get married before I have a chance to do anything. But I won't! I'm going to—"

"Oh, Andrée For pity's sake! *Not* that! *Do* get your shoes and stockings on! It's after twelve!"

They were sitting on the bank of a wide, shallow stream running its hasty course down the mountain side; a favourite spot with them. They liked to come there in the morning and with bare feet and skirts pinned up, to pick their way over the stones, with the cold water lapping about their ankles. It was like a broad and deserted highway, lined with trees. On either side were the dark woods, of which they were both a little afraid. They would ascend the stream, "stepping stones," past the sombre belt of woodland to the wide meadows basking in the sun, and then suddenly the banks grew high and rocky, the stream went out of the sunlight and entered a ravine, gloomy and mysterious, and was no longer a stream but a deep and ice-cold pool, fed by a trickling waterfall. Farther than this they had never gone, the climb up the rocks beside the waterfall would have been a very difficult one, and moreover it was a spot where they didn't care to linger. City born and bred, they had a sort of horror of this silent, imprisoned place.

The stream—the "crick," the country people called it, had an unfailing charm for them. They came to it every fine morning and indulged in pursuits which they were a little ashamed of and which they justified by their ennui—an ennui more pretended than real. They talked to each other and to their mother a great deal about the horrible dulness of the little Catskill Mountains summer resort, but they were really very happy in it, and they secretly enjoyed their infantile amusements. They whittled little boats of soft wood and sailed them; they brought tin pails and scooped up the lazy, fat pollywogs that lay along the edges of the shallow pools in long rows, nasty creatures with a sort of horrible fascination about them. Andrée would watch them wriggling sluggishly in the pail for a long time, with the sun shining through their translucent, speckled tails, and sniff the queer primeval smell of them.

"Aren't they horrible!" she would cry.

"Don't look at them, idiot!" her sister would say. "You'll be having nightmares about them again tonight."

Andrée was very irritating about such matters. She wouldn't keep away from things and people and facts that troubled and tormented her. That pool, for instance... She would argue Edna into going there with her and insist upon lingering beside it, looking into the dark depths of the water, standing in its icy shallows, laying her hands against the wet moss-grown rocks, until she became so filled with her absurd dreads and fancies that even the sensible Edna would become infected.

They had been there that morning; they had sat on a fallen tree and stared at the quiet pool, the dark face of the cliff over which the puny trickle of water ran, ran, ran, had been running, just in this way, for God knows how many centuries. And suddenly they had seen a great black snake, swimming rapidly and silently on its way. They had fled in a panic, barefooted over the stones and rough ground, out to the ravine and into the sun again.

Edna had been angry.

"Why *will* you go there!" she cried. "You're so morbid!"

There was nothing morbid about Edna; she was a distractingly pretty thing of nineteen, very like her mother in her young days as far as appearance went—small, slight, self-confident, with crisp fair hair like a halo about a flower-like face. She was alert, independent and unsociable; her most profound instinct was to keep silent, to stay alone, to be untouched, undisturbed while her strong spirit grew. She was a disappointment to her mother because she was so difficult, so impossible to influence. She wished to take every new idea and run off with it, to examine it alone, in peace; she never wanted to talk over anything. Nor did she care much for reading. She observed, and she made deductions from her observations, she formed intelligent opinions, she judged people with sane and kindly indifference.

But she did not understand, as Andrée did. Andrée apparently never did any thinking. She simply knew things, spontaneously. She knew what people would do, what they were, she loved them or hated them. And she was forced to discuss everything with everybody, to talk, to think, until her brain was sick and frightened. She couldn't quite believe anything or quite doubt anything. She was a thin, tall girl of twenty, pale, distrait, not very pretty, but with a face wonderfully mobile and sensitive. There was a perverse charm about her, about her moods, her immature high-mindedness, her terrible dependence upon others. She would ask your opinion, and if it differed from hers she would begin to doubt herself, and if you agreed with her, she was obliged to change her mind....

They had got their shoes and stockings on and set off by a convenient path for the little hotel.

"If only we didn't have to eat with all those people!" said Andrée, sighing. "It takes my appetite away. I do so *hate* the noise they make ... and those awful babies!"

Edna laughed at her.

"Poor grandma always used to call you 'pernicketty.' And you are, aren't you? They're not such bad people."

"How could they be worse? They're stupid and vulgar and horrible to look at and horrible to listen to. We wouldn't think of bothering with such people when we're at home, and I can't see why we should here. They're not any better in the summer time or in the mountains, than they are in the winter, in the city."

"Mother hates snobbishness—"

"Ha! *Does* she? She's the worst sort of snob in the world. She doesn't like *anybody* at all. She's bored with everyone, just as much bored with right people as with wrong ones."

They had come now to the hotel grounds, and were walking across the lawn with great decorum. And just on time, for a bell rang out with a loud and hostile clamour, and the embroidering ladies on the porch began to collect their work and rise.

Andrée and Edna hurried up to their room for the process of "neatening," which their mother considered indispensable. She was there, in the adjoining bedroom, standing before the mirror.

"How hot you are!" she said. "Hurry, I'll wait for you."

She was a pleasure to the eye, as she always was. She had a well-deserved reputation for being the best-dressed woman in her set, and she took infinite pains to sustain it. She wasn't by any means beautiful, the promise of her young days had never been fulfilled; she was pale, colourless, except for her bright hair still untouched by grey; she was thin and angular, and her features were as tranquil and expressionless as a statue's. But the dignity of the small creature! She was absolutely imposing, she had a look of melancholy and resignation, but a melancholy without lassitude, a resignation without weakness. She had a passion for reserve. Even in her limitless devotion to her children she was a little formal, a little aloof. She was certainly in no way tyrannical or severe, but she commanded unfailing respect. They adored her like a goddess, instead of loving her like a human being. She was a perpetual mystery to them.

Poor Claudine! Like a strayed nymph, forever astonished and affrighted at the strange world into which she had been betrayed! She had known no way of adapting herself, she could never feel at home, her one refuge had been to withdraw into herself.

She was courteous and agreeable enough to all her fellow-guests, but she fled from them. She went off every morning after breakfast, her thin form, straight as a dart, charmingly dressed in clear summer colours, a parasol held over her burnished head, and two or three portentous volumes under her arm, to find a secluded spot in the woods where she could read undisturbed. She read Epictetus and Marcus Aurelius and Schopenhauer and Emerson, with ardent attention, marking passages, meditating on them, trying to appease and fortify her desperate spirit.

The idea of her being desperate would have seemed ludicrous to anyone who knew her. She was calm, so self-possessed, so well-poised! She had a great social success in her own milieu, she was something of an authority upon correctness in dress and manner. She was moreover a lady of unblemished reputation, she was never even indiscreet or stupid. She was quite perfect. Not even the resentful Gilbert could find a flaw in her public demeanour.

And yet, in her own heart, she was bewildered and lost.

II

They went down, all three, to the dining-room, and sat down at their small table, accompanied by a great many glances from the other guests. They never suspected how much they were gossiped about, how much interest they aroused. It was the first time they had come to so small and cheap a place for their summer holiday; heretofore they had stopped at lively and agreeable resorts with others of their own comfortable sort. But

Gilbert had taken one of those unaccountable fancies to which husbands are so prone. It may have been an obscure resentment at the sight of the care-free and pampered existence of his women-folk, or one of those sudden anxieties he often felt at the thought of the future. However, from no matter what cause, he had suddenly required Claudine to retrench and she had obeyed, with her usual profound and polite indifference. Hence the "Pine View Villa," in the Catskills, and two small rooms without a bath.

Their attitude aroused resentment. Claudine had her own special tea, which she made in a pot at the table, and they had extra milk and cream, and various potted delicacies ordered from the city. The landlady took this as a reflection upon her table and it was. And then they had made a special arrangement whereby Andrée was to have the exclusive use of the piano in the mornings, and on chilly or wet mornings, when some of the ladies would have enjoyed sitting in the parlour and rocking and chatting, they were not at all pleased by the vigorous rhythm of her interminable exercises. She regarded them no more than so many chairs.

Edna was the most approachable, but she had a scrutinizing air, an amused sort of interest outrageous in one so young. Altogether a conceited, snobbish, intolerable family; that was the verdict.

"Take the tea and the anchovy paste, Andrée!" said Claudine. "And will you bring them up to my room, please? I'd like to speak to you for a moment. Edna'll wait on the veranda for you."

She closed the door of her room and sat down.

"Andrée, dear," she said. "Was that another letter from Mr. MacGregor this morning?"

"Yes, it was," said Andrée, nonchalantly.

Claudine waited for a moment.

"I wish you'd show it to me!" she said, coaxingly.

"I'd *rather* not, Mother, it's private."

"But Andrée, my dear, why should you have private letters from that man which you can't show your mother?"

She had adopted a very tranquil, reasonable tone, to conceal her own distress and the advantage which it gave to Andrée. She was confronted once more by the terrible *independence* of her children, they all led such busy, lively, entertaining lives in which there was no need at all for her. They loved her, but they would have gone on in exactly the same way if she were not with them. She was unessential, they needed nothing from her. She had never been able to understand how it had happened. When they were little, she was their universe, she consoled, protected, she alone understood them. She had wished to give her life to them. And then little by little they had got upon their feet and walked away, leaving her still standing with empty arms in the nursery. She couldn't follow them; she didn't know how to draw near to them, how to win them. She was helpless, just as she was now helpless before Andrée. The very sight of Andrée frightened her, the fragile and mysterious charm of her beloved child wrung her heart, robbed her of worldly wisdom and common sense. She could have knelt before Andrée and adored her, and wept for the pity that touching youth and ignorance caused her.

"I have loved you every moment of your life, from your first breath!" she might have cried. "There is no one in the world for me but you! I love my other children, but oh, not like you! Not like you! I wanted to give all my life to your service. I wanted to live for you, to wear myself out to give you happiness. And you will not have me!"

She stole a glance at the child's downcast face, mutinous, impatient.

"Andrée, my dear," she said again. "Why should you have letters from that man which you don't wish me to see?"

For answer Andrée put her hand inside her blouse and drew out a crumpled letter.

"Here!" she said. "Read it then, if you want!"

But it was impossible to do so, to pry into her poor little secret.

"I don't want to read it, my darling. I only want to talk to you about—"

To her great surprise Andrée began to cry.

"Oh, Mother!" she sobbed. "That's just what I knew you'd do! Talk it over, and talk and talk, and spoil everything.... Why can't you understand? It's nothing, just nothing at all, and you want to talk it into something. Why can't I be let alone? I'm so unhappy!"

"*Unhappy?* Andrée, why? Tell me! Let me help you!"

"I don't know why—except that I never have any peace or freedom. It's *disgusting* to have to talk about every thought that comes into your head.... How would you like it? How would you like to have to tell exactly how you felt toward everyone and everything?"

Claudine turned away her head.

"I see how you feel," she said. "It must be disgusting, as you say.... But you're surely fair-minded enough to see that I must make every possible effort to safeguard you. You are young and inexperienced."

"When you were my age you were married and had a baby."

Claudine smiled, one of her rare and enchanting smiles.

"That's true. I had *you*."

"So you see I'm not so very young. And as for experience ... well, honestly, Mother, I don't think you've had much."

Claudine was startled. She who had suffered so much, been so cruelly disappointed and mocked by life, who had learned so many, many bitter lessons, to be reproached with lack of experience by this baby? She smiled again, sadly.

"You've never been to Europe, or met any famous people, or anything. And you've never—" Andrée flushed and hesitated. "You've never had any romance. Nothing but just Father, and he's not very thrilling."

"My dear!"

"*Please* don't be shocked! It makes it so hard to talk to you. It's no use my pretending that I want a life like yours or that I'd marry a man like Father. I wouldn't for *anything!*"

"Andrée, I really—"

Andrée shook her head. She alone of the three had never been drawn to her father, had never been influenced by him.

"No," she said. "It's no use talking. I want something *very* different. I don't want any stuffy family life. I'd like to go away, by myself—"

"Andrée! Think what you're saying! How can you be so cruel? What should I do without you?"

"You've got Bertie and Edna. And you're settled down and all that sort of thing. You have lots of things to interest you, but I haven't anything. That's why—" Once more she stopped, her cheeks scarlet.

"That's why I like to hear from—Mr. MacGregor. He encourages me. He says there's no reason why I shouldn't make a name for myself, giving concerts. *He*—well, I know he exaggerates, but he says I'm a—a—sort of— wonder."

"Is he urging you to leave your parents?"

"Heavens, *no!* He just encourages me. He says to keep on practising and practising. And when I get back he's going to give me a lot of extra time."

"Why?"

"Because he thinks I'm—promising."

"Andrée, isn't there anything more personal beneath this interest?"

"I don't know," said Andrée, curtly. "I don't want to know."

Claudine was still for a moment, thinking with supreme displeasure of that man, that music teacher, who had by flattery, by chicanery, won her child's interest. It must be stopped! Should she ridicule him, point out to Andrée that Mr. MacGregor was as old as her father, and a man of no distinction, either mental or physical, a shaggy, lumbering, grey-haired creature only too well used to the silly admiration of young girl pupils? No, ridicule was not a weapon Claudine could handle. She thought for a moment of appealing to her affection, but that too she rejected. She dared not....

"Andrée," she said at last, very gravely. "I am going to ask you to promise me something. If Mr. MacGregor—if this thing—"

"I know what you mean. You mean you want me to promise to tell you if anything happens."

"Yes."

"But don't you see that that isn't a fair promise?"

Claudine was startled.

"Surely your mother has the right—"

"Oh, yes, you have all sorts of rights!" said Andrée, bitterly. "And I haven't any. But if I were you—if ever I have a daughter—I'll never, never ask her to promise to tell me things. I wouldn't want to know them if she didn't *want* to tell them."

Claudine approached and put her arm about the unwilling girl.

"Very well!" she said, with a sigh. "I will leave you free to do as you please about telling me."

Then Andrée bent down and kissed her.

"You *are* a darling!" she cried. "Now I'll rush to Edna!"

CHAPTER TWO

THE FORSAKEN PROVIDER

I

"One of Gilbert's bad mornings!" thought Miss Dorothy.

And she slipped into her place behind the coffee urn, a little more ingratiating, a little more careful not to disturb him, than usual. He sat at the head of the table, glowering behind his newspaper, and by the very sound of the grunt with which he answered the cousinly good-morning, she was warned of what might be expected. She sat very still, in order not to attract the lightning

He ate his grape-fruit, quite reasonably, and a little dish of oatmeal, and then Delia brought in the eggs and bacon. He glanced at the plate suspiciously.

"Are these Murray's eggs?" he demanded.

Miss Dorothy sent the girl a warning glance.

"Yes, sir," she said.

"You're sure?"

"Yes, sir."

"When did they come?"

".... Yesterday, sir."

"Let me see the box!"

"It was thrown away, sir."

His face became alarming

"Dorothy!" he said. "I don't believe it. I don't believe these are Murray's eggs!"

He leaned across the table and sniffed at the dish.

"No!" he shouted. "They are *not!* I know it!"

He flung down his napkin and pushed back his chair. He had for a few weeks past been importing eggs for his special use from a fellow he knew in the country, and he knew that he was being duped, that these immoral women, Miss Dorothy and Delia, used his eggs for other purposes, for the household, for puddings, perhaps even ate them themselves. His appetite was extremely delicate at breakfast, no one could quite comprehend how he felt, especially the morning after a banquet. Suddenly his anger turned into a frightful gloom.

"Take them away!" he said, with a sigh. "Take the damned things away and never bring me eggs again. Never! ... Good Lord! I can't trust *anyone!*"

Miss Dorothy flushed, and smiled nervously.

"Would you like ... a slice of ham, Gilbert?" she ventured.

"Nothing! ... More coffee!"

He had put down his paper, and she was in the full glare of his bilious and lowering regard. He picked the thing up again, not to read it, for he had finished all that interested him, but as a screen to conceal from him this scene which he so hated to contemplate, from that dining-room where he had eaten so many hundreds of breakfasts. Claudine hadn't really changed it, or anything else. By the time the old lady had departed this life, Claudine had no more ideas, no more desire to make changes. The huge sideboard opposite him was crowded with cut glass, silver, hand-painted china, wedding presents, Christmas presents, birthday and anniversary presents, milestones along the road of twenty years of married life. All very neat, comfortable and prosperous, and yet it offended him. He couldn't really find fault with this home or this atmosphere, couldn't well imagine anything much better. If he had been compelled to furnish a dining-room according to his own taste, he would have produced something very similar. He had even a sort of pride in the old furniture and the curtains and the presents. And yet it hurt and angered him so.

He looked up stealthily and saw Miss Dorothy, with such a pleased face, just about to begin her grape-fruit.

The face of a fool he called it to himself, a half complacent, half terrified countenance, a sallow, soul-wearying creature in gold eyeglasses, who existed through his benefactions, one of the thankless crew he laboured unendingly to feed and clothe.

And not one of them made the least effort to comprehend him. He was a man, and therefore to be humoured; he was a man and therefore to be conciliated. Like so many sun-worshippers did they all bow down before the inscrutable source of all comforts, all security, supplicating him to continue shedding his golden rays. Not from humility, you understand, or because they had the least admiration for his productivity, but because only in this way could they obtain what they wished. It was really a worship, with rites and sacrifices, and splendid rewards to be got if you understood how to go about it. Claudine and his two daughters and even the unfortunate Miss Dorothy had all a dearly bought knowledge of what topics would infuriate him, knew his good hours and his bad ones, could read the warning symptoms of his more deadly moods. They knew what he liked to eat and what he liked to hear. And nothing else. His queer, gloomy soul remained mysterious and solitary. In an alien world he groped for light, he existed like a sensitive child among impervious and indifferent adults. Even his children seemed to him possessed of worldly knowledge impossible to him; they were aware of things, they discussed things, of which he was ignorant. They were somehow freer and brighter.

To be considered cross when the spirit was writhing, crying for help ...! He was passionately convinced that his malign fate had driven him into an utterly wrong life and that somewhere else there was an utterly right life, beautiful and satisfying, which he ought to have been enjoying. He had no idea of making adjustments, or of trying to modify his environment; he wanted, most naïvely, to step into another world.

What it was he so thirsted for, he didn't exactly know. It was not peace, or love, or fame, or money, or any of those things a man might legitimately demand from his destiny. He knew only that his daily bread was ashes in his mouth, that his soul found no nourishment, and pined and sickened, that it lived in a universe everywhere insipid and meaningless. And that with all his heart he resented this fate, above all, this marriage of his. Because it was his conviction, that he, as well as every other man on earth, was entitled to an ideal marriage, and a more or less ardent and beautiful wife. The men who got rather less than this had been cheated, defrauded of what he called "the greatest thing in life." It never occurred to him that he was disappointed because he expected too much, he believed himself disappointed because he had received too little.

He never thought of Claudine without a savage resentment. She had swindled him. She was to have brought light, gaiety, charm, into his life, to have transformed it into something resembling her old Staten Island existence, she was to have been perpetually alluring, fairylike, sparkling. And she had failed in all of this. She was nothing more than a decorous and virtuous wife, and she regarded him with something criminally like aversion. She was cold. And he believed, like more than one other man—that her coldness was a fault in her own temperament, and not due to any lack of fascination in himself. It was certainly not a happy marriage. He had grounds for believing that she thought herself a martyr, and he *knew* that he was one.

II

Some occult sense warned him of the time. He glanced up at the clock on the mantelpiece, and caught sight of his own face in the mirror behind it. And he wondered, as he always did when he really, consciously regarded himself, *how* it was he looked like *that,* how it was possible that his appearance should so little express himself. It was another cause for resentment.

A heavy, grizzled man of forty-five with a straggling little mustache over a brutally obstinate mouth. He had a surly way about him, but he was not unattractive; on the contrary, there was something about the gloomy and bilious gaze of his black eyes that engendered pity and good-will.

But neither pity nor good-will dwelt in Miss Dorothy at that particular instant. She was not resentful, because resentment didn't belong in her stock of feelings, but she was *miserable.* He was upsetting all her neat little plans for the day, he was keeping back Delia. He was so late, why on earth didn't he get up and be off to his office, where he belonged? Every moment of these days was so precious to her, when she was sole and undisputed mistress in this house which she had always regarded with awe. She could wish that the summer would last forever, and Claudine and the children never return. Think of the joy of going to market in the electric coupé! Think of the charm of eating her lunch alone, benevolent chatelaine of all this domain!

At last, with his terribly rough gesture, he shoved away the plates before him, so that they upset a milk jug, pushed back his chair in a way that made furrows in the carpet, and got up. He went heavily upstairs and took his straw hat from the gigantic hat-rack. He frowned, there was something he didn't like about that dark hall, with the rug removed for the summer. There were certain changes from his mother's day, the glass top of the front door was covered with shirred green silk, and over the open door of the front parlour hung a portière of bamboo tubes strung together with green and blue glass beads, hung there fifteen summers ago. On the shelf of the hat-rack was a little rubber plant in a horrible green scalloped bowl, and a clumsy bronze statue of a fat shepherd boy, holding out an altogether incongruous little tray for visiting cards, a wedding anniversary present from his senior partner. Each of these objects *per se* he regarded with more or less admiration, but the ensemble disgusted him. He felt that there was something wrong here, and that it was of course his wife's fault. He execrated her in silence.

He set off down the tranquil street, blazing in the July sun, removing his hat now and then to salute a familiar face. He knew so many people in the neighbourhood, through having lived there all his life, but they were not his friends, these people. They respected him as a man who paid his bills promptly and provided well for his family, but they didn't like him, had no warm feeling for him. He was too gloomy, too preoccupied. He had an air of misery about him which was distressing to a hostess. Claudine was obliged to confess, and to apologize for his reluctance to make visits. She said he was such a man's man! He was only happy among his business associates. But what she didn't know, what nobody suspected, was the positive hatred concealed beneath his *farouche* manner for all these respectable people. He despised them and loathed them, and was mortally sick of them, and worst of all, he couldn't feel justified in such feelings. Theoretically they were what he admired, and he couldn't see in what way he differed from them, and, yet he knew that he *did*. This feeling, like all his other feelings, he kept gloomily to himself.

He jumped on a crowded car going across the bridge, very hot, very angry at being jostled, and was carried off to New York, to make more money....

III

Not only at home were his moods known and respected, at his office it was a recognized thing that the early morning was a bad time for him, and that it was most unwise to disturb him. As usual he strode through the outer office and shut himself into his own small room, without exchanging a word or even a nod. He looked through his mail which had been opened and neatly sorted for him, then pushed it aside, staring after it with a distrait and wretched look. He couldn't put his mind on it, he hated every detail, every possibility.

"Why the devil am I slaving away here?" he asked himself. "Working day in and day out, so that she can go flaunting in fine clothes and idling away the whole summer up there in the mountains."

He remembered the extensive wardrobe Claudine had taken with her. Never did she suspect, never could she have suspected, how he resented it. The primeval male in him would deny all luxuries to the unloved woman.

"*She!* In her silk dresses—loafing all day long—servants to wait on her, *never* does a useful thing! Good God! Think of the time and leisure she's got, and she doesn't even read the papers! Not even charitable! Useless, through and through.... Where would she be if it weren't for me? She's got everything she wants, without raising a finger for it. Food, clothes, jewels, money to spend, fool women to jabber with—"

It seemed to him quite intolerable to think of her privileges; he couldn't have endured it at all if he hadn't had a certain very curious consolation for his grievances. His delight was to picture his wife as cast away upon a desert island, and he gloated over her utter futility there. He could imagine how helpless she would be, how incongruous, she with her fastidiousness, her chilly dignity. *She* wouldn't be able to make herself dresses out of grass, sewing with a thorn for a needle. She wouldn't know how, and couldn't learn how, to grind flour from exotic roots, to tame birds, to construct houses. Incurably romantic Gilbert! That was his test for any woman; how she would look and behave on his classic desert isle. She must be lovely, strong, and young, and she must be altogether daring and brave and unwifelike, she must be resourceful and full of alluring wiles, she must urgently *need* him, and yet be entirely independent.

He glanced at the clock, took up his hat, and went out to a celebrated café near by, had two whiskies and soda, and immediately felt much better. He would confess to you that he was rather too dependent upon "bracers," but like all that army, he was merely waiting for a propitious day to renounce the thing entirely. Some day when he wasn't worried or depressed. No hurry about it; it didn't interfere with his business, and it helped him beyond measure through his fits of awful despondency. He was willing to admit that perhaps his health might be better if he drank less, but he couldn't become really interested in his health.

He chatted with the other ten o'clock frequenters of the bar, whom he knew very well, for they came with great regularity. He felt ready for business now; he went back—in fact, he now entered the office officially for the first time, in his proper character, nodded genially to the cashier and to his stenographer, an ambitious young Cuban, and began to pace up and down the big sample room, planning his autumn campaign and reviewing his "line." A very fine line this year; he looked upon it with satisfaction as it lay spread out before him on a big counter sloping steeply on both sides and divided into little compartments filled with red rubber cows and white rubber horses, big, brightly colored balls and tiny hard rubber ones, dolls in knitted dresses, rattles, teething rings. There were among these several novelties which he considered very promising....

"A gentleman to see you!" said the young Cuban, with his alert and zealous air.

"Who?"

"Mr. MacGregor."

"Don't know him. Where's he from?"

"Didn't say," replied the young Cuban, with a creditable imitation of his chief's brusque business-like tone.

"Bring him in!" said Gilbert.

He stood facing the door with a non-committal expression which would be either menacing or genial, as circumstances might dictate. But the man who entered was a type not familiar to him; he couldn't place him; a big, shambling, rugged man of forty or so, a bit uncouth in appearance, but not without distinction. His face was ironic, but his smile was genial.

"Mr. Vincelle?" he asked.

"What can I do for you, sir?" inquired Gilbert, briefly.

"My name is Alexander MacGregor," said he. "I have had the pleasure of instructing your elder daughter in music."

Oh, a music teacher! Probably about a bill, or those outrageous "extra lessons" which his children were forever in need of.

"Sit down, sir, sit down!" said Gilbert.

Mr. MacGregor did so.

"I hope I don't find you very busy?" he said. "This is quite a personal matter...."

"Cigar?" asked Gilbert.

Mr. MacGregor accepted one.

"It's about Miss Andrée," he said. "I understand that you're going out there this afternoon, and I thought—"

They talked for more than an hour, and Gilbert was captivated. He liked this fellow! He liked his cool, manly air, his practical outlook. Mr. Mac-Gregor began his proposal by stating his financial position, which was sound and satisfactory. He put forward his own good points with assurance and he affirmed that his age was an asset.

"Andrée is very temperamental," he said, "and hard to understand. A young, inexperienced man wouldn't be able to. She requires the greatest tact. A rare, peculiar nature. Only men of our age can appreciate it."

Well, thought Gilbert, after all, why not? Wouldn't he himself be a marvelous lover for a young girl, if she were the right sort of young girl? There was a sort of indirect flattery in Mr. MacGregor's idea.

Moreover, he found Andrée an intensely irritating young woman, and he would be glad to see her safely married and gone away. She was a sort of ally to her mother. She was antagonistic; she didn't admire him; she wasn't the sort of daughter he had expected.

And he was delighted with Mr. MacGregor's old fashioned idea of asking his permission before speaking to Andrée. It was really the first time he had ever been treated as a father should be treated. He took Mr. Mac-Gregor out to lunch, to a sedate little second floor restaurant known only to connoisseurs. They ate largely and critically....

By two o'clock indigestion had engulfed Gilbert in black misery. He lingered at the table, chewing a cigar, and meditating. It was Saturday; the office was closed; he had nothing to do until train time. He ordered more liqueurs, more coffee, and refused to be parted from Mr. MacGregor, clung to him, in fact.

Of course, he said, it all depended upon Andrée herself. Of course it did, Mr. MacGregor agreed.

"See here!" said Gilbert. "Come out there with me, and we'll see. You'll have plenty of time to pack what you need for over Sunday. Come on!"

Naturally Mr. MacGregor went.

CHAPTER THREE

THE SUITOR WITH CREDENTIALS

I

It was a filial duty, as well as a wifely duty, to meet Gilbert's train. He wished them all to do so, he liked to see these three charmingly dressed, feminine creatures all looking for and expecting him. But he never showed this; he always wore the distracted and annoyed expression of a tremendously busy man snatching a little time for his family.

He got off the train in his rather clumsy way, and they started toward him, when the sight of Mr. MacGregor following him, bag in hand, changed their politely eager smiles to looks of consternation.

Gilbert kissed them all perfunctorily, and then brought forward his companion.

"I've brought Mr. MacGregor down with me," he announced. "I hope the place isn't crowded."

"It isn't," said Andrée. "I don't see why it should be. I don't see anything to bring crowds of people here, I'm sure."

"Hush, Andrée!" murmured her mother, and bestowed a gracious and expressionless smile upon the visitor. "I'm sure there'll be a room for Mr. MacGregor. Hadn't we better get into the bus now? It's waiting, you know!"

All the way to the hotel she was quite perfect; she told Mr. MacGregor about Andrée's difficulties in practising, she was gay, in a formal, stereotyped way; when they arrived she arranged with the landlady for a room, even went about, picking him out a nice one. Then they all sat on the veranda for an hour or so, in the terrific heat, looking out over the sunscorched lawn and the dusty road, and the motionless fir trees, and talked more. It was not an altogether successful conversation; Andrée was perverse and wilfully tactless, Edna was frankly indifferent, and Gilbert very garrulous. He wished to talk about the wholesale rubber business, and he did.

Then it was time to dress for dinner and they all went upstairs. The door into the girls' room was locked, and Gilbert sat down, prepared for a more confidential talk, and an accounting of Claudine's expenditure. But she attacked him at once, with a fiercely restrained wrath.

"Gilbert, what made you bring that man here?"

"Who? You mean Mr. MacGregor? I wanted to!" he answered, defiantly.

"It was a stupid, meddlesome thing to do!" she cried.

"See here, Claudine—!"

"You don't realize the trouble it may cause.... Why didn't you consult me?"

He laughed unpleasantly.

"I don't think I'll start that now, after twenty years—"

"You've no right to bring any man, where the girls are, without consulting me.... I particularly didn't want this man."

"Why?"

"I don't care to explain."

"It's no use your being so high-handed with me. I'll bring anyone I see fit. I consider my judgment—"

"Then I shall take Andrée away."

"Going to leave me? I've heard that before!"

She was quite white with anger.

"When it's a question of *Andrée*—" she began.

"There it is again—your cursed, unfair, unwomanly favouritism. What's the matter with MacGregor? Not good enough for your princess?"

"Then he's spoken to you!" she cried, in horror.

"Yes, he has, and very decently, too. I don't see how she could do much better, if you ask me."

"Gilbert! Are you mad? That old man—old enough to be her father!"

This touched a sore spot.

"Even that isn't so very ancient," he said, with infantile resentment. "No one but you would call a man of his age old. He's a fine fellow. He has a good name, and he's well fixed, and he's very fond of Andrée—"

"You're—you're positively wicked!" she cried, choking with sobs. "Andrée—that wonderful, beautiful child—and that silly old man ...! I'm ashamed of you! I'm disgusted with you!"

He was astonished and somewhat alarmed. How was he to explain to this unreasonably violent woman his pretty fancies about young brides and adoring, distinguished, grey-haired husbands?

"See here!" he began, but she wouldn't listen to him.

"I won't allow him to say a word to her! Not a word! I'm going to speak to him myself and—"

Gilbert sprang to his feet.

"No, you don't! I'm not going to be made a fool of! I told him he might speak to Andrée—"

"And I'll tell him he can't. I won't have any interference where Andrée's concerned."

"I tell you I have something to say in this matter!"

She looked at him with a cold smile, and deliberately turned away from him. It was a trick of hers, and it always infuriated him. He raged at her in a way of which he was afterward ashamed.

She went on dressing, entirely disregarding him; then when she was ready, she said:

"I'm going downstairs now. Perhaps you'll dress, when you've finished your bar-room tirade."

II

It was a jolly dinner. Both Claudine and Gilbert were in high spirits, as angry people often are, and Mr. MacGregor appeared greatly entertained. The girls were ridiculous; Claudine recognized their mood and frowned. She knew and dreaded this high tension, when every remark provoked a giggle, when they exchanged glances and were scarcely able to control their lips, trembling with laughter. A thought came to her which made her flush with shame. Could they have heard their father ...? He had certainly talked very loudly. And unfortunately that was the sort of thing they considered funny.

Poor woman! She was in misery, before her wretched task. She was afraid of the inscrutable Mr. MacGregor; he was so masculine, so self-assured, so old and sensible. But she was determined nevertheless to drive him away, no matter how outrageous she had to be. He should not be given the opportunity of putting ideas into Andrée's head—silly, headstrong Andrée! She wouldn't leave them alone for an instant.

As they rose from the table, said Mr. MacGregor: "Miss Andrée, shall we have a little music? We might run over that new duet—"

"No, thanks!" said Andrée, laughing. "Not with you!"

"Nonsense! Come along!" he said, with authoritative, professorial air. "I want to see what you've been doing."

"No!" she repeated. "I don't want to! I won't!"

"Come, Andrée!" said Gilbert, severely. "This is no way to behave. When Mr. MacGregor—"

"All right!" she interrupted, and led the way into the parlour where a group of old ladies was already installed. Mr. MacGregor drew up a chair beside the piano stool and they sat down, side by side, the big, stoop-shouldered man with his grizzled hair, and the slight young girl. He spoke to her for a few moments in an undertone, pointing a square finger at the music; and she nodded petulantly.

"Now!" said he.

The four hands were poised above the keyboard in the manner made famous by his teaching. Then they began, a majestic, crashing piece, a prelude in tremendous chords. The group of old ladies was annoyed at first, but some instinct warned them that it was classical music and worthy of respect, and they all sat rocking and listening.

But Claudine could take no pleasure in the noble work. The sight of Andrée and Mr. MacGregor side by side filled her with terror and impatience. She thought of the man's great prestige, the illustrious pupils who publicly lauded him, the recitals given by his conservatory which she had attended, and where he was a demigod, adored by students and parents. He had written books on technic, he was a prominent man, respected in certain estimable circles, he was well-to-do, his reputation was unblemished. His attention must seem such a dangerously flattering thing for his young pupil.

Oh, damnable music! She imagined she could actually see it weave its spell about her child. The duet finished, Mr. MacGregor consented to play alone, and it was marvelous playing. Andrée stood beside him, watching his hands, never raising her eyes. And he never looked at her either; sinister fact!

"And now, you, Miss Andrée!" he said.

She consented instantly. She was fired; she wanted to play now. And Mr. MacGregor crossed the room and sat down beside Claudine.

"She is remarkable," he said.

Claudine looked intently at him.

"You think she would make a concert player?" she asked, briefly.

"She undoubtedly could, if she would. But her temperament is peculiar."

Claudine smiled.

"Her temperament is more or less familiar to me," she said.

"Oh, I wasn't presuming to inform her mother!" he hastened to say. "It was simply that I thought my interpretation—as a musician—might be of interest. I don't hesitate to say that she is one of the most promising pupils I have ever had the pleasure of teaching."

"Then do you think she has a fine future before her?" asked Claudine. She would bring him to the point; he should be made to declare himself so that she could demolish him.

"If she chooses. But I'm not sure that she has the temperament for a public artist. She is too rebellious—"

"Then what do you think she is suited for?" asked Claudine, boldly. But she never had Mr. MacGregor's reply, for Andrée had suddenly stopped playing and got up.

"Mother!" she said, "Do you mind if Edna and I pop over to the drugstore? We want some things—"

Mr. MacGregor had risen, prepared with a gallant offer to accompany them, but before he could say a word, she had gone, her arm about her smaller sister. And with the cessation of the music, Gilbert intended to be heard. Mr. MacGregor was rather interested in the stock market, in a prudent way, and Gilbert had information to give, and prophecies.

Claudine could not endure it; she went out on the veranda to await the return of the children, but though she lingered there for an hour and a half, there was no sign of them. Thoroughly vexed, she went upstairs and there they were in their own room. She heard Edna shrieking with laughter.

Quite shamelessly she stood close to the crack of the door.

"Gosh!" said Edna. "If he married both of us, and another one thrown in, it would just about make a wife of his own age. The conceit of men!"

"Well," said Andrée, "the girls at the conservatory do make awful idiots of themselves about him, you know."

"But, oh!" cried Edna, "you don't know how funny you looked, playing that duet, and both—pouncing—!"

"Shut up!" said Andrée, impatiently. "I knew you were laughing. There's nothing really funny in it, of course not."

There was silence for a moment, broken by giggles from Edna.

"But, honestly, Andrée," she said, at last. "Have you encouraged him? I'm sure he came to woo you!"

"I never dreamed he'd come.... I wish he hadn't! He wrote such heavenly letters. And now he's spoiled everything."

"Father adores him; you can see that. What do you suppose he told Father?"

"Goodness knows! Father swallows everything... Oh, dear! I really liked him—when he was miles away!"

Claudine now knocked at the door; and entered.

"Children," she said. "Where have you been? I waited and waited for you—"

"We just came up here; we didn't go to the drugstore after all. We thought we'd like a nice quiet little talk," said Edna.

"It's very close and hot up here," said their mother. "However I suppose you're not going downstairs again this evening—"

"Not unless Andrée wants to play another duet," said Edna.

Andrée scowled at her.

"Your playing was beautiful, my dear," said her mother. "Mr. MacGregor must be a very competent teacher."

She kissed them both and went back into her own room, unaccountably relieved. She undressed and put on a thin silk dressing-gown and sat down near the window in the dark.

She deliberately tried to banish all thought of Gilbert. He would inevitably go to the large hotel down the road and have a number of whiskies and soda, and come back, either contrite or quarrelsome. One was as bad as another.... She sighed, bitterly. Better think of Andrée.

It was a hot, still night; the world outside seemed restless and fevered, noisy with insects, not sleeping, not tranquil. She could hear dogs barking frantically, and a strain of stupid music from the hotel, chattering voices on the veranda, sounds from other rooms... Oh, my Andrée, how little life has to give you! Even the best of it is so poor! A profound melancholy overcame her; she could not so much as imagine a future for her child that would be happy.

The door opened softly, and Edna's voice whispered: "Mother!"

"Yes, dear?"

"May I come in, just for an instant?"

"Of course!"

"Andrée's asleep.... But I was so afraid you'd be worrying, Mother darling. I knew how you must feel when you saw Mr. MacGregor.... Oh, Andrée's such a chump! But he's done for! I made her laugh at him, and that's spoiled everything."

"You dear girl! How clever and sensible of you! You really do understand Andrée wonderfully."

Edna sighed.

"She is a worry! She'd marry anyone—she'd do anything, if she was caught in a certain mood. I hope you'll be able to keep that old nuisance—"

"Really, my dear!"

"I hope you won't let Mr. MacGregor talk to her tomorrow. It might undo all the good I've done."

Claudine put her arms about the child and kissed her fervently, the sort of kisses she so often gave to Edna in which were all her secret contrition for her favouritism, all her remorse at the inadequate return she made for this honest and, beautiful affection. She had a superstitious dread of being punished some day for her wickedness; some disaster would overtake little Edna, and then she would repent, too late, her idolatry of Andrée.

"Good night, Edna darling!" she said. "You're such a comfort to me!"

And how much dearer was the pain that one caused her than the comfort the other gave!

CHAPTER FOUR

THE UNABASHED OUTCAST

I

Claudine waked up to the dull peace of a mountain Sunday. She could hear the grinding of the ice-cream freezer on the back porch, and far away the bell of the little Roman Catholic church. She rose and dressed while Gilbert still slept, and going out into the hall, knocked on the door of the girls' room. Andrée was up and half dressed, combing her misty dark hair.

"Edna's pretending to be asleep," she said, scornfully.

"There's no hurry," said Claudine. "She can wait for Father and have breakfast with him. Finish dressing, and we'll have time for a little walk."

She sat down and watched her child with tender eyes. There was an awkward, impatient grace about her, in the hasty movements of her arms as she arranged her hair, something so immature, so touching. She slipped on a white frock, because her father was inordinately fond of seeing young girls in white, and announced herself ready. But Claudine saw untidinesses; she tucked in a stray lock of hair, straightened her collar, tightened her belt.

"Now!" she said. "You're nice!"

They went out, closing the door quietly on the motionless Edna.

"What on earth is that row!" said Andrée.

They paused for a moment in the hall to listen. Some outrageous person was playing with vigour on the piano, and whistling, to accompany the vulgar air.

"And on Sunday morning, too!" said Claudine, with a frown, "when so many people want to sleep!"

They went on down; the dining-room was still quite empty at this early hour, and the veranda deserted. But every corner was permeated by that loud, shocking noise!

"Let's see what it is!" said Andrée, and they looked cautiously in at the open door of the parlour.

"Oh, I know him!" said Andrée. "I saw him come last night, on the train with Father and Mr. MacGregor. Horrible, vulgar little wretch!"

Seated at the piano was a slight, fair-haired young man with a minute yellow mustache and a cheerful, impudent face. He wore a new black suit and white buckskin shoes and some awful sort of necktie; he had an air of being specially got up for Sunday. The place was a cheap and obscure one, but they had never before seen in it a guest like this. People of his kind found nothing to please them here.

Claudine was affronted.

"We can only hope he won't stay long," she said, as they turned away.

They went into breakfast, alone in the room, but their peace was destroyed by the playing and whistling; at first they frowned, and Claudine even suggested speaking to Mrs. Dewey; but in the end they were forced to laugh.

They went out for a walk, a carefully selected one, where no cows would be met with to terrify Andrée and a good view might be obtained for Claudine. They talked together in one of their few hours of perfect accord.

"I have some influence over her!" thought Claudine, happily. "If she ever contemplates anything foolish, I am sure I can dissuade her. She is mine! We are bound together by a thousand ties."

Andrée broke into her meditation.

"You're awfully pretty, Mother!" she said, suddenly. "I love the way you look.... There's something—I don't know how to describe it—something old-fashioned about you."

Claudine was not greatly pleased.

"Old-fashioned?" she said, thinking of her new frock, her chic and becoming coiffure, every dainty detail of her costume.

"Yes. You haven't the look other women have. You're so distinguished and—mysterious. Have you had a very sad life, Mother?"

"Mercy, no, child!" said Claudine. She shrank at once from any invasion of her reserve; her dignity compelled her to maintain her aloofness, her air of slightly inhuman tranquility.

But Andrée was insistent.

"But I do wish you'd tell me one thing!" she said. "Did you really mean to marry Cousin Lance, and were you parted by something?"

"Where did you get such a ridiculous idea?" asked her mother, frowning. "No one ever thought of such a thing."

"Edna said she thought so.... Mother, I wish I knew you better!"

Claudine was startled and touched.

"My dear!" she cried. "But don't you....?"

She stopped.

"After all," she went on. "I think it is better just to love people, and not to trouble about trying to know or to understand them."

They had reached a little summer-house built out on a rock over a deep pool in a rocky basin. It had not at all the sinister aspect of that other pool; this was sunny, open and dark blue, with wild flowers growing about it, and ferns. From where they sat, they could see the line of mountains beyond. Andrée didn't like mountains; the sombre and majestic environment exasperated her restless soul. She sighed, but grew quiet looking at her mother's rapt face. She was drawing strength and assuagement from the hills. Poor mother, with her philosophers and her scenery! A phantom existence, Andrée reflected.

"Hope I don't disturb you?" said a cheerful voice, and they both turned, to see with horror the common little man, with a great bundle of Sunday newspapers under his arm. He had politely taken off his hat and stood smiling at them.

"They told me down at the house that this was a pretty walk," he said. "And it certainly is. Fine air to-day, isn't it?"

"Yes," said Claudine, in her most distrait, affable way. "It's a lovely day."

"Would you like to see the papers?" he asked.

"No, thank you. We're going back at once…. We just stopped for the view."

He smiled.

"A tame little view!" he said. "I guess I'll find something better than this before I've finished."

"How?" asked Andrée, abruptly.

"I'm going to climb some of these peaks. I've done a lot of climbing in the Alps," he said. "I've got the head for it, and the legs. Why, there wasn't one of those millionaire sportsmen who could beat me at it. These peaks look like hills to me."

His boasting was somehow ameliorated by his good-humour. And one couldn't help believing that he actually had defeated millionaire sportsmen.

"I suppose you ladies don't climb?" he asked.

"I haven't," said Andrée. "But perhaps I shall some time. It might be rather fun. I'd never thought of it."

"We must go," said Claudine, firmly. "Your father will be wondering what has become of us. Come, dear!"

She smiled politely at the dreadful little man, and they walked off. At a turn of the path Andrée, looking back, saw him spreading out his papers, his straw hat jauntily at the back of his head.

"I'm afraid he's going to be a nuisance," said Claudine.

"I guess you can dispose of him!" said Andrée, grimly. "Lord! How I do hate Sundays!"

Claudine felt obliged to remonstrate, but weakly, because she was quite in agreement with her child. They sauntered back with reluctant steps, each lost in her own incommunicable thought.

II

The great mid-day dinner had been disposed of, the chicken, the ice-cream, and the other decent, traditional things, and the entire party went out on to the veranda and sat down, constrained, almost enraged with one another.

"Let's take a walk, Father!" said Andrée, suddenly.

"Not on your life!" said Gilbert. "*I'm* not nineteen, old girl!"

He took a bill from his pocket.

"See if you and Edna can't find some place to buy yourselves a box of caramels," he said. "I want a look at the papers."

"I shouldn't object to a walk," said Mr. MacGregor.

"Then I'll show you a nice, cool, after-dinner one," said Claudine, brightly, "while the girls go for their candy. Run up and get me my sun-shade, please, Edna!"

Gilbert looked up with a scowl; but he met so cold and steadfast a glance from his wife that he looked down again. Better let her alone; she was capable of the most alarming retaliations. Anyhow, she couldn't do any real harm; love was not to be so easily discouraged. He pretended to be deep in his papers, but he was none the less well aware of his daughters going off in one direction and his wife and Mr. MacGregor in another. He was ready to laugh at the woman's folly.

Claudine had started with the firm intention of approaching and utterly routing Mr. MacGregor. But, to be brief, she didn't so much as mention Andrée's name. She couldn't! Instead they chatted affably as they strolled; Mr. MacGregor gave some information, more sentimental than scientific, regarding Scotch wild flowers. He was really very nice and flattering. She hadn't for years met anyone who took so frank an interest in her. He was by no means a botanist, but he confessed to a love of Nature, and he admired her quite extensive knowledge. Moreover, he too was a reader of her beloved philosophers, and they had an interesting if somewhat superficial discussion of their theories of life. Claudine's idea was that one should try to deny the reality of suffering; she had a pitiful hope that if she were to train her reason sufficiently she would in time be able to reason away her unhappiness. Mr. MacGregor, on the contrary, had a tinge of Calvinism in his philosophy, he thought it better to hug one's pain, to rejoice in its cruel embrace, to be made strong by it.

Then they talked a little of music, Claudine's old love. But Mr. Mac-Gregor was so very practical. He looked upon a masterwork as a thing to be expressed through high technical perfection, he read no meanings, no sentiment into music, he had none of Claudine's mystic delight in sound itself.

They both became mollified. Mr. MacGregor was able to forgive this charming and interesting woman her obvious interference in his love-making, and she was willing to admit that as a man he was strong, sensible, and rather likeable. She couldn't help contrasting his ruggedness, his well-furnished mind, his varied interests, with the bilious and tiresome Gilbert. Here was a companion, who could walk, and who could talk.

They came leisurely home; Gilbert saw them crossing the sunny lawn, both of them annoyingly cool in spite of the midsummer weather. He himself was quite wretched from the heat, and irritated by the newspaper. He got up and went to meet them.

"Tell you what!" he said. "We'll see if we can get a motor somewhere in the place and go for a drive in the cool of the afternoon—about five. The children will like it."

It was of course unimaginable either to him or to Claudine that he should find the conveyance. He was a sort of Sultan; he never did things of that sort. He gave orders, and he paid. So Claudine found and despatched a fat youth belonging to Mrs. Dewey and the thing was done. They then retired to their rooms until five o'clock; Gilbert dozed and his wife gave her attention to her finger-nails.

"What have the children been doing?" she asked suddenly.

"Don't know.... Haven't seen them," he muttered. "Good Lord! This room is *hot!* Can't you find some way to keep the flies out? What good are the screens?"

Claudine didn't answer; an alarming thought had entered her mind. Suppose those provoking girls weren't back when the car arrived? Gilbert would be in a terrible rage; and there would certainly be a scene.... Where could they have gone, on this drowsy Sunday afternoon in that little village so devoid of resources?

Her fears were confirmed; they didn't come back. Gilbert had got into the car, Mr. MacGregor was standing near.

"Call the girls!" said Gilbert, impatiently. "I suppose they're making themselves sick with their caramels."

But they were not in the house, not in the grounds. Mr. MacGregor went down the road to the hotel, and to the drugstore where they must have gone for their candy, but he did not find them. They wasted half an hour, and then went off without them.

Gilbert didn't spare Claudine. He remonstrated all the time, in a manner which, if he had not been a man, would certainly have been called nagging. He said it was disgraceful; hadn't she any control over her children? Didn't she take any interest in them? Was she in the habit of neglecting them in this way? That was the way with women; they hadn't a damned thing to do *but* look after their children, and they didn't even do that properly. And so on. Claudine endured it with a set smile; she scarcely heard him. Mr. MacGregor, however, did hear him; it was not a pleasant drive for him.

III

They got back a little late for the meal known as Sunday night tea. She hurried upstairs to wash and brush her hair, and there in their room were her daughters, both stretched out on the bed.

"Edna!" she cried. "Andrée! Where have you been? Your father had a motor to take you out ... he was so disappointed. You have no right to worry and annoy him so.... Where have you been since dinner time?"

Edna raised herself on one elbow.

"Sorry, Mother darling! We went out with that funny little man. We ran across him as we were coming out of the drugstore and he began to talk. Said he was going to walk to a place called 'The Brave's Leap,' and asked us if we didn't want to go along, so we did. It was heavenly! Miles and miles.... We're awfully tired, but it's a nice tiredness."

"What an outrageous thing to do! I'm surprised at you! The man's a perfect stranger—and not a desirable person at all. I can't tell you how annoyed I am. And your father's plans all upset—"

"But we didn't know about Father's plans," said Edna.

"We didn't miss much," said Andrée. "I hate those silly drives. As it was, we got a lot of splendid exercise and a lot of fun."

"You mustn't do such things without asking me! I thought you both knew better than to go off that way with a stranger. It was very wrong and inconsiderate. Naturally your father expects to see something of you in the little time he's here—"

"But, Mother dear," said Edna, patiently. "We're not children. We couldn't leave Mr. Stephens standing in the street while we ran home to ask mother. He's a very nice little beast, and there was really absolutely no harm in taking a walk with him."

"I have no control over them!" thought Claudine, bitterly. "Gilbert is right!"

Aloud she said, in a tone of great displeasure:

"There is no time to argue with you now. It's late. Please get dressed at once for supper."

"We don't want any supper," said Andrée. "The nice little beast had all sorts of things in his knapsack. We've been eating all afternoon."

"And we stopped at a funny little inn somewhere on the road and had ginger ale and more sandwiches. Mother, I wish you'd been there! It was the only decent time we've had in this place. We saw the most beautiful waterfall, and a wonderful gorge that an Indian's supposed to have jumped across. And the man's really very nice. Of course he's common, and all that sort of thing, but he's the most cheerful creature!"

"He said he was 'athaletic,'" said Andrée, "and he is! He showed off all the time, and it was very amusing."

But Claudine was not listening; she was thinking with dread of what she should say to Gilbert.

And in the end she was certainly not candid.

"The girls went for a long walk in the mountains," she told him. She didn't mention the "nice little beast," and neither did they, whether from dissimulation or carelessness she didn't care to investigate.

On an early train the next morning Gilbert and Mr. MacGregor went back to the city, and she drew a breath of relief. Now she had only two adversaries to struggle against—and perhaps the common little man as well.

CHAPTER FIVE

THE BREATH OF LIFE

I

"Tired?" asked Mr. Stephens.

"Not a bit," said Andrée. "Edna and I owe you a vote of thanks for putting a little life into one of those ghastly Sundays. I loathe Sundays."

"You wouldn't if you'd ever done any work," said he.

She looked at him in surprise. He was sitting on the rail of the veranda where she had found him when she came out after her late and solitary breakfast. He looked well in his white flannels; he wore his great variety of clothes with a sort of innocent gusto, like so many fancy dress costumes, and though so obviously not to the manner born, he had no awkwardness; there was, on the contrary, an engaging and honest assurance about him, and a remarkable vitality. His features were sharp and by no means distinguished, but they were good. His blue eyes were frank and intelligent. He was wiry, well knit, not without vanity in his strength. The cheerful grin had vanished from his face with his last words, leaving it quite serious.

"I have done work," she answered. "You don't know what hard, tiresome work practising is."

"It isn't work," he interrupted. "It's preparation for work. You've never had to go on when you were tired. In fact, you've never had to do it at all. Your conscience has been your master, and I can tell you, it's a darn sight easier master than hunger."

This was extraordinary talk.

"Well, I suppose I'm lucky then," said Andrée. "I've never had to earn money, and I don't suppose I ever shall."

"It's not lucky to be useless," he said.

"Useless!" she cried. "Do you think making music is useless?"

"Of course it is. Lots of people get on without music. Fine, high-minded people, too."

Andrée smiled scornfully.

"I dare say!" she said. "But there are some people who wouldn't think life was worth living without art."

"No, there aren't. Not one. If you gave any human being his choice between a decent happy life without a sign of art, or death, no one but a maniac would choose death."

"*I* should!"

"Then that's because you don't know anything about death, or life either."

She shrugged her shoulders, and half turned away.

"You'd better not bother to talk to such a fool, then," she said. "I'll admit I can't talk to people who despise music."

"I don't despise it. I'm very fond of it. I play a little myself. In fact, I think I've got quite a talent for it. If I could have studied, I'd have been a pretty good musician."

"I don't doubt it, judging by your performance yesterday morning," said Andrée.

She was glad to see his face flush as she walked away. He needed taking down.

Still, she couldn't help thinking of him. He was an interesting, if an impertinent man. Her mother had said nothing further about him, but he was obviously in the category of impossible persons. Perhaps they had encouraged him too much....

But the beastly part of it was, that he was always doing such interesting things, things you couldn't help wanting to do yourself. He lived in a sort of world of his own, quite cheerful in his ostracism. Perhaps he didn't even notice the scorn and disapproval of the respectable old ladies, or the contempt of the matrons. He walked about the corridors with his hat on, he sat on the porch whistling loudly, late at night, when his betters wanted to sleep. Complaints poured in upon the placid Mrs. Dewey. And still, in spite of all this, Andrée and Edna followed his activities with envious eyes. One day a lean, worn horse was brought round for him from some mysterious source, and he came out and packed on it a most peculiar burden in a water-cloth cover. He was there a long time, inspecting the girths, readjusting his load, intensely serious. Then he glanced up and saw the girls in the doorway.

"I'm off for a little camping trip," he said. "A couple of days—exploring the hills."

He mounted nimbly and turned to wave at them, and trotted off, straight and soldierly, in khaki breeches and a white shirt, and a big sombrero on his neat head.

The next thing he did when he returned was to order a canoe from the city and carry it on his back a long way to a suitable little river. He was away in it for three days and came back with a fine basket of fish which he asked Mrs. Dewey to cook for the entire house.

And that evening after dinner he frankly approached Claudine.

"They tell me you know a lot about flowers," he said. "I don't know much, but I know enough to spot rare ones. I've brought back three or four specimens I think you'd like to have."

"Thank you!" said Claudine. "You're very kind!"

She hadn't the heart to snub the friendly creature; besides, it was very nice of him to think of her.

"I'll be very pleased to see them in the morning," she said.

"Do you mind smoking?" he asked.

She was startled; did he intend to stay by her side?

"Not at all! And anyhow, I'm going in directly. I have letters to write."

She left him sitting on the rail in his characteristic attitude, the attitude of a small boy, a rather humorous figure. And yet, in a way, a singularly manly and independent one, quite indifferent to the disapproval of the rocking old ladies, quite sufficient unto himself. Solitary, he was not lonely, not forlorn; he no more objected to being ignored than a cat might have objected. He somehow stood out against the background of mountains and starry sky with a startling individuality, like the epitome of valiant humanity defying nature. She thought of him with great indulgence, in spite of the fact that he had driven her indoors.

II

Claudine came out the next morning, prepared for the excursion she made every fine morning while Andrée practised and Edna sat in the room with her, driven by her sister's industry to the study of Italian. She had with her two volumes of philosophers and a note book and fountain pen, for the studying she did, copying out and commenting upon the passages that impressed her, getting what comfort and peace of mind she could from them.

She put up her dark green sunshade and started off across the lawn, very trim and elegant in starched white; she looked remarkably young, her calm and serious face hadn't a line, a wrinkle, her coppery hair was as bright and heavy as it had ever been, she was straight, her outlines neat and clear. She had never been supple; there had always been a sort of woodenness about her small body, but it had a charm all its own; it gave her a peculiarly "ladylike" air of being not quite human.

She left the grounds and entered upon the highway, inches deep in clean white dust, and she heard no footsteps behind her, no sound until an anxious voice said over her shoulder:

"I've brought those little plants and things for you to look at. I was afraid I wouldn't be there when you got back. I'm leaving at noon for two or three days and they'd be withered by the time I got back."

It was the nice little beast, coatless, in riding breeches and puttees. He proffered a small tin case, and she took it from him with a smile.

"Can't I carry your books and things to wherever you're going?" he asked.

She hesitated a moment, and then said, "Yes, thank you!" and they went on, side by side, Mr. Stephens gallantly holding the parasol very high over her head.

He glanced down at the books.

"Marcus Aurelius and Nietzsche!" he said. "That's a queer combination!"

"Do you know them?" she asked, in surprise.

"Oh, yes! I've read about everything you could think of. I used to read things like this a lot. But not any more. They're not real enough."

"Some people have found them very real nourishment for the mind," she said lightly. She couldn't take this person seriously.

"I haven't any use for mind without body," he answered. "That's what I like about Christianity. It's so solid and material—"

"But it's just the spirituality that is so admirable in it!" she protested.

"Not for me, it isn't. What appeals to me about it is the human, natural, unspiritual part. Tells you to *do* this and that, instead of thinking this and that. It's what you do, not what you feel, that counts there. I've never thought Christ cared whether people believed in Him or not. My idea is that He sort of had an idea that He'd help people by a few practical ideas on how to make the world a decent place to live in. If you behave in this way, He says, you can all be more or less happy. You see," he went on, "I'm a Socialist."

"Oh, mercy!" said Claudine, rather shocked.

"Yes, I'm a Socialist. And the way I see it, to be a good Socialist, you've got to be either an atheist or a Christian. If you're an atheist, and you think this world is all there's going to be, then you feel so d—doggone sorry for the people who aren't getting anything out of it, that you'd do all you possibly could to help them. I used to be an atheist. I was working in a factory when I was about eighteen, and when I'd see those kids starting in—boys, children really—and knew they'd never get even a fair living out of a whole life's work, I guess I was a kind of Anarchist too. I thought the best thing they could do was to grab what they could, to try to wipe out the—hogs that kept all the good things away from them. But then, one day, I thought I'd read the New Testament, along with a lot of other stuff I had in hand. And, Gosh ! ... it was like a—a lamp being lighted in a dark room. Right away I felt that it was *right*. That He'd got hold of the right idea of how to run the world. I'd always hated the idea that we were a lot of fighting animals, all struggling to get food. Evolution didn't suit me altogether. It was too darned unfair to the beginners, you know, the cave men and those fellows who just opened the way for us. Well, I thought after I'd read about Christ, this living's just a job, and here's the way to do it. And after it's done, we'll get a rest. We need it. Why, hang it all! Even a baby a year old has had a hard life, trying to get adjusted.... I don't believe in all this stuff about a whole lot of future lives, and keeping on developing. No, sir! This life is enough; it's hard enough, and we learn enough. I guess we deserve peace after this, and I guess we'll get it. Is this where you always stay?"

"Yes," said Claudine. "But I wish you'd sit down and talk a little. I like to hear you."

"I talk too much," he said, seriously. "Somehow I'm always so full of stuff I want to say that I kind of spill over. And—d'ye know—somehow it seems—valuable—the stuff I want to say. Not particularly because it's me, but because it's—human nature."

"It's really very interesting," said Claudine, blandly.

He laughed.

"Do you know," he went on, "ten years ago the idea of anyone like you—a lady—saying she liked to hear me, even agreeing to listen to me—would have seemed like a pipe dream. I used to think that if I ever got a chance to talk to your sort, I'd give 'em a piece of my mind. But when I got to know more about 'em, why, I saw nothing could be done that way. No, sir; you can't make people understand by talking. They've got to see—and feel. If *you* ever saw or felt what life was really like, you wouldn't be satisfied to—"

He stopped abruptly.

"I didn't mean to talk that way to you," he said. "It's rude. And you're so kind and nice."

"But I want you to! I want to hear what you think! I shouldn't be satisfied to what?"

"Well ... to take everything and give nothing."

"But do you imagine that I give nothing? I have three children."

"That's nothing. I'll be frank, if you really want.... What I mean is, you *don't count.* You don't try to help. You just try to make life bearable for yourself. Don't you see? Even with your children. You don't teach them to serve. You just tell them to live decently."

"Even that is something—in a world like this," she said, with a little smile. He shook his head.

"Not to me! Better to forget your own life—even your own decency—a little...."

"But—since you have so clear an idea of the scheme of things—what would you like people like me—myself for instance—to do?"

"I guess it's too late for you to *do* much," he said, gravely. "All you could do would be to learn to understand."

"Perhaps I do."

"You couldn't. No one understands—really—by intuition. You've got to know, through experience—either inside or outside yourself. And I guess you—"

"Do go on! I'm not easily offended."

"Well, I guess you've felt, instead of experiencing. It's altogether different."

"I wonder what experience you would countenance?" she asked. "Do you consider that the mother of three children, a woman who has lost both her parents, who has lived nearly forty years, is still without experience?"

He made an extraordinary answer.

"Your soul's all right," he said. "It's your heart that's undeveloped."

"Heavens!" she thought. "Is the queer little creature trying to make love to me?"

But he went on.

"The great thing in the world is compassion."

Then he stopped short and pulled out of a breeches' pocket a gold cigarette case.

"Isn't it a beauty?" he asked. "I paid what lots of people I know could live on for months and months for this."

"But—" she began, bewildered.

"I suppose you're wondering what a fellow with views like mine is doing with a toy like that. Well, in the first place, it isn't a dead loss. After I've used it a few years more, I'll sell it or pawn it for quite a lot. It's solid gold, you know; one of the best I could buy. *Isn't* it a beauty?"

"Yes, it is!" she agreed, terribly touched by his naive pride. "It is—a beauty!"

What an extraordinary conversation this was, she and this freckled young man, sitting facing each other on great sun-warmed rocks in the little glade which she had for weeks looked upon as her especial domain! She had certainly never met anything at all like him before, no one so absurd and so honest and so touching.

"But I was going to tell you why I had this thing," he continued. "It's because I think everyone's got a right to a few pet follies. Now, some people think a Socialist can't consistently have a balance in the bank. Well, my idea is this.... I've been able to grab for myself my share in the good things in the world. And that's what I want to see every other fellow do. Not grab, if you could get it any other way, but generally you can't. I want everyone to get a share. And a chance. I've got mine, and I'm going to help other people to get theirs."

"But how did you get yours?" she asked, with an irresistible curiosity. She knew that he wouldn't resent any sort of question.

"Fought for it. Fought for it like a devil. You see, I'd made a little invention—an improvement for a certain type of printing press. I'll explain it all some other time. Well, of course, the fellows on top wanted to take it.... I won't go into that either just now. But, anyway, I knew. I knew the profit it would make, and I made up my mind that a good part of that profit was coming my way. So I grabbed my share. It's what everyone ought to have; a decent share in the profit of his work. It was a good kind of grabbing.... And now I'm able to do what I'd like to see every other fellow in the world able to do—work hard, at some kind of useful, manual work until he's thirty, and then play for three or four years, before he settles down to work his brain. Brains aren't much good until they've had those two things—manual work and play."

"What is your brain going to do?"

"Write. I've got it in me.... But I've got off the track. I was showing you that cigarette case because I wanted to ask you if you could imagine what it was like to be an outcast, to have money enough to buy things like that, and to see how they're begrudged to you. Every time I used to go in to buy things I'd earned enough money to buy, I was made to feel that. My money was good enough, but I wasn't. If you could have seen the swell English tailor I bought my clothes from! He hated me for being able to get them. Because I'm 'common.' Well, as a matter of fact, I'm really very uncommon—darned uncommon.... The point I'm making is, that all the fine, good things in the world are put aside for a few people. Everybody knows it. All the shop people know it. They don't want outsiders to get any of their choice things. They're like watch-dogs—fool watch-dogs, starving to death while they watch other people's meat.... When I was younger and doing more reading and thinking, I used to think the best way to bring about the changes I hoped to see was for the people on top to be awakened. They've got the money, the leisure, the power, the education, I thought.... But I learned pretty soon it would never come that way. They haven't got either brains or compassion enough. They've used all their privileges to corrupt, not to enlighten. And not through wickedness or diplomacy, mind you, but from stupidity."

He pulled out his watch.

"Oh " he said. "I've got to go! Are you all right?"

"Perfectly, thank you!" she answered, railing. "Only a little confused by all you've been telling me."

It was not his words, however, that remained in her memory after he had gone. They meant little to her. It was the curious vitality and force of the man, his candour, his innocence, his baffling air of certainty. She thought of his activities, his ideas, his tireless flow of talk, and the woods, usually so full of interest and charm for her, were suddenly blank. The mystery and wonder she had seen in the smallest plant were suddenly nothing at all in comparison to the wonder of a human being.

She became uneasily doubtful of her philosophic attitude toward her fellows, her great desire to escape them.

"He's ..." she thought, with half a smile. "He's a breath of life in all this stagnation.... A breath of life!"

CHAPTER SIX

THE UNLAWFUL PICNIC

I

After lunch they all, Claudine, Andrée, and Edna, dressed themselves in their ceremonial garments, the modish and immaculate white required by the gold-providing Gilbert, and went down to the railway station to meet him. There were other wives there, and other children, and a little swarm of bucolic onlookers. And there was also the "breath of life" in tramping outfit, with immense waterproof boots and a new Panama hat. He came over to them immediately.

"I'm taking the next train up," he said, with his invariable assumption that everyone was interested in his doings. "They say there's an old fellow away up in the mountains who's a regular wild man. An Italian; he used to lead round one of those dancing bears, but it got away one night and he went into the woods after it, and never wanted to come back. Two or three people have told me about him. His hair's got long, and he has a beard down to his waist. They say he won't speak, but I guess I can make him. He runs away and tries to hide."

"That sounds more like the bear," said Edna. "Perhaps he ate the man and they're both merged into one."

He laughed.

"Well, I'm ready for bears, too," he said. "I've got the best kind of rifle made, and I know how to use it."

"Everything you have is the best there is, isn't it?" said Andrée scornfully.

He reddened, but he answered cheerfully:

"You bet! And I'm proud of 'em, too. I earned 'em. They weren't given to me by anyone else."

Andrée turned away.

"Let's walk up and down, Mother!" she said. "It's so much hotter standing still."

Claudine very willingly assented; the last thing in the world she wanted was for Gilbert to find them talking to that young man. He would be angry, and not without cause, for this was certainly not the sort of acquaintance for the mother of two young daughters to cultivate. Edna might talk to him with impunity, her sensible ideas and her humour legitimatized almost anything. She put her arm through Andrée's and they began to saunter up and down, keeping a discreet distance from Mr. Stephens.

"He needs to be sat on!" said Andrée, with a frown.

"I don't believe you can do it!" said her mother, smiling.

"He is a thick-skinned little beast. He's insufferable!"

"I don't think so. He's polite enough, if he's treated politely."

"But I'm not going to treat him politely.... There's the train!"

They halted and stood watching, while the engine roared past them and stopped neatly at the proper spot, and the handful of passengers alighted.

"O Lord!" groaned Andrée. "Again!"

For she had seen the gaunt, ungainly form of Mr. MacGregor coming down the steps, bag in hand. He lifted his hat and came toward them.

"I am charged with a very unwelcome message, afraid," he said. "Mr. Vincelle is unable to get away this week, and he asked me to come down, and see if I could be of any service to the ladies!"

Oh, cowardly Gilbert! Claudine could have laughed at his infantile ruse. She welcomed Mr. MacGregor with cordiality and beckoned to Edna, who came, but who naughtily brought the little man with her.

"Look here, Mrs. Vincelle!" he said, eagerly. "I've been talking to Miss Edna.... As long as your husband didn't come out, you're all more or less free, aren't you? No plans made, I mean? Well, won't you all be my guests on a little picnic?"

"I'm very sorry—" Claudine began, but he was not to be stopped.

"Why not?" he said. "It's a hot afternoon, and I'll show you a fine, cool spot. I'll arrange everything. I'll see to the supper, and everything else. All you have to do is just get your bathing suits—"

"Bathing!" said Edna. "I didn't know there was any in this place!"

"There's a wonderful swimming pool. And I can lend you a bathing suit," he said, looking directly at Mr. MacGregor, to whom he had not been, and never was to be, introduced.

"I'm afraid we're not the same size," said Mr. MacGregor.

"Doesn't matter. You can get into it. We can start about four and come home by moonlight."

The girls were both frankly pleased with the idea; Claudine confessed to herself that it was an attractive prospect. But impossible! They couldn't be the guests of this man, they couldn't really, openly, admit that he existed. She looked covertly at Mr. MacGregor, hoping for support, for some grown-up, tactful remark that should help her to get away. But he had taken it for granted that Mr. Stephens was a friend of the family, and he wanted to go on that picnic.

"Some other time—" Claudine began, with her most condescending affability, but Edna broke in, with a wail.

"Oh, Mother, I'm so longing for a swim! Do let's go!"

"It'll be very nice, I promise you!" said Mr. Stephens, solemnly. "I'll take all the responsibility for seeing that you all enjoy yourselves."

"After all, Mother, why not?" murmured Andrée, in her ear. "I'd like to eat somewhere except in that disgusting dining-room for once. And a moonlight walk!"

"I'm afraid Mr. MacGregor wants to rest after his journey," said Claudine, and her tone was threatening. But Mr. MacGregor did not understand; he thought that he was expected not to want to rest, and he insisted that he longed for this picnic.

Claudine was miserably conscious of her lack of character; at her age she had no business to allow herself to be entrapped into so undignified a position. She knew she should have prevented this thing, that even now she ought to destroy the project, but she was quite unable to do so. She was committed....

II

It was an imposing safari, observed by the people on the veranda with excessive interest. First went Claudine under a parasol held by Mr. MacGregor, then the two girls, arm in arm, and behind them, alone and unheeded, the young host, carrying a number of things, and behind him Mrs. Dewey's fat youth, and a young man never accounted for, both heavily laden. Like a general the little man called out his orders.

"To your right now!" And Claudine and Mr. MacGregor would lead the march in that direction. Once they had to make a detour to avoid a field of cows, through which Andrée refused to pass.

"Now!" he said. "Just down this hill, and you'll see the place. It's beautiful! Fern Glen, I've named it. It's a regular, natural swimming pool—water cold and clear as can be. And quiet! Lots of nice little birds, too, Mrs. Vincelle, just what you like."

But instead of the exclamation of admiration he had expected, he heard a tragic cry from Andrée

"Why, it's nothing in the world but our horrible old snakey pool!"

"I didn't realize we were getting here," said Edna. "We've always come up the stream."

"But what have you got against it?" asked the young man, horribly chagrined. "It's a beautiful spot, and it's *not* snakey."

"It is!" said Andrée. "We've seen snakes swimming in your beautiful natural swimming pool."

"They weren't poisonous snakes, then," he assured her. "And they'll keep out of your way."

"I won't give them the trouble," said Andrée.

"We'll look after you, Miss Edna and I," said Mr. MacGregor. He always made a point of pretending that he and Edna were the firmest of allies, perhaps because she was the only member of the family he didn't at all fear.

"I believe I'll risk it!" said Edna. "It looks so lovely and cool and I'm so terribly hot."

The fat youth and the young man had gone away again, and Mr. Mac-Gregor and the host withdrew, to return very promptly in their bathing suits. Claudine was filled with quiet amusement at them; each was so evidently satisfied with his superiority over the other. Mr. MacGregor had an air of saying "I don't believe you realized what a fine, big man I am! This poor chap's tights are too short for me, and my chest almost bursts his poor little jersey. I may be an artist, but what a manly one!" And young Stephens, straighter than ever, couldn't keep a grin from his freckled face; he was itching with a desire to show off. He was, moreover, very proud of the arrangements he had provided for the ladies; a little tent to serve as their dressing-room, with a mirror fastened to one of its sides.

It was characteristic that Andrée should be the most daring and reckless of them all. Claudine could not swim; she waded waist deep into the pool and stood there throwing water over her shoulders, like a little statue in a fountain, Edna thought, full of a precise and formal grace, not one burnished hair out of place. Mr. MacGregor swam powerfully all about the pool once or twice, to show his strength, and Edna followed him, and though she didn't go nearly so fast, she wasn't nearly so tired. He felt a little pang of envy for her youth that tinged his admiration for her with an almost unkindly feeling. Seen in a bathing suit, she was more robust than one would have imagined; she was small, like her mother, but it was not at all a fairylike smallness. She had a beautiful, a perfect figure, well-developed, supple, and sturdy; her skin was as white as a Dryad's in that tree-shadowed place, and her blond hair was like sunshine, although her dimpled face had no sort of resemblance to any wild wood creature. Never would she pine or die for love! She was a young woman, not a sprite, and she had all of woman's marvelous resources against suffering. Compared with her, Andrée was an immature and *farouche* schoolgirl.

And yet it was she they all looked at. She was a fleet swimmer, but with little endurance. She had a well-known trick of swimming out too far and becoming panic-stricken and needing help to get back to the shore. She had a positive talent for alarming and distressing the others, for being perpetually the centre of attention. It was not that she consciously tried to "show off," like Stephens; what she did, she did to satisfy some requirement of her own nature. She insisted upon swimming too near the waterfall; she *would* dive, heedless of remonstrance. She was wayward, taciturn, defiant. She was the only one of the women to get her hair wet, the only one who emerged dank, shivering and disheveled. And when they sat down on the pebbly shore for supper, she alone was untidy, she alone out of spirits. Her damp hair hung about her shoulders, her lips were bluish; she had only the curtest answers, and was obviously disinclined to speak at all.

"I'm afraid you stayed in the water too long," said Claudine, with a shade of anxiety.

"No," whispered Edna to her mother. "It's not that. She was simply terrified every minute! That snake, you know! And yet, of course, she would hover about the very spot where we saw it.... Don't speak to her, Mother darling! She'll be all right in a few minutes."

The supper was undeniably a triumph for Mr. Stephens. He had done wonders. Carefully concealed, he had caused to be brought a freezer of ice cream, great vacuum bottles of iced tea, and rum to flavour it for those who liked it. His bearers had lighted a fire before leaving, and in it were roasted potatoes and corn. There were also cold chicken and a fine boiled ham and a great number of other delicacies. The guests were hungry and complimentary.

Afterward he brought out that gold cigarette case and passed it about.

"Do you mind if I have one, Mother?" asked Andrée.

"I'd rather you didn't," said Claudine, coldly. There was nothing she disliked more.

But Mr. MacGregor intervened.

"As long as Miss Andrée isn't a singer," he said, "won't you be indulgent, Mrs. Vincelle? I believe they're very good for the nerves. In my younger days, of course, such a thing would have been out of the question. But live and learn! My own sister—"

"Mercy, what a killing look!" murmured Edna to her sister. "He wants to show you how up-to-date and young he is!"

"Very well!" said Claudine, graciously. But it was not Mr. MacGregor's plea which had persuaded her; it was the peculiar look on her child's face. It would be unwise to cross her, she thought.

And Andrée smoked, leaning back against a tree, looking an abandoned, reckless young creature, surrounded by a subtle and dangerous atmosphere of adoration.

The moon came up ... what further enchantment did she need than that light on her pale, dark face, than all that sweetness and mystery of the mid-summer night about her?

The bearers came back and took away their burdens, and a little later the picnickers followed. Claudine walked a little in advance with Mr. Mac-Gregor, and whenever, with a strange uneasiness, she turned to look behind her, she certainly saw two little points of light from two cigarettes among the shadows.

She condemned Mr. Stephens to Limbo.

III

Naturally when Gilbert came out the next week-end he wished to know all about this picnic, and he wished to know also, although he dared not ask, why his candidate, Mr. MacGregor, had appeared so obviously discouraged. They had become great friends; they dined and went to the theatre together, and maintained a delightful bachelor intimacy, coming and going as they pleased. He had listened to MacGregor's praise of Claudine with a sore heart. She kept her charm, her affability, well hidden from her husband! There she sat beside him, on the veranda, her book politely closed on her lap, just wifely, no more.

"Who was the fellow who gave the picnic?" he asked. "I've never heard of him. You haven't mentioned his name in your letters."

"You'll see him in the dining-room this evening," said Claudine. "He's not—not quite our own sort, you know, Gilbert, but he's very nice and pleasant."

"Well, I'm no snob!" said Gilbert. He was in a wonderfully pleasant mood, his wife noticed, and if she had felt the least assurance of its keeping on, she would have unbent a little. But so many, many times had she hurried to meet him half way, only to see him retreat.... His thoughts would have astounded her.

"Why in God's name can't the woman be simple and friendly with me—

and not so damned suspicious!" he said to himself. "She's always watching me out of the corners of her eyes.... If we're not—in love, there's no reason why we shouldn't be friends."

He was really anxious to be friendly that day, poor devil, who had never had a friend in his life, or ever been one!

"No, I'm not a snob," he went on. "That's a feminine failing. But I don't like my family making bosom friends of people I don't know."

"He's certainly not a bosom friend," said Claudine, "and as for your not knowing him, how could that be helped, when you weren't here?"

"Very well! Very well!" he said, impatiently. "We won't argue. Introduce the fellow to me, and I'll soon see what sort he is."

No one could imagine Claudine's dread and misery. She knew very well what Gilbert would think of Mr. Stephens.

His solitary little table was near a window, and a vagrant breeze that ruffled his light hair gave him a boyish and untidy look. He had a book propped up before him and he was eating absent-mindedly. She pointed him out with a smile which was the equivalent of a shrug of the shoulders, throwing the poor young fellow to the wolves.

"There he is, Gilbert!" she said.

Gilbert stared incredulously at the cheerful young man, with sleeves rolled up on his sunburnt arms, coat-less, innocently absorbed in his book.

"What!" he said. "That fellow!"

"I told you he wasn't quite—"

"And that's the sort of man you encourage—and have hanging around your daughters, while you raise cain about a gentleman like MacGregor!"

He stared again.

"You introduce him to me," he said, "and I'll soon settle his hash!"

"Don't be rude to him, Gilbert! Remember we've accepted his hospitality.... You'll put me in a very undignified position."

"You've done that for yourself," he said.

With what reluctance did she approach the unsuspecting young man, and present him to Gilbert! He got up with alacrity and held out his hand, but Gilbert ignored it. He glanced round, and saw that Claudine had gone, and that he might therefore be rude without fear of interruption. He was terribly upset; he had a dim suspicion that Claudine had set up this man in opposition to his Mr. MacGregor, that it was altogether some beastly feminine plot.

"I want to thank you for your hospitality to my family," he said, slowly. "However—"

"However?" repeated Mr. Stephens, encouragingly, but Gilbert found it very difficult to go on. He stood with his hands behind his back, the very image of respectability and decent prosperity, lowering at "that grasshopper," as he mentally named the other.

"However," said Mr. Stephens. "It mustn't happen again. Is that it?" He was, it must be confessed, rather unduly sensitive to the social disapproval of capitalists.

"Yes!" said Gilbert. "I'm very particular—in regard to the acquaintances—about the people—about people I know nothing about—where my family is concerned."

"Well," said Stephens, "you can investigate, if you like. You can find out all about me. You can write to—"

"No! It won't do .... No, I'll have to ask you to—to discontinue the intimacy."

"There isn't any intimacy."

"There's not to be any intercourse whatever."

"I don't see how you can stop it," said Stephens.

"I forbid it!" said Gilbert, with a scowl.

"You can't forbid me, you know. As for your family, I don't know whether you can forbid them or not. That's their business. If they consider it the best policy to knuckle down, why, I shan't think any the worse of them. It's the way of the world to dance when the fellow with the money fiddles. You—"

"Look here, you damned, impudent, vulgar jackanapes—"

"Don't begin calling names, or I might call you a damn' vulgar bully. But I won't. I don't lose my temper so easily. Fellows like me know that when they do lose their tempers, they've got to back it up with their fists. Something your sort never do, do you? You yell and curse, and that's the end of it."

They were disturbed by the distressful voice of Mrs. Dewey, outraged by these loud voices, but respectful before two such profitable persons.

"Gentlemen!" she said. "Please....!"

Gilbert turned on his heel and strode out of the room. He went, of course, to his wife.

"I've been having a talk with that gentlemanly friend of yours," he said, with a desperate effort to steady his voice. "And I want to tell you, once and for all, I'll have—I'll have ... I'll have ... Understand me, both of you— and I want you to tell Andrée, too—you're not to speak to the fellow again. Under any circumstances."

"I'll have to answer him if he speaks to me," said Edna.

Both her parents were astonished.

"No, you don't!" said her father. "I won't have it!"

"I can't be rude to him," said Edna, in her most tranquil, sensible voice.

"I tell you!" shouted Gilbert. "I won't have it!"

Edna said nothing, but the expression of her face was not obedient.

Gilbert didn't know how to proceed; he hesitated a moment, then he turned away.

"Claudine," he said, from the doorway, "this is your business! You brought them up, and now you can handle them. You see to it that my— wishes are carried out. Understand, I'll have no nonsense!"

"Oh, my dear child!" said Claudine, when the door had banged after him. "I wish you had more—tact! Surely Mr. Stephens isn't worth a quarrel with your own father!"

"I don't know, Mother. I think he's rather wonderful. I wouldn't be rude to him for anything. You know Andrée and I have seen a lot of him this week. We've been rowing with him, and walking, and he's been as nice as could be. You can't imagine! ... He's so different from anyone else we've ever known. And even if he is common, he's not the least bit—objectionable. Why, Mother, you can see how trustworthy and honest he is! It's written all over him!"

"I know, my dear. But your father—"

"Father's not infallible. He makes mistakes. He's not a good judge of people at all. And I'm not going to be rude to the poor man. And I'm *sure* Andrée won't, either. She loves to hear him talk. She says he makes her ambitious."

Claudine was in despair. How did other mothers manage to impress their children? Was the trouble because she was singularly ineffectual or because her children were singularly rebellious? It didn't occur to her that it might be because she was wrong. She decided to try another tack.

"Edna!" she cried, fervently. "For my sake, dear, avoid any trouble with your father! You can't think how it distresses me!"

"Mother!" said Edna, firmly. "That's not fair! That's just as bad as Father's way. It isn't fair to try to make me do what I don't think is right."

But she melted at the sight of her mother's face.

"Very well, darling!" she said. "I hate to do it, but if it'll make you any happier, I'll be tactful. Father won't know a thing about it. I'll give Mr. Stephens a little hint. He's never offended. I'll only talk to him when Father isn't here."

And Claudine must be satisfied with this.

CHAPTER SEVEN

STEPHENS EXPLAINS HIMSELF

It was perhaps a mistake not to have told all this to Andrée. She had been almost all the afternoon in the woodshed with two baby kittens she adored, quite happy there in the dim light and the quiet, and determined to avoid the possibility of a motor ride with her father. When she came in to dress for supper, everyone was calm again, and Mr. Stephens' name wasn't mentioned. After supper Gilbert had to return to the city, and his wife and Edna went with him to the station, but Andrée said she had a headache, and remained behind. She sat in a corner of the veranda, still in the same vague and happy mood in which she had passed the afternoon, glad to be alone.

Presently she saw a familiar figure in the lighted doorway, and she called out, cheerfully—

"Hello, Mr. Stephens!"

"Hello!" he answered, but to her amazement, instead of coming to her, he went on toward the steps.

"Where are you going?" she asked. "To the drugstore? I'll come with you."

"No," he answered. "No ... I was going for a walk."

"Wait a minute!" she said, and jumping up, went over to him.

"What's the matter?" she asked. "You're—queer! Why don't you sit down and talk to me?"

He glanced uneasily at the row of dark figures rocking behind them.

"Well ... under the circumstances ..." he murmured.

"What circumstances?"

"You know what your father said—"

"No, I don't, and I don't care, either. Tell me!"

"Not here."

"Then let's walk!"

They strolled over the lawn, beyond earshot of the veranda.

"Well," said he. "We had—words. He told me not to speak to any of you again. I said, of course, I'd speak to you as long as you cared to speak to me.... But—"

"How beastly!" cried Andrée. "How horrible! But please don't pay any attention to it. Edna and I never do."

"At first I thought I wouldn't. They're free agents, I thought; it's up to them to say whether they want to drop me or not. I've never had much respect for parental authority, in regard to adults. But when I'd thought it over—I saw it wouldn't do. It's not fair to you. You're not free agents. It puts you in a rotten position."

"So you're not going to speak to us?"

"No, not that ... I'm going away to-morrow morning."

"No! No! Don't! I couldn't bear to think you were driven away like that! Please don't go!"

"I must. I've told Mrs. Dewey already. I—the whole thing has made me—sick. I've got to go!"

Andrée stopped short.

"Very well!" she said. "If that's all you care ..."

"It has nothing to do with—caring."

"If you valued our friendship—as I do—"

"You don't!" he cried. "You don't! You can't! You don't know me.... I'm just a sort of—of freak—to amuse you on your holiday."

"Look here!" said Andrée, sternly. "What makes you think that? You're the last person in the world I'd have expected to be—silly and sensitive and imagining things like that. Can't you see that Edna and I like you?"

"I thought you did.... But to tell you the truth, I never know, with people like you, how much is real, and how much is politeness. I'm not polite; I'm not used to politeness."

"No one else ever thought that Edna and I were very polite," she observed, laughing.

"But I can't make you out!" he cried. "I never realized what a difference there was... You're a mystery to me."

"Don't think like that," said Andrée, rather sharply. "What I admired so much about you was your way of looking at everyone as simply *human*."

They had turned down the road in the direction of the big hotel; in the dusk he could see her face, and never had anything seemed to him less simply human. She looked to him so wonderful, so strange, so troubling; all his ideas about the frank and sensible companionship that ought to exist between man and woman were dissolving in her spell. Never had he felt less companionable—or less human. He was exalted and very unhappy. Humility was not one of his virtues; he had an honest consciousness of his own worth, and he did not feel humble now, but he was frightened. He knew very well that he was in love with her, and in a silly, unreasonable way, too. He saw no justification for adoring a woman, but he adored this one.

"Well ..." he said. "Why do you like me, anyway?"

"Because you're *real*," answered Andrée, promptly. "And honest. And specially because you haven't any limits."

"Oh—outside the pale!" he cried, very much hurt.

Andrée was surprised.

"Why do you always think things like that," she asked. "You seem to think that matters so much—that—that artificial difference. It doesn't to me."

"It has to. I know I'm touchy. I'm ashamed of it, but I can't help it. I'm always looking for slights, and I generally find them.... But what did you mean then by my not having any limits?"

"I meant a sort of feeling—that I could tell you anything. You might not always understand, but you'd try. You'd listen. I couldn't imagine you ever saying 'This is *too* much!' like Father. You haven't put up any boundaries."

"I see," he said, gravely. "Well ... it's true, to some extent. I don't pretend to understand everyone, but I can say I've never seen a soul yet that was really—well, altogether strange to me. There's always something in common.... Now, with women, you know. Lots of these fellows—writers and all—they like to call woman a mystery. I know I said you were, but now I'm speaking in a general sense. My idea is—"

He stopped and looked a little anxiously at Andrée and was reassured by her quiet attention. He had long ago grasped that strange quality of comprehension in her; she was not particularly clever or original, but she could grasp everything. She didn't know; she saw. It was like a seeress gazing into a crystal; she might not comprehend the significance of what was presented, but she *saw*, so clearly and justly. Experience in talking to feminine comrades had taught him how dangerously inclined they were to make personal applications; this girl would never do that. He went on, a little more easily.

"I don't see anything mysterious in women," he said. "I haven't any use for what you call 'chivalry.' I'd defend a woman—any woman, anywhere, but it wouldn't be because I—well—felt any reverence; it would be because she was weaker. I wouldn't try to make life easy for women—or for anyone.... Only a fair show. I'm a man; I expect to take a man's part in the world. And I look to women to take their own part, and do their own work, and shoulder their own burdens.... Here's the drugstore; shall we have a soda?"

Andrée assented and they went into the shop, which was filled with couples engaged in the same pursuit. He found a stool for Andrée, but there was none for himself; and he stood beside her, seriously consuming an elaborate thing of nuts, marshmallow, syrup and ice-cream. He was conscious all the time that he was enjoying a luxury; this thing was to him no frappé, but a symbol, a part of his share of the benefits of civilization. He would have liked to arrange for every one of the workers of the world to have a due allowance of such confections. His thoughts at that moment were very far from Andrée; he was, in fact, concerned with the memory of a hokey-pokey vendor on the lower East Side, surrounded by dirty children pitifully eager for his poisonous wares. He might have been disappointed to know how personally Andrée had applied his words—and then, he might not have been.

His words— "I'm a man, and I expect to take a man's part in the world," had given her a curious thrill.

"He is a man!" she thought. "More so than anyone I've ever met." She glanced back over her shoulder at him, but his blue eyes were fixed upon the bourgeoisie consuming their unearned luxuries. She thought that among all the men there he stood forth notably as soldier, sturdier, oddly impressive in his utter honesty. And not bad-looking. His short blond hair showed a neat, well shaped head, the mouth beneath his absurd little mustache was a well cut one, resolute and very kindly; he carried himself splendidly.

"Well!" he said, at last. "Let's be getting on!"

Andrée got up, still thoughtful. He turned in the direction of Pine Villa, but she protested.

"I don't want to go back now!"

"Better," he said cheerfully. "Your mother'll be worried."

This did not please Andrée, for she felt that any such dutiful ideas should have come from herself. She was about to say something a little disagreeable, when they caught sight of Claudine coming down the road, always an unmistakable figure by her gait and her bearing. The young man was disconcerted; he had no way of knowing how she had regarded her husband's hostility, and he was very much in dread of her politeness. It was too dark to see her face; he had to wait for her voice, and to his great relief, it came to him tranquil and friendly. She didn't say anything remarkable, only "Good evening," but it implied for him all sorts of astounding and exquisite things. She didn't mind his taking a walk with the matchless Andrée....

"I hope you're not converting Andrée," she said, in just the light and agreeable tone she would have used toward any of the bourgeoisie. "I shouldn't like her to be a Revolutionary."

"I'm not, myself," he answered, seriously. "Did you ever read Dostoievsky, Mrs. Vincelle?"

"Yes," she answered, secretly amused at his fatal responsiveness.

"Well, I think that fellow's idea is the best philosophy I've ever come across. I believe to some extent in Conscious Evolution, but not so much through the development of a new type of humanity as through the development of compassion. You know. The kingdom of Heaven on earth. I think it's compassion rather than intelligence that can save the world. If you can learn to pity, you learn to help.”

“Presupposing a little energy,” said Claudine. He was very much aware of her resistance; she did not wish to argue; she had a dread of being serious; she was never, never, to be convinced. Her mind and her opinions were unalterably formed; she was willing enough to listen, to think, but she accepted nothing. It was altogether different from talking to Andrée.

“I think it’s quite possible to be compassionate and selfish at the same time,” she went on.

“Well, there’s nothing wrong in selfishness. It’s vital. It’s a force, not a vice. As long as you want the right things.... Specially for women. An unselfish man might be a hero, but an unselfish woman couldn’t be anything but a victim.... Like a child.... Imagine an unselfish child. Of course it couldn’t survive. What you’ve got to do is to learn to feel for other people so much that it hurts your selfishness—so that you can’t be comfortable unless the rest are too.”

Claudine found his earnestness a little wearying; she wondered how the impatient Andrée could endure much of him. He was admirable, and he was very touching, and not for any Gilbert on earth would she offend him, but she wished very much that he might be somewhat less obviously there. He had had his cue to vanish; he could have put such a nice, friendly end to the acquaintance, and been entirely in the right, but instead—there he was. She had no objection to Andrée’s talking to him, but she felt that future walks were to be discouraged.

They crossed the lawn, black and spongy under the pines, and as a matter of course, she began to mount the steps of the veranda. But Andrée lingered.

“Come, my dear,” said Claudine. “Edna’s waiting for you.”

“Half a minute,” said Andrée, and her mother entered the home without her. Andrée leaned against the veranda, her head thrown back, looking up at the sky; Stephens stood before her, and characteristically, he was looking down at the earth, very thoughtful. There was a long silence, which neither of them noticed.

“Good night,” said Andrée, suddenly, and he was startled to see her holding out her hand. He took it, rather reluctantly, and she gave his a firm, strong pressure, and didn’t let go. But he drew away almost roughly.

“Good night,” he said, and walked away.

No other man she had yet seen would have done that; she was accustomed to having her imperious impulses treated with at least a semblance of rapture; she went in, more thoughtful than ever.

The truth of it was, that for young Stephens there were no trifles; everything was significant. He was a man of strong passions and dearly bought wisdom; he knew no middle course between being indifferent or quite otherwise. He had been brought up in a class where a friendship between a man and a woman was unthinkable; or any sort of careless or meaningless intercourse. If you weren't in love with a girl, or on the point of falling in love, you never thought of her. He had developed and he had learnt much; he had a remarkable command over himself; he would have been able to go on like this forever and ever, simply talking and talking to Andrée, and being quite impersonal, but not if she were going to hold his hand. He really resented that. Old ideas which he fancied he had outgrown came back to him now, with force; a venomous distrust for women of Andrée's sort. As a boy, when he had seen them in the streets, exquisitely dressed, in their carriages, it had given him comfort to believe them all wanton and worthless chaff. Later, when he had begun to read novels, all this had been confirmed; he had made more than one fiery and bitter speech to his comrades on that subject; on these pampered women with their jewels, their furs, their inordinate luxuries. He was honest enough even then to admit the existence of a leaven of desire in his sullen resentment.

"It's the dream of most fellows like me," he had thought, "to possess a superior woman. And there's no chance of it. No matter what we do, or become, the finest and best of them are always out of reach."

His candid opinion of the Vincelles would have shocked them one and all. He had studied the social conditions of his country with thoroughness, and he knew they weren't the best, or even the second best. They belonged in a place he could never get to, but there were places above to which they could never attain; he was far better aware of this than they were. He knew that Andrée was half-educated and half-trained, that she was not useful and not, socially speaking, ornamental. And he had been able thus dispassionately to judge her because she had seemed so entirely impossible to him. He knew he loved her, but he had had no hope, and, obliged to withstand her allurement, he had been able to analyze it. The intractable and wayward spirit of her was what he loved; her elusiveness. Always and forever she would do what she wanted; every breath would sway her, but not the mightiest wind from heaven would dismay or turn her from her desire. There was no constancy, no steadfastness in her, but she was honest. She was very largely made up of faults, and they were faults he loved; wilfulness, recklessness, a sort of casual and unconscious cruelty, a marvelous selfishness, innocent, unambitious, like that of a child. She would not strive, never fight for what she wanted, she would stretch out careless hands for what passing things took her fancy.

Just at the moment, he took her fancy. Well, he wasn't going to have it that way. He was going away, to forget her, before there was any more to forget. He wanted not to see that dark, mutinous face again, or to hear that nervous and exquisite voice, that seemed always to have a sob in it. Because he was constant and steadfast, and he had no wish to give so very much and to get nothing in return.

CHAPTER EIGHT

THE THING IS ON THEM

I

There was a very great deal that young Stephens didn't know about himself, some of it that was obvious to other eyes. He did not go away the next morning; Edna met him after breakfast and entreated him not to do so.

"We're so dull and miserable here," she said. "And you're the only hope. Do you know what Mother calls you? The Breath of Life! Now after that you can't go, can you?"

He smiled, a little inattentively. There she stood, so pretty and serene, one of those women who considered it their right to make outrageous demands upon men.... He saw suddenly how difficult it must be to withstand their demands. He did not want to refuse Edna; he liked her very much, because she was frank and friendly; he didn't suspect that her frankness held a hundred times more reserve than Andrée's silences, that she, so smiling and affable, was infinitely more aloof, more mysterious, more unknowable, than her dark sister.

"The Breath of Life!" he said. "Why?"

"Because we're all very nearly dead, and you're so much alive," she said, tranquilly. "Can't we have one more nice day together?"

"I don't see ..." he said, doubtfully. "After—well—your father, you know...."

He had no clear conception of Gilbert's position; he had certainly seen many husbands and fathers who were bullies, but in a more primitive society this bullying carried weight and was not defied. He knew little of the civilized expedients of women; he didn't imagine that Claudine would stoop to deceive. Yet he didn't think her quite capable of independence.

"Oh, Father!" said Edna, carelessly. "He's just melodrama.... And we won't tell Mother, and she'll pretend not to know where we've gone. We can—"

"But I don't like it!" he protested. "It's a humiliating position for me."

"It really isn't, Mr. Stephens. We're the humiliated, deceitful ones, and we don't care. Do you know the country round here?"

"I was born a few miles down the river," he answered, soberly. "In Brownsville Landing."

Andrée came sauntering out of the house, and caught his words.

"I'd like to hear about you," she said, but he shook his head.

"No," he said. "That's a mistake. What used to be me isn't me now. It's—well, it's like these books—they start off when the fellow's a baby, and they tell you all the things he thought and all the ways he grew and changed, until you can't see him at all. I'm darned glad you never saw me or heard of me before, and you've got to see only what I am now." He smiled ingenuously. "It's not much," he said, "but it's what I've worked twenty-eight years on, anyway."

"Come on; let's start somewhere," said Edna. "Or Mother'll come out and have to not 'countenance' it. Let's take a 'ramble'; that's what Father calls a walk."

"It is a 'ramble,' too, with him," said Andrée.

"Well," said Stephens, "there's a nice place up the road five or six miles—nursery for all kinds of evergreens, and a little hotel. If you think you can do it—? It's a steep climb."

Edna ran in to leave a message for her mother with Mrs. Dewey, and they set off. It was a sultry, hazy morning; it seemed unaccountably oppressive to Stephens. He felt unpleasantly like a new toy to these greedy children; they looked to him to provide amusement; they weren't interested in his ideas, which were his life, and they had no faint idea of the wonder of him. He glanced down at his white flannel legs and buckskin shoes; he thought of his appearance in general, his immaculate cleanliness, the comfort of fine raiment, of himself strong, confident, carrying a cigarette case of purest gold and walking by these fabulous girls. And he thought of a sallow youth, ten years ago, lounging outside a pool room in Brownsville Landing, in a dirty grey flannel shirt and a villainous cap, dazed and stupid with incessant cigarettes, engaging in candid persiflage with the mill girls who passed. He had bridged that gulf all alone....

The making of his money he regarded as a minor achievement. It was the regeneration of his spirit that was so remarkable; that, he felt, was little less than a miracle; he would have liked to tell that.

He had been in the hospital with a broken head, justifiably got in a saloon brawl; he had lain in the ward two days, suffering and resentful because he couldn't smoke. No one came to see him; who was there to come? His father, who worked in the brick yards, was always drunk when he wasn't busy, and he had no other relatives; he didn't know what a friend was. He went about in a pack, a gang of youths of his own age, bound by no other tie than that of the pack instinct, all of them more or less vicious, in a pitiful way. They lacked ambition, that is, at eighteen or so, they showed a lamentable disinclination to work every day and all day in mill or factory. They wanted something better, and even now Stephens fancied that their sordid distractions *were* better, had a little more of the stuff of life in them.

In his restlessness and misery, he had turned his attention to the man in the next bed, a portly, pallid fellow of forty-five or so, with a black beard and a severe and dignified manner. He looked like a physician, some sort of professional man; he was actually a mill hand, an Englishman named Simms, a Manchester Socialist of the old school, austere and fanatic. He sat propped up in bed reading Huxley, but he was very willing to talk. And in five days he had expounded the world to the sallow "corner boy." Gesturing forcibly with his bandaged hand—he had been badly mangled at his machine—he set forth his Quixotic and beautiful doctrines. He had little humanity, no flexibility; he was uncompromising and stern as a Calvinist.

They had lived together for two years. It was Simms who had shown young Stephens the charm of cleanliness; he had a bare little room on the outskirts of the town which he scrubbed himself; his habits were, fastidious and ascetic. He taught young Stephens sobriety and continence and his own worth, and he taught him to read. His pupil was not docile; he joined the Y. M. C. A., which was anathema to Simms; he took courses in everything, he frequented the gymnasium. He made use of what the older man disdained; his ideas were more practical and less sublime.

He felt now that he was justified and he wished poor Simms were alive, to be argued with. He stole a glance at Andrée, and he felt a curious mixture of despair and defiance. He was good enough—but she would never think so.

II

Claudine had watched them go from her window, with some uneasiness. People of his sort were so hard to handle! Why hadn't he the tact to go away? It was so difficult to keep a middle course between offending him and offending Gilbert; she dwelt with dismay, not for the first time, on the uncompromising nature of men, how rudely they upset all feminine niceties. Nothing might be implicit or vague with them. Even Bertie, her marvelous boy, had to tell her things, and be frank about his feelings, in a way Andrée and Edna never were.

She spent a peaceful day, reading and writing letters. The letters did her good, put her in touch with her own little world again, restored to her some measure of complacency. She was unhappy and her life very futile and insignificant, but it might have been so much worse; it might have been harmful. She re-read Lizzie Wiley's letter, full of the atrocious Bernardine Perceval, who had left her husband.

"I saw Bernardine," she wrote, "on the street car with the little girl. What she will drag the child into I don't know. I thank God there are still a few like yourself left." And so on. Lizzie Wiley was a wealthy spinster of passionate moral views and her approval was not without weight. Claudine thought with a faint smile of her own bad moment, twenty years before, when she had wanted to leave Gilbert; she had a fairly definite idea that those moments occurred in most marriages; for an instant she wondered what had made her resist it. Duty? Fear? Lance? She didn't much want to know, and put the thought aside. The fact remained that she had stayed and done well, for Gilbert, for herself, for her children.

She wrote a plaintively humorous letter to Nina Sidell, whose Violet was just Andrée's age. Violet was a frightful worry, in a way her daughters would never be. Wasn't that something else to her credit? Then there was Connie Martinsburgh, whose four exuberant and handsome children were all troublesome. Perhaps, although she seemed to herself so entirely negative, she did after all exert a good influence over her family... That absurd young Stephens had upset her, with his terrific vitality; he had made her feel so pallid, so helpless, so useless. Poor Breath of Life, with his gold cigarette case!

III

They returned from their "ramble" early in the afternoon, and the girls at once went upstairs to lie down. They were much more fatigued than they eared to admit.

"Lord! What a cyclone!" said Edna, taking the pins from her crisp, reddish hair and letting it fall about her bare shoulders. "He can do everything and he knows everything. That lecture about coniferous trees....! And yet he's amusing."

Andrée was stretched flat on her back on the bed.

"He's more than amusing," she said, with a frown. "He's very fine. He's a man."

"Oh, hardly that!" said Edna, slipping into her kimono. She was startled by her sister suddenly sitting upright.

"You silly little snob!" she cried. "You make me tired! You don't know anything—you can't see anything!"

"Oh, Gosh!" thought Edna, in alarm. "I *do* see something now!"

Andrée went on, to point out to her younger sister the mental or moral excellencies of young Stephens; all in vain. She neglected to mention his endearing smile, that odd, tender look in his blue eyes.

Edna kept whatever she thought to herself.

"He said he was absolutely going away to-morrow," she reflected. "And she'll forget."

And by the light of this, the relations between Andrée and the Breath of Life seemed rather funny than anything else. Edna didn't mention her discovery to her mother, nor did she attempt to stop them or to go with them when they left the veranda that evening. She looked after them as they crossed the lawn, with a benevolent smile.

"That poor man's going to get a jolt," she reflected. "I dare say Andrée'll get engaged to him this evening, just as she did to Johnnie Martinsburgh last winter. Then she'll get into a panic, and I'll very probably have to get her out of it, the same way. Well! It can't be helped! That's Andrée, all over. She's so darned sincere every time."

"Let's take a walk over to your Fern Glen," Andrée was saying.

"I don't think—" he began, doubtfully.

"Yes," she insisted. "There'll be a moon, won't there, later on?"

"Your mother—"

"It's your last evening."

"I know," he said. "But we can talk here—"

"I believe you're afraid of me," she said, laughing.

"I am," he answered, and she suddenly stopped laughing.

"You'd better let me alone," he went on. "I don't understand your ways. Things you think are funny make me miserable."

"I don't want a bit to make you miserable, and I certainly don't see anything funny in—in this thing. Do come on! Mother and Edna will be home, and then we can't go."

She went on, and he reluctantly followed her white figure. They went along the road, walking quietly on its grassy border, he always a little behind her. It was a mild beautiful night, a night on which one could walk forever. Behind the pine trees there was a marvelous faint radiance, the path of the coming moon. The breeze blowing across the apple orchard they were passing brought a wine-like perfume and an exquisite rustling of leaves. The young man looked steadfastly down at his white tennis shoes moving soundlessly over the grass.

They came to the pasture through which Andrée had once refused to go, and they saw the great, dim shapes of the cows standing motionless in there.

"I suppose you want to go around—" said he.

"No; I shan't be afraid, if you'll stay near me," she answered.

He let down the bars, and carefully replaced them when they had gone through.

"Don't run," he said, "and they won't pay any attention to you."

To his surprise she took his arm and held it lightly. "I do hate them!" she said. "What would you do if they were to run after us?"

"They never do," he answered, briefly, and fell silent. But she was amazed to feel his arm, his firm, strong arm, tremble beneath her touch.

She smiled to herself in the dark.

They came at last to the glen, and sat down on a rock. The moon had risen just above the crags; the air was tremulous with its light.

"It's too bad there are nothing but owls here," she said. "I'd love to hear a nightingale sing."

"I've heard 'em, in England. I was there four years."

"Now, you see! With all the interesting things you've got to tell me, and that I want so much to hear, you talk about going away to-morrow. You can't!"

"I must!"

"Are you—going to write to me?"

"No. What would be the use?"

"Don't you want to go on being friends?"

"Look here—are you going to make me say—what I don't want to say?"

"Yes, if I can! I want everything clear and plain between us. You're the first real friend I've ever had, and I'm not going to lose you through any stupid misunderstanding."

"Well, then; I *couldn't* go on being friends. I'd ... it would have to go on—to something else."

She was perfectly still.

"You know what I mean, don't you" he asked.

"Yes ... I know," she answered, in an odd, flat voice.

"And you don't want that...."

"I don't know," she said, "whether I do or not."

He was so startled that he sprang to his feet.

"What!" he cried. "I don't believe you do understand!"

"I do! You mean you think—you might—later on—fall in love with me."

Her sublime candour touched him almost beyond endurance. He walked a few paces away from her, to the very edge of the pool, and tried to calm his heart with that unutterable beauty, that fall of water, like bright silver hair in the moonlight, like a stream from the moon itself, over the face of the cliff, without sound, into the radiant brightness of the pool. If there had been a nightingale to sing there, he thought, it would have broken his heart.

"As a matter of fact," he said, in a low voice, "I am in love with you now. I shouldn't have told you if you'd let me alone."

"Why shouldn't I know?"

"Because—I don't feel like amusing you that way."

"Oh, but I don't—really I don't look at it like that! How can you always think so of me? I'm not trivial and shallow," she cried, very much wounded. "You ought to have seen that I wasn't!"

"All right!" he said, grimly. "Now you know."

"And you're going away?" she asked.

"I am."

"Suppose I don't want you to go?"

"That would make me go all the quicker."

"You have a—a rather funny way of being in love," she said. "I should think—"

"Now, see here," he said, with a sort of desperation. "Won't you let me alone? I've told you. I didn't want to, but you made me. You can have all the satisfaction of knowing that you've—hurt me and humiliated me. And nothing's going to be any good any more."

"Why?" she enquired, in a reasonable tone. "There are so many things in your life."

"I don't want them. I don't want anything but you. I'm—of course you don't know and you don't care. You'll go home and laugh at the impudence of that vulgar—"

Andrée faced him, very angry.

"That *is* vulgar, if you like," she said. "To imagine my doing that—laughing at you."

She had come down to the edge of the water, beside him, very near him. She was contemptuous, she was indignant and hurt. And suddenly all that went. There, in that enchanted glen, with the moon on him, he was transfigured, or it may be revealed. There was nothing mean about him; his sensitiveness was no longer paltry, but tragic. He was no more and no less than a man; forlorn in his strength and his youth; betrayed by the world he fancied he had conquered. Tears came into her eyes; she laid her hand on his shoulder.

"Oh ...! *I*—laugh at *you!*" she said.

He started away suddenly.

"Don't," he said. "Don't do that!"

A fatal and overmastering curiosity possessed her; her arm went round his neck, her fingers gently touching his cheek. She was amazed, delighted to feel him tremble under that shadow of a caress; she was exultant with a sense of her miraculous power, never before suspected. In all innocence, she could comprehend his passion, in a great measure because she herself was quite devoid of passion, was able to look on at this. She was impressionable, terribly susceptible to the magic of love in others, intoxicated by the emotion she could so easily inspire in others; but within her was always a grain of something hard and cold, never to be touched. An artist, was Andrée, always a little aloof; she could never lose herself.

But she loved him then, humanly enough, with an immature and cruelly exacting love. If he had said one word, made one gesture, to offend her critical and fastidious spirit, she would have hated him. Fortunately he didn't know this, and was not on his guard, not wary. He was as much concerned with his own feelings as she with hers; they were scarcely aware of each other.

"You can't really like me," he said, miserably.

"I do!" she said. "I do!"

"But not—love?" he said, looking at her with profound anxiety. Her glance fell and with eyes veiled, she was no longer so august. "You don't love me?" he insisted. "That couldn't be!"

She had no answer to make, but the very droop of her shoulders was acquiescent. He was astounded, incredulous, more appealing to her in his humility than in any other attitude he could have taken.

"Be honest with me!" he entreated. "I don't ask you for anything but that."

"I love you," she said, quietly. It was to them both a priceless boon conferred.

"But think what I am!" cried the pitifully honest lover. "I'm not in—your class. I don't know your ways. I couldn't live like you—"

Their arms were about each other, and what did all that matter? The strength and tenderness of his embrace, the reassurance she felt in his unalterable sympathy and kindness, made her weep. He was not strange to her; he was dearer and more familiar, even than her mother. There was security in him, and her deepest instinct required security.

"Don't cry, darling little Andrée," he said. "Are you afraid we can't be happy?"

He was, very greatly.

"No!" she said, scornfully. "Of course I'm not afraid."

They sat down, side by side, on a fallen log; he looked into her dark eyes, glittering with tears; he didn't know how to tell her how precious, how adorable she was.

"I'll do my best," he said. "Tell me just what you want, and what you don't like.... I can't help making you happy, when I love you so, can I, darling Andrée? I'll be the best kind of friend and lover I can to you, always. I'll never interfere."

"If you only won't," she said, eagerly. "I've grown to rather hate the idea of ever marrying, because it means so much interfering. I want to be myself."

Stephens privately didn't believe in marriage at all; he had even written a brochure on the subject; he thought it an evil; he would tell you, asked, or unasked, that he had never seen a happy marriage, or even many endurable ones. He didn't believe in women being dependent; he loathed domesticity; he revolted at the idea of vows and promises. And now, at this moment, he became completely an apostate. What else could be done with a creature like Andrée? Of course they must be married; more than that, he voluntarily made to her then and there all those vows he condemned; he promised to make her happier than he possibly could, he promised eternal love and constancy, he promised that as this moment, so should all their lives be; he believed it, and so did she.

"We'll be friends, Andrée, always," he said. "We'll each have our own life and our own interests. We'll make it a different sort of marriage."

"Oh, let's!" said Andrée.

But while he was already envisaging the next ten years, she was held in thrall by this one minute. She listened to him for some time, but the intolerable feeling grew on her that he was wasting precious time.

"We don't know how it'll come out," she said, impatiently. "Let's not bother about it, but just be as happy as we can."

He was silenced by this admirable recklessness. He took her in his arms and kissed her, and this time she kissed him; then he rather abruptly said it was time for them to go home.

"No; why?" she said.

But he was quite firm about it. He knew himself better than she did. He was alarmed at his total lack of views and opinions just then; he was not as reasonable as he wished to be. He was mortally afraid that by some expression of his ardour he might offend his glorious Diana. They walked home with their arms about each other, through the fields and the woods, a walk in a dream, in moonlight and shadow.

He went up to his hot little room and sat there in the dark, heart-sick with the ecstasy of it. He was more troubled and unhappy than he had ever been before in his cocksure existence. This thing, made up of moonlight and Andrée's dark eyes, had come crashing into his life, to break it in two. He had not wanted or imagined anything of the sort; he with his talk about biologic necessities. He was appalled at the idea of going on, because everything within him had stopped.

He was not easily daunted, but it was a long time before his courage was fully restored. He lighted a cigarette, and it tranquillized him.

"All right!" he said, aloud. "I made a new man of myself once. I'll do it again. I've got to."

That was what he thought.

CHAPTER NINE

BERTIE

I

Claudine had put aside her philosophers that morning, and sat in her little glade, listless and wretched. An insufferable, intolerable summer, a summer altogether wrong and harmful. And inevitably six weeks' more of it.

"It isn't right to keep the children here in idleness," she said to herself. "Healthy, intelligent adults, wasting months and months.... They ought to be doing something. They ought to be busy and useful.... I suppose I got these ideas from poor little Mr. Stephens, but they're good ideas. There was something very admirable about him...."

She smiled at the recollection of the "nice little beast," but the smile vanished instantly.

"They're both so discontented and restless—begging me to take them away. And I can't do anything I haven't any power, any authority! I can't do the least thing—I can't even leave this place without Gilbert's consent...."

A few miserable tears started to her eyes.

"That's the reason I have no control over them. A mother ought to be wise and firm and—free. But I can't do what I think ought to be done. I've never been able to. I have to argue with Gilbert, or deceive him. That's what it really is, although I like to call it tact. They ought to go home, and study, or work. They don't need a holiday! But I can't make him see that; not possibly. He sneers about 'a lot of idle women,' but he won't let us be anything else.... And the older I get, the more—cowardly I become. I can't bear to argue and argue with him. I know I can't win. I haven't any influence over him. I can't—charm him, or coax him, and I can't convince him. He's so obstinate."

She clasped her hands.

"Oh!" she cried. "If I could only, only have had my darling Andrée alone, I could have done so much for her! So much! I could have been so wise, so gentle, so patient, that she would have loved me with all her heart! I could have influenced her and helped her—"

She hastily wiped her eyes, ashamed of her emotion.

"How did it happen? Why did I become so helpless? Whose fault is it? Gilbert's? No, I can't think that. Other women with husbands just as bad as Gilbert don't allow themselves to be submerged. It's my fault; it must be. There's something wrong with me, some horrible moral weakness."

Her eye fell upon Marcus Aurelius and Epictetus.

"No; they're no use—only a drug. I call it training my mind, but it's only trying to dull my feelings. I ought to fight and struggle. I must! I must! I must get hold of my children. Now when Bertie's coming, when he hasn't seen me for two months.... I ought to be able to do something with him. He adores me."

She fell into a reverie upon her incorrigible boy. No doubt that Bertie was lazy, frivolous, and something a little worse— "wild," her friends called him. And yet she never worried seriously about him. He was so obviously the sort of person who always comes out on top. It was impossible to imagine him defeated. He was the cleverest of all her children, alarmingly clever, and he was also in some ways the finest of them. He had more sensibility than his sisters, more heart. That was the reason she was so shamefully indulgent toward his follies; she was aware, almost by instinct, that they were of no significance.

She decided upon an attitude; she would not be so fond, and full of half-playful remonstrances. No; she would be friendly, but firm and wise; she would show him the significance of life.

II

They went, one or the other of them, to meet all the reasonable trains.

"Why not?" said Andrée. "For mercy's sake, what else have we to do?"

But he did not come by any of them. As a sort of punishment for his shocking lack of industry during his late year at the Polytechnic Institute, he had been banished to a solitary camp in Maine with Lance, selected as a tutor of the most serious possible sort. And as Lance—who was perfectly indifferent to the boy's moral defects—wrote encouragingly of his mental attainments, he was allowed a two weeks' visit to his mother and sisters.

When he didn't come by the five o'clock train, they gave him up for that day. They were all dressed with an eye to his acutely critical taste, and a little crestfallen at their unregarded condition. They came down onto the veranda to wait until the bell rang for dinner, and sat there patiently with the old ladies.... When there came, along the mountain road, a terrific roaring, a dense cloud of dust, and a motor-car came up at a hair-raising speed, an eccentric, purple car, very low, with a gigantic engine. From this affair sprang out a figure in a duster, wearing goggles and a plaid cap put on backward.

They all started up, joyfully, and Andrée rushed to meet him.

"Where did you get that thing?" she cried.

"It's Pendleton's. What do you think of it? It's a French car."

"It's *très chic*. Come and see Mother!"

He sprang up the steps, pulled off cap and goggles, and kissed Claudine. And try as she would, she couldn't help looking at him indulgently, instead of wisely. There was something about him.... He was a very slight boy, barely eighteen, with an unusually dark skin and sleek black hair; he had a trick of keeping his mouth open, which showed his brilliantly white teeth, and gave him a stupid air; he had a smooth, oval face, narrow eyes, a rather weak chin; he looked at first glance like a silly young ass. But after you had looked again you were more inclined to think him a most engaging young devil. He had an odd, sidelong glance and a grimace of gamin impudence; he was never bad-tempered or sullen, but sometimes a little malicious.

"How did you get on with Cousin Lance, my dear?" asked his mother.

"Splendidly!" he answered. "Aren't you pretty, Mammy! But a bit spindly. Why don't you drink ale?"

"I'm very well, Bertie. Why did you take Mr. Pendleton's car? Isn't it rather a risk?"

"His look out. He offered it. He's a nice little playmate. He took me out to dinner the first night I got home, because the old man said he was busy. *Some* dinner! Andrée, what is there to do here?"

"Lots! You can knit and embroider and play solitaire—"

"We'll change all that, don't worry! Here's the latest thing in evolution, as old Lance would say, come to put a little pep into the fossils. Mammy, don't you think I've evolved a whole lot further than Father? Lance says it takes two million years to grow a new toe, or lose one, I forget which, but it seems to me—"

"That's the dinner bell," said Edna. "Come in just as you are. No one dresses here."

"*Noblesse oblige!*" said Bertie. "I'm going to dress. Tell them to keep the kettle on the hob—whatever that is—for a few minutes."

He came down again very promptly, with his black head sleek as a seal, and a new and marvelous dark suit. He disdained all the various washable materials; they were "a mess," he said, no one had any business to be hot enough to want them. He was absolutely correct in every detail, a very model of fashion and deportment; how were they not to be proud of him and delighted with him? He was very attentive to his mother, and even if it were a rather ostentatious courtesy, it warmed her heart.

She grew annoyed, though, when he persisted in smoking cigarettes between courses.

"It's very bad manners," she said. "It's disrespectful to me and your sisters. And what's more, no one smokes here in the dining-room. It isn't a hotel."

"I'll teach it to be. And it's not disrespectful, dear creatures. It's simply being done now."

"And you're too young to smoke. It's very harmful at your age. I can't bear to see you, Bertie!"

"Mammy, don't spoil my poor little holiday! Two weeks—that's all! Up there with old Lance, I neither smoke, chew, drink, spit nor cuss. Let me have my brief day!"

When they went out onto the veranda after dinner, his quick ear caught the sound of distant Music.

"What's that?" he asked.

"Dancing down at the hotel," answered Edna.

"Free for all, and leave your guns at the door?" he asked.

And after this, nothing would do, but that they must all stroll down to "look it over," and Bertie, entering ostensibly to buy a magazine in the lobby, looked in at the ballroom and said it looked "good enough."

"You and Edna sit out here on the piazza, and I'll take a few turns with Andrée," he said. "The music's not bad and the floor looks good."

"I'd rather you didn't," said Claudine. "They're not at all a nice sort of people here. I don't think it's quite the thing—"

Bertie fell back into Edna's arms like a log.

"Oh—h—h!" he groaned. "Why?"

"It's not dignified—"

"You don't have to be dignified till you get married or inherit money. Tell you what! You come, Mammy! You can dance some nice, old-fashioned sort of waltz. Come on!"

"I ought to!" she thought. "It's my duty to enter into their amusements—as long as I can't stop them."

But after half an hour spent there, she was more than ever determined to influence them—all of them—in an opposite direction, away from this unpalatable and promiscuous vulgarity.

"Don't you think it is better to be bored than to amuse yourselves in such a way as this?" she asked, on the way home.

"No!" said Andrée and Bertie, simultaneously.

"It seems a pity to me that young people like you—intelligent and well-bred, should be so mad about amusement," she said. "I can't understand it! If you were brainless and dull, it would be different. But there are so many really interesting things in the world, so many wholesome and fine recreations—"

"Never heard of them, Mammy! What are they?"

"When I was a girl, we thought it a pleasure to take a country walk with an interesting companion—"

"You wouldn't like the companions that we'd think were interesting," said Andrée.

"No," said Bertie, sadly. "There aren't any nice amusements left,

Mammy. Evolution has done away with 'em."

She looked at the three faces, at that clever and devilish Bertie, at the sensible, clear-sighted Edna, at Andrée, filled with a strange and wayward inner light.

"But you can't enjoy that sort of thing!" she cried. "You can't like to be there, in a room crowded with vulgar, noisy people whom you don't even know! You must see that these new dances are—to say the very least—ill-bred!"

"I accept!" said Bertie. "Lance was telling me about some fellow that made that his motto, and I think it's a gol-durned good one! I accept—anything that comes my way."

"But it doesn't mean that, Bertie. It means resignation."

"I know. And we are all resigned, except you. You want to—let's see—put back the clock of human progress. Very wrong Mammy!"

III

The next morning Bertie went again to the big hotel, and came back innocently with a new magazine for his mother. In the afternoon he went down to the garage and drove back in the startling purple car, and asked his mother to come for a drive. Filled with terror, she accepted, and spent two hours in mortal anguish, flying perilously along the edge of precipices, breathless from the terrific speed. There was no chance then for the serious talk she wished to have with her son, and after dinner he disappeared again, and didn't return until midnight.

But she was waiting for him on the veranda.

"Bertie!" she said. "Where have you been?"

"Dancing around a little, Mammy!"

"With whom?"

"Some girls at the hotel. Very respectable and humble, Mammy. I didn't have any trouble with them at all."

"I don't like it. And I'm sure your father wouldn't like it."

"So am I. But I'm used to that. It's crabbed age and youth—"

"Don't be disrespectful to your father! Bertie ...! Did you—have anything to drink?"

"Oh, yes! A couple of seltzer lemonades."

"I mean—anything—intoxicating?"

"Nothing that intoxicated me, Mammy!"

"Don't be so flippant and provoking! Bertie, I really feel in despair about you. Haven't you any serious or—worthy thoughts or ambitions?"

"They haven't come yet. But I'm only a child. Give me a chance!"

"What do you expect to do with your life?"

"Don't you know," he said, solemnly, "that that's really a ridiculous question, Mammy? It doesn't lie with me. I'm a puppet in the hands of Nature. I'm going to be used by a Blind Force—"

"Please don't joke!"

"I don't think I am. It seems to me it really is like that. I don't see much use in spending all your life squirming. I'd rather go along with the rest of the crowd—wherever they're going. We don't count much. We're just one more generation. It'll take about a billion years to change us or improve us. So what care I?"

"Bertie!" she cried, quite shocked. "Where did you get such ideas?"

"Lance has corrupted me. I was a poor innocent child who wanted to be an engineer and build bridges. But when I was taught to think a million years at a time, I lost interest."

"But you've got to pass your life in some sort of work, dear."

"I'll go into Father's office and show him how to run the show. Then I'll take a wad and buck the stock market and clean up a few millions and never worry again."

"Go to bed!" she said, half-laughing. "You're too silly to talk to! I suppose some time you'll grow up and be a man. And I hope with all my heart I'll be able to be proud of you."

His exploits that week, however, were certainly nothing to be proud of. He took a golden-haired maiden from the hotel out one afternoon and quite wrecked Mr. Pendleton's car, leaving it helpless on a mountain road to be taken back to the garage on a truck. He ran up a startling bill at the hotel for cigarettes, candies, and "seltzer lemonades" which she suspected strongly, and when she confronted him with it, he said, with chagrin:

"Pshaw! I told 'em not to send it till after I'd gone!"

She paid this herself from her own allowance, but the bill for the garage was beyond her. It was going to cost six hundred dollars to repair Mr. Pendleton's car.

"But he'll pay it himself!" Bertie protested. "He's a good sport. He knows I'm a young and inexperienced driver, and sure to have accidents."

"I'm ashamed of you, Bertie, to think of such a thing. I shall have to tell your father, and I'm afraid he'll be very angry."

"I don't believe in family rows. It might give him apoplexy. I should think you'd rather sell your jewels."

But she did tell Gilbert, and he was furious. It was not a pleasant weekend, but it didn't depress Bertie.

"I'm the reed, you know, Mammy, that bows its head to the storm," he said. And the very next day, told her he wanted to, and was socially obliged to, give a dinner-party to some of his friends at the hotel.

"You can't, my dear. Mrs. Dewey wouldn't—"

"She says she will. I hinted at it. We can have it at eight, when the others have finished. She says she'll do it in grand style, for my sake."

"It would cost a great deal. Your father—"

"Andrée and Edna will pay for it, out of their little savings, like sisters should, for their brother's honour. All you have to do is to look lovely and be dignified."

"But I don't care to encourage those hotel people!"

"They won't bother you when I've gone. Besides, you can freeze 'em thoroughly at the dinner. I don't care how rude you are to them."

It was a horrible dinner, of the sort that Claudine most thoroughly detested. Silly, over-dressed girls and one or two of their mothers, and a handful of boys who seemed to her prejudiced eyes nothing but cheap travesties on her fascinating son. She was quite perfect, with the affability and politeness she never displayed so well as when among people she disliked.

But after he had gone away, she was very glad she had done this for Bertie. She missed him beyond measure; of all her children he was the one who had most of her own detached and fatalistic point of view, and he, like herself, could find but cold comfort in his own heart. She understood him, how futile all achievement seemed to him, how terribly necessary was happiness. He *must* be happy; it was that alone which he required from life, not success, like Andrée, not self-approbation, like Edna, but joy in the moment, like herself.

She remembered him as a little boy, a beautiful child, a gay and cajoling little thing, his grandmother's favourite ... certainly a very much spoilt child. She liked to remember his passionate admiration of her, how she had always stopped in at the nursery to let him see her, dressed for the evening. How he had called her "pretty Mammy," quite unabashed by his father's disgust for his effeminacy.

Even now, with all his weaknesses, his petty vices seemed to her very innocent, very unimportant. It was only his way of looking for happiness. She felt sure that when he grew older, he would find a better way. And if he remained as he was, frivolous, reckless, pleasure-loving, wasn't it better, after all, than being stolid, prudent, money-loving?

"My dear, dear boy!" she thought, with tears in her eyes, but a smile on her lips. "Poor Bertie!"

IV

The long, long summer wore away; wasted and arid days they seemed to her. She found but little pleasure in her flowers and birds, no more consolation in her philosophers.

"I suppose I'm growing old!" she thought, and she allowed herself to dally with the idea of growing really old, when nothing would be expected of her, but dignity, which would be no trouble at all.

"But I'm barely forty!" she reflected. "I suppose there'll be at least twenty years more of this!" And her heart sank.

"It's peace I want!" she said. "I'm not made for struggling or achieving. I've been a wretched failure.... I suppose I've even failed Gilbert—in some sort of way. All I can do is to go on blundering and trying—for all that terribly long time.... If I can only see the children on the right road! .... And I don't even know what the right road is!"

She was happy to see her daughters so full of new interest and energy when the time came for going home.

"I can live in them!" she said. "If they'll let me!"

BOOK THREE
THE CUP IS OFFERED

CHAPTER ONE

ANDRÉE'S RECITAL

I

Gilbert was certainly very nervous. His nervousness took its usual form of a great rage and distress about his shirt, which he believed was inclined to bulge, and therefore to ruin and destroy him in the eyes of society. Moreover, his own image in the glass filled him with resentment, that portly and ungainly figure, his grey hair, his unromantic aspect. Nothing but a father, that's all he was, a money-maker. He strode around the bedroom, swearing bitterly and scowling, but toward this exhibition of ill-temper Claudine was neither frigid nor superior. She felt sorry for him. She chatted as she brushed her hair, and she succeeded in soothing him a little.

"You look very distinguished, Gilbert!" she said, and she was ready to believe it.

"Humph!" he said, hiding his pleasure. "That tailor's a fool. The coat wrinkles there, over the shoulders."

"Not when you stand up straight. I suppose you do, when you're being fitted, you know."

He straightened himself and looked again. It did look better.

"I hope she won't get into one of her freakish humours," he said. "Get stage fright, or anything of that sort."

"She won't," Claudine assured him. "She's not nervous in public. She's not the least bit upset. Listen! She's playing over her pieces now.... Oh, Gilbert! Isn't she wonderful?"

He went over to open the door into the hall, so that the sound might reach him better, and the great volume of it impressed him. It must certainly betoken a remarkable skill to do that with such sureness; Claudine had never played so loudly and majestically.

"You'd better hurry a little, Gilbert," said his wife. "I told Mary to serve dinner promptly at six, to give us plenty of time. I think I'll go and hurry Bertie a little."

But really the vain woman wanted her son's approval and admiration. She went upstairs to the room Gilbert had occupied in his bachelor days, and knocked at the door.

"It's I, Bertie!"

"Come in, Mammy!" he called, cheerfully, and as soon as she had entered, he cried:

"Oh, I say! Queen of them all! You *are* lovely! You'll be a riot!"

She smiled happily.

"You silly boy! Is it really a nice dress?"

"I wish you were going to sit up there on the platform and play. I'd rather hear you, and look at you, Mammy!"

"It might have been I," she thought to herself, with a shade of bitterness. "I might have been a mother really to be proud of—a musician—a somebody."

But she smiled again, and glanced at herself in the mirror. It was the most shockingly expensive dress she had ever had, a real Paris frock of satin in an exquisite shade of green that became her perfectly, and set off her coppery hair and pale skin to their best advantage. She was proud of her small waist, her little feet, in spite of the fact that they were old-fashioned, she was pleased with her miniature neatness and delicacy.

She turned to her son. Gilbert had angrily insisted that a boy of eighteen had no business in evening dress; a dinner jacket was the thing for him. But Bertie had pointed out the fact that the thing had already been ordered and fitted, and would have to be paid for.

"I never imagined you'd kick," he had said, plaintively. "You're always so generous, Father."

He finished scrupulously tying his white tie.

"Do I look like a monkey?" he asked. "Father said I would."

He followed his mother downstairs into the dining-room, and the others joined them promptly. There was an air of general satisfaction at the dinner table. They were all pleased with themselves, individually and as a family; they were all unusually festive and spirited. Andrée, the heroine, was blazing with excitement.

"You'd better eat," said Lance, warningly to her. Music was no more to him than a passing phenomenon in the course of man's history; it served to show something of the development of his brain and esthetic sense, but it would, he felt, in the course of time be regarded as nothing more than a frivolity. It was interesting to see how seriously it was now regarded. Still, he was fond of Andrée, and he wished her to be successful, if only for her mother's sake. He had an unwavering loyalty for Claudine, never expressed, never quite comprehended by her, something which in a less preoccupied man might have been called devotion.

Bertie had once said that Lance had "mastered evolution"; certainly he never seemed to grow older. With his light, rather long hair parted in the middle, his tortoise-shell spectacles, his slender figure, he looked like a sober and enquiring youth, a juvenile professor. He was quite illustrious, in the not very extensive circles where paleontologists may shine, he had been on two noteworthy government expeditions, and had written a large book, but he hadn't made money. The most profitable thing he had ever done, financially, was to tutor young Bertie. But he was able to exist in comfortable independence, and he wanted no more. He had a calm self-assurance which impressed everyone, even Gilbert, and he was a guest not without honour, a friend of prestige.

He took out his watch.

"Time to start!" he announced, and they all rose.

II

Mr. MacGregor expected a triumph that evening. He had hired a large hall, and had been promised the presence of several well-known musicians and critics, to say nothing of the important "society element." He had been for years steadily growing in favour, until he now held a unique position as a master who was not only able to give to débutantes a very attractive accomplishment, but a man who trained and developed genuine artists. There was a certain youth from the Ghetto at present creating something of a furore as a concert player whom he had "made," and several lesser stars. And he had now up his sleeve two or three surprises, to be released this evening. He had a boy—a young Pole whom he had been teaching gratis and more or less supporting, he had a young woman of buxom charm and amazing technic, and he had Andrée, whose chief claim was not so much in technic—though hers was of a high order—but the originality of her interpretations. He knew that some of the critics would be indignant at a lack of classic reverence, but others would be charmed, and all of them would talk.

He himself didn't appear; he stood in the wings, watching and listening, his attention divided between his pupils and the audience. And there wasn't one chagrin; everything went beautifully. His young Russian aroused a sharp interest in the critics, the buxom young woman was at her best, and Andrée ...! He was entranced with Andrée. She looked like the very spirit of music, filled with an innocent wild ardour, young, lovely, proud. His hopes, his personal hopes, that is, of ever becoming her husband had very nearly faded away, and he was able to regard her with a more impersonal eye. He had never summoned the courage to propose to her; he knew it would only make him ridiculous, and he was beginning to feel rather glad that he hadn't committed himself.

"She'll go a long way beyond me!" he reflected, candidly. "She has a wonderful future before her—if she doesn't make a fool of herself!"

Her family sat listening to her with ecstatic pride, even Gilbert, who was constitutionally opposed to public life for women. They listened to the enthusiastic clapping, they watched her come back onto the stage again and take an encore, not at all the timid novice, but cool, careless, aloof as Diana herself. They heard whispered comments upon her all about— "a beautiful girl," "so distinguished," "a magnetic personality," and even a few remarks about her music, and when she joined them, when it was all over, they were at a loss what to say to her. Edna wept a little.

They got into the motor; even the chauffeur, who had been given a seat in the balcony, was beaming. They drove home, and went into the dining-room for a little supper, with champagne, to celebrate her triumph.

III

Claudine was nearly asleep when she heard that light tap at the door, but any voice calling "Mother!" could have aroused her from any sleep but death. She hastily put on her dressing-gown and opened the door. It was Andrée.

"I want to speak to you!" she said.

All sleep or fatigue fled from Claudine at once. There was something in that tone, something in the expression of her child's face seen in the dim light of the hall, that froze her heart. She followed her to her own room, which was brilliantly illumined; it had somehow the appearance of a stage, a place pitilessly to expose a secret tragedy; and Andrée in her white dressing-gown and her soft black hair unbound looked a fit figure for any drama. Claudine asked herself, with a sinking heart, what was to be her part....?

"Is anything wrong, darling?" she asked.

"There's something I want to tell you."

Claudine smiled mechanically, but her knees were weak, and she sank down on the bed.

"What is it, dear?" she asked.

"It's very hard," said Andrée. "It's going to hurt you...."

"Don't keep me waiting," her mother said, almost sharply. "Tell me, Andrée!"

Andrée sat down beside her, and lifted one of her mother's hands, looking at it with curious abstraction. Claudine didn't stir.

"Now it's come," she thought. "That horrible, nameless disaster I have always dreaded for this creature I love too much. This will be something I cannot endure."

At last Andrée's voice came, steady and low.

"You remember Mr. Stephens, don't you, Mother?"

"Yes...." she murmured.

"We're going to be married to-morrow."

"Andrée! *Andrée!* What do you mean?"

"Just what I said, Mother."

At first this seemed to Claudine merely preposterous, almost laughable; one of Andrée's freaks.

"But, my dear, you don't know the man," she protested.

"Oh, yes, I do," said Andrée, calmly. "We've been writing to each other since last July, and I've seen him quite often lately. And I've made up my mind. I knew everyone would make a row; that's why I didn't tell you until the last moment. Al's going to Europe on Saturday, and I'm going with him."

Nothing in that speech made the slightest impression upon Claudine except the name "Al." That seemed to her of tremendous significance; the vulgar name of a vulgar young man; it made the affair a fantasy. She was not so much worried now as surprised.

"My dear Andrée—" she said. "You...." She paused, aware of the need for caution.

"I knew you wouldn't understand," said Andrée, bitterly. "You can't see beneath the surface. I knew all the arguing and talking and reasoning there'd be, but it's not going to make one bit of difference. I'm the one to decide, and I have decided. I want to be married quietly at the City Hall to-morrow, without any fuss and—talking. I wasn't even going to tell you until afterward but—" She frowned. "Somehow I couldn't. I wanted to make one more attempt to get you to understand."

"To give you your chance," was what she meant, and what her mother understood. This was the supreme moment to come close to her child—and she sat spellbound, like a figure in a nightmare, unable to speak, unable to make even a pretense at comprehension.

"He's the finest man I've ever seen," Andrée went on. "He's honest and kind and—rather wonderful, I think."

"But—he's not suitable—" faltered Claudine.

"I knew you'd say that! You'll tell me it's disgraceful to marry a man 'beneath' me. Well, I don't think he is, in any way. You'll say—"

"If you're going to take my part as well as your own, Andrée, there's not much use in going on. I'm not so unsympathetic—or so narrow as you think.... I shouldn't have opposed you. I should only have asked you to wait a little—"

"Because you think I'd change?"

"Only until I felt you were sure."

"I am sure! I love Al! You don't know how I feel about him. He's so dear and—"

"Hush, Andrée!" she interrupted, almost sternly. There was a faint flush on her cheeks; this unrestraint, this vehemence, caused her a sort of shame. She had suddenly a thousand things to say— "Think if there should be children"— "Think of the personal habits of a man of his class"—And not one of them could she utter. Her almost morbid modesty, her long habit of restraint, forbade her. She grew desperate; she could urge nothing but her own love.

"Andrée," she said, "I will tell you what I have never told anyone else in the world. I love you more than my other children! I always have. I— I think I don't really love anyone else. You are all my life. You are all I care to live for. If you *knew* ...! When you were a baby.... Oh, Andrée! I used to sit watching you when you were asleep ... you were so pretty—and so strange.... It—made me turn away from God—I loved you so much more.... If you do this...."

"Oh, how cruel you are!" cried Andrée. "And how—unfair! How can you want me to spoil all my life and give up all my happiness, if you love me? How can you not let me alone? Don't you see—don't you understand—how I love him?"

"Andrée, that love is nothing to mine—I know!"

"And you don't try to argue, or give reasons, or convince me. Or listen to my reasons. You only want to play on my feelings!"

"You have no feelings!" cried Claudine. "You have no heart! You don't care!"

"Oh, don't I?" said Andrée, and she suddenly began to sob. "Go away! Go away! I've told you—now let me alone!" she sobbed.

Claudine crossed the room to the bureau and began moving about the little jars and bottles with trembling hands.

"I won't—reproach you," she said. "I won't.... I'll try to understand.... I want to see—Mr. Stephens. Where does he live?"

"I shan't tell you."

"Yes, you must. You can trust me, Andrée. I won't—I promise you I won't tell anyone else. I won't do anything to stop you.... I only want to hear him. I want to hear—all he has to say."

Andrée hesitated a moment.

"Very well!" she said at last. "I think I'd like you to. I'll trust you.... He's at the Biltmore.... I'm not afraid of anything you can say to him!"

"No," said Claudine, dully. She was folding up some bits of ribbon, quite mechanically, and putting them into the bureau drawer. The room was very untidy; there lay Andrée's pretty dress across a chair, and her beribboned petticoat fallen on the floor. And her slippers on the dressing-table.... Was it worth while to pick them up? Was it worth while ever to draw another breath? She looked at Andrée, lying face downward on the bed, and her heart was not moved. No; this was the last possible sensation, the very end of everything; she was going to sink now and be drowned. She went out of the room and closed the door.

Gilbert hadn't stirred. She lay down beside him and closed her eyes, and at once anguish, like a fierce beast, sprang at her throat.

CHAPTER TWO

THE BITTER TRIUMPH

"I'm going shopping early this morning," said Claudine, at the breakfast-table the next morning. "There are some very good bargains advertised.... How soon do you think you could send the car back, Gilbert?"

Now Gilbert, although he scoffed at feminine shopping and bargains, nevertheless respected all this as one of the bulwarks of family life. Women must and ought to go shopping. So he said:

"Take the car. I'll go in the Subway," in the tone of an exasperated martyr.

Her destination, however, was the Biltmore. She was filled with a feverish anxiety to get there; she was in terror lest Mr. Stephens should have gone out, that he would be beyond her reach, that Andrée might see him or hear from him before she did. She was going to the desk to enquire for him, when she caught sight of him, standing up, reading a newspaper, and she approached him and touched him on the arm.

"Mr. Stephens!" she said. "Have you a few moments to spare?"

He was not pleased to see her; she fancied that his face turned a little pale; but he greeted her with a sort of subdued courtesy.

"Where can we talk?" she asked. "I have something to say...."

"I have a little sitting-room; if you don't mind—" he said.

She followed him into the lift, still smiling brightly, a smile which he saw reflected in the looking-glass and which alarmed him by its expression of triumph. If he could have read her thoughts as well, his alarm would have vanished. It was her firm resolution to look bright, brave, self-assured; she hoped that her air would not only impress him but herself as well.

"Oh, God!" she was praying under her breath. "Oh, just this once, make me equal to the situation! I always fail; I'm always beaten! Oh, let me, only this one time, win!"

He opened the door of his sitting-room, and they entered. She began at once, the instant the door closed behind them.

"Mr. Stephens," she said, "I have heard from Andrée what you propose to do."

He bowed his head, and said nothing. She realized, with surprise, that he was not without dignity; that there was nothing in any way contemptible either in his manner or his appearance.

"I am astonished," she went on, "that you should have done such an—unworthy thing. Andrée is very young and impressionable, and you have taken advantage of this to influence her. She neither knows nor realizes what she has undertaken."

"Excuse me," he said. "But I'm sure she does. I haven't tried to influence her. I've—I've given this a lot of thought, Mrs. Vincelle. At first I was afraid Andrée couldn't be happy with me ... but ... now I do think so."

"Why, Mr. Stephens?"

His fair face flushed.

"It's pretty hard to explain," he said, "but I think—well, I think I understand her, and can get on with her. I—well—I know I'm—different, in some ways—but I can't see that that matters."

"It does matter," she said, gently. "More than you realize. It may be quite wrong, but it is a fact, Mr. Stephens, that marriages of—of this sort are very, very rarely successful."

"What kind are?" he asked, with equal gentleness. "As far as I can see, the chances are overwhelmingly against any marriage being really successful. It's—I see it like this: if two people love each other, they ought to take the risk, they ought to face all the chances as—as gallantly as they can, and do the best they can in what's bound to be a difficult position. Personally, I don't believe in marriage, but I can see that nothing else is practicable just now. All I can do is to make it as little like an ordinary marriage as possible—leave Andrée as free as I can—"

"Mr. Stephens—I'm sorry ... but I cannot consent to this."

He looked full at her with a level and grave glance.

"The way I see it—it's a personal matter between Andrée and me. No one else has any right to interfere. And no one *can* interfere. I—you don't know how much I admire you, Mrs. Vincelle, but—I didn't think it was necessary to consult you, or anyone else. That's all very well in the case of a man who wants money—any sort of favours from his wife's family. But I don't. It's only for Andrée to decide."

"And I simply don't count," said Claudine, with a slight smile.

"I know a mother's love is a very strong—" he began.

"You don't know anything about it! You think it's a sentiment; you think it's beautiful to see a mother bending over a cradle. You understand that women love their babies. But when the babies have grown up, you forget the mothers. Do you think they evaporate, or disappear? Or turn into troublesome, ridiculous mothers-in-law? But we don't! We go on! If Andrée were a child, you'd think I was right to struggle for her. You talk about mothers being left free to do what they think best for their children. But because she's older, and I still want to protect her—"

"But—don't you see?—you don't need to protect her from anyone—like me—who—who worships her! Do listen just for a moment! All I want in the world is to make her happy. I want her to have a splendid, free life. I don't want to tie her to me. I want her as she is now. I don't want to change her and—fetter her. I understand her. She'd never endure being bound; she's so proud and independent—"

"And so silly and unstable. That's what you don't understand! But it's no use arguing. I know what it would mean for her. I'm not talking about convictions. I'm talking about life as it is, as she will have to live it. Andrée's an egoist. She's fickle and headstrong, and so terribly unstable."

"Let her be," he said, stoutly. "I'm not. I'm strong enough and—and earnest enough to put up with anything like that."

"Oh, don't you see? She'll think anything you want to suggest to her, but she'll always act according to her own impulses and desires."

("Just the contrary to me," she reflected, irrelevantly. "People can make me do anything, but they never change my ideas....")

"But that's just what I want her to do!" protested Stephens. "That's my idea of marriage—that we should both—"

"Don't argue!" she cried, with sudden violence. "You cannot do this! If you really think any of the things you once said to me—if you have any compassion, and kind human feeling, you can't try to make your happiness on another person's pain. You can't ignore me!"

"But—" he began, "isn't that just a little—selfish?"

She clasped her hands desperately.

"You can't do it!" she cried. "You're kind. You cannot hurt me so!"

He wished to point out to her the extreme unfairness of her position but the sight of her anguish was too much for him. Even when he looked away, he seemed still to see her tear-filled eyes, her face suddenly so worn, so much older, its fine tranquility, which he had so much admired, its dignity, gone. It was like a sacrilege.

"Please don't! Please don't!" he entreated. "I can't bear to see you suffer ... If you'd only realize that I'm trying to make Andrée happy—"

"Can't you have a little mercy on me?" she said. "Even if you think I'm wrong? Andrée is—my whole life; I've let everything else go. I haven't any life of my own, or any hopes.... Nothing but her. Oh, I'd go on my knees to you!"

"No, no!" he cried, shocked profoundly, both by her suffering and by her amazing unscrupulousness. "Mrs. Vincelle! I beg you!"

"Then listen to me! Think of me! Put aside your theories and your principles.... Isn't it something to be kind—even to me? Isn't it better to be kind than—"

But she could not go on; she buried her face in her hands and wept silently. She looked so small, so helpless, so terribly fallen from her almost superhuman aloofness....

"Please don't!" he entreated, again. "I've always had such a great respect for you.... I—you don't know how I've thought about you.... I wouldn't hurt you for anything in the world! Look here! Really! ... Please listen! We'll wait."

She looked up, careless of her tear-stained face, quick to seize her advantage.

"Give me my chance?"

"What do you mean?" he asked, a little alarmed.

"You've done all this—you've persuaded her secretly—behind my back. Let me have a little time!"

"To turn her against me?"

"Yes, if I can."

They were both silent for a moment.

"All right!" he said. "If she can be as easily turned as that, it had better be done before it's too late.... But I don't believe you can. I'm not afraid to have you try. I trust—Andrée."

"How long will you give me?"

"I'm going to England and Germany on—business. I'll be gone about two months."

"And will you promise not to write to her or to see her for two months?"

"I'll have to see her once before I go, to explain. That'll be to-day. After that, I'll—" He paused and smiled a little, very kindly. "You'll have your chance, Mrs. Vincelle!"

She rose and held out her hand, and he took it, rather timidly.

"Good-bye!" she said.

"But—if you find you can't change her—" he said. "At the end of two months—will you consent to our being married?"

"What difference will it make, whether I do, or not?" she asked, bitterly.

CHAPTER THREE

ANDRÉE'S WEDDING

I

Gilbert was alone in his office, working in one of his characteristic fits of great energy. A sort of inspiration would seize him, he would map out astounding campaigns, design advertisements, write letters to his travelling salesmen which filled them with admiration and enthusiasm, humorous, racy letters, replete with valuable suggestions. The greater part of his time he was cross and wretched, but he had his glorious hours, his days of geniality and amazing penetration. The entire office staff would be enchanted, and ready to adore him, for he had a perverse charm about him, an elusive loveableness, a touch of the fascination so marked in his eldest child.

He always addressed his salesmen in his own writing, a very neat and legible one, and he was doing that now, his plump, well-kept hand travelling deliberately over the paper, and a faint smile on his lips, when there was a knock at the door and his young Cuban entered.

"Your daughter is outside, sir!" he announced, with all the homage of a courtier. He was profoundly attached to "the family"; he was not without hope of something happening similar to the things he had read of in French romances—that, as a reward for his furious zeal, he would one day be invited to dinner, for instance, when he could be presented to the young ladies with due ceremony. After that, the rest would be easy....

"Ask her to step in," said Gilbert, and looking at his watch, decided that he would take Edna out to lunch. He took it for granted that it was Edna, because it always was. She was sent as an emissary by both Bertie and Andrée when they wanted money or permission for any unapproved enterprise, because she knew how to handle him.

He wheeled round in his chair, and was surprised to see Andrée standing there.

"Well, well!" he said, good-humouredly. "What do *you* want, eh?"

He thought she looked "queer," and he stared at her more closely. She had a sort of desperate, defiant air, an unchanging smile.

"Sit down! Sit down !" he said. "What brings you here, Andrée?"

"I wanted to talk to you. I wanted to tell you something.... I wanted you to hear it from me instead of from Mother, so that you—wouldn't fly at her."

She knew that she was antagonizing him, but she could not help it. The only way she felt able to tell her monstrous piece of news was rudely and sternly, to deny even to herself the dread and shrinking she suffered. Her father's face changed perceptibly.

"Well!" he said, impatiently.

She laid her pocket-book on his desk, a beautiful little pocket-book, for she had all her mother's elegance in trifles—and stood looking down at him.

"I'm going to marry Mr. Stephens!" she said.

"Who the devil is Mr. Stephens?" he cried.

Andrée began to laugh.

"That man you had a fight with last summer, in the mountains."

"What!" he cried, springing up. "What! That common, worthless little cad!"

"Yes!" she said, looking him steadfastly in the face, and smiling. "That common, worthless little cad. Don't begin to rave at me. You can't stop me. Mother's been trying for weeks."

"I'm not going to 'rave,' young woman. I have more effective means than that to put a stop to your nonsense. You're not so independent as you imagine—"

"If you'll just take it for granted that *I'm going to do it*, we can talk," said Andrée. "Otherwise it's no use, and I'd better go."

"I see your mother's hand in this!" he said. "Some of her—peculiar ideas—"

"No, you don't. She doesn't even know I'm going to tell you. She's done all she could to persuade me—"

"Persuade isn't the word I'd use. Look here, Andrée, my girl, I'm not going to argue with you. Put this idea out of your head once and for all—"

"Why?"

"Why? Because I tell you to. You're too young to know what you're doing, and you'll have to listen to people who are older and know better."

"But—about this—you don't know better. You don't know anything about him. And anyway, it's not a question of knowing, it's a question of— of feeling. I—like him. I'm older than Mother was when she married you. I know what I'm doing. His only crime is being—what you call 'common.' He's very remarkable. If you knew him, you'd soon see it."

"You don't know enough of the world to realize that marriages between people of unequal social position are always unhappy."

"They're just as unhappy in other cases," said Andrée. "I don't believe social position has anything to do with it. It's—disposition. And Al has a wonderful disposition."

"Al!" her father repeated, contemptuously.

"Yes, Al! That's what he calls himself. I like it! It's so nice and jolly and—

common!"

"Andrée!" said her father, sternly. "This is nothing but a whim—a freak of yours.... I think you're only trying to torment and worry the people who love you."

"You'll see if it's a whim!" she answered.

Suddenly he was disarmed; some gesture, some intonation of hers, had brought back to him the naughty little girl who had so perplexed and amused him, the scowling little rebel he had so often wanted to shake— and never had. He remembered her with surprising vividness as a child of six, spending a Saturday morning with him, sitting in the corner of this very office, cutting out paper dolls, while she waited for him to wind up his business and take her out to lunch and the circus.

"Andrée!" he said. "I'll tell you what. I'll let you go over to Germany with your mother to study music for a year."

"But I'm going to study here! That's what Al and I have arranged. I'm going to go on just the same!" she said, triumphantly. "And he's going to give me a grand piano for a wedding present!"

This put an end to his softness.

"If you don't renounce this—mad idea—at once, and finally," he said, "it will mean—that I wash my hands of you. That you'll be entirely cut off from your family, including your mother, whom you pretend to love so much. You'll disgrace—"

"Nonsense!" she interrupted. "It's not true to say I'll disgrace you, because I want to marry someone you don't like. It's—"

"Enough!" he said, frowning. "I've said all I'm going to. If you're not prepared to tell me *now* that you will—obey me in this matter ... or at least, agree to wait a year—"

"No, I'm not prepared to do that!"

"Then you may consider that you are no longer a member of my household!"

"What does that mean?" she asked, scornfully. "Does it mean you're turning me out?"

"Yes!" he shouted. "If you haven't the common decency to appreciate, or feel any gratitude for all that's been done for you, you can try doing without for a while. You can go back now and talk it over with your mother, and when I come home this evening, I'll tell you what I've decided."

"No, thanks! I won't go home. I'll never go home again. It's your home, not mine, I see. Good-by!"

He caught her by the arm.

"I won't allow this! I insist upon your going home at once. Do you hear?"

"Of course I hear! Everyone in the office must. But I won't go!"

"Yes, you will!" he said. He was furious, and very much frightened. He had no idea what she might do. "I'm going to call a taxi and send you home."

"You'll have to get a policeman to go with me!" she said, laughing again. "I won't go! I don't mind a row once in a while, but I don't like the idea of a whole lot of them. It was hard enough to come and tell you about this, but you've made things impossible now. You won't treat me as a woman—"

"You're not a woman!" he cried. And certainly she had never looked less like one. She looked like a schoolgirl, reckless and ignorant of the consequences of her folly, her face alight with a defiance that was more mischievous than resolute.

"Good-by!" she said.

"Andrée! ... Confound you! ... Think of your mother! Go home, and we'll talk the thing over thoroughly this evening!"

"All right!" she said, suddenly, and left him without another word.

II

It was due to Claudine that she remained in the house until her wedding three weeks later. The distracted woman went from one to the other of them, seeing the breach widen every day. She implored and entreated Andrée, she faced Gilbert with unparalleled firmness; she was able to keep up an outward semblance of dignity in the family. But it was a monstrous thing. Andrée and her father never spoke to each other. The meals were a nightmare, to see them there side by side, so bitterly hostile. She dreaded to speak herself, for fear of hurting or angering one or the other of those inordinately sensitive creatures. Edna was grief-stricken; she had tried to remonstrate in the old friendly fashion with her sister, to make her realize the prodigious unfitness of Mr. Stephens, but she had been rudely rebuffed. Bertie was gravely displeased; he disapproved of Andrée and also of his parents for not preventing such a marriage.

"And these are the last days I'll ever have Andrée with me!" thought the poor mother. "These bitter, wretched days! This is the end of her girlhood—and what an end! What a memory to take with her!"

The day after Stephens had returned from Europe he had invited her to tea with Andrée, without having made any attempt to see Andrée alone, or even to write to her. He had no need to ask Claudine whether she had succeeded in alienating Andrée from him; her face told him everything, her smile. He had a little table reserved for them in a corner of the tea-room, and they all sat down in silence.

But Claudine, glancing up, saw them looking at each other, and it was horrible to her. She saw in his kindly, honest face that least kindly, least honest of human desires, his mouth had a kind of grimness; he looked so entirely a man.... And Andrée! Was that the way a woman should look, who is about to decide her destiny? Her brilliant eyes were full on him, provocative, equivocal....

They talked, very harmoniously. He told them about his trip in dutiful fashion, because he wanted Claudine to know his position.

"You see," he said. "I've put about everything I own into this English syndicate. It pays me well, but I put the biggest part of my income back into it again. I calculate that inside the next five years I and three pals of mine can pretty well buy the rest out, and then we expect to turn the thing into a co-operative enterprise, with the workers sharing the profits. Then, of course, I won't get so much as I'm getting now, but I'm getting too much now. But it'll be a good living—something more than that—for both of us, for the rest of our lives."

"But I'm going to work too, you know," said Andrée. "I'm going to study a few years more, and then I'll give concerts. All over Europe!"

"You won't have much of a home, will you?" asked Claudine

"We don't want one!" said Stephens, cheerfully. "I never could see any reasonable connection between—well, marriage and housekeeping. Because I—love a woman, that doesn't mean I want her to look after my personal needs. I'd hate to see anyone like Andrée tied up to a house and a lot of dull, petty details. I'm not going to interfere with her life. Never! If I can help, I will, but if I can't, at least I won't hinder her."

"But—" began Claudine, and she was conscious of a slight flush which mortified her. They didn't mind talking, of such things! "A home is supposed—isn't it?—to be a place for—bringing up children."

"Sure! But that doesn't imply that the mother and father have to spend all their time in it. There are people specially qualified to bring up children. Then let 'em do it!"

"That doesn't seem—" Claudine began, but she stopped. What was the use? Perhaps he was right; if he wasn't, they would soon find out.

"You'll have to live somewhere," she said. "What will you do?"

"A suite in a nice, quiet hotel," said Andrea, "where I can have my piano."

So there was nothing to prepare for this young bride, no house-linen to mark, no silver to buy. Even her trousseau she insisted upon buying ready-made. Her mother did sew a few little things for her, but she felt all the time, with every stitch, how superfluous they were. There was nothing required of her; she too was superfluous.

III

They sat in the motor car, well wrapped in furs, holding each other's gloved hands. In the corner was Lance, who was to give Andrée away, and facing them, Bertie and Edna. But the mother was not conscious of them; she felt quite alone in the world with her child.

They had left Gilbert in the most painful way. He couldn't really believe that Andrée would so flout him; he had continued to hope that at the last moment she would capitulate, and he longed for that moment. He had never asked about the progress of the affair, and Claudine had said nothing until a few days before the wedding.

"Remember, Andrée," he had said then, "if you do this outrageous, disgraceful thing, I'll never see you or speak to you again."

And the morning of that day he hadn't gone to his office; he had remained in the dining-room, after breakfast, smoking and reading the newspaper. Claudine had come in to him.

"Gilbert!" she had said. "Gilbert! Please, please come to her wedding No matter how you feel about it, she's your own—"

"No!" he had cried. "I won't sanction it! It's altogether wrong, and I won't countenance it! She's marrying a vulgar, underbred cur who's a disgrace to the family ... the first and only time I saw the fellow he insulted me grossly. She's absolutely disregarded my authority. She's doing this against my wishes, and she knows it!"

Through the open door of the dining-room he had seen Andrée come down the stairs, quite ready, with her hat on. He had gone out into the hall and stood looking at her, with a terrible twinge of pain.

"Remember!" he said. "If you go out of this house—to marry that man, you can never set foot in here again!"

"I didn't expect to!" she answered, briefly. "Good-by, Father."

But he would not say good-by, he went back into the dining-room and from behind his paper he saw them all go. It was as if he were being deserted, rebuked by his family. His hand trembled, he bit his mustache. Andrée gone! And gone to her certain unhappiness.... She would be married, and her father would not be standing beside her.... He couldn't endure it. He sprang up and hurried to his bedroom, in a blind desire to escape his thoughts. But there was no comfort in that silent house. He could think of no better refuge than his office. His child had gone without him....

"And yet I'm right!" he cried to himself. "I'm right! I've done what I ought to have done! I've refused to sanction this thing!"

IV

Not one of the party gave him a thought. They reached the church and entered, and Mr. Stephens was waiting there, with two friends. No one else had been invited. Like a woman in a dream Claudine went into the vestry with Andrée, to take off their furs.

"Am I all right?" asked Andrée.

"Yes, darling, very nice!" she answered. She wanted to look forever and ever at that girl in her plain dark suit, her small hat, that gallant and heart-breaking young figure.

Suddenly Andrée crushed her in a fierce embrace.

"Mother!" she said. "Mother!"

"Don't cry, my heart's darling!"

"I won't; just in a minute.... Mother, are you satisfied—now?"

"Yes, my darling!"

"Tell me, Mother—I don't understand ... why do you care so much about this—about this ceremony? What does it matter, if we care for each other?"

"I think it's this, Andrée. I think marriage is the only way to impress upon a man what a woman is giving to him. You know—almost all women know—how sacred and wonderful and terrible a thing it is. But I don't believe men quite understand. I think they would take it very casually—if it weren't made as solemn and impressive as—"

Andrée flushed.

"It isn't sacred and wonderful!" she said. "I hate that sort of talk so! I don't want to impress poor little Al with my preciousness. He's just as valuable and good as I am. He gives up just as much."

"Andrée—my baby—if you'll—"

"Don't give me any advice about managing him!" said Andrée, with her sudden laugh. "I'll never try! Hadn't we better go in, Mother?"

Claudine took her seat in a front pew.

"Now I must sit here and watch this horrible thing!" she said to herself. "Oh God! Oh God! Do other mothers feel like this? How can they smile? ... How can they be pleased—and try to make matches? ... Am I a morbid, perverted woman? It's her destiny to marry someone—and he's a kind man... I must be glad!"

She heard their responses, both of their voices steady and clear, both of them making those promises.

"I must be happy!" she said, again. "It's just the beginning of her life. There is sure to be so much joy and accomplishment in it.... This is only one step.... I must have fortitude. I can't live her life for her...."

She rose, to face the little man's wife. She kissed her pale, sombre face, she clasped his hand.

"Be happy!" she said.

Then she looked round in a sort of panic for Bertie.

"Bertie!" she whispered. "Take me home! Take me home!"

CHAPTER FOUR

THE BEGINNING

I

That day she brought an electric tea-pot. They laughed when she took it from its box, for she always brought something, she was trying to introduce an element of house-keeping into their business-like existence.

"But it will be very nice," she said. "We can make our tea up here, all by ourselves, just as we like it. And I've brought a box of cakes from Sherry's, the sort you like."

Andrée was sitting at the piano, weary and a little disheveled.

"It will be nice," she said. "Better than going down to the tea-room, or having a tray sent up.... Gosh! I've been practicing over two hours!"

Al smiled.

"Doesn't she look like a musical genius?" he asked Claudine. "With that hair?"

"Give me a cake!" said Andrée. "Mr. MacGregor came in last evening, Mother, and we played until someone downstairs asked us to stop.... But this one part of 'Thais' is lovely, even with a piano alone, isn't it? We're going to hear it again to-night."

Claudine announced that the tea was ready and Andrée came over to sit beside her on the sofa. Al waited on them with a clumsiness which Claudine found very pitiful; she saw too that he was attempting an improvement in manners, not in a shamefaced way, as another man might have done, but carefully and frankly, watching them with earnestness.

Andrée rose.

"Come into the bedroom, won't you, Mother?" she said.

Claudine followed her into the little room, so bare, so impersonal, and stood for a moment by the window looking out over Central Park, bright under a new fall of snow.

"It's a rather nice view," she said, politely.

"Mother, look here, darling! I want you to help me to get up something for Christmas, will you?"

"Of course I will! What had you thought of?"

"I don't know.... Something nice and human ... You and Edna and Bertie.... Something like old times.... How's Father?"

"Very well...."

"Does he ever mention my name? Lord! Isn't it romantic? A young bride, cut off by her father.... I wish there were someone to appreciate the situation—and me."

"I'm sure Alfred appreciates you, Andrée!"

"Well, he doesn't. He doesn't care about my music, and that's me. He's awfully fond of me, I know that, but he doesn't think I'm really any more important than all the other young females of twenty with black hair. My 'group,' he'd call it. I wish he'd think a little more about me, and less about social justice. I'm sick of it!"

"My dear!"

"I am! Not sick of him, but just of his talking. Just imagine! When I've been playing extra well, I sometimes ask if I've been disturbing him—hoping he'll say he liked it. But what do you suppose he does say? 'Not a bit! I don't hear it at all when my mind's concentrated on my work.' He's writing some sort of silly book, you know."

"You shouldn't call it 'silly,' Andrée. It's not fair. He's not silly. He's a very intelligent, earnest man."

"That's the trouble with him! He's too earnest. When I want to talk to him about nice little things—about us—he's always so—oh, so *mighty!* We're all types, and everything we do is typical of something. Imagine! Last night Bertie brought in Gaston Matthews and Johnnie Martinsburgh—darling children—Bertie says it's chic to live like this in a hotel, without any squaw atmosphere—and Al would talk to them about his theories. Of course, they listened to him; he's generally interesting enough, but it's—I hated it! I suppose I wanted to do the boring myself, about music. And I know so well what they'd think of him if he weren't rich.... They call him eccentric now, but if he were poor!"

Andrée was lying on the bed, her arms clasped behind her head; how—intractable she looked, thought her mother!

"I'm thoroughly sick of it all! All this busy life.... I can't be busy. I don't know how. When I look back on the old days, it seems to me I spent most of my time sitting around with you or Edna. That's what I want now, but there's no one to sit round with. Even when Al isn't working, he wants to 'take advantage' of his playtime and rush around and see instructive things and—"

"Andrée, it's not kind or wise to dwell so much on his little shortcomings. He has so many, many fine qualities—"

"He adores you. Mother, do you want to go and talk to him while I'm dressing? It's very unselfish of me, because I want you every moment.... And you're right. He is rather wonderful. He's not common inside of him, a bit. I don't believe he ever had a vulgar thought in his head. He's—really delicate. He's a nice person to—to live with.... If he only wouldn't talk so much!"

Claudine went back into the sitting-room and found her son-in-law hard at work with a German magazine and a dictionary.

"I've taught myself enough German to get the sense out of things," he explained. "We get out a little magazine we call 'Comrades,' with all sorts of stuff in it from the European Socialist papers, as a step toward Internationalism. I'd be satisfied if I could get just that one idea more generally accepted in my lifetime—that all the people in the world are just about the same, everywhere, that they all want the same things, and suffer from the ˌsame causes."

He stopped suddenly.

"Do you think Andrée's well and happy?" he asked.

"Yes.... She was speaking about Christmas. She thought it would be nice to have some sort of little celebration."

"Sure! We'll invite some people, and I'll reserve a table downstairs in the dining-room—"

"I don't think that's quite what she meant. I think something more—intimate, Alfred...."

"I see! Then how about having a supper sent up here—champagne and so on?"

"That would be very nice, of course.... But—you know she's very young for her years.... I thought if you and I could arrange a little surprise—a Christmas tree—"

"Great! I've never had one in my life!"

"You see, she's always had one, since she was a baby. I suppose it seems silly—"

"Not to me, it doesn't. It's just one of those nice, pretty little ideas that I fall short in. My one idea is to buy things. It seems so wonderful to buy what you want. I'm not used to it yet.... Gosh! You can't imagine how much I learn from you! That's what we need—my kind. We need to learn how to live—oh—poetically, from the people like you. We never get those ideas. We're too darned worried about food. At first I used to be pretty hard and vindictive, and talk about bringing the comfortable people down to earth. But now I'd like to take the other people a little bit *off* the earth— a little bit up."

She thought as she went home in a taxi, what a loveable creature he was. He was everything that she had always imagined a husband ought to be, a comrade, kind, loyal, never interfering, never attempting to impose his own will. Their life was what she had often dreamed of; Andrée had freedom combined with love.

And yet—it wasn't satisfactory; it was so little satisfactory that it frightened her.

"Somehow," she thought, "all that isn't enough.... That bond—that tie of sex alone—isn't enough. Even love isn't enough.... Perhaps there must be more obligation with it."

II

It was a charming Christmas. Claudine had her Christmas dinner decorously at home with her husband and various members of both families; there were all the proper presents and ceremonies, and she was happy. Happy because she could fly to Andrée in the afternoon. Her visits there were a secret of Polchinelle; Gilbert never mentioned them, nor Andrée. And yet to-day, as she was putting on her hat, he entered the bedroom and gave her a crumpled handful of bills.

"Buy something for her!" he said.

She was terribly touched, but she knew better than to show it.

"I will!" she said, brightly.

After he had gone, she smoothed out the bills and put them into an envelope, on which she wrote— "From Father."

She gave it to Andrée with a smile.

"Is he coming round?" asked Andrée.

"I don't know."

"I didn't expect him to until there was a little grandchild. That would be the proper thing, of course, and Father does love to do the proper thing.... I wish there was a little grandchild! That would be something important and interesting. Something real."

"Andrée, you're not going to be trying to-day!"

"No, I'm not! I'm going to be lovely—the spirit of Christmas," she said.

And she was. She was delighted with her glittering little tree, and with all their gifts. She was gay, loving, almost tender. She dominated everything; they all watched her with pleasure, moving about the little room; they listened while she played for them. At the end of the evening she and Edna and Bertie sang a Christmas carol they had learned as children, and it made her cry a little.

"Dear people!" she said. "Thank you all, so very much! You've given me such a happy Christmas!"

No one thought of denying that it was *her* Christmas, or that the common object had been her happiness.

She went out to the lift with them and kissed each one with particular ardour, her mother, her sister, her laughing brother.

"Good night!" she said, still looking after them, still smiling, as if she could not bear to see them go.

They were always glad to look back at that Christmas, for they were never to have another like it.

III

Andrée went back into the room where the little man was sitting, under the Christmas tree. She fancied he looked a little disconsolate and forlorn, and her heart smote her.

"Al!" she said. "Are you happy?"

"Not so very!" he answered, candidly.

"But why? Haven't we had a lovely, happy time?"

"I feel—a million miles away from you," he said. "I wonder if I'll ever get any nearer to you."

She sat down beside him and drew his head down on her shoulder.

"I wish you wouldn't!" she cried. "It—chills me so! I want us to be so very near to each other. I must have it so! I can't bear it if you don't understand everything about me. *Why* did you say that?"

"To-night," he said, "with this Christmas tree and all—I don't know—but you—it seemed to me that you were like a child—just playing at life.... And I can't play! I never did, in my life. I can tell you, that chilled *me!* You seem so very young and so pretty, and so—heedless—that it makes me feel so very old and worn—"

"You idiot!" she cried, laughing. "It's just the other way! You're a little boy; you're always talking and thinking about such new things, things that come and go. It makes me feel such a wise woman, a sort of Sibyl. I think that's why I love you—because you're so awfully earnest and serious about things that I know don't matter."

"What things don't matter? Human wretchedness and cruelty and pain?"

"You don't even know what makes human wretchedness. It isn't poverty. Why, Al, if you could make everyone perfectly comfortable this very night, if you could take away all hunger and want and injustice, it wouldn't give one little bit of happiness to any of the people who had lost someone they loved. It wouldn't help a woman who had lost her man, or a mother who'd lost a baby. That's what you don't know. Nothing can ever, ever be done to spare people their anguish.... I always know—it comes across me in my very happiest moments—that the day is coming nearer and nearer when we'll have to part—one of us to leave the other forever.... What do you think you can do for that?"

"That's morbid," he said, curtly. "No healthy person thinks about death like that."

But he caught her close to his heart and looked down at her bent head with troubled eyes, stroked her soft hair with an uncertain hand.

"I've never heard you talk like this," he said. "I don't like it, darling! Don't you believe that we'll meet again—afterward?"

"It doesn't matter. It wouldn't do any good, even if we knew. People who do believe that suffer just as much. More, I think, because they haven't as much fortitude as the ones who don't believe. Look at you. You think all these miserable people are going to be made happy somewhere after they're dead, but it doesn't seem to give you much comfort."

"I don't look at it that way, Andrée. The world seems to me like a—sort of school, and I want to see everyone get a chance to learn all there is to know, in decency and—dignity, before it's over."

"Maybe your way isn't a good way. Maybe they learn more as things are."

"Injustice never teaches anyone anything but resentment and malice."

"I'm going to play!" she said, suddenly. "Oh, Al! Al! Why didn't you let me be happy? It may be only for such a little while!"

"I didn't mean to make you unhappy! I wouldn't for anything in the world. I'm sorry! Don't play! That damned music sets you all on edge. Stay here and talk to me!"

"I'm tired of talking.... Al, you take up too much time! I'll never amount to anything with you around. You're always bursting into my nice, quiet little art world, and you're so earnest and busy and disturbing!"

"I know it!" he said, contritely. "It's one of my limitations, old girl. I don't appreciate art in any shape. I don't take it seriously. But I do take you and your development seriously. Very seriously. You go ahead with your own work, and I'll try to shut up about mine. We'll let each other alone, and just love each other."

"Love's a terrible disturbance!"

"It shouldn't be. It ought to be peace and completion. It's a help to me. Why, do you know, I have ten years' work planned out—three books. I have the data ready, but I haven't begun them yet. I've never worked so well in my life. And it's simply because I've found you, after looking for you all my life."

She smiled at him.

"But you see, I never expected you!" she said. "I never looked for you! You're a surprise—and nuisance!"

She seized his hair in both hands and pulling down his head, kissed him roughly.

"And yet I suppose you're a sort of help," she said. "Because I'm determined to astonish you. I'm going to spoil all your nice peace and satisfaction, and trouble you and worry you and make you think about me and nothing else!"

"Perhaps I'm still a little dazzled and stupid by having got you," he said. "But don't think for a moment I take you for granted. You're the greatest wonder in the world to me. You're not the companion woman I thought I wanted. You're not a pal. You'll never be a friend. You're strange to me, and you always will be. When I look at you, I see some sense in poetry. I know what those fellows mean with that woman-worship I used to hate so."

"I *am* a friend to you!"

"Oh, no, you're not! You don't care a rap about my work and my plans. I don't exactly want you to. You haven't anything to do with everyday life. You're—you're my love."

"I'm afraid I'll have to be awfully nice," she said, "not to spoil all that."

"No. It doesn't matter what you do. You couldn't change what I love so in you. It's eternal."

"Till death do us part!" she said, with a sombre little smile.

"And after," he added.

CHAPTER FIVE

THE HOUSEWARMING

I

Al didn't say what he thought; it seemed to him a singularly infelicitous time for that. He was beginning to learn the rudiments of a lamentable sort of tact; he followed Andrée about the new flat and admired all that was pointed out to him; seven rooms and two baths, fronting on Riverside Drive, all furnished now and ready for their installation. Claudine had so urged them to have a home that she had won over Andrée, and according to his principle, he had yielded to Andrée. He said to himself, in his customary struggle to square facts with ideas, that it might be a woman's instinct to have a home, and he was prepared to admit that women had almost all the instincts left to the race. He couldn't quite classify the instinct that made her spend so much money on the furnishings; she wasn't ostentatious, didn't do it to "show off"—a thing he could have understood—she didn't do it for him, nor was comfort her object. It was, he decided, her artistic desire for beauty.

Personally, he was ashamed of it. Riverside Drive itself had long been for him a sort of symbol; many, many times he had come to sit there and feast his eyes upon the opulent women with their pet dogs. As a fat man in a white vest and a silk hat typified the Capitalist, so was a stout, well-dressed woman with a Pomeranian the outward and visible sign of all this inward corruption of private life. He saw many such from his windows; there had been one that day in the very lift with him.

On the question of servants he had been firm. And had been diddled.

"No," he said. "I can't have people paid to wait on my personal wants."

"People wait on you in hotels," said Andrée.

"Professionally," he said. "They serve the public, not me."

"But if we don't have servants, how can we be free to do our work?"

"That's one of the reasons these private homes are so bad," he said. "It means nothing but an autocratic—"

"I know," said Andrée, hastily. "Well, then, we can go out to dinner every night, and we'll have a visiting maid and a Jap for a few hours every day. They can still be serving some more of the public when they're not with us."

"That's nothing but compromise. But it's better than having anyone's life entirely given up to our personal service. I suppose it's a necessary part of— all this," he said, looking about his domain. He was inwardly miserable and humiliated; Andrée knew it, but she felt that he would soon enough get used to it. She wanted beauty and luxury about her, and she considered that several grosser souls might well be occupied in ministering to her.

"Servants aren't unhappy, Al," she said, "if they're well treated."

"No, I dare say they're not. Neither are kept women. Or imbeciles," he replied. He suppressed the rest of his thoughts, in deference to Andrée's instincts, both feminine and artistic. As a woman she was apparently obliged to have a home, and as an artist, it had to be this sort of home. He was conscious himself of a very unreasonable instinct to give her everything she wanted; he consoled himself by the reflection that this desire to please women was what stimulated men to supreme effort—a condition which gave more credit to his sex than to hers, he thought. He had by this time almost entirely discarded his idea that men and women were not very different, were all simply human beings. He considered it generously; which, he asked himself, was the true normal human being, Man or Woman? Not both of them....

"Perhaps what we call feminine traits are the really human ones," he thought. "Woman's compassion, her intuition, her flexibility.... Our masculine justice and logic may be aberrations from the normal.... Women are primarily concerned with realty—birth, love, death—"

Only Andrée was not. He felt discouraged, and went into his brand new bedroom to dress for this party he so dreaded. He had flatly refused to wear a dinner jacket—and not entirely from principle, either. Andrée had been unexpectedly nice about it. She came into his room now as he stood before the mirror in his shirt sleeves, and rumpled his wiry hair.

"That's the way you ought to wear it," she said, laughing. "Every inch a Socialist! But you are a darling."

He saw her in the mirror, and it gave him a shock. She was lovely, radiant, in a low cut frock of silver cloth; he might have admired her impersonally on the stage. But as Mrs. Al Stephens, as his wife and comrade, it made his heart sink. He fastened his low collar and made a neat little bow of his neck-tie.... The two clear eyed and fearless comrades who were to face life together—to solve problems of living—this earnest young man in a blue serge suit, and this slender, seductive creature in silver.

"My God!" he said to himself. "The Life Urge works the wrong way— no doubt about it. It's *against* progress and clear thinking."

He was not given to facile caresses; he only looked at Andrée, with eyes sombre and doubtful.

"Am I outrageous?" she asked, smiling, utterly sure of her power. "Would you rather I had short hair and wore a red flannel blouse?"

"I don't know ..." he answered, with a sigh. "I'm no better and no worse than lots of others ... I'd be damned eternally for you."

She threw her arms about his neck and kissed him.

"That's dear of you!" she cried. "Only I don't want you to be. I don't want to be a drag on you."

"A drag," he repeated, thoughtfully. She appeared to him not at all a drag, but a terrific impetus—in the wrong direction.

II

Mr. MacGregor was watching Andrée with mild amusement. He had pupils who played better than she, who were undoubtedly more gifted, but he had never had one of whom he expected a more brilliant future. He was careful not to tell her that not through talent alone would she conquer, that, on the contrary, her greatest advantage was something quite different. It lay in her extraordinary and provocative charm. He believed that her beauty, the ardour and grace of her playing might atone for certain undeniable imperfections not only in technic, but in interpretation, a certain perilous latitude, an alarming tendency to anarchistic originality. She was standing in the centre of a group of her guests, all men, as befitted her; she was listening with her moody, unsmiling air, quite indifferent to any whisper of admiration. She knew very well how to take care of herself; she had her own particular sort of rudeness, an odd, innocent sort of bluntness; she wasn't in the least like a married woman. Mr. MacGregor was glad of this, because her husband was a grave error, and it was necessary to keep him in the background. Fortunately, he seemed willing to stay there; he appeared to be neither jealous nor usurious. Mr. MacGregor had told her that if she wished to appear in public she couldn't possibly be called Mrs. Stephens, and he hoped that she would have sufficient tact not to look or to behave like Mrs. Stephens either.

He was approached by Claudine, who had a secret atonement to make; he understood how she felt; she had, in the matter of Andrée, gone farther and fared worse. He was sorry for her, for having sent him away and thus left the field to Stephens. He liked Claudine; she was one of those agreeable people who took everything for granted and never said what she meant; there was a feeling of security in talking to her. She looked charming that evening because she was happy, bright with pride in her marvelous children. She was enthralled by Andrée in her beautiful dress; this was how she liked to see her; Andrée was born to be worshipped. The somewhat scandalous Bevan Martinsburgh stood beside her, and obviously approved. He was a fair, very tall young fellow of twenty-eight, casual, magnificent, good-humouredly regal; he had a habit of looking down from his great height into adoring feminine eyes uplifted—Andrée's were not. He approved all the more. She was the only girl present who was making no effort to attract; she had the attitude of her father in his young days; it was for others to please her. She was notably unresponsive, not even critical. The conquering Bevan compared her with Vi Sidell, who was quite as goodlooking and apparently as indifferent, but Vi's was a false indifference which covered a smouldering readiness to be pleased. Vi was insolent, while Andrée was only distrait. He had known Andrée more or less all her life, but never before had he bestowed attention upon her. It was her *cachet*; Claudine saw it as such. She couldn't help a little pang of regret at the sight of Al in his blue suit, off in a corner talking to that eccentric Cyril Smith— talking so much and so earnestly. Of course, Smith always looked blank and supercilious like that; and never answered, but she had an unpleasant conviction that he must be bored and indignant. He surely hadn't come that evening for this. It was, she reflected, like the wedding guests and the Ancient Mariner, only that Al's tale was frequently by no means absorbingly interesting. No one else paid the least attention to the host; it really wasn't right. She smiled brightly at Mr. MacGregor, but her mind was on the Breath of Life. She saw him run his fingers through his hair in that familiar gesture, making himself so untidy and so touching. It was cruel to put him here, where none of his good qualities were visible.... Her belief, never shaken by experience or observation, that in a marriage, one or the other of the couple would inevitably change and conform to the other, was slightly disturbed at that moment. What if Alfred never became less opinionated, or Andrée more amenable? If they didn't change ...?

She was glad as a relief from this oppressive fancy to look at Edna with that young Malloy. He was entirely right. He had been brought over by Mr. Quillen from the English branch of the Line, and was reputed as promising; he was altogether a gentleman, and very handsome, and there was about him a romantic air which charmed her mother heart. When he first arrived in the country he had been instantly smitten by the graceless Vi Sidell, but quite of his own accord he had turned toward the simpler charms of little Edna. They were progressing slowly; Edna was not the sort to smite; she grew on you little by little, with her thoughtful, gracious air, and her infantile, dimpled smile. That would be such a good thing....

Bertie too was entirely reassuring. He was never infatuated, like those other silly boys; he had a gallant and delightful air, but it hid a secret indifference. He always knew what he was doing; he was no passionate fool, that boy of hers. He could be silly enough, but never without a certain grace; it was impossible for him to be ridiculous. He had characteristically passed over all the younger and prettier girls and concerned himself with poor Phyllis Jenkins, who already at twenty-five had learned not to take anyone seriously. She was penniless; years ago this had had a sort of romantic appeal, and she had been many times on the point of becoming engaged, to quite nice men. But that has its limits; it was a horrible fact, now, known to all men, that to be engaged to Phyllis Jenkins would be a joke. She knew it herself, and was obliged to be sprightly. She was an angular, almost pretty girl, nervously vivacious; she had had to be grateful so much that it had rather worn her down. She was wearing a superfluous bouquet of Edna's and a necklace universally recognized as a former possession of Mrs. Arnold's; she had come with the Sidells in their motor and someone else would be morally obliged to take her home. Let Bertie flatter and cajole her as much as he wished; it did him only credit and no harm.

It is probable that no one else enjoyed the evening quite so much as Claudine. Andrée was an inexperienced hostess and by no means solicitous for the pleasure of her guests. There was a sort of formality and stiffness that didn't wear off; there was dancing—Bertie saw to that—but it was dutiful and polite. The supper, provided waiters and all, by Santi, was good enough, but trite; Andrée lacked all hostess alchemy. Only Claudine retained the joyous air of a proud mother at a children's party.

At last it was over. Bertie had taken Phyllis home, everyone had gone but Claudine and Edna and the attentive Malloy. Andrée stood yawning by the piano.

"I'm glad it's over," she said, frankly.

"It was very nice," said her mother. "Where is Alfred?"

"I don't know. He went out with Cyril Smith long ago," Andrée answered, carelessly. Claudine didn't like that; she frowned slightly, but the presence of Malloy restrained her from speaking further. She kissed her beloved child and prepared to go; she took it for granted that the young man was coming with them, but Edna, with a nice perception for the psychologic moment for parting, thought otherwise. She and Malloy had had a little conversation to which she desired no anticlimax.

"Good night, Mr. Malloy," she said, with a smile there was no mistaking. The young man looked after her, astonished and rueful. He was for the moment forgetful of Andrée.

"That's that," he said aloud.

Andrée laughed, and he turned quickly; the light of a red-shaded lamp gave a strange lustre to her silver dress; she was sitting in a big chair, with her hands clasped behind her head, and she looked—she looked very unlike a Vincelle, he thought.

"Sit down, if you like," she said, "and smoke a cigarette before you go."

He was willing enough to do that.

"I thought I was taking them home," he observed, "but it seems I wasn't."

"Edna's like that," said Andrée, smiling. "Misleading."

He considered that the privilege of pretty girls. He was a chivalrous and rather artless young fellow, with a kind and susceptible heart; he was a little vain and unduly anxious to please; he was what would have been called a "flirt" in Claudine's day, with all the innocence the word implied. He gratified Andrée's aesthetic eye; he was faultless, an ornament to the room. He was supple and tall, with a punctilious grace; he had a dark, lean face which might have been too regular in its beauty but for the attractive defects of cheek-bones that were too high and an upper lip a trifle too long. Andrée had long ago put him down as stupid as an owl, and had expressed to her mother her dislike for the way he "hovered" about Edna.

"He's like a stage lover," she had said.

But to-night she was tired, and his stupidity was agreeable; moreover she was annoyed at Al and wished to keep this handsome creature sitting here until he returned, to punish him.

He talked about her music, and very agreeably remembered all the various times he had heard her play, and gave her ardent praise.

"Oh, but you're not a critic," she said.

"No," he said, looking at her with a smile. "I'm certainly not a critic—of you."

It was agreeable of him, she thought, not to be serious, like Al, but to be frankly interested, just in her. She offered him a cigarette from a box on the table and lighted one herself.

"Al's late," she observed. "I suppose he's gone to a meeting. He can't keep away from them.... Are you a Socialist, Mr. Malloy?"

"I don't really know what a Socialist is. I may be one without knowing it. But I'm afraid I'm frivolous."

"You're in business, though. That justifies you. I've heard often enough from Father what a prodigious struggle that is!"

"I've dabbled in music, too."

"What a horrible thing to say!"

"I'm not a bit ashamed of it. If you asked me, I'd sing for you."

"I couldn't accompany you now. I'm too tired."

"I accompany myself."

"Go ahead then! But don't forget that I *am* a critic!"

"You'd never have the heart to criticize my artless efforts."

He sat down at the piano and began playing in a loose, execrable style which made her frown. But when he began to sing, her frown vanished. He had a delightful voice, true, strong, and full of touching fervour. He emphasized his Irishness, he sang old Irish ballads, exactly as they should be sung....

Andrée, leaning back in her chair and listening, was half amused at her own pleasure.

"Have I 'worked up' this mood?" she reflected. "What a darling he is! I'll be glad to have him in the family.... He'll be a nice foil for little rumpled Al."

With his strong and tender voice still sounding in her ears, she held out her hand to bid him good-by. And perhaps without quite meaning it, she gave him a glance that went to his head. She saw him kindle, and she smiled, withdrawing her hand.

"Indeed I didn't want to criticize!" she said. "It was very lovely!"

"You'd inspire a donkey!" he cried.

"Don't be a donkey!" she said, laughing. "It's late. You'd better go."

"May I come again?"

"Of course!" she answered, and almost without meaning it, smiled again, a little too nicely.

"You're wonderful," he cried, impulsively. "Like—"

"I know," she interrupted, laughing. "Never mind! Good night!"

"I shouldn't have been like that," she reflected, when he had gone. It had been the most insignificant little conversation in the world, and yet it took on the aspect of a betrayal. She was really uneasy about it; she wandered about the room, waiting for Al, in a most unpleasant frame of mind. Certainly she hadn't said or done anything to feel guilty about; it must have been some secret mutiny in her heart of which she was only half aware.

"Very silly of me," she said, almost surprised. "It might help Edna.... He's a dilatory suitor.... I can talk a lot about her, in an artful way.... If I see him again...."

CHAPTER SIX

DISCORDS

I

"Twice in one day," thought Al. "It won't do! We can't go on like this!"

He was walking up and down that bedroom he so hated, with its silly little four post bed and the thick carpet, and the offensive, dainty imitation masculinity of it—a woman's idea of a man's room. Two little blue shaded electric lamps, a fool of a little table—he kicked at the table as he passed it, and Andrée's photograph on it fell down. He was profoundly disturbed, not so much angry as dismayed. Trapped; no way of getting out....

"Why, damn it all!" he cried. "I can't be like this! This isn't me! This isn't what I meant! We are interfering—every hour of the day, with each other. It won't do!"

The first thing had been his fault, he admitted; he shouldn't have been so vehement, or so hasty. But it had been the sort of thing hardest of all for him to endure with patience.

He had gone into the kitchen, where he was not expected to go, because he had been hungry at a wrong time, and there he had seen a hideous thing. It might have looked to other people like a char-woman scrubbing the floor, but to him it was very much more than that. She didn't even look up; what concern was it of hers who came and went in this house? She was a wretched little old woman; he stood in the doorway looking down at her, at the tiny knob of white hair on her bony skull, her narrow shoulders working stiffly, at her clumsy hands pushing the brush back and forth. She breathed hard from her puny effort; she tried to appear more vigorous when she heard someone enter, being well aware that for the char-women of the world effort is accounted of more worth than accomplishment. He stared and stared at her, crawling slowly on her hands and knees, doing this work in the stupidest and cruellest way.... On the kitchen table her lunch was set out for her on a newspaper by the superior visiting maid; no one would come near her or speak to her; she was shut up here to scrub alone.

"Here! Get up!" he said, abruptly.

She looked round with bleared and watery eyes.

"Get up!" he said, again.

"But I ain't done," she protested.

"Get up!" he shouted. He could not tolerate for one instant longer the sight of this old creature at his feet; it was obscene. She clutched at the table and pulled herself to her feet.

"I can do it, if yer give me time," she said, with quivering indignation. "If I take longer, I don't charge so much."

Al knew everything in the world about her; she was the typical "case"; he knew where and how she lived, what she earned and how she spent it. He cross-examined her and she answered him mendaciously, but he was able to sift the truth from the lies.

"Now, see here," he said. "You're sixty-five or so." She declared, for working purposes, that she was fifty. "You've earned a rest. You've worked all your life."

"I'm able—" she began.

"You're not. Now, see here! I want you to go home—now. I'll see that you get a living allowance from—from a certain source every week. It's not charity, d'you understand, not charity. It's what you have a right to demand from society. You can consider me the agent of society."

Her education was incomplete and she did not understand the meaning of his terms.

"The Society give me coal last winter," she observed. "I didn't never—"

He didn't trouble to explain that he represented nothing more than impartial justice.

"Take this now and go home," he said. "And for God's sake, don't go crawling round scrubbing up anyone else's floors, ever! Get drunk, if you want—"

"Oh, I never, never, never—"

"It's better," he said. "Better than this. It'll be your money—the allowance you'll get. Little enough, but you can waste it any way you like. Try to live."

From behind the kitchen door she took down a heartbreaking fuzzy black cape trimmed with jet, and the disreputable ghost of a hat; she tucked the money he gave her into a tremendous hand-bag and retied the clasps with string. She was not grateful, any more than one is grateful for sunshine; in an inexplicable world these benefits came sometimes upon the just and the unjust. She had had a neighbor, mother of nine children, who had been miraculously sent off to the sea-side for two weeks of rest out of forty years of life; she knew of other things like that. She was only in a hurry to get away before further investigation revealed little weaknesses that might repel the Agent of Society.

Al had gone to his wife about this, and she had been angry.

"Who's going to finish the floor?" she demanded. "Jennie won't do that rough work."

"I don't care if it's never finished. I won't have that sort of thing in my house. It's just what I'd give my life to put an end to. It's—"

"I suppose you'd admire me if I did it?"

"Yes, I should," he answered. "You're better able to do it than that poor old skeleton."

"I don't care much about your admiration," said Andrée, slowly. "This is *your* house, is it? Not mine? That's just the way Father talks. '*My*' house ... '*I*' won't have this and that—"

"I didn't mean to be arbitrary," he said, quickly contrite. "Only, don't you see ...?"

He went on, to explain. Andrée could, as usual, see his point of view, but she didn't agree.

"She's a wretched, drunken old creature," she said.

"But, damn it all, why shouldn't she be?" he cried. "What's that got to do with it? You know plenty of people who drink, but you don't suggest condemning them to servitude for life, do you?"

"If you want to run the house, you can," she said. "You can settle this now. Jennie won't finish that floor, and I certainly won't."

"Then I will," he said, and he did. Andrée hated him for that; she was not too aloof to be unconcerned with what Jennie would think and say of that performance.

They had lunch in absolute silence; and yet, little by little, they were weakening. They were neither of them quarrelsome or resentful, and they had a marked respect for each other's obstinacy. One hour more would probably have seen them reconciled and laughing, if Tomlinson and Bucks hadn't appeared. These comrades were more than Andrée could endure; she had in the beginning made a frigid attempt to be polite on Al's account, but her politeness was neither desired nor understood. Tomlinson was a big, stout, brutal fellow with a jaw shaved blue; he didn't hesitate to express his opinion of Al's mode of living, and he did it profanely.

"How the hell you expect to have any influence?" he shouted. "You preach one thing and you practise another. You and your—flat and your servants and your—fine clothes!"

He was a professional Socialist, a politician; he was honest enough in his aims, but quite otherwise in his methods. He had to consult Al frequently, because Al had a considerable personal following in various clubs and centrals, and was quicker and more intelligent than he. He admired Al; he told him frankly enough of his shadiest transactions, because Al, although tiresomely honourable, knew life and was not squeamish. He wanted him now to accept a nomination on their ticket, which Al refused. He had a great many reasons for refusing and Tomlinson a great many for his accepting;

it was a very loud and furious argument, although neither of them was really angry.

Bucks didn't enter into it. He was a bald, scholarly little man with a full brown beard, a sort of secretary and mentor to Tomlinson. He rarely talked; he sat and smiled and watched, and was ready to give data at any moment. Andrée would have rather liked him for his mildness and courtesy, if his collars had been cleaner; she was not constituted to rise above that.

She shut herself into her room while they stayed this day; every sound of that loud discussion reached her, and filled her with rage and disgust. And then, to cap it—

"It's your wife!" shouted Tomlinson. "That's what it is! Your damn society lady with her fine airs—that's what's ruining you!"

"You shut up and mind your own business!" said Al, and no more than that, no other defense or praise of her.

Perhaps she didn't realize how tired he was, or how secretly guilty Tomlinson's reproaches had made him, for after the comrades had gone, she took occasion to speak her mind, and she found him unusually irritable. They took a long stride forward in frankness that afternoon. She called him vulgar and coarse, and he said she was idle and selfish.

All this Al remembered now, walking up and down the room.

"It mustn't be this way," he thought. "It must not be. And I'm the one to change it. I'm older—I'm responsible. I knew there'd be difficulties— it's my job to explain and to reason, and not to quarrel with her. There must be some common ground...."

"And even if there isn't," he went on. "Even if we never think alike, it needn't matter. Good God! Haven't I enough restraint and common decency to get along with the woman I love, even if she has different opinions? Let her be herself!"

He washed his flushed face in cold water and brushed his unruly hair; he subdued his spirit, and went to look for Andrée. He found her in the library, dressed for the street, drawing on her gloves.

"Going out?" he asked, unnecessarily.

She said "Yes," curtly, and then her heart melted; he looked so neat and subdued and good.

"I'm going for a walk," she said. "Do you want to come?"

They went out together into the bright Winter air; but try as they would, no words of reconciliation came from either of them. No words at all....

Was it some subtle reflection of her own mood that made him feel so wretched? He was quite as tall as she, he was properly dressed, he carried himself well, he was strong, vigorous, not bad looking. Why then should he feel so small, and so—he had no other word for it—so cheap—as he walked beside her that day? Of course she was beautiful, but she always had been; of course she was proud and a little disdainful, but that also was nothing new. She looked very lovely in her furs; he saw people turn to look at her.... And suddenly, as plainly as if she had spoken the words, he knew that she was ashamed of him.

He stopped short.

"I forgot ..." he said. "There's something I must finish. I'll go back."

She made no attempt to dissuade him, she let him go without a word, with a smile which he knew was one of relief. When he turned back, he saw her, still walking down the drive, a distinguished and beautiful creature.

"Snob!" he said to himself. "Vain, fickle, coldhearted snob! She didn't want me with her. She doesn't give a damn where I go, or what I do."

A terrible grief assailed him, which he imagined was anger.

"I might have known it!" he told himself. "They're all alike—her sort. Pampered and flattered...." He struggled desperately back to justice.

"I'm making a mountain out of a molehill.... She simply wanted to be alone.... Nothing very bad in that! ... She's only a kid, after all.... She cared enough for me to marry me.... She does care for me!"

II

If he had been able to measure the molehill, he might not have been so sure of exaggeration. Andrée went on as if she could never walk enough, block after block, until the sun had gone, and twilight come, and lights began to glitter. She stopped in at the Plaza for a cup of tea.

"I'm ashamed of him! I'm ashamed of him!" she said to herself. "I'd be ashamed to have him here, with me. I only like him when we're alone. I can't bear for other people to see him. It's like a nasty secret—*amour*.... It degrades me.... Oh, I ought to have had more pride than to throw myself away on a common little man like that! Oh, why didn't someone stop me?"

III

The next afternoon, at exactly the same hour, she was walking down Fifth Avenue with Malloy, and with him, went again into the Plaza for tea, no doubt to vindicate her pride.

And if it was a test, it was successful, for she was not ashamed of him.

CHAPTER SEVEN

THE PASTRY-COOK'S DAUGHTER

I

Claudine mounted the front steps with an unusual languor. "I'm afraid I'm going to be ill," she thought. "This cold hangs on so.... I must have some hot tea and lie down."

To tell the truth, she would not really have been sorry to be ill. It would have been a respite from the nightmare life of the past weeks. Nothing but worry and distress about her son, nothing but disgraceful quarrels between him and his father, and an exasperation and irritability on the part of Gilbert which terrified her. He blamed her for everything, for his disappointment in the boy, for the costly folly of the boy's existence. Claudine was neither able to quarrel nor to keep silent. She felt obliged to defend Bertie, to make excuses for him, she even told lies for him, and paid his debts herself when she was able. Gilbert frequently found this out, and said that she deceived him treacherously, which was true. She was not at all contrite; she knew that with Bertie threats and bluster were of no use whatever; one had either to convince him by reasoning—which she was incapable of—or to win him through his affection, which was what she tried to do. She knew that he loved her perhaps more than anyone else had ever loved her.

"How can you bear to make me so unhappy, Bertie!" she had asked him.

"It isn't me that makes you unhappy, Mammy," he had answered. "It's Father. You wouldn't worry about me, if he didn't make you. You know I'm all right—a heart of gold under a rough exterior. A harmless buffoon. I'm just consciously being wild, as is proper for my years. It's all Father's fault."

She acknowledged to herself, with some surprise, that he was right. Left to herself, she would not have worried over Bertie; there was a quality in even his most grave follies, a grace, an innate delicacy which in her eyes quite redeemed them. He didn't love his vices, he played with them.

She rang the bell, and the door was opened instantly, not by the maid, but by Bertie himself.

"Hello, Mammy!" he cried. "I've been waiting for you! Your tea's ready!"

She followed him into the front room, and found it charmingly prepared for her. He had lighted the gas logs, and had drawn up before the blaze a little gilt table never before used for such a purpose, on which he had arranged a silver tea-service always kept in state on the dining-room sideboard, and a bowl of red carnations.

"Why, Bertie!" she cried. "How dear of you!"

"Wasn't it? Sit down, Mammy, and try a cake!"

"My dear boy! Did you buy the flowers and cakes for me yourself?"

"I bought the flowers. The cakes were a gage of love. Mammy, lookin' about you, don't you feel convinced that I'd be the best husband that ever was?"

"I dare say!" she answered, smiling.

"Mammy, don't you smell a rat?"

"What *do* you mean?"

"Why these preparations? Why this introduction of the topic of husbands?"

"Do explain! what new nonsense is this?"

"I'll tell you, Mammy! I'm going to be married!"

"Bertie!"

She frowned with displeasure.

"True!"

"I don't like to hear you say such things, even in joke. A boy of eighteen—"

"Oh, it wouldn't be for five years, Mammy!"

"You mustn't think of binding yourself to anything of that sort at your age. Surely you're sensible enough to know that you're sure to change—"

"I never do. But don't you see what a good idea it is? How it will keep me safe in the midst of all sorts of temptations which beset a handsome youth? I suppose I am a youth, aren't I? Although no one ever called me one."

"It's not right to expect any girl to wait five years for you. And what makes you think you'll be able to marry in five years, you silly boy? You've never earned a penny—"

"I'll explain all that presently. Mammy, seriously, I've arranged my future in a very remarkable way."

"And who on earth do you imagine will marry you, after waiting five years?"

"She is beautiful, good, and rich," said Bertie. "She's the daughter of the King of the Pastry-Cooks."

"*Who?*"

"Her name is Giulia Santigiorni."

"But who is she? An Italian?"

"Yes, her father's Santi, the caterer."

"Oh, Bertie!"

"I only ask you to see her. She's altogether lovely, and she's had one of those marvelous *nouveau riche* educations. You know the sort of thing—lessons in everything from the most expensive teachers. Sings, plays, paints, speaks all known languages, studied deportment and household management and First Aid. She's been for the last two years in a convent in Paris, and they've made one of those regular foreign young girls out of her. You know, modest and gentle, always on the alert to be respectful and polite to old people.... The King of the Pastry-Cooks is rather keen on society. He gives monster parties—you never saw anything like them; they're awfully pathetic. He gets paid entertainers, singers and dancers and—oh Lord!—wizards! He loves wizards. We sit in rows in the ball-room, while the wizard holds a show on the stage he's had put up. Then he serves a supper! Oh! Never in your life have you dreamed of such suppers! ... And when you're going home, you each get a present. Not a favour, Mammy, but a genuine present—silver cigarette case, and so on.... Of course, he doesn't know half the people who come. He prowls around, a poor, fat, gloomy devil, and no one bothers with him. But he sees a crowd in his house, and that satisfies him."

"Where is the mother?"

"Dead, long ago. He has two daughters and two sons. They're all very nice and respectful."

"But do you think it's quite a suitable match?"

"Couldn't be more so! My Giulia is the most well-bred thing that ever drew breath. You'd feel quite ashamed before her. I believe she took lessons in how to behave in all European courts, and how to entertain royalty."

"But, my dear boy, how do you propose to live? On the—the pastry-cook father?"

"No; I'll get on, Mammy. I always do. I'll either go to Princeton next autumn, or go into Father's business, whichever you advise."

"No, Bertie, you're the one to decide. What do you want to do? What do you want to make of your life?"

"Whatever I can," he said. "I don't really care very much. I want to make a good show, that's all—earn a living."

"Bertie, dear boy, with your intelligence you ought to aim higher than making a living. Isn't there something you can put your heart into? Some sort of work you could really—"

"Not any more, Mammy. It's this ice-cap."

"What do you mean?"

"You ought to know. Old Lance talks enough about it.... It's going to cover the earth—a new glacial period—going to destroy life on this planet."

He rose and began walking about the room and when he spoke again, his voice had changed.

"I've always wanted to be useful. I'm so dam' sorry for people—for almost everyone. I welcomed Evolution like a long lost brother. I thought I could do something to help it, perhaps.... I imagined us all evoluting along into something magnificent. I didn't see any end to our possibilities. I agreed with Al that, if we got together, we could make a heavenly world out of this.... But then Lance sprang this ice-cap on me. And—"

He paused.

"It was something pretty much like despair.... Nothing seemed any use. The happier we got, the less would we want to be frozen, don't you see?"

She was terribly touched by the pain in his voice, by the suffering she divined in his queer soul.

"But it's millions of years away," she said.

"That doesn't matter, as long as it's sure."

"We might find a way to live in it, by the time it comes. It might even be a mistake."

"Lance couldn't be mistaken. You have only to look at him to know he's infallible. And—have you seen their fossils, and their reconstructed pre-historic animals? Those chaps know everything, Mammy, past, present and future."

"Come here!" she said. "Sit beside me, dear."

She drew his sleek head down on her breast.

"Did this idea bring you to—to any sort of—faith?" she asked.

"No, Mammy. I simply felt that the ice-cap ought to be kept a secret. I'd have been glad to be a martyr to humanity and kill all the scientists who knew about it, only I knew more would crop up. I even thought of being a fake scientist myself, and getting up something more cheerful, but that wouldn't get by."

She cried over him a little, and he sat quite still, with his head resting on her shoulder. She wished so passionately that she had something to give him, some invincibly right word.

"I think you'll get over this, dear boy," she said.

"Of course I shall," he answered promptly. "I'll get fat and pompous in fifteen years or so. You know that dish, Mammy—Angela on Horseback—oysters wrapped up in bacon? I'm in a hurry to wrap my little oyster of a soul in a lot of nice fat bacon. Then I'll be comfortable. Nothing better, is there, than making money and getting married?"

"Don't be cynical," she said, gently.

"You know I'm not. I'm only trying to do what I can. I know what's good for me. Little Giulia's good for me. She's all spirit, but it's the nice, old-fashioned, hopeful kind. I never could tell her anything about the ice-cap, for instance; nothing that would hurt her; and being by nature very candid, that'll help me to learn not to have anything to tell. I'll have to grow placid, don't you see?"

He sat up and looked at her, with his diabolic smile and his soft eyes.

"Now, then, will you tell Father in some nice mendacious way that I've got serious and want to settle down to something? Is it to be college or business?"

"I think college," she said, smiling back at him. "You know, after all, Bertie, there may be something left for you to learn."

"All right!" he answered, cheerfully. "And then—come with me to see my pastry-cook's daughter."

"But shouldn't you bring her here?"

"I want you to see her in all her gorgeousness."

"But it isn't quite the thing. You see, you're not—you can't be actually engaged to her."

"She considers that we are. Anyway, their code of etiquette isn't inflexible. Please come! And—look here, Mammy, if you don't like her, if you don't agree that I've done a masterly thing in getting her, I'll give her up!"

"I'll go, Bertie," she said. "But bear this in mind, dear boy. If you change your mind, for any reason whatever, about either of your plans, don't hesitate to say so. Don't go on in a wrong course, simply because you've entered upon it."

"You know I wouldn't. But this time I'm righter than I've ever been before."

II

She went with him the next afternoon, to the house near Prospect Park. The door was opened by a man servant in an elaborate livery.

"My idea of a flunkey, whatever that is!" Bertie murmured.

They were ushered into a drawing-room, an immense room, furnished with an out-of-date sort of magnificence; it gave Claudine a sudden insight into the pathos of the household.

"Look around you!" said Bertie. "You will see a pastry-cook's dream. But you won't have long to observe; Giulia would prefer death to keeping my mother waiting."

He was right; she entered almost at once, and came up to Claudine with a most polite, a supplicating air, held out her hand, raised to her face a pair of sorrowful and beautiful eyes. They sat down to talk but it was too much of a task even for Claudine's experience. She was as affable and impersonal as it was possible to be, she was really well-disposed toward this pretty little thing. But she could evoke from her nothing but a humble sort of politeness. It was evident that she adored Bertie, and that his mother was to her a person of superhuman augustness. She was well-bred, she had pretty manners and a sweet little voice; she was dressed very nicely in a dark blue crêpe de chine, which was simple, but excessively expensive. And she herself had an innocent and spiritual charm, like a little strayed angel. She was small and fragile, and she hadn't the least hint of a womanly figure—a child's body, with flat wrists and a tiny neck. Her dark, pallid face was broad at the brows and very narrow at the chin, which made her childish mouth look larger; she had a wonderful profile, a nose straight with the forehead, a short, full upper lip, a minute and heart-breaking perfection. But it was not her beauty which captured Claudine, it was the transparent sweetness and fidelity of the little soul. She was stupid, she was pliable, she was a baby, but she had a heart to appreciate Bertie, and a charm to hold him.

Tea was brought in by two men servants on a tea-wagon, and the signorina dispensed it with deftness. There were cakes and cakes and cakes, cheese straws, rolls, all sorts of sandwiches, and when these had been sampled, the servants returned with ices in the form of lilies lying on leaves of green almond paste.

Bertie didn't say much, but from time to time Claudine caught him looking at his Giulia with half a smile, a look tender and a trifle amused. He wasn't going to take her too seriously, or expect too much of her. It was, in short, one of those loves which cause a mother very little pain; she knows she is not supplanted, not diminished. Singular that two of her children should "marry beneath them"!

She took leave of her future daughter-in-law with a kiss, and the man servant in the hall opened the door for them.

"It's pouring!" said Bertie. "Go in again, Mammy, and I'll send a few flunkies for a taxi."

"I'd rather not. We'll find one."

"You mustn't get wet, especially with that cold. I can't allow it!"

But she was briskly descending the steps, and he had to hurry after her.

"How obstinate you are, Mammy! If you won't think of your health, have some regard for your pretty little hat!"

She shook her head, laughing. She was so happy with this son, with his affectionate, half effeminate ways, his open admiration. She had with him a gay and coquettish little air no one else ever saw.

"Come along! We'll be sure to pick up a cab in a minute, Bertie! Look at the streams of them going by!"

But all the cabs were full. It was quite fifteen minutes before they stopped an empty one, and by that time Claudine was chilled to the bone, and shivering in her wet shoes and dripping skirts.

"I'm sorry, Bertie!" she said. "I was very stupid!"

He looked at her in silence, and when she was home and safely in bed, he telephoned for the doctor.

III

Andrée and Al had been to the opera that evening and to supper afterward, so that they were late in getting back to the apartment. The desk clerk handed them a message received hours ago.

"Please ask Mrs. Stephens to go home at once. Her mother is ill."

CHAPTER EIGHT

MUTINY

I

Andrée was wandering about the "second parlour" that Sunday afternoon, in a state of joyful idleness, humming to herself. It was so blissful to be at home again, now that the horrible shadow was lifted from her mother. She felt a new and precious sense of lightness and irresponsibility, a return of girlhood. She loved the old life, the kindly servants, the jolly breakfasts with Bertie and Edna, she was even ready to love the stuffy and decorous Sundays she had once found so hateful. Her father was sitting by the open window, reading the paper, and she loved him too, because he looked just as he had always looked to her. She went over to him and kissed the top of his head. He glanced up and smiled.

"Well!" he said.

"Well!" she answered. "Are you happy? I am!"

They were thoroughly and beautifully reconciled now. In spite of his disappointment over the conduct of other people under the shadow of death, Gilbert knew that he had acted properly. He had forgiven his daughter, and he intended, in due course of time, to forgive his son-in-law. He had been profoundly affected by Claudine's illness; he had wished to be with her constantly. But she had not wanted him; she had turned always to Andrée. He had certainly expected, although they had been more or less estranged for some years, that under the shadow of death she would come back to him. She *should* have said, "After all, we have lived more than twenty years together in storm and sunshine. Let us forget our differences!" But she had not. She had said nothing at all, except to thank him for the profusion of flowers he sent. They hadn't had a single touching conversation. On that night, which he had spent at her bedside, in agony and fear, she had not even seen him; she had lain gasping, exhausted, bathed in perspiration, with half-open eyes, as far away from him as if she were already dead. It was Edna who had consoled him, and led him away, and it was Andrée who had stayed by Claudine until the crisis was past. It was always Andrée's name she had murmured— "Andrée! Baby! My baby!"

He had done his best to be just and temperate about this, but it hurt. And as she began to grow better, and the danger was over, his old exasperation at her aloofness returned. He had really longed for a reconciliation; he would have told her frankly that he was sorry for many things in the past, and that he hoped with all his heart to understand her better in the future. It was his eternal passion for something perfect and beautiful in life; if only these twenty years could be crowned now with love, he could have been content. It was easy for him to forgive and forget, the sins of other people as well as his own. But it was not easy for Claudine. He clung to her, for he had nothing else, but she had turned away from him to her children, and she had forgotten him.

He had made a very thoughtful provision for her convalescence. He had learned from her lawyer that her old home in Staten Island—which her father had left her at his death—was temporarily vacant, and he had secured it for a year. Half of it, that is, for her father had converted it into a double house, an improvement by which she had profited, for she had received rent for both halves for years. With the help of Edna he had removed from the storage warehouse as much of Mrs. Mason's old furniture as they thought good, and later in the spring, when Claudine was strong enough, she was to go there with Edna, to find it all prepared for her. This plan had touched her, she had thanked him with tears in her eyes. He would have gone there with them, if it had been suggested....

"What's this?" asked Andrée.

He roused himself from his unpleasant meditation, and turned to look at the object she held in her hand.

"That? It's a game—'Pigs in Clover.' I remember your mother was very much amused with it when she was first married."

Andrée smiled and began to manipulate it, singing again.

Now Gilbert had been brought up to distrust happiness, especially feminine happiness. His mother had never been happy. Claudine was never happy; the only permissible thing in that line was the benevolent, and possibly alcoholically stimulated, high spirits of the *pater familias*, coming home bearing gifts. He loved Andrée, he was delighted to have the pretty, willful creature about him again, but still, he could not help distrusting such gaiety.

"When do you expect to go home?" he asked.

"This is home!" said Andrée.

"Your home is with your husband, young lady!" he said, severely.

"I know! I'm going—pretty soon."

There wasn't the slightest need or reason for staying another hour. She had been there for four weeks, and her mother was now well on the road to recovery. Al telephoned every day, first he asked about Claudine, whose illness he had taken terribly to heart, and then he always said—

"When are you coming home, old girl?"

And she always answered "In a day or so."

"You know your old father likes nothing better than to have his girl at home," Gilbert went on. "But you're a married woman, and you have to think of your duty."

"I do think of it. But not all the time.... I think I'll run up and see if Mother's dressed."

She had started up the stairs, when the telephone rang, and she ran back to answer it. She was quite sure it would be Al; this was his regular hour.

His voice responded.

"Mrs. Stephens in?"

"This is Andrée!" she answered, brightly. "How are you, Alfred?"

"Your mother doing well?"

"Yes, very!"

And then, instead of his usual query, he said—

"It's about time you were coming home, isn't it?"

His voice was somewhat alarming, and she answered in her very pleasantest manner.

"Yes; I'm coming in a day or two, Al."

"Suppose you come this evening?"

"Oh, I couldn't! Not possibly!"

"Why not? I'll come for you about eight."

"No, Al, it's not possible. My things aren't packed."

"Edna can pack them and send them after you tomorrow."

"But how ridiculous! Why should I rush off like this?"

"Well," he said slowly. "Suppose—because I particularly ask you to—?"

"You're very unreasonable!"

"Humour me, then, for once."

"No, Al!" she said, firmly. "I can't come to-night. To-morrow—or the next day—I'll let you know—"

"Look here, Andrée; I'm coming for you to-night!"

"But I tell you I'm not going home!"

"I insist!"

She laughed.

"What in the world is the matter with you, my dear boy? Do you imagine you can bully me?”

"I don't want to. I'm asking you—to do me a favour."

"It's a ridiculous, selfish, unreasonable favour, and I shan't do it."

"I'm coming for you just the same, at eight o'clock!" he said.

She was going to remonstrate with him, but she found that he had left the telephone. Her cheeks flushed, and she bit her lip.

"Little beast!" she said to herself. But some secret thought made her unusually indulgent, she shrugged her shoulders and dismissed the thought of him.

She went on up to her mother's room and knocked at the door.

"It's Andrée!" she announced in her triumphal voice, as if that name were a talisman to admit her anywhere.

Claudine was sitting at her dressing-table, brushing her hair. There was grey in it now, on the temples, and her face was thin and drawn. She wore a negligée with high collar and long sleeves, to conceal the pitiful emaciation of her neck and arms. Andrée couldn't look at her without a twinge of pain.

"I'll do your hair for you, darling!" she said, and Claudine willingly relinquished the brush to her. "I am some use to you, aren't I, Mother?"

"I don't know what I should have done without you, dear!"

"'Should have done!' Then you don't need me now?"

"You know how dearly I love to have you with me, but—"

"But I ought to go home? I'm not useful any more, and I'm not wanted—"

"Don't be so unreasonable, my dear! It's only that I think it unfair to Alfred—"

"Why?" she demanded, impatiently.

"You shouldn't stay away from him."

"Why not? He's always saying he wants me to feel free. He certainly shouldn't object to my taking a little holiday."

"And you ought to be at your work again."

"I can practice here for Doctor Jaas. The Conservatory can wait."

"You ought to go home!" her mother repeated.

Andrée frowned.

"Al's just been telephoning, to 'insist' upon my coming home this evening. I suppose you think he's right?"

"Yes."

"You mean you'd like me to rush off like that?"

"Yes, I should."

"I shan't!" said Andrée. "I don't suppose you'll mind my waiting until to-morrow to pack my things?"

"If I were you, I should go with Alfred this evening—"

"I wouldn't for anything! Just give in to his silly whim—"

"It's not a silly whim... Andrée.... I wrote to him."

Andrée stared at her mother's reflection in the glass.

"What!" she cried.

Claudine opened the drawer of the dressing-table and looked into it.

"I thought—the sooner you went home, the better," she said, in a low voice.

Andrée did not ask why. She understood very well.

II

It was a marvel to Claudine that no one else had noticed. There was a certain effrontery about them both, a smiling ease, but it should not have deceived Edna. She herself had observed it the first time she had gone downstairs and seen them together. Andrée had been at the piano, and Malloy standing by her, to turn her music. She had looked up at him, and met his eyes, and it was not possible for Claudine to doubt that they understood each other too well. She could not help watching them. Malloy was attentive to Edna—rather too much so—but it was with an air of bravado, of displaying his versatility, his irresistible fascination. With a sidelong glance he would follow Andrée with his idiotic infatuation, his bedazzlement, plain in his face. The very fact that they so seldom spoke to each other made her quite sure that there was a great deal of which she knew nothing. She regarded Andrée's cool triumph with an aching heart. She was not shocked or astounded; it is a sad truth that no perfidy or evil could shock that woman. She was willing to believe both the best and the worst of anyone; whatever was presented to her, she accepted. She believed that now she was seeing the very worst of Andrée, the selfishness, the recklessness, the cruelty, which she knew better than anyone else. She didn't blame Malloy; not much was to be expected from him. He was kindhearted and manly, and so on, but wax in hands like Andrée's. He didn't love Andrée; he wouldn't have thought of her if she hadn't made him. He had been happy with Edna, and he would be again—if he were let alone. And Andrée didn't love him; she would forget him. If it were stopped *now*.

That is the reason that Claudine had written to her son-in-law.

"I really think, Alfred, that for several reasons it would be wise to induce Andrée to go home to you as soon as possible, and to take up her work again," she had written, and she had left it to his common sense to comprehend and to follow her hint.

But she hadn't reckoned with his unruly passions. He had put two and two together, to make a sum considerably more than four. He had seen Malloy once in their sitting-room at the hotel, where he had come to sing for Andrée. He had decidedly not liked him.

"If he's engaged to Edna—or going to be—why does he hang around here?" he had asked.

"I suppose he hasn't the same idea of etiquette as you," Andrée had answered, with an unpleasant smile. "However, if you don't like him, I'll tell him not to come. He'll understand."

She had intended to wound and anger him, and she had succeeded. But she had done something more; she had awakened in him that old and buried suspicion for women of Andrée's class.

Years before he had met Andrée that idea had been superseded. He had made his money, and had begun to know at least a little of that other world. And he saw that the women there were no more or less than human beings, very much hampered and hurt by their idleness. He had tried to see in Andrée not only the beloved woman, but a human being entitled to as many faults and weaknesses as he had himself, entitled to the same moderation of judgment that he himself required. He had deliberately put aside his suspicion of Malloy, he had conquered Andrée's irritability with his patient good-humour, and they had been getting along very nicely the week before Claudine's illness.

And now, by the words of Claudine's letter, all the fruits of his reason were destroyed, and the old distrust and envy and utter misunderstanding came rushing back. He saw Andrée as a stranger of whom he knew really nothing, an unaccountable, alien creature. He knew at once that Claudine's letter referred to Malloy. No doubt the fellow was hanging about the house there all the time, singing to her....

It was on Saturday night that he got it; he had reflected upon it all that night, and the next morning, and by the afternoon he was in a humour which would have caused Andrée no little astonishment. He hated the Vincelles and all their entourage; he believed that they were laughing at him, that he had been played with all these weeks, that now they fancied they had got well rid of him. All except Claudine; she wasn't like the others, of course. He wished that he could see her and talk to her, but that couldn't be. She had at least indicated to him what should be done.

III

At eight o'clock he rang the door bell.

"I want to see Mrs. Stephens!" he said, curtly, to the servant.

"She's at supper, sir. Will you wait?"

"No; just ask her to step here and speak to me!"

"What name, please, sir?"

"Her husband," he said, grimly.

They were all in the dining-room, enjoying the "Sunday night tea" of their tradition. Gilbert sat at the head of the table and made jokes, like a patriarch; opposite him was Claudine, on one side Edna and Malloy; on the other, Bertie and Andrée. They lingered; they had not yet thought of rising from the table when the maid entered with her message.

"Mr. Stephens is upstairs, ma'am!" she whispered to Andrée.

"Who is it?" asked Gilbert, in the tone of a man who is master in his own house.

"Mr. Stephens, sir," answered the girl.

He turned red; he was sorry he had asked; he was very much at a loss. And so was everyone else. This proscribed man actually under this roof! Gilbert was torn between his anger at the fellow's audacity and the respect due him as a husband. Propriety conquered.

"Ask Mr. Stephens to come down here and join us," he said. "Bertie, bring up another chair to the table!"

But the girl returned almost immediately.

"Mr. Stephens is sorry, sir, but he is in a hurry, and he would be obliged if Mrs. Stephens would come upstairs."

Andrée rose. But her expression alarmed her mother.

"Andrée!" she murmured, but her warning was unheeded. Andrée went slowly upstairs, and into the hall where her husband stood waiting. He had not removed his felt hat, but he had thrown open the fur-lined overcoat of which he was so absurdly proud. Never had his appearance so profoundly displeased her.

"What do you want?" she asked.

Her tone excited him to instant hostility.

"I told you I was coming," he said.

"And I told you not to come."

She looked at him.

"I didn't think even you would do a thing like this—coming here—waiting in the hall—like a servant with a message—"

"That's enough," he said. "I only want to know whether you're coming back, or not."

"When I'm ready, I'll come."

"I'm ready now. I've waited as long as I'm going to wait."

"Are you trying to threaten me?" she asked with cold surprise.

"No, I'm simply giving you your choice—to come with me, or to stay."

"I'll stay, thank you," she said.

She had a sudden impulse of pity for him, he looked so desolate and lost. She thought it would be nice to have her cake and also to eat it.

"Let's not quarrel!" she said. "Come downstairs and have supper with us!"

"No!" he said. "I'm going.... The servant's delivered his message."

He opened the door and went out, slamming it after him with a crash.

Andrée struggled against a great desire to cry, or to shout after him, she didn't know which.

"Little beast!" she said, aloud. "Vulgar little bully!"

"What's the meaning of this?" said a severe voice behind her, and she turned to see her father.

"There's no meaning in it at all," she answered. "Al's gone home, that's all."

"Did you quarrel, Andrée?"

She was surprised; she had forgotten that fathers were supposedly authorized to ask such impertinent questions.

"No," she said. "He thought I would come home this evening, but I wasn't ready."

Gilbert saw some feminine mutiny in this.

"Did you refuse to accompany him?" he asked, in a portentous voice.

"Yes," she answered. "Of course I did. Is that a crime? Am I supposed to humour every caprice?"

Gilbert stopped her with a gesture. He put himself in Alfred's place; he knew how he would have felt under the circumstances, how humiliated and furious.

"No doubt he had very good reasons. You've already remained away for over five weeks—"

"Four weeks."

"Four weeks, then. You have—in my opinion—you have neglected him."

Andrée made no defense, but her air was not acquiescent. Gilbert became more fatherly.

"Now, I'll tell you what you'll do, Andrée. Telephone your husband, and tell him you'll be home in an hour or so. And I'll take you myself, and make the young man's acquaintance, eh?"

"No, thank you, Father. I'm not ready to go."

"Get ready then! Get ready! Bertie will telephone for you. Bertie!" he called. "Bertie! Just a moment, please!"

Bertie came running upstairs.

"Your sister's going home—"

"I'm not!" said Andrée.

Gilbert was astounded.

"This is a serious matter," he said. "I can't permit it. It's your duty to go home to your husband."

"I'll just postpone the duty for a few days," said Andrée.

"I say no! He came for you this evening and—"

"What is the matter?" asked Claudine's low voice. She had come up after Bertie, and was standing in the shadow, outside the circle of light cast by the lamp on the newel post.

"I am telling Andrée that she must go home tonight. It seems her husband came to fetch her and she refused to go with him."

"She'll go to-morrow," said Claudine. "It's rather late now."

"Father," said Andrée, "I don't want to be rude—but it's my own affair. I can't let anyone tell me what I shall do. I'll go home when I think best."

"This is outrageous!" shouted Gilbert. "You can't adopt that tone toward me, young woman! You've been spoilt and indulged long enough! Bertie, go down to the garage and bring the car!"

"No!" cried Claudine.

"Do as I tell you! Now, Andrée, I'll give you fifteen minutes to pack what you need, and then you'll go, ready or not. This is my house, and what I say shall be done. Do you understand?"

"I believe I do!" she answered, carelessly. "You're putting me out, aren't you? Very well, I'll go!"

She turned and ran up the stairs.

Claudine turned upon Gilbert with desperation.

"Gilbert! Go after her! Tell her she can wait! Tell her—"

"I'll do nothing of the sort!" he answered. "I won't be defied in my own house—"

She seized his arms with her weak hands and actually tried to shake him.

"Stop her!" she cried. "Stop her! You don't realize what you're doing!"

He looked down at his wife with stupefaction.

"Stop her!" she cried, again. "Go after her and tell her to wait!"

"You ought to be ashamed of yourself," he said, severely, "to suggest—"

But she didn't wait for him to finish.

"Then I'm going with her," she said.

With trembling knees she ascended the stairs, entered her room and began dressing. She hastily put into a little bag a few necessary clothes, her jewel case and her bank books, and came out again, just as Andrée had gone downstairs.

"Gilbert!" she whispered to her husband. "I must stay with her until they are reconciled. It's a matter of vital importance!"

He was touched; she was so ill, so weak, so terribly upset.

"Very well!" he said. "Bertie will take you to their house. Take care of yourself! You're not fit to go out."

She gave him a hasty kiss, and taking Bertie's arm, left the house. Andrée was already in the street, standing beside the car.

"I'll have to drive you," said Bertie. "Donald was out."

"But you won't drive me home, my child!" said Andrée. "You can take me to some other hotel."

"Take her wherever she wants, Bertie!" said Claudine, with a sob.

CHAPTER NINE

HOME AGAIN

I

Claudine sat down to answer her distressing correspondence. She took a long time to arrange her writing materials, to adjust the light, for her heart failed her, courage and hope were nearly gone. She sat before the same little rosewood desk she had used in her girlhood, in that little bedroom she had passed so many happy years in, she was at home again, in the house in which she had been born, and she had at this moment no better wish than that she might die there.

She had brought Andrée here the day after their flight, nearly a month ago. She had felt a presumptuous and sublime joy; for the first time in her life she was going to have Andrée alone, alone there in that house of gentle memories. She would take her for walks, show her the places she had so loved in her own young days, she would soften her heart and win her utterly. She would teach her to see the worth of her husband, the sacredness of their bond, with all her love, all her sad wisdom she would lead her back from this morass into which she had strayed. She had felt sure that she could do this, now that they were alone. Andrée was susceptible, she could be persuaded. She had shown a passionate affection for her mother; she had wept in her arms that night, she had accused herself of selfishness and ingratitude.

There had been just two days of Paradise, two long days spent together in exquisite companionship. The granddaughter of Selma, Mrs. Mason's most devoted old servant, had come to wait on them, and she made them entirely comfortable. There was nothing to worry or disturb them. They had had their meals together alone, and quiet evenings in the drawing-room before a fine log fire. They hadn't mentioned Andrée's affair; Claudine was content to wait for that, filled with hope by her child's new softness.

And then on the third evening Malloy came. Evidently Andrée had sent for him, for she greeted him without surprise. He was troubled, anxious, very ill at ease; he had the unmistakable air of a man tormented by an unwelcome passion. He was afraid of Claudine, he was ashamed of his treachery to Edna, he was ashamed of his terrible bondage. But he could not escape. Andrée's mocking smile turned his heart to water. He adored her; he was unable to hide his madness.

Andrée didn't attempt to see him alone. She brought him into the room where her mother sat before the fire, and kept him there. She asked him to sing, and he did so, his fervent and touching voice sounded through the fire-lit room and moved the wretched mother to tears. What was she to do? She could see him with Andrée's eyes, she could so easily understand what it was that had captured that reckless and beauty-loving heart. He was so handsome, so ardent, so entirely a lover. He had none of Alfred's preoccupations; he hadn't, she thought, any thoughts at all, nothing but sentiments and traditions. But a gallant gentleman—

He left early. It certainly had not been a pleasant evening for him. He had scarcely been able to speak, with Claudine present. But when he was going, and had said good-night to Andrée, who hadn't risen, she followed him out to the front door.

"Mr. Malloy!" she said. "Have you told—Edna?"

"No ..." he said. "I'm ashamed to say I haven't.... But of course I shall ..."

"Don't!" she entreated. "Please don't! Not just yet! If you can—won't you go to see her as usual?"

"But—do you think that's—honourable?" he asked, shocked.

"It's kind, Mr. Malloy!"

"But—isn't it—only putting it off, you know?"

"Sometimes it's better to do that," she said. "Please, Mr. Malloy, if you are able to—?"

"I'll try!" he said, quite miserably. "I suppose you don't want—me to say anything—until you're home again?"

"Yes," she answered.

The door closed behind him.

"Because I'm going to stop this!" she said to herself. "It can't be! I'm going to stop it!"

That was her one object—that nothing irreparable should be said or done. She was absolutely certain that the infatuation would not last, there was not one element in it to make it permanent. She was certain that if no monstrous irrevocable folly were committed, Malloy would thankfully return to Edna, who really suited him, and that Andrée would go back to her husband.

But she was filled with terror at the possibility of that evil chance. She lay awake all that night, trying to plan how she could prevent it.

No enlightenment came. Malloy came again and again. She dreaded to speak to Andrée, for she knew how speech solidifies and strengthens the vaguest thoughts, but it could no longer be avoided. She could no longer be complaisant. She waited until Andrée was in bed one night and then she went into her room and sat beside her in the dark, at the foot of her bed.

"Andrée!" she said. "I must know!"

"I want you to, Mother. I've been waiting for you to ask me...." She sat up and flung her arms round her mother.

"Oh, my darling!" she said. "I'm so terribly, terribly sorry! I know I've made you suffer. I know it's a dreadful thing to do to dear little Edna! But I can't help it! I thought at first it would only be a lark. I didn't mean any harm. I never imagined *this* would come! But now it's too late! I love him so, Mother! I never knew what love was before. I never, never felt like this about Al.... Oh, Mother! I'd stop if I could! I don't want to hurt you or Edna. But I can't help it!"

"You can, Andrée! It's not necessary to do what you want."

"You're so cold and so—good, you can't understand! I love Francis so that I can't give him up. No matter what harm it does, to me, or anyone else."

"What do you intend to do?"

"I've written to Al, to ask him to—for a divorce."

"Oh!" cried her mother. "*Why* did you do that?"

"What else could I do? You didn't think I wanted a nasty underhand intrigue, did you, Mother? I wouldn't—I wouldn't even kiss Francis until I was free from Al. I'm not that sort."

"What did Alfred say?"

"Nothing. He didn't answer. But I know he'll do it. He's always said he'd never try to hold me if I wanted to be free."

"I think you ought to see him, my child."

"Why?"

Claudine had no intention of telling her true reason.

"It's the best and frankest way to do," she said. "If you like, I will write to him and ask him to come here. I wish you would see him—for my sake, Andrée."

Andrée sighed.

"I will, then, if you like, Mother. But it'll be horrible. We'll be horrible. We'll quarrel. All his commonness comes out when he's angry."

"You needn't quarrel. Then it's agreed that I'm to write?"

"Yes," said Andrée. "But it's not a bit of use to try your diplomacy, Mother dear! I see through you!"

And this very evening she was trying to write that letter. Andrée and Malloy were sitting on the porch, almost under her window, now and then she could hear the murmur of their voices.

"I'll write the other letters first!" she decided, in despair.

She wrote to Gilbert, the same sort of thing she had been writing all the month.

"I think it is very necessary to stay with Andrée, until she and her husband are reconciled. It is a critical time. I hope and believe that all will turn out well."

He, of course, knew nothing at all of the Malloy complication; he believed it to be a simple quarrel.

Then she wrote to Edna:

> My dear little girl:
> It is always a pleasure to receive one of your cheerful letters. I can't thank you enough for taking such good care of Father, Bertie, and Cousin Lance. I am very glad you like Bertie's Giulia; she is a charming little creature, and very devoted to him. Your description of their ball was amusing, and, I thought, rather touching. Bertie had told me of Mr. Santi's predilection for wizards; I think I should enjoy them myself. Your dress must have been lovely. I am sorry your father thought it too short! Personally I think that style suits you; you don't look any older than when you were a little girl going to dancing school.
> Write to me often, my dear little Edna. And don't expect any news from me, because there is none. I am very much better; you are not to worry. As soon as this most unfortunate affair is settled, I shall be at home again.
> Very lovingly and gratefully,
>
> YOUR
> MOTHER.
> P. S. Be sure to send the furs to cold storage *this week!*

She looked again at the little pile of letters she had had from Edna, gay, pleasant, commonplace. And yet alarming. There was not a single mention of Malloy. Edna was not one to wear her heart on her sleeve; she had no ability and no desire for expressing her emotions. Her mother blessed her for her seemly reticence; how easy it was to deal with people who didn't talk, who took so much for granted! She was quite certain that the poor little thing was very unhappy, but she was also certain that she was not desperate. She had no doubt noticed the change in her handsome lover, but she wished no consoling for it; she would console herself, she would endure with dignity and common sense.

And now for Alfred.

She hesitated for a long time, then began to write, in her careful and delicate hand:

> My dear Alfred:
> I have just learned of Andrée's decision, and I think I need not

tell you how it grieved me. Not only on your account, but on hers, I believe that a divorce would be a terrible mistake, and I beg you to oppose it resolutely. I beg of you, Alfred, not to consent to it. No one understands Andrée as I do and I know that this would be the very worst thing possible for her.

She has consented to see you and I entreat you to come and talk it over with her. I trust to your deep affection for her, and to your humanity. I know that she can never be happy and *safe* with any one but you.

Will you come on Sunday, if convenient for you?

Always your friend,

CLAUDINE
VINCELLE

She stamped and sealed it, and lay down on the bed, to read, to try to read and to forget her bitter anxiety.

II

Sunday came, and no word from him. And on Sunday evening Mr. Malloy appeared. Claudine was very much taken aback; he had never before come on Sunday, and she had very humanly taken it for granted that he never would. She hadn't told Andrée that she expected Alfred; she had planned to take her by surprise, before she could adopt a difficult and dangerous mood. If he should come now! She sat upstairs in her room, in a state of tremulous agitation, looking out of her window, trying in vain to see the street through the fog that had risen, listening for his footfall, though what she could do to forestall him she didn't know.

Outside on the porch Andrée and Malloy were sitting, well-wrapped, coat collars turned up against the thick, chill mist of that April night. Their hands were clasped, but they spoke very little. They were in a mood of sombre depression, not unknown to lovers. Now and then Claudine heard the sound of their voices, forlorn and detached; if it had been Alfred, she thought, how different it would have been! A continuous flow of talk, and retorts from Andrée, irritated perhaps, but certainly interested....

She fancied she heard a footstep on the hilly street; she opened her window softly and leaned out. The trees were dripping on the gravel drive; hoarse whistles sounded from the bay, and—yes, undoubtedly, that was the garden gate! A step on the porch, and Andrée's voice—

"I want to see Mrs. Vincelle!"

She flew down the stairs and opened the front door.

"Come in, Alfred!" she said.

He followed her into the sitting-room and stood before her, still in his overcoat and cap.

"So she's out there with him?" he said. "Do you think that's a fair way to treat me?"

"I'm sorry, Alfred. Very sorry. I had no idea he would come this evening. I wouldn't for worlds have—"

"He does come to see her then? In your house? And you don't mind?"

"Please sit down!" she said, gently. "I am so glad you came. I wanted so to talk to you—to explain—"

He took off his overcoat and cap and threw them on a chair. He was thinner; his face had lost its boyish and alert expression, it was set in an expression of bitterness and misery.

"I didn't want to come," he said. "It can't do any good. I knew what you thought would happen. You thought if we saw each other we'd—melt. That she'd change her mind. Well, I don't want that. We've had enough emotion. I don't want any—love that comes from caprice. No more moods and impulses. I—it wasn't that way with me. It was—real."

"Alfred, you mustn't be hard! It's not like you. If you love her, you must forgive her a hundred times. She's silly and—"

"It's not a question of forgiving. I don't see it that way. She's free to do as she pleases. It's simply that now I know she's not capable of loyalty."

"Alfred, I give you my word there's been nothing wrong—"

"Oh, I believe it! She's *respectable!*" he said, bitterly. "I'm not afraid of her being too generous with—anyone. She'll be like some of those singers and geniuses I've read of. She'll have half a dozen husbands, but she'll never do anything wrong."

"That's very cruel and unjust! Surely you've seen enough of the world to understand these—infatuations…. He's a very handsome and attractive man, and she has lost her head. That's all it is! It won't last!"

"I know it won't. But it will happen again. It isn't the infatuation that hits me so hard. I can understand that. It could happen to almost anyone. But it's the—the rank, beastly cruelty of it! To walk off and leave me without a word. I—you don't know—leaving all her little things there—all her little things—telling me all the time she'd come back in a few days…. It's …"

He got up and walked over to the fire.

"No," he said. "She can have her divorce. I always told her I'd never try to keep her against her will. But—I wish to God we'd never got married. If we could only part now with some sort of decency … if she could just say, 'It's over. Good-by!' But now—I guess you don't realize—I'll have to be caught in a compromising situation—all the dirty, filthy business will have to be written down and talked about by a lot of lawyers…. The sort of thing I hate worse than death. It's what they call acting honourably for me to do that."

"Don't do it, Alfred! Don't do it, I beg you! I am sure she loves you!"

"She has a damn peculiar way of loving, then."

"I know she has. There are horrible things in her nature. But I am sure that you know the good in her too. She is honest and—"

She covered her face with her hands.

"Can't you see, Alfred? She needs you so! No one else can help. No one else can help her to grow into something better."

"Please don't cry!" he said, in great distress. "I'd do anything for you. You're an angel!"

"I'm not! I'm not! I once—long ago—thought I'd leave *my* husband. But thank God I didn't!"

"But it might have been better for you if you had," he said, frankly.

She looked up in surprise.

"No!" she said. "It would have been—I am sure that self-sacrifice is the best way in life."

"That depends on the object. If you sacrifice yourself for—well, humanity, it's fine and good. But for one other human being, no!"

She had no intention of permitting an argument to begin. She pulled the conversation away from reason back to emotion, where it belonged.

"I don't ask you to sacrifice yourself, Alfred. It would make you both happy."

"I can't do it!" he said, quietly. "She wants to leave me, and I must let her."

"But you'll see her?"

"No. Please don't ask me any more. It's settled. I'm sorry—on your account. I should be glad to do it for you—if I could. But I can't."

He went toward the chair where his coat lay and was about to put it on, when the door opened and Andrée entered. He turned and faced her. Her cheeks were rosy from the damp air, her black hair curled about her forehead; her mother looked at her loveliness with a beating heart. Surely he could not resist her!

But he picked up his cap and threw his coat over his arm.

"Good-night!" he said.

The front door closed after him.

III

Not fifteen minutes ahead of him Malloy was making his way to the ferry.

"My God, what a mess!" he was saying over and over to himself. He had never in his life felt so shabby, so shamefaced, as he had felt that evening.

There was no triumph in this love; he was a thief. He had mortally stricken that poor little chap. He had humiliated and hurt Edna. He had involved himself and Andrée in a disgusting scandal.

"We never can be happy," he said. "Not on such a foundation.... But I don't care! I'd rather have her and be miserable all my life!"

CHAPTER TEN

DESTINY INTERVENES

I

Andrée was very late that evening. She had gone to the city to do some shopping, and at eight o'clock she had not yet returned. Claudine sat down to supper alone, but she could not eat. She was filled with apprehension. She couldn't imagine what was keeping Andrée.

The weather had suddenly turned mild, the dining-room windows were open and a sweet damp breeze was blowing in from the garden. Rose had prepared an especially appetizing supper; she hovered about the silent woman, very anxious that she should eat it. The shaded lamp threw a warm light on the table, set out with Mrs. Mason's glowing old Crown Derby; there was the same order and quiet all about her that had so delighted her a few weeks ago. But now it frightened her. It was death-like...

"There's no use trying to go on," she thought. "This must end! I'll have to tell Gilbert—and poor little Edna. I'll have to go back.... I've done all I can."

It was nearly a week since Alfred had come, and in the meantime Andrée had begun her divorce proceedings. No miracle had happened; heaven had not intervened. This disaster, this ruin was approaching with a sure step.

"I really don't believe I can eat, Rose!" she said, apologetically. "I'm sorry; your little supper was so nice. Be sure to put something aside for Mrs. Stephens."

"I think I hear a taxi coming now, ma'am," said Rose.

They both listened. Rose was right, a taxi was stopping outside the house; a man's voice said "Thank you, Miss!" and there was a step on the veranda. Rose hurried to open the door, and in an instant Andrée entered the room.

Claudine sprang up.

"What is the matter?" she cried, alarmed at her child's face.

Andrea at once began to cry hysterically.

"Stop, child!" said her mother. "What is it? What has happened?"

Andrée sank into a chair by the table and leaned her head on her arms, shaking with sobs.

"It's too much!" she cried.

"Go away, Rose!" said Claudine. "Go into the kitchen and make Mrs. Stephens a nice hot cup of tea!"

Rose vanished.

"What is it, Andrée?" she asked again. "Don't torture me so! What has happened?"

Andrée sat up suddenly and began to laugh through her sobs.

"I went to see Doctor Lawrence!" she cried. "I was afraid—It's true! ... There's going to be a baby!"

She began to shriek with laughter. Claudine seized her by the shoulders, and shook her.

"Be quiet! Be quiet, Andrée! Come upstairs!"

Andrée shook her head.

"No!" she cried. "No! I'm expecting company! Francis is coming! Oh, Lord! Oh, Lord! Isn't it funny! Won't he be pleased!"

"Hush! Come upstairs!" Claudine repeated, and half dragged her to her feet. She put her arm about her and supported her up the stairs to her own room.

"Lie down!" she said. "I'll bathe your face in cold water. Try to control yourself, Andrée!"

But Andrée could do nothing but weep and laugh.

Claudine sat by her, patting her cold hands and stroking her hair, silent, waiting for her to become tranquil. The doorbell rang, and Andrée sprang up, suddenly sobered.

"Mother! ... It's Francis! You'll have to see him!"

"We'll tell Rose to say you're not at home."

"No! I want you to see him! Listen, Mother!"

"Yes?"

Andrée looked at her with a stern glance.

"You'll have to send him away," she said. "Tell him it's all over. I'll never see him again."

"Do you mean that, Andrée?"

"It would hardly do to introduce a little Stephens into our household," said Andrée, with a frigid smile.

"But what shall I say?"

"I don't care. Anything! Only, Mother, if you ever let him guess the truth, I'll never, never forgive you! My life is ruined. I've got to give him up. But— it's so ridiculous and humiliating. No one must ever know!"

"But they can't help knowing!"

"Francis won't. He's stupid. He won't put two and two together. Tell him—anything. Say I've repented on account of Edna. Only get rid of him, for God's sake!"

"Hush, Andrée!"

"Oh, I'm so ashamed and wretched! Why did this horrible thing happen! I wouldn't believe it at first! It was too ridiculous and shameful! I won't have Francis know. I'll go away somewhere."

Claudine rose.

"You'll lie here quietly, won't you?" she asked.

Andrée assured her that she would, and closing the door after her, Claudine descended the stairs.

Of all the painful and awkward tasks she had yet had to do for her child, this was the worst. She couldn't suppress a wry little smile. She who so loved peace and dignity, who was so constitutionally averse to plain speaking!

Mr. Malloy was in the drawing-room, walking about. He stared a little at the sight of Claudine.

"Good-evening!" he said.

"Good-evening!" Claudine answered, brightly.

How was she to begin? She stood quite still, and her silence warned him of something unpleasant to come.

"It's very difficult—" she said. "Please sit down, Mr. Malloy!"

He did so, and she seated herself opposite him.

"I must be very firm!" she thought. "Oh, if I only can get rid of him!"

He waited for some time.

"I hope there's nothing wrong, Mrs. Vincelle," he said, at last.

"No ... I should not call it wrong.... Indeed, I think I won't try to conceal from you, Mr. Malloy, that all this has been very painful for me. I have always had the greatest respect for Andrée's husband and I thought it a great—a terrible mistake for her to leave him."

He flushed.

"I'm sorry ..." he said.

"Naturally I think first of her. I knew that this was not for her good. I knew—please forgive me—I knew she wouldn't be happy with you. But I couldn't stop her. She is very willful."

"But—"

"But she has—changed, Mr. Malloy! She sees now that she was wrong. She has asked me to tell you so!"

He rose.

"No!" he cried. "No! It's impossible!"

"She asked me to tell you. She could not bear to do so herself. She—and I too, Mr. Malloy—we both rely upon your—fine feeling to understand. And to go away."

"But I can't believe it! Why, only three days ago—"

"I know. But you must believe me. She—it's so hard to tell you—she doesn't wish to see you again."

"Please let me see her!"

"She doesn't want to see you. I am sure you will understand that it is best so."

"What has happened? What has made her change?"

"It is impossible to say. A—a change of heart.... But I beg you to accept this as—final—and to go!"

"Very well!" he said. "I'll go!"

She held out her hand to him.

"Mr. Malloy!" she said. "Can't all this be as if it had never happened?"

"I don't see how," he said. "I'm afraid I can't forget so easily."

"But—some day I hope you will marry happily and—"

He shook his head.

"You will!" she assured him. "You are too much of a man to let this really hurt you! If you cannot have—exactly what you want, you must—"

She stopped, in confusion, and suddenly, in some inexplicable way, he guessed her meaning. He was astounded.

"You don't mean—" he began. "... Edna?"

"Yes," she murmured.

"But—after I've deceived her so?"

"The only question is—if you—care for her?"

"I do! I always have! Not as I did for—Andrée.... But she's the finest and truest girl in the world.... I can't tell how unutterably ashamed I've been of the way I've behaved toward her—"

"Repair it!"

"Don't you see that I can't!"

"She doesn't know, does she?"

"No.... But she's suspected that—there's something wrong—"

"It's not too late. If you really care for her, if you're really sorry for what you've done—"

"I do care for her. Too much to make a—second best of her."

"Oh, stupid! Stupid!" she cried to herself. "What does it matter!"

He went on, in a horrified voice.

"You surely wouldn't recommend a marriage founded on a deception?"

A cynical thought occurred to her.

"They're all founded on deceptions," she reflected. "On lies that people believe about each other."

"I'm not recommending anything," she said, aloud. "I only want to say again that I'm very sorry for all this, Mr. Malloy."

He went away, down the little garden walk for the last time.

"She's not the high-minded woman I thought her!" he reflected. "She's—her ideas are absolutely—sordid."

And then he forgot her in his profound sorrow.

Claudine remained for a moment in the drawing-room.

"He'll go back to Edna," she said to herself. "I'm glad.... He'll do as well as anyone else. He's kind. And rather attractive.... She won't expect too much."

II

She was just falling asleep that night, after having seen Andrée comfortably settled. She was mortally weary, unable even to think. She had a light burning low, as was her reprehensible custom, and she had a book beside her, in case she could not sleep. But, in spite of her trouble, the murmur of the night wind soothed her, and the air blowing across her face. She had closed her eyes, and a blissful numbness was stealing over her, when she was startled by Andrée's voice.

"Mother!" she cried. "Mother!"

She was instantly wide awake. Andrée stood beside her, like a spectre in the dim light, in her night dress and her dark hair about her shoulders.

"I want Alfred!" she said. "Oh, Mother ...! I began to think—"

Claudine took her dressing-gown from the foot of the bed and laid it about her child's shoulders.

"I've been so wicked!" she went on. "It frightens me! I want Al back! I want to see his kind face.... He's so kind and so good! I want to go home to him! I want just him—and this baby. Please, please send for him!"

"I will, pet, as soon as it's morning!"

"I can't wait! I'm so unhappy! I want to hear his dear, kind voice!"

"Come in here and lie down beside me, darling. Talk to me!"

With that beloved head on her shoulder, Claudine grew calm and strong again. She would have listened to her all night. What did it matter if this were only a new caprice? It was a good one, a safe one.

She thought of her own life, of how her child had assuaged her bitterness and given her peace. She thought of the hopes she had relinquished—such little hopes compared with Andrée's inordinate ambitions, and she believed that all that was to happen again. Andrée would be saved, if she would love her child better than herself. And she believed that this would happen. She looked very earnestly into her face; it was imperious, even cruel, but it was the cruelty of blindness, of one who inflicts suffering without knowing what suffering is.

She didn't care in the least that Andrée's brilliant future was endangered. She didn't care how fettered and narrow her life might become. Better narrow and deep, she thought, than broad and shallow.

She listened quite unmoved to her child's tears and sobs. It didn't matter. She kissed her with a sublime sort of indifference. She had won; God had helped her, and she had won.

III

Alfred came, promptly, the next morning, and Andrée received him alone.

"Al," she said. "Can we make a new start?"

He didn't look at her. When Claudine had telephoned so urgently for him to come, he had expected something of this sort.

"I suppose we could make any number of them," he said. "The question is, would there be any use in it?"

"You said—"

"I know all that I said. I said you could be free whenever you wanted. And that implied the same thing for me, Andrée."

"I don't want to be free."

"Why don't you?"

"Because—I want—"

She held out her arms, her eyes filled with tears. But he did not move toward her.

"Al!" she cried. "Do please come here!"

"No," he said. "Let's not complicate the thing with—*that*. Just tell me what's changed you. I'm here to listen."

"Suppose—it was only that I'd found out I was wrong—and that I missed you, and wanted you back? Wouldn't that be enough? Haven't you missed me?"

In spite of himself he was touched.

"I won't pretend I haven't.... It was a bit of a shock to me, you know. I'd never expected anything like that. I thought that you—that we were so—close—nothing could come between us."

"Couldn't you forget it? Al, it's hard for me to—to beg like this! I can't say anything more. I only ask you if you're willing to start again."

That was a voice which he found it hard indeed to withstand, a face that moved him beyond measure. Yet he was passionately anxious that no new mistake should be made.

"But what guarantee would we have that we'd do any better?" he cried.

"I think—" she began. "I think it would be different—now."

"But why, Andrée? Do you see things differently? I mean—"

She had begun to cry a little.

"You see, Al ... there's going to be a baby...."

"What!" he cried. His face had turned quite pale. "What! My God! Really?"

"Very really!" she answered, with a faint smile.

He sprang up and caught her in his arms, in a sort of desperation.

"Oh, Andrée! I'm so sorry! My lovely, beautiful girl! I'm so sorry!"

"Don't!" she cried. "You make it worse! Be glad, can't you? I thought you would be. I thought everyone would be—simply beaming.... I wanted you to be!"

"I'm not!" he said, doggedly. "I love you too much!"

"*Do* you?" she said, triumphantly.

"Now you've got it out of me," he said. "I knew you would! Yes, I do love you—too much, I guess. I don't want anyone but you, ever."

"Oh, Al! Al! It's so heavenly to have you back again, and hear you again, and see you—with your dear old rumpled hair. There's no one like you!"

"I wish to God you didn't have this before you!" he said, sombrely.

"But I'm glad, Al!" she told him. "It's life!"

EPILOGUE

I

It struck Claudine with the force of a blow. She put down the book and the night wind at once fluttered over the pages, as if by command of nature trying to divert her. But she turned back to the place again, all her heart fixed on the words like the eyes of a frightened child fixed upon an approaching light; she did not all at once grasp the meaning, but the significance was coming to her, illuminating and dispelling a familiar dusk, revealing to her what had always been there, but what she had not seen.

She had been turning over the pages of an old copy of Browning's poems, given her by Lance years ago, because he had fancied that so small and delicate and pretty a creature must necessarily feed on poetry. As a matter of fact, she had never been poetic, not even very romantic; she had always had a love for indigestible ideas, which had, in the main, done her very little harm. She might read Nietzsche and Schopenhauer; she remained none the less the Claudine who could wander gay and happy in a garden.

And now suddenly stood up this robust dead poet to look into her soul and accuse her, to judge and condemn her. The thing had all the solemn horror of what her ancestors would have called the voice of an awakened conscience; it was the handwriting on the wall.

> The sin I impute to each frustrate ghost
> Is—the unlit lamp and the ungirt loin,

Though the end in sight was a vice, I say.

That was for her! That was an arrow for her heart.

She was quite alone in the house; Rose had gone out to a lodge meeting of the Lady Pioneers. Claudine was always glad to let her go; she was never so happy as when alone with her ghosts. When the stairs creaked, that was the stout figure of her mother in dull black silk, going about her benevolent household affairs; there was a rustle of paper; that was the boy Lance studying in his room upstairs; a faint tapping; that was her father emptying his pipe. The wind blowing across the garden brought back to her unblemished the old emotions, the sheltered security, that careless and formless hope that had filled her girlhood; she would forget, alone in her room, the reality she had found so bitter.

But to be a ghost among these other ghosts! That frightened her. She looked about the quiet lamp-lit room; in the bookcase her old books, on the walls her old pictures, on the bureau the photographs of her father and mother, and a pitiful little bottle of that Cherry Blossom perfume; only the old things; it was as if twenty years had been a dream. She was aware that she had tried to make them so, that she had tried with desperation not to live. Blasphemous effort, rewarded now by this numb anguish!

"A frustrate ghost!" she cried aloud, and her voice seemed to have no sound. She had a preposterous idea that she was invisible and inaudible, that there was nothing in this room but the memory of her. She was only her own dream. She sprang up to look in the mirror, and saw there a white face and wide eyes; an apparition.... The wind blowing on her was suddenly chill, like a cold breath.

"No, no!" she said: "Oh, no! I want to be alive!"

There was for once no solace for her in that dear garden; she closed the window and pulled down the blind, to shut away the dark and the troubling sounds; she sat down and clasped her trembling hands; she tried to see herself once more in the stream of life, let it be never so cold and violent. She thought of Andrée, nothing but pain in that thought. Poor young Andrée and her poor little baby! Poor Al! She thought of Edna, hiding under her tranquility an unforgettable humiliation, of Bertie, with his gallant despair; of Gilbert, unaccountably forlorn. There was a thin veil hung between her and these living, struggling creatures; she could see them but not reach them; she fancied them being swept past her and calling to her and needing her, while she looked on, standing apart.

"Oh, why haven't I done something? Why haven't I helped?" she demanded of her shrinking heart. And the inexorable response was "Begin now!"

But remorse came easier than effort. She passionately condemned herself. She saw herself an egoist; in her young days she had been gay and gracious because she had had what she wanted. And when that had been withdrawn from her, she had grown cold, aloof, finding peace in indifference. She thought of all she might have done, of the influence she might have exerted. Not that she believed herself stronger or wiser than these four adult human beings for whom she felt responsible; it was a mystic belief in the power of a woman and a mother. She was convinced that she could give more than was in her, more than she had; she loathed herself for not having done so. She believed, as was natural, that if she had tried she must have succeeded. She knew that in her garden everything grew only according to its type; she believed nevertheless that human creatures might be so warmed by her love, so nourished by her tears, that they would grow not according to any laws, but according to her own desires.

She felt that this was the turning point in her life; she had wasted twenty years, dreamed them away; only God knew how few or how many remained to her. She was making the most painful effort of her life; it was not a struggle, she wished it were; it was an attempt to struggle. The lamp must be lit, the loin girded; she must no longer pass among the living as a gentle phantom. She must help all these people who belonged to her; she must by her valour and devotion compensate for what they were denied; she must inspire and fortify. But what was to breathe life into her? Love— even such love as she had for Andrée—had not done it. She was not religious; she could not turn to prayer. And her philosophers had nothing at all to give her. She sat up almost all that night, trying to fan her shrinking and mutinous spirit into a blaze…. Her life should be service; she clung to that idea.

It was the inevitable moment, due to everyone whose work is finished, to women whose children have grown; it was a little death. But she did not recognize it as that; she felt it to be a spiritual re-birth. The world was empty and she was obliged to fill it with herself. And she was by no means large enough.

II

She telephoned to Gilbert in his office the next morning; she was so affable that he was upset. She should have been home long ago, anyhow, instead of staying down there alone on Staten Island in that peculiar way. He felt that she was trying to be ingratiating, and this of course aroused his hostility and distrust. Her quiet, clear voice reaching him in the midst of his morning mail caused him all the usual feelings of annoyance induced by any thought of home life. She asked him about his health, and he knew she didn't care; she even asked that supremely irritating question "How is business?" Well did he know why his family asked that.

Then, amazingly, she said:

"If you're not too tired, Gilbert, won't you come down here for dinner? The garden is so lovely."

"Suppose you come home," he said, surlily, but it was only an instinctive reaction; the bear hitting out with his paw.

"Do come," she said, pleasantly. "It would be nice to be by ourselves. And the garden—"

"Very well! Very well!" he said. "I'll come. I can't spend the morning at the telephone. I'll come, Claudine. Good-by."

Now this disturbed him. He was inclined to suspect, with reason, all advances made by his family, and yet he liked these advances. He felt fairly sure that his wife had some favour to ask, some feminine chicanery to execute, but he was like a king with his courtiers; he was grimly contemptuous of all this beguilement, but he relished the homage.

The idea of going back to that house on the hill to see Claudine stirred in him old and unpleasant memories. He felt himself no phantom; he was poignantly aware of the passing of twenty years and youth with them; he didn't feel that he had not tried, but that he had not succeeded. He had made money, just as he had intended, but the rewards of his activity had been unjustly withheld. He had the wrong sort of wife, the wrong sort of children, the wrong sort of life altogether. Still he would do the right thing, as he had always done. He stopped on his way to the ferry and bought Claudine a five-pound box of chocolates, the kinds she hated most and which he had bought for years and years, never being undeceived.

III

But long before he got there, all Claudine's plans had been upset. She had gone about all the morning, seriously intent upon her scheme to win back her husband. This, she felt, was the first step along her new road; once he was won back, she would make him into something different, as it was her womanly duty to do; she would take him to concerts and persuade him to read. She had that idea common to good and inexperienced women, of the fascination she might wield if she chose, an idea in no way related to vanity, but a conception necessary to existence. She had never yet consciously tried to be fascinating, but at the back of her mind had always been the thought of how powerful she might be, if she weren't so nice. She was obliged to believe this. If Gilbert, by analogy, had realized when he went out to lunch, that perhaps seven out of ten men that he passed could have knocked him flat on his back, he couldn't have endured life; he had to believe that he could hold his own, if he wanted. And she, too, must have her belief in her mystic power.

She had been sitting down to a delightful, solitary lunch; the dining-room with its shining waxed floor and well-polished mahogany furniture, the yellow roses in a great Delft bowl, the dim, cool peace all about her, filled her with serenity and courage. Certainly she would change Gilbert and everything else in her life; she intended to ask him to stop here with her for the rest of the summer; a real sacrifice, for it meant the end of this delicate and immaterial existence, and a hateful preoccupation with roasts and wines and laundry. Edna had gone to Easthampton with the Ryders, Bertie was away with Lance; Miss Dorothy could have the Brooklyn house to herself. This transplanting would make her work easier, but she realized that she would have to be notably charming in order to win his consent. She thought a good deal about what she should wear; she was engaged in this when Al came in. He was very hot and crumpled and cheerful.

"Oh ... Alfred!" she cried. "Andrée ...?"

"Fine!" he told her. "But I had a free afternoon—she had some friends there, and I thought I'd like to see *you*."

"There's nothing at all wrong?"

"Not a thing! Only—I don't know—I've been wanting to have a talk with you for a good while.... I know I talk too much, but just the same, it seems to me the best way to get anywhere."

"Sit down," she said, smiling. "I think you're very fortunate to be able to talk, Alfred. I can't think of anything nicer than to be able to express what you feel."

He did sit down opposite her, and at once assumed his serious, conversational look.

"It's a lot more than that," he said. "I have an idea that you can't really feel a thing until you do express it. That's the value of talking; not that it conveys your ideas to someone else, because generally it doesn't, but that it wakes up your own brain.... But this was going to be about Andrée.... There's something I want to get from you—something I can't get hold of."

"If you mean how best to get on with her—" she began, but he interrupted.

"No; it's not that. That's all a mistake—this 'getting on' with people. It means either humouring her, like a spoiled child, or trying to dominate her. Well, what I want is, to *let her alone*. And that's what I can't do. I'm always trying to make her see things my way."

"But you can't help doing that when you know you're right."

"I don't know; I only think. I'm only an experimenter. I may be wrong about lots of things. Anyway, she's experimenting, too, and she's altogether too fine to be bothered. I've spent the best part of my life shouting people down, and now it's hard to stop. It isn't that I've tried to cram my ideas down anyone's throat," he assured her, earnestly. "All I ever wanted to do was to start people thinking. I've always tried to keep hold of that idea that I was an experimenter, but I'm too darned sure. I'm—well, I'm not humble enough, d'you see? I interfere.... Now, that's what I've always admired so in you. That's what makes you so wonderful. You *don't* interfere."

"But—Alfred!" said the frustrate ghost, with something like a gasp.

"I wish you'd explain to me—give me some idea how you do it.... How your mind works," he went on. "I mean, how can you watch, the way you do, without interfering?"

Many reasons prevented her from telling him that she had very often tried to interfere, and had invariably failed. She was silent for some time, while he waited anxiously for her words.

"I'd been thinking, only last night, that I didn't help—interfere—nearly enough," she said, at last. She raised her eyes to his face with a look he had never seen before, a glance troubled and appealing; she was making a heroic struggle for candour with her reticent and uncandid soul. No other living creature had seemed to her so human, so impersonal, so secure, as this young man; she felt that she could say to him as much as her heart would ever permit her to utter. She quite forgot that he was waiting for wisdom from her; she grew pale with the intensity of her desire to hold communion with her kind, to hear the truth without entirely telling it.

"Alfred ..." she said. "It seemed to me—I'd wasted my life."

"But how?" he demanded.

"By not helping."

"Well ..." he said, honestly. "Of course there's a lot that needs doing in the world, and the people with money and leisure—"

"I don't mean *doing* anything," she said, with an impatient little frown. "I mean—influencing. I haven't tried to influence the people about me."

He uttered a mild oath of himself. It was startling, to say the least, that she should talk like this, as if she hadn't heard a word he had spoken— when he had been waiting for the secret of her non-intervention.

"I should have tried to help my children—to influence them," she went on, with increasing agitation. "I've stood aside—"

"But don't you see?" he cried. "That's what's so wonderful! That's the fine thing about you—you've let them alone. Even if you haven't accomplished much yourself, you've given other people a chance."

He was distressed to see tears in her eyes.

"My children aren't happy," she said.

"They're living," he said. "They're growing. They're learning their own lessons in their own way. If you'd done what you call influence them, it would only mean that they saw things through your eyes."

"I've accomplished nothing. I've only passed through life like—"

His glance fell on the Delft bowl.

"Like a flower," he said, thoughtfully. "You've just existed, in a very sweet, gentle way. I think that's a mighty fine thing.... I don't believe there are many people who have done so little harm."

He got up; he took her outstretched hand, and went off, without the sage advice he had come for, but consoled for lack of it by a variety of new ideas. And he left Claudine strangely assuaged.

IV

She went walking along, gravely inspecting her sweet peas, bending over them to inhale their perfume, to touch with a delicate finger their exquisite petals. They had done very well; she was proud of them. People passing along the street stopped to look at them in their incredible variety; a great bloom of colour against the high board fence, faint pink, pale yellow, lavender, rose, a strange, deep purple brown; they looked like little winged things, alighting for the moment on the fragile vines.

She came to the end of the row and turned the corner to the bed where the verbenas stood, and beside them a turbulent little sea of petunias, closely massed. The smell of the moist earth, of the grass freshly cut, of all the little flowers she had planted and tended, came to her on a tiny breeze, and a limitless joy filled her. Never before in her life had she felt so happy, so tranquil, so strong. Her glance embraced the smooth lawn stretching to the gravel drive that encircled the house, and the flower beds against the walls, filled with nasturtiums, thickly bordered with sweet alyssum, drenched in the sun, hot, fragrant, valiant little things. She was one with all of this, with no more purpose than they had.

Alfred's words had filled her with actual bliss. She might be a ghost, but she was no more frustrate than that sweet pea that had swung loose from the string upon which it should have climbed, and swayed in the breeze, holding by nothing. She was an unlit lamp, but by the blaze of the sun, who needed her little flame? The world wanted nothing from her, and she had nothing to give. The turmoil of the night before was gone, her little effort ended.

She saw Gilbert coming up the hill; he looked hot and cross, with his straw hat pushed back on his head, and the box of chocolates under his arm. But now his crossness didn't seem to her alien and alarming; he was nothing but Gilbert, a familiar mystery. There was no need to understand him, no need for any excessive interest in him. She wasn't required to explain herself to him, or him to herself. She believed that she could never again be repelled by any strangeness in him, or disturbed by what he did. Her soul felt relieved of all its burdens, light, almost gay. He was one person, and she was another; they couldn't gravely affect each other, they were not inter-dependent; they were allied, but it was an alliance only for their interest, not to hurt or to hamper them. She went out to meet him, with a friendly smile she led him up on the veranda and left him there while she made an artful mint julep. Her friendliness didn't depend upon his being friendly; it was her own independent emotion. But it provoked an instant response from him.

"What's come over you?" he asked, curiously. "You haven't been like this for I don't know how long."

"Perhaps it's this dear garden," she answered, vaguely.

"You'd better stay in it, then," he said, with a sulky smile. "It agrees with you."

"That's what I'd like to do. Won't you come down here for the rest of the summer, Gilbert? It's very cool and quiet."

"I might," he answered, to her surprise.

The sun had gone down and a cheerful dusk had fallen, lively with the chirping of insects. They talked carelessly, of the small things that interested them; he too grew affable, almost tranquil. Astonishing how little he wanted! Not to be charmed, not to be comprehended, only to be accepted, casually and kindly, just as he was.

An absurd idea came to her of their two souls, sitting side by side, in rocking chairs, absorbed in the contemplation of life; she saw these souls as pliable white things, his half-melted candles, with great black eyes. It made her laugh aloud.

"What's the joke?" asked Gilbert.

"Only the silliest sort of fancy," she said, in a comfortable tone that didn't irritate him. He didn't ask again, because he didn't care. His desire had been always to be understood, never to understand others. And any woman who could sit in the dusk by him while he smoked, who talked so little, who made a julep like that, undoubtedly understood him. He was content.

THE END

Selected Stories

by Elisabeth Sanxay Holding

Hanging's Too Good for Him

He first emerged from obscurity at his father's funeral. He was the only son and the heir to everything, and therefore, of course, the center of interest; but immediately and forever he destroyed all the tepid sympathy and good will of the assembled relatives by his curious air of immense carelessness, his foppish nonchalance.

He hadn't even the decency to wear a dark suit, they observed. He was dressed in light gray, evidently quite new, and he kept his hands in his pockets. It never occurred to any of them that his indifference might be a clumsy effort to conceal an immeasurable embarrassment. Neither did any one else remember what he remembered—that his father had detested any sort of formal mourning. And it was Tommy's destiny always to do a thing in the wrong way, always to antagonize, invariably to blunder.

It was not regret for the loss of his father, or any great regard for his opinions, that caused Tommy to remember and to respect his wishes. It was nothing more than a naïve and kindly sentimentality. His father had been a horrible bully to him, the great bogey of his childhood. His mother had died when he was very little, and he had been sent off to boarding school at once.

It seemed to the family that Tommy had always been at school, winter and summer. Once in a great while he had emerged at some cousin's Christmas party, a rather silly blond boy in military uniform, always spoken of as "poor little Tommy Ellinger." There were no family rumors or traditions about him, no reports of his behavior at school.

Now, however, that he had definitely come to life, it was necessary for the family to decide upon him, and they decided unfavorably. He got, then and there, the name of being "defiant" and "conceited."

His father's elder brother was to be his guardian until he was twenty-one—a task which disgusted and appalled Uncle James. He was an old bachelor lawyer, living in a hotel. Naturally his first thought for Tommy was college, which would remove the boy for all his minority, and even longer; but Tommy fought desperately against that. His hatred for books, for herding with other young males, for all the bullying and chaffing which terrified his awkward innocence, for the competition which dazed his lumbering mind, made him unusually resolute. Business, too, he summarily repudiated.

"Then what do you intend to do?" his uncle demanded, with false patience.

"Well," said Tommy desperately, "why couldn't I be a lawyer, like you?"

His uncle looked at him with a grim smile, and answered nothing. The subject was dropped for the time being, and Tommy went to live at his uncle's hotel, to make up his mind about his very important future. He lived a wretched sort of life, forever hanging about the lobby, or sitting through vaudeville shows and musical comedies. He ate breakfast with his exasperated old uncle every morning, and dinner almost every evening.

There was something peculiarly and intolerably irritating about Tommy—some quality which, in spite of his invariable good temper and his ingratiating manners, infuriated his uncle. A perfect young ass, the old lawyer called him.

Why was it that the qualities which would have been so endearing in a girl of eighteen were so maddening in Tommy? Why was he, with his youth, his boundless good will, his plaintive innocence, really nothing on earth but a young ass?

He was a great lanky boy with a naïve, good-humored face and a preposterous foppish air, a man-of-the-world air; wearing clothes ostentatiously correct and an amazing eyeglass with a broad black ribbon. He imagined that he looked like a foreign diplomat, while at the bottom of his heart he was quite conscious of being and looking a puppy. He swaggered, but without any self-assurance.

He devoted great thought to his clothes, and he could not refrain from mentioning his sartorial inventions and improvements to his uncle.

"What do you think of the cut of this coat?" he would ask. "Do you notice this shoulder? Rather good, eh?"

"Beautiful!" his uncle would say. "I never saw such grace and elegance—a regular Beau Brummel! You're fascinating. There's nothing that interests me like the cut of your coats!"

Then Tommy would open the evening paper and laugh loudly and ostentatiously at something in it, to show how undisturbed he was.

"Why don't you go out?" the old gentleman used to ask, often and often, when, their dinner finished, they went up together in the lift to the little sitting room they shared. "What's the matter with you, Thomas? A boy of your age, sitting at home here with an old fellow like me, night after night! Why don't you go out somewhere and enjoy yourself? Haven't you any friends?"

Well, he hadn't. All the boys he had known and liked in the military academy up the Hudson had come from the farthest ends of the country—from Texas, from California, from Maine. He had never been particularly popular, anyhow, and he was too shy and too ridiculous to make friends now.

His uncle attached great importance to this, for he himself had scores of friends. He wished Tommy to be a sort of creature the like of which is no longer to be found—the traditional, old-fashioned beau, the arbiter of elegance, welcomed everywhere, affable, agreeable, but forever unattached, the society man of a past generation. He supplied the boy with spending money, and introduced him to a few charming young married women and a great many old bachelors.

"Now go ahead!" he told him. "Make yourself popular! Make yourself liked! A young man of your age, of good family, with a little money in your pockets, with good prospects!"

He was invited to one or two sedate houses, for his uncle's sake, but nothing came of it. The society life toward which his uncle urged him forever eluded him. In fact, he had no life of any sort. He was only waiting, hanging about in innocent and dreary idleness, unable to believe that life should so cheat him of every joy, every excitement.

It was spring when Tommy's father died and he left the military academy. He spent a horrible summer with his uncle, in a hotel in town, or at other similar hotels in the mountains, on the coast, anywhere and everywhere. Then came a still worse winter, during which the old gentleman's exasperation rose to a fury.

They would go now and then to a musical comedy of the liveliest sort, this being the Uncle James's idea of what the boy ought to like. When the old man saw him sitting there not liking it, when he saw him not caring for or comprehending wines, a barbarian as to food, absolutely indifferent to the arts, and hopeless in regard to sport, he became almost homicidal.

"Go away!" he shouted at him. "Go and spend this summer by yourself! I won't waste the money on taking you to a decent place. Go on a farm! Go to some cheap, miserable, damnable little country boarding house, where you can sit and gape all day, like the booby you are!"

Tommy felt that it would be paradise now to get away from his uncle, no matter where. The idea of going off alone, unbullied, unthwarted, quite dazzled him. He was only too ready to go anywhere his uncle suggested.

So Uncle James answered several newspaper advertisements, and at last found a place which he felt would be suitable. He wrote and made all arrangements, and then gave Tommy his directions, money that was to last him for a month, and the following advice:

"Don't make a fool of yourself about any of the girls there. Remember, you haven't a penny for the next three years except what I choose to allow you; and if you get yourself mixed up, or compromised, I won't help you. I won't recognize any responsibility of that sort!"

Tommy turned scarlet.

"Not in my line, Uncle James!" he replied, with extreme jauntiness. And off he went.

II

His uncle almost forgot about Tommy for some time. He had a letter from the boy every week—a stupid, schoolboy letter which he hardly bothered to read. "The weather had been very hot. I guess you are glad not to be here, aren't you? There is a lot of hay fever around now. It is certainly a lucky thing that you didn't come"—and that sort of thing.

Then, while Uncle James was enjoying his little breakfast at the corner table in the grill room, which he had occupied for years and years, just as he was about to taste that invariable bowl of oatmeal with cream and powdered sugar, his eye was caught by a headline on the front page of his paper. He dropped his spoon on the floor.

FATHER SHOOTS GIRL'S BETRAYER—
TRAGEDY NARROWLY AVERTED AT THE
HOTEL TRESSILLON—SON OF THE
LATE THOMAS ELLINGER WOUNDED

He stared and stared at the thing. The paper crackled in his trembling hands, the letters swam before his eyes. Nonsense! "Son of the late Thomas Ellinger"—must be a mistake!

He read the story with a furious sort of incredulity. It was a nasty story of a young city man going out to a little country town for a vacation, boarding in the house of a decent farmer, and running off one night with the poor little sixteen-year-old daughter. He had taken her to a disreputable hotel and registered as man and wife, which they weren't. And the decent farmer, the outraged, the desperate father, had tracked them, and, standing in the doorway of the crowded and noisy restaurant, had fired two shots at the girl's betrayer—at Tommy! At the boy who a few months ago had been sitting opposite Uncle James at this very table!

"No! Nonsense!" he cried, crumpling up the paper and throwing it under the table. "One of those beastly newspaper stories! Damned lies, all of them!"

He went up to his room, got his hat and stick, and hurried out, furtive, terrified, afraid that every one was pointing him out as the uncle of that fellow. He wanted to telephone, where he would not be seen or heard, somewhere outside of his hotel. He went into a booth in a cigar store, and called for the Hotel Tressillon.

"Mr. Ellinger," he demanded.

In a moment he heard that familiar young voice, with its exaggerated accent. "This is Mr. Ellinger speaking."

"Thomas!" cried the old gentleman.

The boy gave a sort of gasp. Then, with his unfailing genius for doing the wrong thing, he assumed an airy and offhand tone.

"Hello, Uncle James!" he said jauntily. "I didn't know that you were back in town again."

"See here!" shouted the old gentleman, in a tremendous voice. "Is it true—this abominable thing I saw in the papers? Is it *you?*"

"Yes," replied Tommy.

"Yes?" repeated his uncle's voice, incredulous. "Yes? *You* did a thing like that? Good God! Explain yourself, Thomas!"

"I can't!" said Tommy.

There was a brief silence.

"You—you young cur!" The old man's voice was trembling. "Don't ever come near me again. Don't let me see you. I'd like to shoot you! You miserable, dastardly cur! You've disgraced the whole family. You've disgraced your father's name. I'd like to see you hanged—only hanging's too good for you!"

III

Tommy's face was scarlet, as if he had been struck. He went across the room, as far as he could get from the telephone, sat down, tried to smoke a cigarette, and tried to smile carelessly. He had to give it up. He hid his hot face in his arms, and sat there, amazed, confounded, utterly overwhelmed, at his own deed and at the awful consequences of it.

His uncle's voice he recognized as the voice of the world in general. That was how he was to be regarded in the future—a cad, a cur, hanging too good for him. A pariah—he who so valued the good opinion of others! It was the sort of thing one couldn't live down, ever. His life was blasted at its very beginning.

He knew that he could never justify himself. There were the facts in the newspapers, and he couldn't deny any of them. How to explain, even try to explain, what lay behind them? He himself didn't comprehend it. He was more surprised, more shocked, than any one else could possibly have been.

He looked at his wrist watch, which lay on the table because it couldn't be put on over his bandaged wrist, and saw with dismay that it was only ten o'clock in the morning. The thought of the hours he would have to pass, shut up there alone, overwhelmed him. He was ashamed to go out, even into the corridor. He had already had to face a doctor and the waiter who had brought up his breakfast, and his raw sensibilities had made each of these encounters an ordeal.

He imagined a quite preposterous hostility. He was already an outcast, he was deserted, no one would come or telephone; he had nothing whatever to do now, or in the future. He looked around the ugly little hotel bedroom, and he felt that he was in prison, judged and convicted by his fellow men, and already banished from them.

Nothing to do, but plenty to think of, to recollect, and to examine. He leaned back in his chair, staring at the ceiling, and tried his honest best to retrace all the steps of the affair and to discover the true measure of his guilt.

He remembered every minute detail. He saw himself getting on the train at the Grand Central, saw himself in the train reading magazines, hoping that the other passengers admired his clothes and his luggage, and fearing that they didn't. He remembered the dust and the heat and the tedium.

It was late afternoon when he reached Millersburg, and he was gratified to see from the window that a fair proportion of the population was assembled to see the New York train arrive. He was confident that he was causing more or less of a sensation as he descended, with his irreproachable tweed suit, his imposing eyeglass, and the latest thing in traveling bags.

He walked leisurely over to a solitary old carriage, climbed in, and directed the driver to take him to Mr. Van Brink's. Then he leaned back carelessly, prepared to review the landscape, when the jolting old vehicle stopped. They were not yet out of sight of the station, from whence the natives were still watching his progress.

"Well, what's wrong?" he asked the old driver. "Horse given out already?"

"Here ye be!" the driver answered dryly. "Here's Van Brink's!"

Tommy knew very well that he was being laughed at by the loungers at the station, as well as by the old driver, and he liked it no better than any one else would have liked it; but he was a genuinely good-natured sort of devil, and he grinned, in spite of a very real chagrin at so unimposing an arrival.

Having paid the driver lavishly, he walked along the little garden path before him, and up some steps to a little veranda. The door opened at once, and a hand reached for his bag.

"Come right in!" entreated a gentle young voice. "This way, please!"

The little house was cool and very dark, every shade pulled down, every shutter closed. Tommy followed the white dress that was ascending the stairs, and was presently led into a dim, breezy room, smelling of verbena.

The white dress flitted over to the window and threw open the shutters.

"There!" she said, looking back over her shoulder and smiling.

That smile! Tommy looked at her, enchanted.

You could see that she was very young, although her figure was almost matronly—short, full, agreeably rounded. She had calm, clear gray eyes, fair hair neatly arranged, a rather pale, chubby face with blunt features, pretty enough; but what was she but a nice, ordinary little country girl in a calico dress? What was there, or could there be, in such a young person to arouse the faintest interest in a man of the world like Tommy?

Ah, it was something to which far more sophisticated souls than his must have succumbed—a lure so flamboyant, a charm so candidly voluptuous!

She was serenely aware of her carnal fascinations. She was ignorant, but not without a certain experience, and she had a fatal sort of instinct. She knew her power, and knew how to employ it.

She looked at Tommy with complete self-possession. She was not in any way awed by his clothes, his eyeglass, or his magnificent air. Indeed, it was he who grew red and confused before the calm gaze of the girl in the calico dress.

"Is there anything you'd like to have, Mr. Ellinger?" she asked politely. "There's towels—"

"No, not at all!" protested Tommy, in his best manner. "Thanks awfully, but there's nothing."

The little thing in the white dress went out.

Tommy unpacked his bag, and then, restless and hungry, wandered about the room, looked out of the window, yawned, whistled, brushed his hair again, wondered what was expected of him. At last a knock at the door, and the gentle young voice said:

"Supper's ready, Mr. Ellinger!"

She was waiting to show him the way to the dining room. She behaved, in fact, like a very nice little hostess, properly concerned with his comfort. He liked that, of course, and he liked the supper, too. It was a novel sort of meal to Tommy—cold meat, fried potatoes, little glass dishes of preserves and pickles, cakes, pies, strawberries, and coffee, all on the table together.

Old Van Brink and his wife made no impression on him at all. They were what he had expected—what they ought to be. He talked to them in his best manner, genial, very much at ease. He was ingenuously sure that they were kind and honest people, and that they admired him. All his interest centered on the calm little thing across the table.

Supper over, Van Brink retired to a rocking-chair with the newspaper, and his wife began to carry the dishes into the kitchen. The little thing looked at Tommy.

"Would you like to take a little walk?" she asked. "'Most every one does—down to the village."

"Charmed!" he assured her, with his inane magnificence. "Will you wait till I get my stick?"

So they set off together down the dark, tree-bordered street. It was cool and very quiet, with a wistful little breeze stirring in the leaves.

"Peaceful, isn't it?" said Tommy contentedly.

"Oh, yes! I hope it will do you good," the little thing answered benevolently.

Thanks, said Tommy, there wasn't much wrong with him he needed a rest, that was all.

"Well, you'll get it, here!" said she, with a deep sigh.

"Why? Not much excitement?"

"Oh, you can't imagine! Year after year!"

He was sorry for her.

"But you'll be getting married one of these days," he assured her gallantly.

"There's no one here to marry," she said.

They had come into the brightly lighted Main Street, and Tommy became somewhat distrait. He was wondering what sort of impression he was producing on the natives. They were observing him. He saw girls turn to stare after him, and a group of youths on a corner snickered as he passed.

All this pleased him. He swung his stick and strolled on with exquisite indifference. The little thing, he fancied, must be admiring him tremendously.

But she wasn't. He was undoubtedly causing a sensation, this lofty stranger from the city with his remarkable clothes; but his smooth face was too innocent, his manner, for all its swagger, too ridiculously boyish. He was more or less stupid to this maiden accustomed to the loutish gallantries of the corner loafer, to facile caresses and furtive advances. He was insipid— "slow," she called him to herself; but of course he could be taught.

Coming to Egbert's Drug Store, they went in, at Tommy's suggestion, and each of them had a glass of soda. She did feel a certain triumph then, at his manners and his handful of change.

It was dark when they returned to the house.

"Would you like to sit on the porch?" she asked. "All right! Let's bring the hammock around."

So they brought the hammock from the little back garden and slung it on the veranda. They were hidden from the street by a tangle of honeysuckle. The window behind them was unlighted, and there wasn't a sound from the house. They might have been alone in the universe. No one disturbed them, no one came into sight. There they sat, in the sweet-scented dark, Tommy on the railing, the little white figure swaying in the hammock.

"Don't you want to smoke?" she asked.

"Thanks!" he answered. "Yes, I will, if you don't mind."

"If it's cigarettes, I'd like to have one, please."

He was surprised and rather offended, because this wasn't according to his idea of her.

"Sure it won't make you sick?" he asked.

"Oh, no!" she answered pleasantly. "We used to smoke at boarding school, you know."

He proffered a lighted match, and in its glare he caught a glimpse of her face, quietly smiling. Again he was fascinated, suddenly, unexpectedly.

They smoked for some time in silence. Tommy could see her curled up in the hammock, swinging just a little. All of a sudden she sighed.

"Oh, dear!"

"What is it?"

"Nothing much. For goodness' sake, Mr. Ellinger, how old are you?"

He tried to laugh in an amused way, but he was chagrined and puzzled by her tone.

"Why do you want to know?" he inquired.

"Never mind, if you'd rather not say."

"I've no objection to telling you, my—my dear young lady," he answered, nettled. "I'm—eighteen."

"Are you? I'm only sixteen. We're only kids, aren't we?"

He didn't like that. Moreover, he perceived something sinister beneath the words.

"I suppose so," he assented, in a tone of paternal indulgence.

"Call me 'Esther,'" said she. "Don't let's be silly! What's *your* name?"

He hesitated, and finally decided upon "Tom"; but she, like every one else, saw the inevitability of "Tommy."

There was a long silence. Then out of the dark came her calm little voice.

"Tommy," she said, "you're a funny boy!"

"Am I?" he said, with an uneasy laugh.

The situation was quite out of hand now. He didn't know what was expected of him as a man of the world. He did know, though, that he was failing.

"Tommy," said she, again, "come and sit here, beside me."

With a quite artificial alacrity he jumped up, went over to her, and sat down in the hammock, close to her. He called himself a fool, an imbecile, a contemptible ass.

"I ought to kiss her," he said to himself, "or put my arm around her, or at least hold her hand!"

But he couldn't. He couldn't even talk to her. He wanted, above everything else in the world, to run away. He was not flattered or in any way stirred or excited—only miserably ill at ease and instinctively alarmed. He dared not move, even to turn his head.

At last Esther got up with a sigh.

"Good night, Tommy," she said. "I hope you'll sleep well!"

"Thanks," he answered, feeling utterly foolish and miserable.

IV

He did not sleep well. He lay in bed, his hands clasped under his head, looking out at the summer sky.

"She's a queer girl," he thought, with a sort of resentment. "She's bold—runs after a fellow; and yet you can see she doesn't care two straws for him."

In long imaginary conversations with Esther he regained his lost advantage. He was affable but cool—very cool. He could see her round little face quite clearly before him, her serene eyes, her neat fair hair.

He awoke after his restless night to a hot, still morning. He could not find a bath tub. Dressing reluctantly, unrefreshed and a bit irritable, he went downstairs. It was a few minutes after eight by his watch—a very decent, early hour, he thought; but, looking into the dining room, he saw only one place laid on the long table.

Mrs. Van Brink hurried in from the kitchen, limp, hot, and painfully anxious.

"Set down to the table, Mr. Ellinger," she cried in her shrill voice. "I'll bring your breakfast right off. We're all done. You won't have to wait more'n a minute."

He ate alone, a little resentful that Esther didn't appear. Then he went out on the porch. No one there—the shady street was quiet and empty. He went around the house to the sun-baked little yard at the back, where he discovered Mrs. Van Brink hanging dish towels on a line in terrible haste. Her face became positively convulsed with worry at the sight of his listlessness.

"Now, then!" she cried. "You don't know what to do with yourself, I'll be bound! And I haven't got a minute to spare, with the dinner I have to get up for Mr. Van Brink at noon. His farm's four miles off, you know."

She stared at him, frowning, until an inspiration came.

"Maybe you'd enjoy to play on the harmonium," she suggested. "Esther's got some real sweet music."

Tommy did not know what a harmonium was; but she showed him a queer little organ in the parlor, and he sat before it all the rest of that intolerable morning, picking out tunes and experimenting with the stops.

At noon old Van Brink came driving home in his buggy, and his hot and anxious wife began hurrying back and forth between the kitchen and the dining room, bringing in an enormous hot dinner. The farmer had nothing to say to Tommy. He sat there with his napkin tucked in his collar, consuming one dish after the other as fast as his wife brought them in, absorbed and ravenous, like a feeding animal. Now and again Tommy caught the old man's small blue eyes surveying him with an expression which he could not comprehend, but which he didn't like.

Van Brink drove off directly after eating, and his wife withdrew to the kitchen again. With growing resentment, Tommy seized his hat and went out, followed the route of the night before, and reached the village. Entering the only hotel, the Gilbert House, he ordered a cocktail and bought a newspaper; but the drink was shockingly bad, and he couldn't endure the stale dullness of the place long enough to read the paper there.

He had never before in his life suffered from such boredom. He went back to the house, determined to write at once to his uncle and say he couldn't stand it any longer.

And there, rocking on the porch and enjoying the cool of the afternoon, sat Esther.

"Hello!" she said cheerfully.

"Good afternoon," he replied stiffly.

"Well! What makes you look so cross?"

"I've had a rotten day."

"I'm sorry; but it wasn't my fault, was it? You needn't be cross at me."

"It was your fault, in a way. You might have told me what there is to do in this place."

"Oh, but there isn't anything! I'll take you for a walk after supper, if you want."

So after supper, when Mrs. Van Brink had gone back to the kitchen, and her husband, in stocking feet, sat reading his newspaper, Esther and Tommy set out again.

"Shall we go right out in the country?" Esther asked him. "Or would you rather go through the village and see some of the fine houses?"

Tommy preferred the country.

They turned north, followed the dark and quiet street past all the little houses, and into a road soft with dust, under the black shadow of great trees, with a sweet breeze blowing from the meadows.

"One day's enough for you," said Esther. "How would you like to spend *years* here?"

"By Jove! How do you stand it?"

"Well, I won't, any longer than I can help!"

They were going uphill steadily. The fields were left behind, and the pine forest was closing in on them, dark and fragrant.

"This is my favorite walk," said Esther. "I often come here by myself."

"Rather lonely, isn't it?"

"I'm never lonely."

Again that vague alarm came over the boy. He felt defenseless, lost. He dreaded to go farther; but, chattering pleasantly, Esther went on and on, and he had to answer and to follow.

The road grew rougher, and his little comrade stumbled often.

"Hadn't we better turn back?" suggested Tommy. "You'll be tired."

"Oh, no! I don't call *this* far!"

"And it's getting late. Your mother and father—"

She laughed.

"You needn't worry about them! Let's sit down and rest a few minutes, if you like."

There was a great flat rock a little way up the bank from the roadway. Sitting there, they could catch a glimpse of an enormous orange-colored moon through the branches.

"It's nice, isn't it?" said Esther. "And doesn't my ring look pretty in the moonlight?"

She held up a plump little hand for him to see.

"Are you engaged?" he asked, for even he knew that the question was expected of him.

"Yes—to the young man you saw last night in the drug store. It's a secret, though; mommer and popper don't know."

"I hope you'll be happy," said Tommy, after a pause.

"I don't see how I can be," she answered plaintively. "I don't really like him; but oh, dear, what else can I do? Why, I've only seen one real *refined* man in all my life. He was a traveling salesman. He wanted to marry me and go and live in New York; but popper wouldn't let me. He said I was too young."

"Well, you know, you are, rather. You don't want to be hasty, my dear young lady!"

She sighed.

"I don't know why I'm telling you all this; but I'm so unhappy!"

He felt very sympathetic, but could think of nothing to say.

"I'm going to take off this ring now, while I'm with you," Esther went on. "I want to forget all about Will for a while." She slipped her warm little hand into his. "Oh, Tommy!" she said coaxingly. "Be nice, won't you?"

The light of the moon shone clearly on her pretty upturned face, her white throat. He stared and stared at her. She leaned back, more and more, until her head was resting on his breast and her smooth hair brushed his lips.

The first wave of some immense and terrible emotion, something he had never before experienced, came rushing over him. He clenched his hands, struggling against a fierce desire to push her away.

"What are you doing to me?" he wanted to shout. "What's happening to me? Go away! Get out!"

But she did not stir. She rested against him, contented as a kitten, soft, gentle, and still. Little by little his mood changed, his panic was allayed, and he bent over and kissed her. Then he wanted never to let her go again. He kissed her violently, time after time. He couldn't stop.

A sort of madness possessed him. A terror greater than ever assailed him—a terror of himself. He knew he wasn't to be trusted. He put her aside brusquely and got up.

"Come on!" he said. "It's late. Let's go back!"

V

He sat at the open window of his room that night, oppressed by guilt and dread.

"I shouldn't have kissed her," he said to himself. "Now she'll think I'm in love with her."

He knew well enough that he was not. He disliked her—almost loathed her; she was so soft and clinging, so irresistible and so inferior. He didn't want to see her again.

He hadn't yet been able to devise a suitable attitude when he met her the next morning. Seeing her so perfectly unmoved helped him, and they sat down to breakfast in friendly accord.

"It's another hot day," she said. "Mommer thought maybe you'd enjoy a picnic."

"A picnic—just you and me?" he asked suspiciously.

She nodded, and waited for his reply, watching his face with candid eyes. He grew red and hot.

"Very nice idea," he said loftily.

He was racking his brains for some means of avoiding the excursion.

"Not if I know it!" he said to himself. "She won't get me alone again!"

But his reflection in a distant mirror caught his eye. What? Here he was, six feet tall, dressed in absolutely the latest fashion, a thorough man of the world, and yet uneasy in the presence of this sixteen-year-old country girl! "Dumpy," he called her—stolid, ignorant, rustic, in a cheap cotton frock.

His good humor came back. He smiled down upon her kindly, all alarm gone. Let her make love to him if she liked—there was no harm in it.

They started directly after breakfast, walked mile after mile through the fields in the full glare of the hot August sun, up stony hills, through bramble-lined woodland paths, until Tommy, carrying the big lunch basket and a walking stick, and wearing a rather heavy Norfolk jacket—the only correct thing for picnics—was dazed and tired. Not Esther, though; she was as fresh and cheerful as ever.

In the course of time they reached the place predestined by her for lunching—a little clearing on the slope of the pine-covered mountain, a sort of sunny nest in the forest, where a brook ran by, rapid and cool.

When he had at last satisfied his appetite—a strangely hearty and indiscriminate one for such a man of the world—Tommy lay back against a sun-warmed stone, smoking a cigarette and looking up at the bright sky. It was nice to have Esther there, he admitted to himself. It was nice to see her, contented and blessedly quiet, sitting beside him.

He turned his head to see her better. What a round, pretty, white throat she had! And her lashes were almost dark against her cheeks. He was annoyed by a sudden great longing to kiss her again. He tried to put the thought out of his mind—tried desperately; but in some inexplicable way, even as she sat there with her eyes closed and her little face so tranquil, she conveyed the fact to him that she was waiting to be kissed.

He did it, with a violence surprising to them both. She struggled half-heartedly, then settled down, close to his side, with his arm about her, and said no more. He kissed her again and again, stroked her hair, looked at her in delight. Dear, gentle, ardent little soul! Truly it was an afternoon on Olympus!

Tommy was done for now. She had awakened his innocent, primitive manhood, had aroused in him a feeling which he was too immature to appraise. He believed that he was, that he must be, in love with her. How otherwise explain his joy in kissing her, his immeasurable admiration for her charms?

"By Jove!" he said to himself. "I'm *in love!*"

He said it with amazement, with pride, with profound distress, because his passion tormented him. He was ashamed of it. He knew very well that it was not spontaneous; Esther had forced its growth. He had not wooed and won her; he had been captured in a most obvious way. He was a slave, and he knew and resented it.

Not that Esther was at all a difficult lady to serve. She had no whims, no caprices. She was neither jealous nor exacting. Indeed, she required nothing at all of Tommy. She let him alone. She was very affectionate, whenever he was; but if he were moody or anxious, she was peacefully silent.

There was always an air of content about her. She might have been the personified ideal of the man of forty—the woman who is always responsive, and yet who exacts nothing. Very, very different from the ideal of generous eighteen!

Precious little joy did poor Tommy find in this his first love. He was perplexed and confused; he couldn't imagine any sort of end to it. He couldn't contemplate marrying Esther, and the idea of any other sort of arrangement never occurred to him. In his eyes she was simply a respectable young girl, under her father's roof, not good enough, or not suitable, to be the wife of a man of the world, but far too good to be thought of in any improper way.

He didn't even know what he wanted—whether he wanted to leave her, or whether he couldn't live without her. He was weary beyond measure, those hot and sleepless August nights.

VI

At last, one evening, there came a sort of crisis. It was a sultry, rainy night, and they were in the little parlor, bored and constrained by the presence of old Van Brink in the next room, with the door open. Esther had been playing hymn tunes on the harmonium, and Tommy had been watching her, feverishly impatient to kiss her. She had stopped playing, and they sat in silence, listening to the squeak of the old man's rocking-chair and the rustle of his newspaper.

The room irritated Tommy by its amazing tastelessness. Even Esther looked different in it, he thought. Outside, under the summer sky, alone with him, she was a goddess. In here, what was she more than the plump, phlegmatic Esther Van Brink?

A door opened, and Mrs. Van Brink came in to her husband, her work in the kitchen finished until the next sunrise. She looked exhausted. It occurred to Tommy, not for the first time, that Esther was not a remarkably kind daughter. He had never yet seen her do any sort of work for her mother.

Immediately, with artless tact, Mrs. Van Brink closed the door. Tommy sprang up and caught Esther in his arms.

"My!" she cried, laughing. "Aren't you in a hurry, though?"

Tommy reddened, painfully aware of his disadvantage.

"I don't know what you'll do to-morrow evening," Esther went on. "Will Egbert's coming to see me."

Tommy could scarcely grasp the idea. An evening without Esther! Another man!

He was silent for some time. He realized then that he would rather marry Esther than lose her, than be supplanted by any Will Egbert.

"Look here, Esther!" he said at last. "I know I haven't any right to complain. I'm not—anything to you; but I'd like you to know something. Before I came here, my uncle—"

He paused so long that Esther frowned.

"Yes?" she said. "What about your uncle, Tommy?"

"He warned me—told me I couldn't get engaged, or anything of that sort. You understand, don't you, Esther? You see, I haven't any income. I depend on him, and I *know*, very well, that he'd never consent to—to anything."

She didn't answer.

"I've thought it over a great deal," he went on; "but I don't know what to do exactly."

To his chagrin and surprise, Esther got up and, going back to the harmonium, began to play loud, triumphant hymns. He could not guess her mood. He was afraid he had offended her; and with that a shade of the old magnificence returned.

"Esther darling, you're not angry, are you?" he asked.

"Oh, no," she replied cheerfully; "but I want to think. Let's sing."

She had a book of "College Songs," ugly and tasteless, like everything else in her life, and they sang them, one after the other, until bedtime. In the next room the mother and father listened, proud and pleased.

"Hark to sis!" said old Van Brink. "Sings and plays pretty good, hey, mother?"

"My, yes! It's real sweet!"

"I'll bet you that young man don't see many girls like sis, city or country, hey, mother? He's no call to turn up his nose at our gal, hey?"

"He don't," she answered thoughtfully.

The next morning, at breakfast, as soon as they were alone for a minute, Esther whispered:

"Tommy, I've got a plan! Let's go out on the porch," she suggested aloud, as her mother came in to clear the table.

"Well!" said Tommy, when they were alone again.

"Well!" she repeated. "Come on—sit down and listen. I want you to take me to the city to see your uncle."

"No!" cried Tommy, startled. "No, my dear girl! That wouldn't do at all!"

"It would! I'll be so nice he'll *have* to like me. I thought and thought about it last night. *Please* do, Tommy!"

"But, my dear child, don't you see that you couldn't go off with me that way? You'd—you'd compromise yourself!"

"Not if we got married right away."

"But suppose Uncle James said no?"

"But he wouldn't—especially when he sees how I trust you."

Tommy put forward all the objections he could think of, but she was able to answer them all.

"*I'll* manage him," she insisted. "Only let me see him! And then, Tommy," she went on, "it's getting horrid for me here. Egbert is jealous. He says he won't give me up, and won't take back his old ring. And"— amazing invention!— "mommer and popper say that you're just trifling with me, and they want me to take back Will. Every one says I'm a silly little fool to think so much of you!" Tears came into her gray eyes.

"Oh, *do*, Tommy, *please*, take me away! I'm so miserable here!"

And at last, because she wept, and because he could see no other way, he agreed to take her.

VII

Reluctant and harassed as he was, he couldn't help a certain delight in the adventure. He hadn't yet lost a boyish relish for running away; and this getting up after the others were asleep, stealing downstairs, bag in hand, and meeting Esther in the dark little hall, thrilled him to the marrow.

They hurried through the empty streets, black beneath the shadow of the old trees, and entered the station, where an oil lamp burned. The ticket office was closed; there wasn't a soul in sight. They sat down side by side on a bench, to wait for the New York train.

In her usual way, Esther put her hand in Tommy's. He turned to look down at her in the dim lamplight, and the sight of her flushed, excited little face, combined with the pressure of her hand, nearly brought tears to his eyes. How she trusted him, poor little girl! Leaving her home and her parents and going off with him this way! He swore to himself that she should never be sorry for it; that, even if she were not quite the wife he would have chosen, he would respect her forever for this generous, this noble trust in him.

He had, in short, never in his life been so overwhelmingly asinine. His fair, infantile face was pale from the intense seriousness of his resolutions and the weight of his responsibility. He would at that moment have been ready to assure you that it was he who had implored and persuaded Esther to run away with him—that it was his idea and his wish.

It was midnight when they arrived at the Grand Central. The moment they stepped off the train, a realization of his colossal folly rushed over the boy. The subtle excitement of the hurrying crowds, the sophistication of this environment, suddenly destroyed his rustic romance, and he grew cold with fright.

What was this that he had done? What was he to do with Esther? He couldn't marry her without a license. He had thought of taking her at once to Uncle James, to convince him on the spot of Esther's desirability as a wife. Uncle James might be asleep; or, if he were awake, he would surely need some preparation. He was courtly toward ladies—ladies with money; but one never knew—

"Oh, Lord!" he thought. "Oh, Lord! What can I do with her?"

They had eloped from the girl's home. He was now and forever responsible for little Esther. There she sat, waiting for his wise decision.

They sat down on a bench in the immense hall, he with his latest thing in traveling bags, Esther with a shabby little wicker suit case. Forlorn, young, weary, they sat in silence—waiting, both of them, for Tommy to become a man.

"I know!" he cried suddenly. "Esther, you go into the ladies' waiting room while I telephone. I have a cousin. I think she'd be willing to do something. At least she'll put you up overnight."

But in the telephone booth his courage fled. He couldn't explain all this over the wire. He ran out and got a taxi, and at one o'clock he arrived at his cousin's little flat uptown.

She was a charming, gracious, good-natured young widow. She got up, put on a dressing gown, and sat listening with angelic patience to Tommy's story; but she could not conceal her horror.

"Oh, Tommy, my *dear* boy! You're so young! Don't be hasty! Oh, Tommy, don't rush into—anything!"

"Now, look here!" said Tommy, sick with nervousness and alarm. "Don't lecture me, Alison. It's done. Just suggest something. She can't go back now. I'll have to see Uncle James about getting married; but what shall I do now? I can't leave the poor kid sitting there in the Grand Central Station all night."

"No, of course you can't," Alison agreed. "Bring her here, Tommy—and hurry! I'll wait up for her."

She set about making preparations for this most unwelcome guest, thinking and hoping all the time that Tommy might be saved—that this distressing thing might blow over without hurting him.

She pictured Esther as a poor innocent little rustic, as simple as Tommy. She never saw the girl, and so was never enlightened. She waited for two hours, but no one came. Then, worried, heavy-hearted, she went back to bed.

VIII

Tommy had hurried back to Esther, and found her just as he had left her—a model of patience and propriety, with her little bag beside her. Though she was pale and heavy-eyed with sleep, she was as neat and fresh as ever. He told her his plan.

"Come on," he said. "Hurry up! Alison said she'd wait for you."

"I'm not going there," she said. "I can't, Tommy."

"You'll have to, dear!"

Her eyes filled with tears.

"I can't! I can't! I just couldn't face a strange woman now. What would she think of me, running away with you like this?"

"But what can I do with you, Esther?"

She clasped his arm and looked up into his face with streaming eyes.

"Oh, Tommy! Please don't leave me! I'm so frightened and so lonely! Don't send me away!"

"But you must be reasonable, sweetheart," he implored. He began to realize how terribly he had mismanaged this affair. He cursed himself. Why hadn't he made plans? "You know we've got to consider your reputation," he said.

"Oh, that doesn't matter!" she cried. "No one'll ever know about it. Only don't go away from me, Tommy! I couldn't bear it!"

He yielded. He was so distressed, so confused, so alarmed, that he had no moral strength to withstand her. He took her to the Tressillon, a quiet, dingy place where he had once or twice had dinner. He took two rooms for them, on different floors, and he registered as "Mr. and Mrs. Thomas Ellinger, Jr." What else could he have done?

He slept soundly, although he hadn't expected to close an eye. The first thing he thought of upon waking was to telephone to Esther's room. He was told that she wasn't there.

He dressed and hurried down to look for her everywhere—in the dining room, the grill, the lounge; but he couldn't find her. He was seized with panic.

When he found that her bag was still in her room, he resigned himself to wait; but he was angry—more angry than he had ever been in his life.

She came back at lunch time, composed and smiling. He was sitting on the lounge when she entered. He got up, took her arm with a nervous grip, and led her into a quiet corner.

"Look here, Esther!" he said. "You mustn't act like this! Where have you been?"

"Oh, nowhere special—just for a walk."

"I'd planned for us to go to the City Hall and get the license this morning, and get married."

"Oh, Tommy!" she said, with a pout. "I don't want to get married. I'm too young!"

"Don't be silly!" he said impatiently. "We'll have a bite of lunch and then we'll hurry down town."

"I think it's silly to get married. We're too young. What could we live on?"

"You needn't worry about that," he said, wounded. "I dare say I can manage to take care of you."

"I don't think you could, Tommy. We'd only be miserable. No, let's not be married."

"Esther!" he cried, appalled. "What's the matter with you?"

"I think we've made a mistake. Let's not be silly and make it any worse. The best thing would be for us to part. I can look out for myself perfectly well. I know a man here in the city—I dropped in to see him this morning, and he said he'd get me an engagement to go on the stage. He's an advance agent, or something. I met him out in Millersburg. He has lots of pull."

"Don't talk that way!" he thundered. "Don't you realize what you've done? Haven't you enough sense to see that you're compromised?"

"No one knows anything about it, and there's no harm done. I'll write to mommer and tell her I ran away to go on the stage."

"No, you won't!" said Tommy. "I sent them a telegram this morning to say that we were married. I thought we would really be by the time they got the message."

She looked at him in silence.

"Well!" she said at last. "You *are* a fool!"

"I suppose I am," he replied bitterly. "However, it's done now. They know you're here with me, and they think you're my wife, so you'll have to see it through."

"Not I!" she said cheerfully. "I'm not going to marry a kid like you!"

"For God's sake, why did you come away with me?" he cried.

She smiled.

"I guess I liked you," she said.

"Don't you like me now?"

"Don't be silly!" she said. "Of course I do; but I think we're too young to think of marriage. It was a mistake."

She was absolutely incomprehensible to him; but she could read him through and through, and the better she knew him, the greater grew her contempt.

"It was only a joke," she said.

"Is that your idea of a joke? It's a pretty dangerous one."

She shook her head.

"No, it isn't. I knew you were a nice boy. I knew I could trust you. I'll always remember you, Tommy—always. You're the nicest—"

"What do you propose to tell your parents? They'll write to you here, or they may come."

"They won't find me. I'll leave tomorrow morning. Mr. Syles told me of a nice boarding house. You'll go back to your uncle. He'll never know about it, and we'll both forget the whole thing, won't we?"

They went up into her room, and they argued all afternoon. Tommy tried to show her the enormity of her conduct, but she insisted upon regarding it as an escapade. She emphasized her sixteen years. She behaved with an airy childishness which she had never shown before, and which he knew to be false.

He had played the part she had determined he should play, and there was an end to him. Her modest little pocketbook was well stuffed with his money. She was in the city where she wished to be.

Sixteen? Esther sixteen? Preposterous idea! She was as old as the earth.

At last she said she was hungry, and reluctantly he took her downstairs to the dining room, crowded and noisy, with dancing going on to the music of a fiendish orchestra. Gone was his pride, gone was his kindly protectiveness. He was overwhelmed with shame; he saw himself a dupe, when he had fancied himself a hero.

He couldn't eat. He sat there across the table, in sullen wretchedness, keeping his eyes off her detestable face, listening to her calm voice, telling him that it was "better for them both to part now." She was affable, but she made no effort to be kind. She had nothing to say about love, about grief at parting. She placidly ignored their romance. She urged him to be "sensible," and a "good boy." And with every word she made a fresh wound in his quivering, childish soul—scars never to be healed.

He was sitting with his back to the door, and he hadn't seen old Van Brink enter. He had looked up in alarm at a shriek from Esther, and there was that face, convulsed with hatred—hatred for *him*. Then the shot, the crowd, the atrocious sense of unreality, of insane confusion, the pain in his wrist.

Some one had hurried him off in a taxi. He had looked back blankly from the doorway at the brightly lighted room, at an old man held by force from following him. It wasn't, it couldn't be real!

Once again he picked up the newspaper and looked at that shameful headline:

TRAGEDY NARROWLY AVERTED AT
HOTEL TRESSILLON

It occurred to young Thomas Ellinger that perhaps the tragedy had not, after all, been averted.

IX

"Everything passes," runs the old saying, and the contrary is also true. Nothing passes.

If you had looked at that stalwart and serious gentleman in the box, correct, evidently prosperous, with his honest and rather blank gaze, you would certainly have imagined him to be one of those fortunate creatures without a history, a soul without a scar. He was there with an agreeable, well-bred wife and a pretty young daughter, and he was apparently enjoying the play with a temperate and sedate enjoyment—interested, but not very much interested, you know.

And yet he is none other than the black sheep of twenty years ago, the disgraced and abandoned Tommy. Moreover, the actress whom he is watching with so tepid an air is Esther herself, and he is very cunningly concealing a great confusion of feelings.

He had casually suggested going to see her act that evening, as he had done four or five times before, since he had by chance discovered that Esther and the celebrated Elinor Vaughn were one and the same person. He had no knowledge of the means by which she had risen, but he was by no means surprised to find her at the top. Why shouldn't she be? Indeed, how could she not be? She was certainly born for victory.

Each time that he watched her magnificent outbursts of dramatic passion, her rages and her griefs, he felt a secret and delightful joy. Only imagine what he had escaped! Only think what such a woman, capable of moving the most cynical heart, could have done with him! He looked cautiously at the people about him, saw them stirred to horror, grief, or delight, and he felt himself superior to them all. They didn't know that it was only Esther Van Brink!

He watched her to-night, at the end of her famous second act, winning by heartbreaking entreaties the mercy of a vindictive and obdurate husband. Never could he have withstood her. He would have been lost!

The curtain fell, rose again, fell, and she came out to stand for a moment before the footlights, bowing, smiling a little wearily; and then she saw him.

He drew back hastily, but it was too late. When she came before the curtain again, she looked at him and smiled. Before the third act began, a boy came to the box with a note:

Please, Tommy, come behind and see me for a moment.

ESTHER.

"It seems she's some one I used to know," he explained to his wife. She raised her eyebrows and smiled politely, but he knew she wasn't satisfied. "I suppose I'll have to go," he said.

"Oh, by all means!" replied his wife. "Alice and I won't wait."

He was uneasy and annoyed. That was just like Esther—no consideration!

He found her in her dressing room, with a crowd of people, but she sent them all away.

"He's an awfully old friend," she explained, "and very shy. I'll never be able to catch him again."

The little country girl had certainly become a handsome woman, he reflected, and she had lost none of her impudent charm, her mocking tranquillity.

"Well, Tommy!" she said.

"Well!" he answered, and he had exactly his old air of a boy acting the man of the world.

"My, you've got on!" she said admiringly. "You're really splendid, Tommy! Are you a millionaire?"

"No," he answered, flushing, well aware that she was laughing at him. "I'm in business."

"How did you do that?"

Naturally he didn't care to talk about his heroic effort to rehabilitate himself—how he had actually found himself a job, and won his alarming uncle's forgiveness for his one wickedness by patient industry and some years of complete self-effacement.

"And you're married, if my eyes do not betray me."

"Yes, I'm married," he answered stiffly.

He wasn't going to permit any Esther on earth to make light of that respectable and very happy union.

"Oh, Tommy!" she sighed. "I'm glad! I'm glad it's all turned out so well for you—and for me, too. I don't believe I would ever have become the actress I am if it hadn't been for all I suffered through your desertion."

"What?" he cried, astounded. "*My* desertion?"

And there were actually tears in her eyes.

"Yes," she said. "You nearly broke my heart, but it made me."

He could scarcely believe his ears.

"But—but—" he stammered, with a feeble effort to remind her of her own treachery.

"I only wanted to see you and tell you that I forgave you long ago, Tommy—forgave you frankly and freely. I owe my success to that suffering."

She held out her hand. He grasped it, and hurriedly took his leave. She forgave him! She forgave him his desertion, which had nearly broken her heart!

He stopped in the street outside the theater, ready to denounce her to the silent sky; but in spite of himself began to smile, with reluctance, with an immense and grudging admiration.

"Upon my word!" he said aloud. "What a woman!"

A Hesitating Cinderella

"I'm no jazz baby," Madeline declared indignantly.

"Well, I never said you were, did I?" demanded Mr. Ritchie.

"Well, you think so," she replied.

"Well, if you can read my mind, it's no use me trying to talk," said he.

"I never asked you to talk!"

They were both aware that their badinage had lost its fine edge.

"Well, I never asked you to listen," Mr. Ritchie said valiantly, but he knew very well that this was not a clever retort.

At that moment he was greatly dissatisfied both with his wit and his person. He thought it brutal on the part of fate that a young man as passionate and resolute as himself should have so frail a form, and that after having taken a correspondence course in rhetoric and oratory he should still be so tongue-tied—especially with Madeline.

He could see himself in the mirror opposite. He sat so straight that he leaned over backward a little, but this did not disguise the fact that his shoulders were narrow and not quite even, and his chest somewhat hollow. Neither had his studies or his burning thoughts left any visible impress on his sallow, rather ratlike face; and all this hurt his terribly sensitive soul.

"I never said you were a jazz baby," he insisted. "I only said lots of girls were—and that's a fact. Why, a lot of those girls wouldn't spend a cent to get a decent, well balanced meal! All they care about is clothes and—"

"I don't guess you know such a lot about girls," Madeline interrupted.

Her tone was scornful, and the outrageously sensitive Mr. Ritchie at once saw all sorts of implications. She meant that girls wouldn't bother with him. She meant that he was nothing but a mechanic. She meant that his clothes were shabby, and that he was small and slight. She meant everything that could affront his manly pride.

His face grew crimson.

"All right!" he said loftily. "Have it your own way!"

He turned away his head, though he was a little alarmed as he did so. He had always felt that chivalry required him to keep his head turned rigidly toward Madeline, to atone for the fact that she stood while he sat. Of course, that was not his fault. Madeline being a waitress, and he a customer, anything more gallant was impossible.

He certainly did not enjoy being waited on by this splendid girl. In fact, he so bitterly disliked it that he would have ceased coming to Compson's Chophouse, if he had not realized that in his absence she would very likely be waiting on some other man, possibly not so chivalrous.

It was altogether a sacrifice on his part, because the food did not conform to his standards. He could not get here the well balanced rations necessary for building up his physique. Of what use to work night and morning with a patent exerciser, if he did not get the proper muscle-building foods? This worried him very much, for he desired a fine physique as greatly as he desired a master mind.

Then, too, he often had to wait a long while for Madeline to be free to attend to him, and he fretted at the waste of time. He couldn't light a cigarette to beguile his tedium, for he knew that the smoker cannot have a fine physique. If he saw a smoker who looked as if he had one, Ritchie knew him to be a whited sepulcher, with a failing heart, exhausted lungs, and no will power.

To be sure, he might have passed the time with some improving book. He always carried in his pocket a volume of a set he had bought—a set guaranteed to broaden his mind, and to contain all that he ought to read; but he couldn't keep his mind on a book when Madeline was about.

"Have it your own way," he repeated.

This time he said it with a new significance. He meant that, as far as he was concerned, Madeline might have everything her own way forever.

Unfortunately, she wasn't there to hear him. She was waiting on a man at another table. She never so much as glanced at Ritchie. He knew she wouldn't look at him, and he took a gloomy pleasure in staring at her.

She was worth looking at, was Madeline. Tall, spare, straight, in an austere white uniform and a sleek coiffure, she was a miracle to irradiate any chophouse. Her features were subtle—a delicate nose, a rounded chin, a mouth very red in her pale face. Her black brows made an incomparable line above her dark, steady eyes.

In spite of her thinness and her pallor, in spite of twenty years of bad air and wretched food, she was strong and tireless, with muscles like steel— a heritage from ancestors of Slavic peasant stock. She had a cool, careless manner, inclined to sudden hauteur when she thought it necessary, but she could also chat with the greatest affability—as she was doing now.

"Trying to make me jealous!" thought Ritchie. "What do I care?"

He had merely invited her, very politely, to a dance to be given by the Coyote Club that evening. He worked very hard all day as a mechanic in a garage. In addition to building up a fine physique and broadening his mind by reading, he was taking a correspondence course in mechanical draftsmanship; and the Coyote Club, of which he was treasurer, was his one frivolity.

Every week they engaged a pianist, a saxophonist, and a drummer, and had a dance in a hall over a restaurant on Eighth Avenue. There was no "rough stuff." It was a seemly and refined entertainment—Madeline ought to have known that. Ritchie only meant that some of the girls brought by some of the Coyotes were jazz babies. The remark was not intended as personal, and she shouldn't have taken it as such.

"Don't know much about girls, don't I?" he reflected angrily.

Nothing could have been more galling, especially as it was true. Ritchie had noble ideas about girls, though. He was not exactly in a position to marry at the present moment; but later on, when his heroic efforts began to show results, he intended to have a home, a garden, and a wife whom he would venerate and take to lectures and concerts.

He did not care to admit that that wife must be Madeline or no one. He was far too proud to acknowledge how much he cared for a girl with her silly ideas; but unhappily he was not clever enough to conceal it, and Madeline knew only too well.

These were her silly ideas. Knowing herself to be rare and seductive, she intended to marry a millionaire. She was weary and disgusted with her present condition. She wanted a life of exquisite refinement and languor. She hated the restaurant, she hated her home, her uniform. She turned up her delicate nose at everything about her, including Ritchie. Not that he wasn't "refined," for he surely was, and she secretly admired him; but it was not the right, the princely, sort of "refinement," and she would have none of him.

Still, she felt a pang of regret when he went out. A girl as attractive as she, alone in the world, could not well help learning to appreciate the chivalry and restraint of Mr. Ritchie. He never "said anything," and never would, until encouraged. He came every night to Compson's for his dinner, and of late he had fallen into the habit of being on the corner when she came out, at ten o'clock. He never said that he was waiting for her, and she had manners enough to be surprised every time. He walked home with her, both of them conversing with the utmost formality.

He had never invited her anywhere, except to this dance at the Coyote Club. He had never so much as shaken hands with her. She knew very well that the reason for this was his severe sense of respect for her. While she admired this, she would have been better pleased with a little more impetuosity.

Still, it was no use denying that he left a gap. Madeline missed him. Even when she was busy, she had found comfort in the sight of his head bent over one of his little books.

"Now he's mad," she reflected. "He won't come back. All right! I don't care! Let him go to his old dance and have a good time with the jazz babies!"

She consoled herself by imagining the balls she would go to in the future, when the millionaire arrived—balls like those she saw in the movies. She herself would wear a long, swathed dress and carry a feathered fan. She would be languid and scornful, and would flirt in a refined manner impossible to one who was at present a waitress in Compson's Chophouse.

II

By eight o'clock the room was growing empty. As a hint to possible intruders, each time a table was left vacant the lights near it were turned out. A few solitary men still ate, in bright oases, but they had a hasty and guilty air; they knew that their tardiness was resented.

One by one the waitresses disappeared into the little back room where they changed into their street clothes, and returned, crossing the restaurant with eager steps, until there remained only Madeline and Miss Sullivan. Miss Sullivan remained because her customer was a pig-headed old gentleman and refused to hurry; but Madeline was there because Mr. Compson had great confidence in her, and allowed her the privilege of turning out the lights and locking the door.

The proprietor himself had gone, with the cash box. Madeline would have the responsibility of guarding, until morning, whatever sum the pig-headed old gentleman might pay.

"Gosh, I could stick a pin in him!" murmured Miss Sullivan. "Twenty past! There goes that dishwasher, even!"

"I'll look after him," said Madeline. "You can go, if you like."

Toward her own sex Madeline was not haughty, but quite good-natured.

"I'll do as much for you some day," declared Miss Sullivan, like a creature in a fable, and off she went.

The room was very still. At intervals the elevated trains went by with a thundering roar, leaving behind a sort of vacuum of quietness. The old gentleman looked up.

"Piece lemon meringue pie," he said briefly.

"Kitchen's closed," Madeline replied, with equal brevity.

This annoyed him very much; but in view of the fact that he was known never to leave more than a nickel for a tip, his annoyance never caused much concern in Compson's. He got up, folded his newspaper, felt in all his pockets, and very slowly took down his overcoat.

Madeline, leaning against the wall in a careless attitude, refused to show signs of impatience. Indeed, when she saw him struggling into the tight sleeves of his shabby old coat, she felt an impulse of scornful pity, and came to his aid. He didn't thank her. Apparently he preferred to consider it her fault that he was old and slow and stiff, and couldn't enjoy his dinner.

After he had gone, she began turning off the few remaining lights. The place was nearly in darkness when the door opened and two men came in.

"Closed!" said Madeline.

But the taller of the two led his companion to a table and pushed him into a chair.

"Can't you manage a cup of coffee?" he entreated. "My friend's ill."

Madeline was not very credulous. She snapped on the nearest light, so that she might look at the alleged invalid.

One look was enough. She hadn't lived twenty years without learning something, and she knew at once what ailed the fellow; but she didn't care. She felt instinctively that he was a victim. He had been led astray, very likely by this burly ruffian with him.

"Poor feller!" she said softly.

His curly head was thrown back, his eyes were closed, and he seemed sunk in innocent slumber. Not only was he singularly handsome and engaging, but he wore a dinner jacket. Never had Madeline seen one so close at hand before. It invested the suffering hero with a high, romantic interest. It thrilled her. He was a creature strayed from another world. He was helpless and abandoned, and not for anything on earth would she have forsaken him.

"I'll get him some coffee," she said.

She said it rudely, because she hated the other man, and knew it was all his fault.

There was a little left in the coffee urn, and it was still warm. She brought it promptly, but the sufferer could not be roused to drink.

"Good Lord!" said the other impatiently. "I don't know what to do with the young idiot! Pour water on him."

"I never!" cried Madeline, with passionate indignation. "And get his nice clothes all wet?"

"Well, do something with him," said the other. He showed an alarming tendency to shift the responsibility for his unconscious companion to Madeline's shoulders. "I can't take him home with me. Lock him in here till the morning, and let him sleep it off!"

"I never!" she said again. "Just suppose he waked up all alone in the dark, and couldn't get out! Don't you know where he lives?"

"Of course I know, but he wouldn't thank any one for sending him home in this state. He's the only son of wealthy and respectable parents," the other answered, in a flippant tone that was obnoxious to Madeline. "It would bring their gray—or dyed—hair to the grave in one swoop. This fellow, my dear girl, is young Benny Bradley!"

"I don't care who he is, he'd ought to be took care of. He's got to be!" Madeline said sternly.

"Not by me," returned the other. He rose, and looked at Madeline with a smile. "It's time for me to clear out."

"You can't!" the girl protested.

"I shall," said the man. "I make you a present of Benny Bradley."

He was actually going, but she caught him by the sleeve.

"Oh!" she cried. "You ought to be ashamed! What ever can I do?"

"I don't know. Why not call the police?" said he.

He unclasped her fingers, and, raising his hat gallantly, went out.

"Oh, my!" cried Madeline, in despair. "Oh, my! What ever will I do with the poor feller?"

She dipped a folded napkin in water, and laid it on his forehead. A glance in the mirror startled her. In her white uniform, wasn't she just like a trained nurse with a wounded hero? The vision inspired her. She felt that she must be calm, brave, resourceful.

Somewhat timidly she lifted his limp, white hand, to feel his pulse; but, having little idea how a pulse should behave, she gained no reassurance.

"Poor feller!" she repeated. "Anyway, I'm not going to leave you, if I have to sit here the whole night!"

She would have done that, and would have faced Mr. Compson and her sister workers the next morning undaunted, if she had not been saved by the entrance of Mr. Ritchie.

III

To the casual observer there was nothing heroic in Ritchie's coming, but truly it was heroic. It had cost him a horrible effort to subdue his outrageous pride, to forego the Coyotes' dance, and to return here for the ungracious Madeline. And how did he find her? Bending over a strange man in evening dress, all alone, long after the place should have been closed!

"Well!" he said. "What's all this?"

With vehement indignation Madeline told him the story of the base desertion of the helpless sufferer.

"And what am I going to do with him?" she ended. "It's the worst I ever heard—going off and leaving him like this!"

"Well, send for the police," said Mr. Ritchie, but he regretted his words when he saw her eyes blaze.

"Shame on you!" she cried. "The state he's in!"

"Well, now, see here," said Ritchie. "guess you don't know what's the matter with him. He's not sick; he's just—"

"Hush up!" she interrupted fiercely. "I guess I do know! It isn't his fault—he got in with bad comp'ny."

"How do you know?" he inquired.

"I *do* know," she replied firmly. "Never you mind how! And I'm going to see he gets taken care of till he's all well again."

All this did not contribute to Mr. Ritchie's happiness. Wasn't it just like a woman, he thought, to be captious and haughty to a devoted young man of blameless life, and an angel of compassion to this unknown profligate?

Nevertheless, in spite of his jealous alarm and his pain and his distrust, it was Ritchie's sure instinct to behave generously. Heaven knows where he got his magnanimity. He hadn't learned it in the mean and sordid little home of his childhood. He hadn't been taught it in school, and it had been a part of his nature long before he had read a line of those improving little books.

His sallow face flushed.

"Well!" he said. "I'll take him home with me."

Madeline didn't know how to be gracious, but she appreciated this.

"He can't walk," was all she said.

"All right!" said Ritchie grandly. "I'll call a taxi."

He had never done this before. He hastened to a cab stand on Fifth Avenue, and it seemed to his proud soul that all the chauffeurs knew he had never used a taxi, and despised him. He was very truculent about it.

An infinitely greater humiliation was in store for him. When he returned to the restaurant, he couldn't lift, or even move, the helpless young man. All those hours with the exerciser availed him nothing. His physique was shamefully deficient.

"Let me," said Madeline. "I'm real strong."

Without much trouble, she took the fellow under his arms and got him to his feet. He opened his eyes, then, and smiled a dreamy, innocent smile. Supported by Madeline and pushed by Ritchie, he made a sort of attempt at walking to the cab.

"I'd better go with you," said she, "or you'll never get him up the stairs."

Sick with shame, Ritchie was obliged to consent. Neither of them for an instant contemplated asking the chauffeur's assistance; and the chauffeur, being class conscious, did not volunteer it.

Ritchie had the worst fifteen minutes of his life during his first ride in a taxi. He felt himself a mean, contemptible, worthless thing, with his lack of bodily strength. He contrasted his worn, shabby suit with the stranger's expensive clothes. He knew that Madeline must despise him. She would despise him far more when she saw his room, yet he could devise no way for preventing that.

When the cab stopped before his door, he paid the fare, torn between a certainty that his natural enemy, the chauffeur, was cheating him, and his desire to appear lordly before Madeline. Then, together, they began to get the stranger up the stairs.

The noise of the operation made Ritchie's blood run cold. Suppose some one saw him with a drunken man and a girl? He hauled at the fellow's arm in no very gentle manner.

At last, at the top of the house, he unlocked a door, and, supporting the stranger against the wall of the corridor, he brusquely said to Madeline:

"All right! You might as well go now."

"I'd like to see him settled," said she.

So Ritchie had to light the gas and had to let her in.

The room was a bleak, bare, cold little cell, with the exerciser fastened to the wall, and the window nailed open, to admit all the hygienically fresh air possible. On the bureau, instead of the little accessories of a fastidious gentleman, were a pair of military brushes, the vital library, all in a row, and a bottle of ink. On the table were an alarm clock and the apparatus of the correspondence course. There were no other visible articles personal to Ritchie, except a razor strop and six cakes of carbolic soap, economically unwrapped to dry.

He pushed the stranger down on his cot.

"All right!" he thought defiantly. "Now you can see just how I live—and hope you'll like it! Go on—laugh, if you want to!"

But she was not laughing.

"Oh, my, what a dusty towel!" she was thinking, in distress. "And no curtains. The woman that runs this house ought to be ashamed of herself!"

She turned to Ritchie without the least trace of haughtiness.

"Well, good night, Everard," she said.

It was the first time she had used his name. He needed that assuagement to compensate for the lingering glance she gave to the prostrate unknown.

IV

Ritchie came home in a somewhat bitter humor, partly due to his having spent the night on a hard chair, and partly to other and finer causes. He hoped that drunken fellow would be gone. He wished never to see him again; but when Ritchie opened the door, there he was, lying on the bed and reading one of the little books.

"Hello!" he said, as joyously as if Ritchie were his heart's dearest friend.

"Are you feeling better?" Ritchie curtly inquired.

Without waiting for a reply, he began to take off his grimy work clothes.

"I don't know how to thank you," the other went on. "Absolutely the whitest thing I ever heard of! I must have been pretty far gone last night—can't remember a blamed thing."

He was not discouraged by his host's silence.

"I shan't forget this, you know," he continued. "You darned nearly saved my life. Can't imagine what my people would have said, if I'd come home like that. You know how it is—"

"No, I don't," interrupted Ritchie. "I'm a teetotaler."

"Shows sense," said the other warmly. "I think I'll have to be one myself. My name's Bradley." He waited. "What's yours?" he asked.

"Ritchie," responded the other. "And as good as Bradley any day," he added mentally.

In some respects, however, honesty obliged him to admit that he was not so good as Bradley.

Bradley, after stretching, got up. He was in his shirt sleeves, and Ritchie surveyed his tall, slender figure with the eye of a connoisseur in physiques. The fellow was young yet, not fully developed, but certainly those shoulders, that solid neck, that broad chest, were promising very promising.

"Well, he probably eats too much meat," thought Ritchie, with dejection. "Living like he does, he won't last!"

In order to show his perfect ease and indifference, he began to wash, whistling when the process permitted.

"I must be badly in your way," said the other, in his good-humored manner. "I'll clear out, I think. Got a spare overcoat? I don't like to go out like this."

Ritchie grew scarlet. His overcoat—certainly spare enough—was in that place where winter overcoats naturally go in the spring.

"No," he said sullenly.

"Then I—" began Bradley.

There was a knock at the door. Ritchie flung it wide open, with the air of one who has nothing to conceal. In the hall stood two resplendent young heroes, broadly smiling.

"Still alive, Bradley?" said the taller and older of the two.

They both came into the room as if Ritchie did not exist. Trembling with resentment, he stood aside, collarless, in his cheap striped shirt, with his black hair still wet on his forehead. These three well fed, well clothed creatures, with their vigorous voices, completely filled the room—filled, he thought, the whole world, squeezing him out of it.

In an affectionate and blasphemous manner Bradley reproached his friend for deserting him the night before.

"You ought to thank me," said his friend, "for leaving you in the care of that peach of a girl!"

"What peach of a girl?" asked Bradley, pleasantly surprised.

The friend recounted the circumstances. No one observed Mr. Ritchie's rage and dismay.

"I went there just now to make inquiries," the friend went on, "and she told me where I'd find you. Bradley, old son, if you're a man and a brother, you'll go there at once and thank her! She's a beautiful girl, and—"

"Here!" interrupted Ritchie. His voice was so strange that they all turned to look at him. "Leave her out!" he cried. "You can thank me!"

Bradley was smitten with compunction. He began thanking Ritchie with energy, introduced his friends, and invited him to dinner.

"No!" said Ritchie. Like many teetotalers, he had acquired the habit of saying "no" somewhat ungraciously. "No! But you can just leave her out!"

Again he was thanked by all of them, and at last they left his room; but he knew that Madeline would not be left out. He felt certain that they would go at once to Compson's Chophouse. He could see them talking to Madeline. He knew how she would admire their dress, and their silly language, and their frivolous and disgusting manners.

"*All right!*" he said to himself. "You're welcome to 'em; but you don't catch *me* going there any more, to be made a fool of. Not much!"

Suddenly he decided that he wanted no dinner—not at Compson's, or at any other place. He threw himself down on his cot, with a scornful laugh that sounded like a sob. Fellows like that always got everything. They thought they owned the earth—and very likely they did.

V

Young Bradley was not subtle or astoundingly clever, but he did know better than to go to thank a beautiful girl in the company of his two friends. He went alone.

He was instantly struck down, completely conquered, by Madeline's haughty glance. It was the first time he had met a haughty girl. He found most girls very much otherwise. He was accustomed to the ardent pursuit of mothers and aunts, and not much coyness on the part of their *protégées*. He had no conception of Madeline's idea of man as a dangerous and persistent hunter, with woman as his prey. In his circle the girls did the hunting and he the evading.

He was captivated by her severity. She refused to go out with him that evening; so he came again the next evening.

"Please come!" he entreated. "I've got the car outside. I'll wait for you as long as you like, and then we'll run up to a little place on the Post Road."

"No, thank you," said Madeline. "I never go out with strange gentlemen."

"How am I going to stop being a strange gentleman if you'll never go out with me?" he complained.

Madeline didn't know, and didn't care to encourage strange young men by trying to explain. She knew perfectly well that he would come back.

To be sure, he did, and this time he was dreadfully insistent. Now perhaps the cause of Madeline's hauteur was the take-it-or-leave-it attitude of the men she knew. Certainly she had never before encountered a persistent suitor, or one who was not offended by rebuffs. Customers inclined to gallantry were very much annoyed if not encouraged. Even Mr. Ritchie was fatally ready to be insulted; but this young fellow didn't care in the least. Let her be haughty, captious, even cruel, still he was charmed and delighted.

Though she did not think this quite manly, Madeline could not withstand the cajolery of the handsome and good-natured boy. She was thrilled with pride that this splendid creature should come to seek her in Compson's lowly chophouse. She was secretly overwhelmed when he brought her orchids. She didn't really resent the innuendoes of the other girls. They were simply jealous because no such hero ever had or ever would come to seek them.

In her heart she was grateful, almost humble. She regarded her incomparable Bradley with something very like awe. To placate Compson, he would order coffee and pie while he waited to talk to her; and his manner of eating and drinking, the way he rose and remained standing when she approached, all the careless ease and grace of him, were a marvel and a joy. Moreover, even in her most fervent admiration, she had never lost the protective tenderness she had felt the first time she had seen him. She worried about him, about his health and his morals.

This was really the reason why she finally consented to go out with him—so that she could talk seriously and firmly, and perhaps reclaim him.

"Well, you can be waiting for me tomorrow at nine o'clock," she said. "You'd better go along now."

As he was leaving—a notable figure in a suit such as never entered Compson's, and a straw hat, and a walking stick—he was met by Ritchie coming in. Ritchie was dressed in threadbare serge, and wore brown shoes, which he had attempted to make black. Bradley went by without a sign—not by intention, for he would have saluted his benefactor joyously if he had known him; but Ritchie, to him, was exactly like countless others, and quite indistinguishable.

Of course Ritchie took this apparent neglect as a personal insult. He sat down at his usual table, burning with shame and fury. When Madeline approached, he said truculently:

"I suppose you don't want to go to the movies to-morrow night?"

It was an announcement, rather than a question.

"Well, I'm sorry," replied Madeline, "only I got a date."

"Him, isn't it? All right! Go ahead! That's just like a woman," said Ritchie. "If a feller has good clothes and a fine physique, what do they care if he drinks, or anything?"

"I wasn't aware I was requesting your valuable advice, Mr. Ritchie," observed Madeline frigidly.

"I wasn't giving it," said he. "All I was saying was, women are all for show. They never see below the surface. Anyway, I'm going to Chicago the end of this week. I'm sick of New York!"

"My! Poor New York!" murmured she.

"I'm sick of the girls here," he went on vehemently. "Just a lot of jazz babies—that's what they are!"

"Here, now!" she cried.

"Jazz babies," he repeated. "There isn't one of them with—with any brains or any feelings."

Madeline had turned pale.

"I'm not paid to be insulted by customers," said she. "I'll send some one else to wait on you. I'm sure I hope you'll find some one in Chicago that's good enough for you, if such a thing is possible!"

And thus terminated their acquaintance. They were now complete strangers.

VI

In the course of her twenty years Madeline had not shed so many tears as during this one night. There was time for a deluge, for it was surely the longest night that had ever covered the earth. It had the interminable confusion of a dream; and, like a dream, it was made up of vivid and apparently unconnected flashes.

First there was herself leaving Compson's with a not very genuine air of composure, entering Bradley's car, and settling herself by his side, determined not to be impressed or perturbed either by his magnificence or by the rakishness of the small car.

Then there was the flight through the bejeweled and marvelous city—a delight seriously marred by her companion's sinister silence. Not being a driver herself, she had mistaken his preoccupation with traffic signals and so on for a grim and alarming determination. She had, as etiquette required, tried to talk, but he scarcely answered.

Then they shot out into the country—a world dark and unfamiliar to her. Almost the first thing Bradley did was to draw up the car by the roadside and produce a pocket flask. He had been surprised and amused at her indignation, and not overawed by her firm principles. She had said that she wished to go home, but he had been so very persuasive about the supper agreed upon that she had yielded.

She had regretted her weakness. The road house was an awful place. It was like the "haunts of vice" that she had read about in the Sunday newspapers. The prices on the menu appalled her, and the dancing was beyond imagining. Bradley knew some of those people, and had danced with a girl, leaving Madeline alone and unprotected at their table.

He said that what he had to drink was ginger ale, but she didn't believe it. Ginger ale couldn't have made him so flushed and silly; and when at last, after he had sat there smoking cigarettes and dawdling, they rose to go, she had noticed that his gait was unsteady. He had grown talkative, too, and never had she heard such silly conversation.

And now here they stood, on the brow of a hill. It was dark, but the dawn was already tingeing the sky. The birds were awake all about them, each one giving his own note—a reedy quaver, a chirp, a clear, exultant carol, each one indifferent and independent, but part of a glorious orchestral symphony. It was dawn, and here they were, for the graceless Bradley had lost his way in the dark.

They had gone jolting up lanes that ended in walls and fences, they had rushed across bridges, they had turned this way and that. Bradley made inquiries, but was not quite capable of profiting by them. Moreover, Madeline's tears and reproaches had made him frantic. Dawn, and here they were! So fair and tranquil a dawn, it might have inspired to poetry the most insensitive soul; but to poor Madeline it meant only another working day. It made her think of Compson's.

"Oh, my!" she cried. "Oh, what shall I do? Oh, how could you do such a thing?"

"I'm very sorry," was all that the sobered young man could say. "I didn't mean to."

"My aunt'll never let me in the house again!" she lamented. "Somebody's sure to come from Compson's and ask where I am, and my aunt'll say she don't know. I wish I was dead!"

"But can't you explain?" Bradley asked patiently.

She was amazed at his stupidity, but the poor chap was quite unaware of the villainous aspect he had in the eyes of Compson's staff. He had never considered himself a villain—certainly not where Madeline was concerned. He was very grateful to her, and he had tried to show his gratitude. That had not been at all difficult, because she was so pretty; but, thought he, what an awful temper!

Bradley was used to girls who concealed the most fiendish rages when in his company, and he believed that all girls were amiable. Ritchie would have understood Madeline's outbreak. He might perhaps have quarreled with her, but all the time he quarreled he would have been terribly moved by her plight. Bradley couldn't see that there was any plight. If she hadn't been so terribly upset, he would have thought the thing a joke.

"Explain!" she cried. "Who do you think would believe me?"

He was about to speak, but when he looked at her, he could not. Some faint comprehension of her point of view came to him. The more he looked, the better he understood.

Grief had dignified her. Her tear-stained face, her brimming eyes, her trembling lip, distressed him beyond measure. He was an honest and kind-hearted fellow, and even something more than that. In his way, he was chivalrous. He felt deeply ashamed just then to remember that only a few hours before he had thought it rather comic to be taking out a waitress. He regretted the harmless but not very decorous jokes that he and his friends had made about the episode. He wished he had shown his grati-tude in some other way. She wasn't a waitress—she was a forlorn and miserable girl whom his ill-behavior had got into a situation which she re-garded as serious.

"I'll make it all right," he said earnestly, wondering how this might be done.

"Well, you ought to!" she replied.

She didn't mean to be ungracious or unkind, but she was in anguish. Nei-ther she nor any of the people she knew could take such things lightly. She saw herself irretrievably disgraced, her haughty respectability forever tar-nished. She knew so well what the girls at Compson's would say!

She had been so proud of her discretion, of her superiority! She had been so very cautious about "strange gentlemen"! And to be away from home all night! She couldn't bear it. Grief and resentment drove her to tears again.

"Don't!" entreated Bradley. "Please don't! I'll make it all right, some-how—I give you my word I will!"

What he meant was that he would fly to some sympathetic feminine spirit, who could and would make it right for him.

VII

Madeline's aunt didn't believe one word of her niece's story. Madeline quarreled haughtily and scornfully with her, but in her own heart she could-n't blame her. She wouldn't have believed it herself. Getting lost in a mo-tor car with a millionaire! That was simply nonsense.

She lay down on the bed in her dismal little room, as close to despair as she was ever likely to be. One of the girls had come from Compson's, and her aunt had said she didn't know where Madeline was.

"I can never go back there!" she thought. "Never, never!"

She might have been mourning for a lost paradise. After all, it was as hard for her to lose her standing among her peers at the chophouse as for a duchess to lose prestige in the drawing-rooms of Mayfair. She had noth-ing else.

She neither expected nor wished to see Bradley again. He was a sinister mystery to her; she couldn't understand him at all. She was convinced that he had got lost on purpose. The very fact of his not having tried to make love to her made the case all the more perturbing. He must have some deep design which she could not yet fathom.

He was bad. He drank. He went gladly to road houses where every one was bad, and drank, and danced improperly. His fascination was the fascination of a villain. His whole life must be a phantasmagoria of splendid evil.

As the room grew dark, she shuddered at the very thought of him. She dozed, and dreamed nightmares, and woke and cried and slept again. The blessed security of her honest, hard-working life was gone. She would have to give up her job. She couldn't face the other girls again. Perhaps she was caught in one of those awful snares elaborately laid by millionaires for the daughters of the poor. Perhaps it was Bradley's purpose to see that she never got another job—to hound her to the brink of starvation, that she might be obliged to listen to his evil proposals.

"I'd rather die!" she cried to herself with a sob.

There was not a soul in the world to assuage the heartsick young creature, no one to speak a word of common sense or solace. Her preposterous fears were terribly real to her. She had eaten nothing all day. She was exhausted, frightened, illimitably wretched.

She heard her aunt moving about in the kitchen. She knew that nothing on earth could induce the older woman to bring her even a cup of tea, and nothing could persuade her to ask for it.

"Not after what she said!" thought Madeline. "It would choke me!"

She fell asleep again, and was awakened by her aunt's hand on her shoulder.

"Here's that Mr. Ritchie," the aunt announced.

"Well, tell him to go away!" replied Madeline.

"Tell him yourself," said her aunt promptly. "I guess I got something better to do than carry messages for you!"

Her aunt was a severe, stout, bespectacled creature of fifty, a woman of invincible propriety, and Madeline's conduct had stricken her to the heart. She was as glad to see Ritchie as if he were an angel, because obviously he could remedy all that was wrong; but she had no other way of expressing gratification, affection, or the most profound grief, than by her habitual disagreeableness.

"That's just like you," said Madeline.

She rose, too wretched to care how she looked, and went into the lugubrious little parlor where Ritchie waited.

"Well! I thought maybe you were sick," said he.

"Well, I'm not," she replied.

There was an awkward silence.

"Well!" he said at last. "Then what about going to the movies?"

Although he refused, as always, to look squarely at her, he had none the less observed her wan and tear-stained face, her untidy hair, her piteous dejection. Something which he imagined to be anger came over him.

"You been out with that feller?" he demanded.

"That's my business!" returned Madeline valiantly.

"Well, if you—if you had more sense," he said, and paused. He could not well have been more miserable than he was at that moment, nor could he have concealed it better. "Well!" he said again, with a sort of fury. "All right! It's nothing to do with me. Go ahead! Suit yourself!"

He drew one of his books from his pocket, opened it, and held it out to her in a shaking hand.

"You can just look at this, if you like," he said. "I'm going away to-morrow—that's all I've got to say!"

She did look. Heavily underscored were two lines unfamiliar to her, and of striking beauty and significance:

> 'Tis better to have loved and lost
> Than never to have loved at all.

Mr. Ritchie flung the book down on the table and walked out.

VIII

The very next evening, when he should have been on his way to Chicago, he was ringing the door bell of Madeline's flat. His presence brought ineffable consolation to the aunt, and was not displeasing to the girl herself.

"My!" she said loftily. "I wouldn't have thought you'd come back!"

"Well, I did," said he. "Aren't you going back to Compson's any more?"

"That's my business!" she answered, but she let him in, and he did not appear rebuffed.

"Well, I guess they miss you there," he observed.

"Let 'em!" she retorted with spirit. They were both too polite, too formal, to take any notice of the tears rolling down her cheeks. "I went out with that Mr. Bradley, and we got lost in his car. We never got back here until near noon. There's no use telling those girls that. They're awful spiteful, and they'd never believe me."

"Well, I do," said Ritchie.

"I should think you ought to!" said Madeline, with a sternness that concealed a very warm gratitude.

"Well, I said I did, didn't I?" pursued Ritchie.

There was a pause.

"He was here to-day," said Madeline; "him and his sister. I must say I didn't think much of her—all painted and everything. She wants to get me a job with one of those Fifth Avenue dressmakers, as a model, to show off the dresses."

There was calm triumph in her tone, but despair seized Ritchie's heart.

"She says I'd be an elegant model," observed Madeline.

"All right!" said Ritchie. "Go ahead! Be one! Suit yourself!"

Another pause.

"That po'try you showed me," said Madeline. "I thought it was sweet."

"It's not meant to be sweet," replied Ritchie severely. "It's more like, now, tragic. If you'd read more—"

"I always admired the way you read such a lot," said Madeline.

In spite of himself, he was mollified. He glanced at her covertly. She was quite as lovely and disturbing as ever.

"Well," he said, "of course I got to read. I want to get on. I'm making twenty-seven a week now, and more when there's overtime. I spend a good lot on those correspondence courses, and the Coyote Club and all; but I guess I could do without them, if I felt like it."

"I'm not going to take that job," said Madeline suddenly. "I wouldn't— not for anything. I guess I've had enough of that kind of people—all that drinking and all. I'd never get on with that kind!"

"Well, twenty-seven a week, *clear*—" said Ritchie.

The collapse of castles in the air doesn't make a sound. Down came the magnificent edifice of Everard Ritchie's ambitions, and the airy palace of Madeline's dreams. In their place was instantaneously erected a three-room flat in a respectable quarter.

Their hands met, but not their eyes. They were timid lovers; but by that handclasp they could say all they wished.

"Those people just make me sick," said Madeline. "You ought to have seen them dancing out at that place!"

Then their eyes did meet, full of profound confidence and understanding. His arm went round her shoulders, and she drew close to him.

"I know!" said he. "Fellers like that are no good at all; and those girls!" He looked at his haughty and incorruptible Madeline. "Those girls," said he, from the depths of his vast worldly knowledge, "are nothing but a bunch of jazz babies!"

Like a Leopard

It was a frightful night. Brecky turned up the collar of his overcoat, pulled his cap lower over his eyes, and left the shelter of the railway station for the open road. He heard the train that had brought him from the city pull out again and rush whistling through the fields and marshes. When it had gone, everything human had vanished, leaving him alone with the great and terrible wind and the cold rain.

He made what haste he could along the muddy road, his head down against the gale. The driving rain half blinded him, the tumult confused him, with the unceasing rush of the wind and the dull sound of the sea. His way lay through immeasurable desolation, past house after house empty and black, shops all closed and shuttered, streets in which there was not one human creature. It was a sort of Pompeii, a deserted village, a nightmare; but to the practical Brecky it was nothing more or less than Shorehaven, a summer resort, quite naturally deserted in midwinter.

He was not a man of imagination, this Johnny Breckenbridge. He was a wiry young chap with an impassive, weather-beaten face. He dressed very soberly, but he had an incorrigibly sporting air, and there was something rakish and jaunty about him. He was nimble, alert, and just a trifle bow-legged. He was never tired, never discouraged. He had all his wits about him, and knew his way in the world.

He had been, one might say, born a jockey, and he had been a good one, too, for years; but he had grown tired of the restrictions of a jockey's life. He was fond of eating and drinking, and he liked to be his own master.

He had continued his activities on the race track in a less official capacity. He had done well as a bookie, too, for he was shrewd, cautious, and trustworthy; but he had suddenly fallen in love and married.

"And that's no life for a married man," he observed to his many friends. "Got to settle down now."

Brecky was thorough in everything, and he wished to be a thoroughly married man. He took his new obligations with great seriousness. He intended to do well for his jolly little Kathleen. He knew that his duty in life was to make money for her.

He never thought of consulting her, however. She had been a waitress in a little restaurant in the city, and he had admired her brisk good humor and her common sense. She was a pretty kid, too—dark, small, vigorous. She had received a great deal of attention, but she was never silly or vain about it. She knew how to take care of herself. She liked a good time, but no monkey business. She was mighty independent, Kathleen was.

To Brecky's uncomplex mind, the wedding ring was to transform her completely.

She was to be no longer Kathleen, but a wife; and to him all good wives were alike. They were kind, gentle, contented, and very helpful. You made money gladly for them; but if you were a real man, you didn't let them spend much of it.

He had looked about the world thoughtfully for a few months. Then he had taken nearly every penny he had saved and had bought a hotel at the seaside, with a heavy mortgage on it. To this place he had brought his Kathleen, that she might help and comfort him while he mastered his new business.

Extraordinary friends of his used to come down and give him advice. He listened and learned. He knew a number of men connected with hotels, night clerks, head waiters, and so on; and they were willing and anxious to help him, because every one liked him.

He had no iconoclastic ideas. He wished to run his hotel according to all the tried and tested rules of the business. He wore out his advisers. Those who came down to look over Brecky's hotel went away exhausted and squeezed dry, leaving whatever valuable knowledge they owned in Brecky's possession.

In midwinter, when the place lay like a frozen village on the shore of an inhuman sea, lights used to shine from the windows of Brecky's immense hotel, and to flit from one floor to another. That meant Brecky and some consulting friend, muffled in sweaters and overcoats, inspecting the rows and rows of bedrooms, discussing the wall paper, the flimsy furniture, debating with breath that congealed in the frigid air, whether this or that room was going to be cool enough, shady enough, airy enough.

But however the lights might flit about the building in those winter nights, there was one that remained steady and constant as the beam from a lighthouse. It came from the kitchen window. It sprang up every evening when dusk began to close in, and it always burned until nine o'clock or so. Brecky saw it now, as he turned the corner and struggled down the street at the end of which his hotel stood.

This was the hardest stretch, in the teeth of the terrific wind blowing inshore. It was like leaving the world and plunging into chaos. He went at it, head down, his eyes fixed upon the cheerful light, an agreeable hunger rising within him. That light meant Kathleen and the excellent dinner she was sure to have ready for him.

II

Brecky stamped up the wooden steps and across the veranda, opened the front door with his latchkey, and entered the house. It was colder in there than it was outside. The place wasn't designed for winter occupation, and there was no means for heating it. Moreover, its construction was flimsy, and a wind like that now blowing found its way in without trouble, and went moaning through the hall, rattling the doors and windows.

He passed through the dining room. It was entirely dark, but there was no fear of running into anything, for all the tables were drawn back against the walls and the chairs piled on them. He pushed open the swinging doors into the pantry, and another door, and was suddenly in a different world, warm, light, filled with delightful savors.

"Ah!" he said, with a sigh.

He slipped off his overcoat, cap, and rubbers, and went over to the stove, holding out his numb hands to its welcome heat. Then he turned and kissed his wife, absentmindedly, almost without looking at her, in spite of the fact that she was well worth looking at.

"Did Mullins come about those sash cords?" he asked.

"No—no one came. I haven't seen a soul all day," she answered; but he missed the significance of her tone.

She hurried back and forth with steaming dishes, and at last informed him, rather curtly, that his dinner was ready. He sat down at once and ate with good appetite, but in silence and abstraction, because he had to think about those sash cords. At last he finished and leaned back in his chair, ready for the amenities of life.

"Well, Kathleen!" he said. "You're one fine little wife!"

He was innocently oblivious of his wife's state of mind. It hadn't occurred to him that she kept on existing and thinking when he wasn't there. His remark was a match to dry straw.

"A fine little *cook*, I guess you mean!" she said with sudden asperity. "That's your idea of a wife!"

He laughed.

"Well!" he said. "They kind of go together, don't they?"

"Looks like it," she said; "only some cooks get paid."

It was his habit to ignore remarks like that. Women, he considered, were often fanciful and "touchy." It was better to leave them alone at such times. He lighted a big cigar, deliberately took his mind off his wife and all domestic concerns, and began to meditate on his business.

But the perverse creature continued to exist and to speak.

"I didn't start out in life to be a cook," she said, in an ominously calm and reasonable tone. "I'm glad enough to do it for your sake, Johnny; but I'd like you to remember that I'm not used to this kind of life."

"Yes, yes!" he said soothingly, and continued to smoke and stare at the fire.

"You never even look at me!" she cried suddenly.

"Yes, but I do!" he protested. "Sure I do!"

He looked at her then, with a smile, and saw that she was crying.

"For the Lord's sake, what's the matter?" he asked, with despairing good nature. "I'll look at you for an hour, if you like; only don't cry, that's a good girl!"

She put her handkerchief to her eyes, and went on crying. He swore under his breath, and, getting up, went around the table and put his arm about her.

"Come now!" he said. "You're as pretty as a picture, and you know I love you."

"Yes!" she said. "You want to make it up quickly and forget all about me!"

He couldn't help laughing at the woman's cleverness.

"Well!" he said. "If I do think such a lot about this business, who's it for? Don't be silly! It's all for you."

"It isn't! It's because you like it. You'd go on with it just the same if I was dead!"

He was a little in doubt what to do. Should he ignore her, and let her get over her inopportune temper alone? Or should he wheedle her?

He was really annoyed. He thought it all rather touching and feminine. They were all like that—wanted a man to spend his time making love and playing the fool; and yet, if he didn't provide all they wanted, or thought they wanted, they'd nag him to death. He kissed her again.

"We'll go in to the city some day next week," he said. "We'll take in a show, and all that. That's what you need."

"It isn't! What I need is some one to talk to. You never want to listen to me. You never ask me what I've been doing."

"But there's nothing you could do," he, answered innocently, "except cooking and sewing and—"

He was really surprised at her outbreak, she was usually so cheerful and equable. He looked at her flushed and furious face, the tears still in her eyes, and an unpleasant conviction came to him that this was going to be serious—and lasting.

"You come in," she went on, "and you sit down and eat your dinner, and the only thing you can find to say to me is to call me a *cook!*"

"I said you were a fine little cook," he began ingratiatingly. "Nothing wrong in that, is there? Why, I'm proud of you, Kathleen! Only this afternoon I was telling Sawyer how you could cook."

"Well, you'd just better find something else to praise me for!" she cried. "I'm something more than a cook, and the sooner you learn it the better!"

He was astounded and somewhat shocked at her violence—dismayed, too. He had an uneasy feeling that he couldn't handle this situation adequately. So, according to his habit, he decided to go away, believing, as many other people believe, that if he weren't in the situation, there would be no situation. But his cool deliberations were upset. Moreover, his cigar was out, and he didn't like relighted cigars.

He got the books in which he was trying to work out a new idea of hotel bookkeeping, but he couldn't do a thing. He couldn't put out of his mind the image of that girl, that provoking and beloved girl, with her angry, rosy little face and her eyes full of tears.

"Women!" he thought savagely.

No denying, though, that she was a wonderful wife and companion. She had never complained before, she had never failed him. Out of the corner of his eye, he saw her get up and begin carrying the dishes over to the sink. He thought he would help her, and then he thought he wouldn't. It would be weakness.

Still, it would do no harm to conciliate her. Perhaps, if he did, his working mood would return. He watched her for a few minutes longer, bending over the dish pan. Then he got up, went over to her, and, putting an arm about her, drew her close against him.

Then a devil entered into him.

"Why, you silly kid!" he said, kissing her. "You're the best little cook!"

She turned and gave him a smart box on the ear.

He was so astounded that he couldn't speak. He stared at her flushed and furious face, his own perfectly blank. Then, very slowly, the color began to rise in his lean cheeks.

He was a man slow to anger, a man of self-control and *sang froid*; but when his temper was aroused, it was a bad one. His wife was secretly horrified at what she had done. She hadn't meant to do it. She knew he was only trying to be funny. She was ashamed and alarmed.

"What made you do that?" he asked slowly.

"Because I'm sick and tired of being called a cook, that's why!" she answered valiantly.

"Well, you'd better apologize!" he said.

"Well, I won't!" she answered promptly. "I'm glad I did it. I'm just sick and tired of—of all this—shut up here alone all day long!"

"All right!" said Brecky. "*All right*!"

She looked at him steadily for a moment. Then she began, very deliberately, to dry her hands. He turned away and walked back to his books, but she saw that his hands were clenched, and she knew that he was filled with fury. She was elated, and she was sorry.

He began figuring, but he grasped his pencil so fiercely that it broke, and he had to get up and look for another.

He saw Kathleen standing before the little mirror she had hung up on the wall, dressed in her fur coat and engaged in pinning on her hat.

"What are you doing?" he asked.

"Putting on my hat," she answered calmly.

"Where do you think you're going?"

"I'm not going to tell you."

He smiled.

"Well, good-by!" he said.

Taking the key out of the lock, he went out of the kitchen, slamming and locking the door behind him.

"She can stay in there and think it over!" he said to himself.

III

Brecky made an effort to be light, careless, superior. He whistled as he went upstairs to the two rooms they used on the floor above—one as a bedroom, the other as a sort of office, where Brecky "saw people." He had plenty of material to occupy himself with here—letters and catalogues and estimates and so on. A little gas stove was burning in one corner, and the room was as neat, cheerful, and comfortable as it could be made by Kathleen's benevolent genius.

He had scarcely set foot over the threshold before a pang of remorse assailed him. Wherever his glance fell, there was something to speak of Kathleen and her care for him. He was by no means imaginative, but he was suddenly able to imagine his young wife alone all day in this huge, cold place. He began to have some idea of what her life must be.

"By gosh!" he thought. "After all, I don't know that I blame the poor girl for landing on me!"

And all at once the pathos of the thing overcame him—that poor little bit of a thing flying out at him like that—at him, who could have picked her up and shaken her like a kitten. He shouldn't have teased her. After all, there was more to her than her cooking. He hadn't fallen in love with her for that.

His impulse was to hurry downstairs and make it up; but he didn't see how one could make up a quarrel with a woman without giving her a present. It wasn't decent. Moreover, it would be too difficult. A present relieved a man from the necessity of making any sort of explanation, or of talking at all. You give the present, with a kiss, and it's done.

He walked up and down the room with his hands in his pockets, haunted by the image of Kathleen angry and Kathleen gay. The more he reflected, the more mysterious and oppressive was his sense of guilt, the more contrite and tender his heart. In the end he came to a decision extraordinary in one so stiff-necked. He resolved to go downstairs and say, quite frankly, that he was sorry, and that he loved her and didn't care whether she cooked or not.

The house seemed blacker and colder than ever as he descended the stairs. He wondered if she was crying in there, or scornfully washing the dishes. He unlocked the door, opened it, and entered.

He couldn't see her at all. He stared about the huge kitchen, which was well lighted. There were the dishes, just as he had last seen them, but no human being. Kathleen had gone!

He couldn't believe it at first. She couldn't have got out by the windows, for the heavy shutters were locked on the outside. There was no possible means of egress from that room except an incredible one; and yet, as she wasn't in the room, she must have got out that way. She must have gone down the flight of rickety wooden steps and through the cellar.

She had always been in mortal fear of the cellar, because there were rats in it. Brecky had always brought up the coal for her when she wanted some. In order to pass through it at night, she must have been in a desperate mood, he thought.

He was more disturbed than he cared to admit. Where could the girl go, alone, on a night like this, with a regular hurricane blowing? There was nothing for it but to put on his cap and overcoat and go in search of her.

The wrath of a woman had in it something peculiarly alarming and mysterious for Brecky. He felt that Kathleen was capable of the most amazing deeds, that she was not bound by any of his rules or scruples. He couldn't imagine what she would do. He was completely lost.

He opened the front door and stepped out into the tumultuous night. Fortunately there was only one direction in which to go, unless one wished to walk into the sea, and he didn't think that even an enraged wife would do that. There was nothing suicidal about Kathleen, anyhow. She was too sane, too solid, too honestly fond of life.

He was also aware that she was well able to withstand this weather. Where he could go, sturdy as he was, she could go, too. She was vigorous and resolute.

The wind was at his back now. He went with fierce impetus along the empty streets, and he went, inevitably, to the railway station. He entered the warm little waiting room, where a white-bearded agent dozed in his ticket booth.

The man looked up and nodded at Brecky.

"Too late!" he said. "She's gone!"

This might mean either a train or a wife.

"Ten minutes ago," the agent went on, full of the secret triumph he always felt at the spectacle of a thwarted traveler. "You'll have to wait two hours, and mebbe more."

Brecky sat down near the stove and set to work to frame a question which should in no way compromise his wife. He wished to seem aware of all her doings. He couldn't ask whether she had been at the station; but the agent assisted him.

"Your missus would 'a' lost the nine o'clock train herself, if it hadn't 'a' been near half an hour late."

"I'm glad she caught it, anyway," replied Brecky. "It's a case of serious illness. I told her to hurry along, and I'd follow as soon as I could."

"Your phone out of order?" asked the agent.

"Yes," said the quick-witted Brecky, "Did she telephone here?"

"Yep—said to meet the train when it got to the station."

"I wonder who she got on the phone!" said Brecky. "Probably her aunt or her cousin."

Splendid improvisation, for Kathleen hadn't a single relative in the city, to his knowledge!

"It just happens I heard the name," said the agent. "'Charley,' she says, 'I'm coming in unexpected, and you must come and meet me!'"

"I didn't know Charley was in New York," said Brecky thoughtfully.

"She didn't phone New York," said the agent. "I just happened to hear. It was New Chelsea."

"I see!" said Brecky.

IV

He took a cigar out of his pocket and began to smoke, and to think. His impassive face showed no trace of emotion. He was simply waiting for a train; but within he was in a panic, torn with rage, fear, and a frantic desire for action.

Who the devil was Charley? After all, what did he know of Kathleen? What did he know of women, anyway? He had left her alone for days and days, while he looked after business matters in the city. He had left her alone, partly because he wanted to go into the city, because he disliked solitude and quiet. How did he know what she thought of when he was gone? Charley!

He could scarcely endure it. His lean body trembled, like that of a nervous horse held brutally in check. He wanted to bolt. Charley!

Unfortunately, Brecky did not find it difficult to believe evil. His experience of life had been hard and definite. He had as high an opinion of Kathleen as he had ever had of a human being, but he was not trustful. He knew too much, and it was a one-sided knowledge.

It was possible that Kathleen was merely a fool, and didn't realize what she was doing; but this Charley wouldn't be like that. If women were more or less a mystery to Brecky, men were not. He had a sudden and very clear picture of Kathleen, neat, rosy, pitifully self-assured, alighting from the train, to be met by Charley.

All at once he knew who Charley was—that fat, owlish fellow who used to sit so often at Kathleen's table in the restaurant. Sands, his name was. He had money of his own, and used to bother Brecky for tips on the races. He used to sit for hours absorbed in the form sheets, trying to figure things out for himself—with the usual results. And Kathleen had turned from Brecky, the shrewd, the alert, the competent, to that fellow!

"I've got nearly an hour to wait, haven't I?" he asked.

Brecky's voice rang out sharply in the quiet little room. The agent opened his eyes, more startled than the words warranted. He fancied there was something in the other man's tone. He stared at him, instantly wide awake.

"I guess I have time to run home and get something," Brecky went on.

"Don't be late, though," said the agent. "This'll be the last train to-night."

Brecky vanished, slamming the door behind him. He retraced his steps with dreamlike ease. He was not conscious of progressing until he found himself once more at the hotel. He was filled with emotions so violent, with such a confusion of hatred, jealousy, and pain, that he was truly overwhelmed. His inarticulate soul could find no other words for his anguish than—

"No one's going to make a fool of *me!*"

He put his hand into his coat pocket for the key of the front door, but it wasn't there. He was obliged to go around to the back of the house and enter through the cellar. He felt his way through the piercing cold of that black underground cavern, and ascended the shaking wooden steps to the kitchen.

The kitchen gave him a shock. It was exactly as he had left it, neat, quiet, warm, with the clock ticking, the kettle gently steaming, Kathleen's apron across a chair. It was like the memory of a past irretrievably gone. Brecky's heart contracted with pain. He stopped for a moment, to muster all the resolution he had.

He went upstairs into the bedroom, and from a drawer of the bureau he took what he wanted. He caught a glimpse of himself in the mirror, saw his face strained and hard beneath his inevitable cap, and he thought he looked like a criminal in the movies. Well, why shouldn't he?

He caught the train. He got in and settled himself comfortably in the smoking car, deserted except for two men playing pinochle.

The train ran on smoothly, stronger than the wind. Brecky could see very little from the window except the slanting rain and now and then a blurred light. The turmoil in his brain never ceased. He looked unpleasantly wide awake, staring, like a somnambulist. His gray eyes never seemed to blink, or his face to move a muscle.

And for all his grief and fury he had no other words than that pitifully inadequate refrain:

"No one's going to make a fool of *me!*"

His cigar was out, but he did not notice it. He sat with a curiously alert air, like a pointing dog, immobile, but terribly ready. He was thinking.

He stopped the conductor as he passed through the car.

"Can you stop at New Chelsea?" he asked.

The conductor shook his head,

"It's not an express stop," he said. "You'll have to go on to New York and then take a train back. You'll have to wait till to-morrow morning, too. No more trains to-night!"

Brecky reflected. He took it for granted that if Kathleen had telephoned to the fellow at New Chelsea, that was where he lived, and where he was most likely to be found. He pulled at the conductor's sleeve as the man was moving away.

"Do you slow down anywhere near there?"

"Not enough for—"

"Just you tell me when you're going to slow down a bit," said Brecky. "I've got to get there. You won't be responsible."

"I should be," said the conductor sententiously. "Morally speaking, I should be responsible."

Brecky knew every inch of that line. As they approached the desired destination, he got up and went out upon the platform. The pinochle players saw him standing there, in the wind and the rain. Then, suddenly, he vanished. He had climbed down the steps and jumped.

The fall stunned him, and he lay still for an instant. When he could breathe freely again, he rose, and mechanically tried to brush himself off. He was always a neat fellow.

The train had disappeared, and he was alone in the universe. He could still hear the sea, dull and menacing, and the demoniac wind still blew. He didn't quite know where he was. His plan was to follow the tracks.

Wet to the skin, a sinister enough figure with his face nearly hidden by pulled down cap and turned up collar, he went doggedly forward toward the next station. He presented the appearance of a highwayman.

Before long he saw the feeble light of the New Chelsea station ahead of him, blurred through the rain. With a sigh of relief he mounted the wooden platform, where he was for the moment sheltered from the weather.

He tried to open the door, but it was locked. He looked in through the window, and saw the dimly lit room, quite empty, and the stove, without fire. Evidently the station master had gone for the night. This was a blow to Brecky, for he had counted upon making inquiries here.

He prowled around the platform, scowling, trying to plan his course. To his right he saw a few scattered lights, which must be, he thought, the village of New Chelsea; and he went toward them, along a muddy road. In due time he reached the main street. There was a drug store, closed and locked, with a ghostly green light in the window. There was also a protective light in the window of a well stocked grocery; but not a human being to be seen, not a sound to be heard, except the yelping of a dog somewhere in the hills that rose behind the town and partly sheltered it from the wind. Only a sudden cruel gust, from time to time, met him full in the face.

He turned a corner, and at the end of the street he saw a distant form, walking with a slow and deliberate step very familiar to him. It was a policeman, and Brecky hastened after him.

"I've lost my bearings," he said. "Is Charley Sands's place anywhere near here?"

The policeman hesitated for a moment, with rural caution.

"What do you want to go there for?" he asked.

"Well," said Brecky, laughing, "I suppose because I don't want to walk around New Chelsea all night in this weather. Three of us started here in a motor, but we broke down a little way up the line, and we couldn't get our bearings. We each tried a different direction, and I guess I'm the lucky one. Charley will have to turn out with a lantern to find the other fellows."

"Oh, they'll be all right!" said the policeman, disarmed. "There's houses and little settlements all around this part of the country."

He directed Brecky to the house of Charley Sands. A good walk, about three miles, he should say—uphill, and mighty hard to find in the dark.

"Oh, I'll find it all right!" said Brecky cheerfully.

V

He very nearly found something else that night. He lost his way entirely. He went on, as in a dream, along muddy roads, up hills so steep that he thought his weary heart would burst. He would not admit his intolerable fatigue, and the frightful ravages made by passion and bitterness. He wished to continue, inexorably, until he had accomplished his object.

The country was unfamiliar and hostile to this denizen of cities. When at last his strength was wholly gone, he did not know where to turn. He dared not wake any of the people in the dark farmhouses he passed. He crept up to a barn once, but a dog drove him away.

At last, at very last, he found an open shed behind a church, used as a shelter for the buggies and the Fords of the worshipers; and he crouched in there, relieved for a time from the unendurable confusion of the dark and the wind. His cigars and matches were dry and safe in an inside pocket, and he began to smoke. He hadn't the slightest wish to sleep. He didn't even feel tired. He only wanted to stop for a moment, to secure a pause in his superhuman exertions. He knew very well that if he hadn't found this refuge, he would have been defeated.

Wide-eyed and reflective, he sat in his corner until he observed that the stormy dark was changing its aspect, that it was growing faintly and drearily gray. It surprised him. He had forgotten that morning was ever coming again. He got up and set out on his way once more.

An extraordinary thought occurred to him. It would have been better, he said to himself, if he had died. He had lost Kathleen; why was he to live? What had he left?

He had no longer any heart for revenge. He was sorry he had to see it through; but, according to his queer code, it was absolutely necessary to vindicate himself. Otherwise his self-respect would be gone, and he could neither live nor die in peace.

It was nearly eight o'clock when he approached the house of Charley Sands, which an early stirring laborer had pointed out to him. He had planned that hour. He had also looked up the time of the train he meant to take—when he had finished. It was due to his self-respect to make a valiant effort to escape, although he didn't really care.

It was a trim white house surrounded by placid lawns. He went up to it with careless audacity, his hand grasping the revolver in his pocket. What did he care? Let Sands see him, let him ask what he wanted; he would soon find out!

Brecky had made himself neater, after his horrible night, than almost any other man could have done; but at best he looked haggard and menacing. He knew it, and was glad.

The weather had cleared, but he was still wet to the skin and cold, although he was not aware of it. He walked along the gravel path, which crunched under his firm tread. He was making no effort to conceal his presence. He wished to be observed, to bring this thing to its climax, to be done with it.

He ran up on the veranda, and, with one of those queer impulses of an abstracted mind, instead of ringing the bell, he knocked sharply on the door.

He heard some one coming down the stairs, and he smiled. If it was Charley—

But it was not. It was an entirely strange young woman, who looked at him with distrust. He was so taken aback that he could not speak. He stared and stared at her.

"Well?" she demanded impatiently.

"Sands here?" he managed to ask.

"What do you want with him?"

Brecky hesitated. His tired brain, flung loose from the pivot of his fixed idea, spun round helplessly. He couldn't really think at all. Another woman here!

He was roused by the sight of her preparing to shut the door in his face. He set his foot against it.

"I want to see him," he said. "You call him!"

She was alarmed then, and began to call "Charley!" in a shrill voice.

Down the stairs came bounding the fat and owlish young man.

"Well!" he cried. "Brecky!"

The young woman frowned.

"He didn't say who he was," she said. "I didn't know. Come in!"

Brecky entered, still dazed. They didn't seem at all surprised to see him, even at that hour of the morning, and in the lamentable state he was in. He sat down uninvited, threw off his cap, and lighted a cigar.

"This is my wife, Brecky," said Sands, in a tone of severe rebuke. "Kathleen's second cousin, you know."

"All right!" said Brecky.

His manners, usually punctilious, had deserted him entirely. What he wanted was for these people to clear out of their own room, and let him think for a moment; but the young woman sat down opposite him. She was rather nice-looking, in a shrewish way, but obviously hostile.

"She's here," she said.

Brecky sprang up.

"Let me see her!" he cried.

"I don't think she wants to see you," said the young woman. "I don't blame her. If she takes *my* advice, she'll never go back to you!"

Brecky looked at her steadily. He felt, however, that it was better not to say what he thought just then.

"You're just making a drudge out of her," the other went on. "It's a shame—a pretty, lively young girl like Kathleen shut up in that awful place! All you care about is getting your meals cooked. I wouldn't do it for any man. She's sick and tired of it, I can tell you—being your cook. If she takes my advice, she'll go back to her old job, where she'll have a little money to spend and see a little life."

"All right!" said Brecky again. "But maybe she doesn't want to take your advice. Anyway, I'd like to ask her."

"Well, I hope she won't see you. I know what you'll do—make all sorts of promises, till you get her back there again, and then she can go right on cooking!"

"Do I see her, or don't I?" asked Brecky, still quite calm.

"I'll see," said the peppery young woman, and went off and left him alone.

He had a new idea to contend against, and one for which there was in his experience no precedent. He could comprehend an elopement, but any subtler reason for his wife's leaving him was extremely hard for him to grasp. It was his habit, though, to face facts, and he tried now.

He tried to imagine Kathleen as a human being, and not as his wife; but he failed. What more could the girl want? He was filled with rage at her ingratitude, and at the humiliating position she had got him into. He was certainly being made a fool of, for the first time. He had done his best, had worked for her, had been sober, kind, loyal. What more could the girl want?

Whatever it was, she wouldn't get it—that she wouldn't! She had left him, and she could come back, if she wished; but he wasn't going to ask her.

"That's not my way!" he said to himself, with a grimace. "I won't crawl for any one. I haven't done anything. It's all her fault!"

He was half inclined to walk out of the house then and there, but if by any chance Kathleen was going to be sorry, he didn't want to miss it. He discovered that he was extremely anxious for her to be sorry, and that if she were, he might perhaps not be so very angry. She needn't even say it. One nice smile, and the thing would be over.

"I don't know," he thought. "Maybe it has been hard for her. She's only a kid. Of course, it doesn't excuse her running away like that, and making such a fool of me, but—well, I don't know. Maybe, later on, I'll get a servant for her. I could afford it."

VI

Brecky wheeled about, for some one had entered the room. It was the rebellious Kathleen herself. She seemed to him to have grown miraculously prettier overnight, and he was still less angry.

"Well, Johnny?" she demanded.

He resented that tone very much.

"Well!" he said affably.

There was a long silence.

"I'm taking the nine forty train home," said Brecky. "Coming?"

"No," said she.

Without another word, he picked up his cap and made for the door; but he was met by Charley Sands.

"Here! Here!" said he. "Stay and have some breakfast first, old son!"

"All right!" said Brecky.

He wanted breakfast badly. He also wanted to show Kathleen how unconcerned he was, that he was not hurt and bewildered and angry. He stood in the hall, talking to Charley. He was aware of Kathleen's voice in a near-by room, talking to that vixenish young woman.

"Married life's a great thing!" said Charley dismally.

"Sure is!" said Brecky.

He couldn't imagine how any man could marry if he couldn't marry Kathleen. He despised and hated Kathleen, but in common justice he had to acknowledge to himself that she was the prettiest and sweetest girl in the world, and utterly superior to all other women. She was—

Just then he heard her speaking. She had a clear voice that carried well.

"No," she was saying. "I think I'll make some pancakes for Johnny's breakfast. But see here—you needn't tell him I made 'em, Grace. I don't want him to think—but he looks dead tired, and he does love pancakes!"

That did it for Brecky. He ran down the hall and pushed open a door. It opened into the kitchen, and Kathleen, in an apron, stood at the table, before a large bowl. He paid no attention to the second cousin. He darted around the table and took Kathleen in his arms.

"Oh, come on home!" he said.

She began to cry at once, very comfortably, with her head buried in his coat.

"Don't be silly!" he said anxiously. "See here, Kathleen! Listen! We'll get a cook. We'll go to the theater, and—"

His wife raised her head and kissed him vehemently.

"Oh, Johnny!" she began, but stopped short, dried her eyes, and went on with great dignity. "Johnny," she said, "I wouldn't mind cooking and all that, for you, if you didn't—kind of expect it. That's what made me mad last night. You just expect—"

"Well, I won't any more," he assured her. "You come home, and I'll be darned surprised every time I get a meal!"

A few minutes later they all sat down to enjoy Kathleen's matchless pancakes. Eating them, Brecky also partook of the fruit of knowledge.

"You're one grand little cook, Kathleen," he thought; "but this time I won't say it!"

The Aforementioned Infant

The lawyer read the document aloud to her, but she did not understand. "What was that?" she asked timidly. "Free—"

"'Free access to the aforementioned infant,'" he repeated. "That means that you may see your child at any time—any reasonable time, of course," he hastened to add.

It did not take Maisie long to discover that there was no reasonable time. No matter at what hour she came to the house, she had to wait in the hall, sitting in a high-backed chair against the wall, humble, patient, like a child herself. The servants passed and repassed as often as they could find pretexts, for the sake of staring at this creature who had trapped young Mr. Lester into a scandalous marriage. The fact that she had not been notably successful as an adventuress stirred no one to pity. They had married, and it must have been due to Heaven knows what beguilement on her part.

Maisie had little charm for the casual observer. She was small, fragile, with untidy black hair and gray eyes immense and sorrowful. She dressed like a schoolgirl in a blue sailor blouse and a short dark skirt. Her pale face had the rounded contour of extreme youth. If the reckless Mr. Lester had betrayed her, one might have felt compassion for her as a forlorn and lovely child; but the fact that he had married her proved her to be basely calculating.

After a long time she would be taken up to the nursery. If the baby was asleep, she would stand beside the crib, her hands clasped, tears raining down her face. She would wait patiently until it awoke. Then she would lift the sturdy little thing, strain it to her childish breast, kiss its faint, silky hair, and press her own cheek against its plump one. She scarcely dared to whisper her passionate endearments, for the trained nurse was always there, looking at her critically.

"I don't like to see her pick up the baby," the nurse said to Mrs. Tracy. "She doesn't look healthy."

"I dare say she's not," replied Mrs. Tracy, with a sigh; "and who knows what she's been doing, or where she comes from? But I suppose it can't be helped. She had a legal right to see the child, of course. My son is very strict about her rights, and so on—very generous."

Her son himself was not always so sure of his generosity. He had moments when he thought himself little short of contemptible. Only moments, though; he was no rebel, and if his world was inclined to condone his offenses, or even to deny them, who was he to contradict it?

He was young himself—only twenty-two; a good-looking, silly, sweet-tempered boy. His life was one folly after another, always repaired by some one else. He did not imagine that he could do no wrong, but he felt pretty sure that any wrong that he might do could easily be undone by some one else.

He had found Maisie behind the counter of a candy shop, where he went to buy lavish presents for other girls. Her luminous and innocent eyes, her soft little English voice, had taken his fancy. She was quite alone in the world. She had come to America with her brother, a third-rate actor, a hard-working, ambitious fellow, for whom she was to keep house.

"But he died," she said simply. "So I'm working here."

She had been pitifully ready to love. She had taken all Lester Tracy's extravagant speeches in perfect seriousness. She didn't know how to conceal her sweet delight; and he had been very much touched by her artless affection. There was no one like little Maisie.

He often took her out to dinner, and to save his life he could see nothing in her to find fault with. She was always gentle, quiet, appealing. What if she was a shop girl? He knew plenty of girls of his own sort who might have learned much from Maisie. She was no gold digger, for she demanded nothing, expected nothing. She was happy if he took her out, but she was quite as happy if he stood in the vestibule of the wretched apartment house where she lived, and talked to her and kissed her.

She cared nothing at all for his money. He had tried to explain that, but no one would believe it.

He couldn't explain his marriage very well. He had come into the candy shop, one day, on his way home from a wedding breakfast, where he had had a good deal too much to drink. He had leaned across the counter and said to Maisie:

"Come on, Maisie, darling! Let's go and get married!"

She had got her shabby little hat and walked out of the shop with him, and they had gone down to the City Hall. He had been well aware of his condition, and a little afraid that he wouldn't be granted a license; but he had made a great effort, and had carried it off splendidly.

He had been very happy with Maisie. He had run away. For a time no one knew where he was or what he had done, and they had lived in a big seaside hotel, undisturbed by any thought of the consequences of the thing. He did not like to remember how sweet Maisie had been. He tried to forget the innocent gayety of that fortnight.

Of course he had been discovered, and the monstrousness of the escapade had been shown to him. He had been hectored and wept over and bribed, and he had given in, as he always did.

Maisie was no less docile. She had been told that she must give him up, and she did as she was told.

Her docility was a sore temptation to the Tracys' lawyer, who saw no reason why they should throw money away on a girl who didn't want it. He advised them to waive the question of a divorce for the present, but to ask her to sign an informal—and infamous—separation agreement, to accept a very small cash settlement, and to vanish. She saw clearly that no one on earth—alas, not even Lester—cared where she went, or what happened to her.

To the lawyer she seemed to be a singularly insensitive creature. Even Lester was surprised that she gave him up so readily, without even a word of farewell. She would have got more sympathy—and more money—if she had made a scene; but that never occurred to her. She accepted whatever life offered with the blind resignation of a child. She felt herself entirely helpless and ineffectual, and took refuge in a strange inner life of her own, in the most piteous dreams and fancies.

II

Without energy, without bodily or mental vigor, Maisie had the immeasurable strength of fortitude. She could live one day at a time, endure each misery as it came; and in her baby she found a sublime compensation for every sorrow. Her money was exhausted when she left the hospital, but she was accustomed to the idea of a lifetime of work; and now that she had something to work for, a new ambition had awakened in her.

Her brother had taught her to dance. Indeed, they had once laboriously rehearsed a "turn" of his invention which was to thrill the music halls. She knew all the hackneyed steps, the conventional gestures, and performed them with a conscientious and touching grace.

The stage was out of the question—she knew that. She had no stage presence, no commercial value; but she could teach. Her naïve confidence in her ability to do so convinced the manager of the Palace Dancing Academy, and he engaged her as a "lady instructor." The hours were irregular. She had to be on call from ten in the morning till ten at night, and was paid by the lesson.

She bought an evening dress from a secondhand dealer, an amazing affair of tarnished spangles and frowzy net, in which she looked incredibly dowdy. She could never learn to dress her hair. There were always silky threads waving as she moved, and one dark lock that insisted on falling across her forehead. One of her pupils said privately that dancing with her was like dancing with a rag doll. She seemed boneless and unsubstantial.

On the whole, however, she was well liked, for she took the greatest pains, was never impatient, never discouraged. Neither did she resent anything whatever. Some of her clients went far in their compliments, but her pale cheeks never flushed. She simply didn't care. She had done with men, and all her steadfast and gentle heart was given to her baby. The Maisie who went dancing about in the Palace Academy was an automaton, whose soul was locked up at home.

She knew nothing at all about babies. She didn't even know that there was anything to know. She read the label on a package of infant food, and followed the directions given. For the rest, she had vague ideas about keeping it swathed in flannel, giving it a daily bath, and taking it out in the fresh air whenever she could. She knew nothing of infant hygiene, and had never been told that the child should be let alone in order to develop naturally and healthily. She never let it alone, if she could avoid doing so; and still it developed mightily.

When she went out to give her lessons, she simply locked the room and left the baby in the crib. Sometimes she worried about fire, but she had no idea that what she did was wicked and shocking. On the contrary, she thought it inevitable.

She hadn't told any one that there was a baby, but Mrs. Tracy found it out, and was very much agitated. Her grandchild! Try as she would to let well enough alone, the idea tormented her. It was an intolerable shame that her grandchild should be brought up in squalor and degradation by this girl!

She went again to her lawyer, and he gave her sage advice.

"I've no doubt she'd be willing to give up the child for a suitable consideration," said he. "She seems to be a matter-of-fact young person."

So he went with Mrs. Tracy to offer the suitable consideration. They found the miserable furnished room and knocked at the door. It was locked, but the baby inside began to cry.

"I guess Mrs. Tracy's out," said the landlady, who was interested in these imposing visitors.

"Does she leave the child locked in the room alone?" demanded the outraged grandmother.

"Well, what else can she do?" replied the landlady. "But she's always home by quarter past ten."

So they came again at that time. Maisie had brought in a sandwich and a piece of cake for her supper, and had spread them out on the table. The baby's food was simmering over the gas jet, and the baby itself was propped up with pillows on the bed, jolly as a sandboy. Maisie had taken off her evening frock and put on a short, old-womanish sort of flannel dressing sack. Her short dark hair hung loose about her neck. She looked startled when she opened the door.

The senior Mrs. Tracy was an impressive woman, tall, slender, straight, with a high-bridged nose and pale, restless eyes. She had an arrogant spirit, but she came prepared to hold it in subjection, and to cajole, if necessary. She must and would have her grandchild.

Moreover, she fell in love with the baby at once. It was a vigorous, wild little thing, with rough dark hair and a glance farouche and bright. It was rather undersized, but perfectly formed and healthy.

"And she's dressed it like a monkey!" she thought angrily. "The child is certainly ten months old, and still in those ridiculous long clothes, and that absurd jacket! And *why* a bonnet in the house?"

Mrs. Tracy considered all this as evidence of Maisie's lack of maternal feeling, and she was astounded when the girl refused to sell her baby.

"Oh, no, thank you!" she persisted. "Oh, thank you very much, but I'd rather not. Thanks, but really I can't!"

The lawyer and Mrs. Tracy pointed out to her how grossly selfish she was, and told her that she thought only of her own pleasure, and not of the child's advantage. Maisie kept to herself certain ideas she had about these advantages. She was terrified, but resolute. She would not give up the baby.

III

Several times, after that, Maisie was summoned to the lawyer's office to be bullied and cajoled. She came as promptly and obediently as if a letter from him were an order from the Inquisition, but she would not abjure.

One evening, when she came home, the baby was gone. She might have protested against the illegality of her locked room being forcibly entered; but, as the lawyer well knew, those who are not aware of their rights are little better off than those who have none.

She came to his office early the next morning. He had expected her to come. He had also expected her to be somewhat lacking in self-control, but she was worse than he had imagined. He was very reasonable. He explained that the child was now in the custody of its father, and she would have to show cause why it should be removed therefrom. He hinted that she would not find that easy to do.

"Now, then, my dear young woman," said he, "you mustn't be selfish. Your child will be brought up with every possible advantage, and you shall see her whenever you wish. Compare what her grandparents have to offer her with the life that she would have with you. Your—er—young Mr. Tracy has no money of his own, you know, and there is no way to force any sort of—"

He saw with alarm that she was likely to become troublesome. She no longer wept, but her mouth twitched and her eyes burned.

"Then let them give me the money to take care of the baby, instead of their nurses!" she cried. "I'd do it all alone! The baby was always well with me, and so happy you can't think!"

It would have been convenient to expel this naughty child from school, but it could not be done. She would not consent to write a letter refusing to return to her husband. On the contrary, the mention of such a thing caused her a most ludicrous hope. Perhaps Lester really wanted to ask her, and these people were trying to stop him. She had strangely little affection for him left. She was, in fact, perfectly indifferent in regard to him; but if she got him, she would get the baby. That was all she wanted.

Mrs. Tracy went to see her again.

"Now, my dear child," she said, "you're very young. For your own sake, you don't want to go on like this, married and yet not married. You want to be free, so that you can make another choice, and, I hope, a happier one."

She went on to explain that if Maisie would only do as she was told, she would soon have a dazzling freedom. She might marry again; she could do exactly as she pleased.

Maisie had an ignorant fancy that she already possessed about as much freedom as she was ever likely to get, and she said she didn't want to marry any one else.

"But I'll do anything you want, if you'll give me my baby," she said.

She held firmly to that. Lester could have everything there was—freedom, money, as many wives as a Turk; she wanted nothing but the baby.

Mrs. Tracy desired and intended that her son should have everything desirable, and the baby as well; and she felt sure that in time this would come about. She had observed that everything comes to those who can afford to wait. If poor people were simply let alone, their own poverty would drown them.

IV

Lester Tracy was alone in the house, technically speaking. To be sure, there were four servants drawing the breath of life on the premises, but even they would have admitted unanimously that Mr. Lester was alone. He was dressing to go out, moving about in his room, and whistling cheerfully.

He was a lean, blond young fellow, his face already marked by dissipation; yet it was not a coarse or an evil face, only a frivolous one. He was little more than a tragic buffoon, and sometimes the poor devil was aware of it. Not now, however. Now he was happy, with his unfailing infantile zest for facile pleasures. He stopped whistling for a moment, to examine his closely shaved jaw; and then he heard a stealthy footstep in the hall.

Because nothing had ever happened to him, he was afraid of nothing. He had a vague belief that his person was sacred, that any evildoer would fall back abashed before Lester Tracy. He hoped it was a burglar; that would be something to tell his friends. He turned out the light and pushed open his door without a sound, very much excited.

But it was only Maisie, stock still, with her hand at her heart, and a white face. She wore a scanty rain coat over her tawdry, bespangled frock, and one of the big, floppy hats that she fancied. She had somehow the look of a masquerader, in clothes that didn't belong to her, and she certainly did not belong there in the Tracys' hall.

A very unpleasant emotion came over Lester at the sight of that little figure. He had grown accustomed to thinking of Maisie—when he thought of her at all—as one of his follies of which some one else was disposing. He had forgotten that she was real; but now that he saw her, she seemed more real than any one he had ever seen or imagined.

She was pale and motionless, and yet she seemed as startling as a blaze of light. Her forlorn and betrayed loneliness was like a halo about her young head.

Recovering from her momentary alarm, she went on toward the nursery. Lester was miserably irresolute. He wanted to go out and tell her to go boldly to her baby, to go arrogantly, proudly. He couldn't endure her furtiveness.

"After all, it's her baby," he thought. "My God, what an awful thing we've done!"

He imagined her in the dimly lit nursery, standing beside the crib, and looking into that chubby little face. It suddenly occurred to him that the nurse might be about, and might send Maisie away. He decided to stop that.

He had come out into the hall on that errand when Maisie, too, came out from the other room. She had the baby in her arms, huddled in a blanket.

They faced each other for the first time since their honeymoon. In spite of all that they had forgotten, in spite of the gulf of injustice and suffering between them, some little spark of honest and beautiful good will was in their hearts. It was not love—that had been murdered—but loyalty to their past love.

"Maisie!" he said. "Oh, Maisie! I'm sorry!"

She bent her head in an attitude of sublime and humble resignation.

"Just let me have my baby!" she entreated softly.

V

Mrs. Tracy turned the world upside down. Not a soul in that house could sleep, could rest, could eat, during her reign of terror. It was not only her personal grief at the loss of the child that distracted her, but the monstrous affront to her pride.

She was informed that Maisie had called to see her, and had been told to wait in the hall until she returned from the theater.

"And the treacherous, wicked creature must have crept up the stairs and *stolen* the child!" she cried. "She must have taken the poor, helpless little thing while it slept! Didn't you hear a *sound*, Lester?"

"Not a sound," said he.

"If there is a law in the land, she shall be punished!" said Mrs. Tracy.

If she could have had her way, she would have made it a criminal offense for any one to harbor the treacherous Maisie, to give her a morsel of food or a roof to shelter her. Her haughty spirit brooded over the insult until she was ill from it. The lawyer dreaded the sight of her haggard face.

"It's very difficult to trace so obscure and ordinary a person," he protested.

"My grandchild is neither obscure nor ordinary," she said. "Set your wits to work. The child *must* be found!"

As Mrs. Tracy had large resources and Maisie none at all, this was accomplished. The girl was discovered acting as general servant in a lonely country house—a wretched, ill paid position, with work beyond her young strength; but she could have her baby with her, and she fancied herself safe. From the kitchen window she could see her small idol staggering about in the grass. She could lie at night in her attic room with the child in her arms. They had food to eat, clean air to breathe, and a roof overhead.

Mrs. Tracy's idea was to go out there by motor and simply take the child away, but the lawyer dissuaded her.

"No," said he. "I shouldn't like that done again. It's apt to create prejudice against you if the case comes to court."

"I fancy I should only need to inform the judge how the child is living— sleeping in a servant's room—"

He shook his head.

"No," he said. "You never can tell how those things will go. I advise you to compromise with her—to leave the child in her custody six months—"

"With a servant? When she can have every possible advantage with her father? I will not do it. Let the case go to court. I fancy—"

"But you see," he explained, "after all, the mother is supporting the child more or less decently; and as far as I can ascertain, there's nothing against her character—no evidence to prove her an unfit guardian."

"Something *could* be found," said Mrs. Tracy.

The lawyer understood her very well, but he did not care to go so far. That sort of thing was done, of course, but not by him.

"I'm going to save the child," said she. "If you don't care to help me, I'll do it alone!"

He quite believed that she would, and he felt a small twinge of pity for Maisie.

VI

Maisie accepted blessings as she did curses, patiently and incuriously. She was not startled when a young man came out to the country, told her that he had noticed her dancing at the Palace Academy, and made her an offer to be his dancing partner for two or three cabaret turns.

She was no analyst of character, either. She took people on their own valuation, which is generally a flattering one. She was pleased and a little touched by Mr. Denbigh's friendly interest. It was a long time since she had talked freely with any one near her own age. She told him that she had studied stage dancing with her brother, and was sure she wouldn't be shy in public. She told him how anxious she was to get on in the world, for the baby's sake.

He offered her a loan as an advance, and she accepted it, agreeing to go back to the city at once and to sign the contracts he would bring her. She was so artless, so impersonal, so ignorant, that Mr. Denbigh went away a little disconcerted by the facility with which the first step had been accomplished.

"Mr. Ainsworth Denbigh," his card read. That, however, was not his name, and though he spoke with the slurred, agreeable accent of the New Yorker, he was not one. He was a slender, supple young fellow, with the queer beauty of Heaven knows what mongrel blood. He had dark, narrow eyes, olive skin, high cheek bones, and a delicate jaw. He had sprung up from nowhere; he had no tradition, no background, no scruples, no country, no friends.

In the middle of the dancing craze he had come to the surface. With his adroitly acquired manner, he had some success as a professional dancer in hotels, because women liked him. Then, as his vogue fell off, his means of living became more and more unsavory. Through a new and unmentioned lawyer, Mrs. Tracy had got hold of him. It was to be his role to prove Maisie an unfit guardian for the baby, and the thing was to be done thoroughly. Mrs. Tracy intended it to appear natural, inevitable, without the faintest trace of her guiding hand. She couldn't have found a better tool than Ainsworth Denbigh.

He had no trouble in teaching Maisie. She had a remarkable talent, a matchless grace, and she was docile. She learned the steps exactly as he wished. She was light in his arms as thistledown, but she was not passive. Her movement had a strange, exquisite quality; with all her supple body apparently at rest, she moved through space like a floating leaf, like a wind-blown flower.

She was utterly devoid of any sensuous allurement. Dancing to vulgar music, wearing the insolent dress he had advised her to buy, before gross eyes, the plaintive innocence of her beauty was unimpaired. Her gray eyes could meet any regard with the same clear wonder, her pale cheek never flushed.

Ainsworth Denbigh was decidedly overshadowed, but this didn't trouble him. Maisie was welcome to all the credit provided he got the cash, and their partnership was very profitable. They were making a name for themselves in a second-rate sort of way— "Mr. Ainsworth Denbigh and Miss Maisie Kent in ballroom dances *de luxe*." Better still, they were making money.

He often regretted that he had entered into an agreement to remove Maisie from the Tracys' path—not because he was touched by her forlorn youth and sweetness, or had any scruples of honor, but because he was well satisfied with affairs as they were, and resented the effort required of him. He made no headway with Maisie, and he had the wit to see that he never would. She was polite enough, and very easily swindled out of her fair share of their profits. Apparently she had confidence in him; but that was not enough. She was expected to fall in love with him, and obviously she was not going to do so.

She had taken a small flat near Morningside Park, and had engaged a colored woman to look after the baby. When their last turn was over, she was so eager to get home that she couldn't even attend to what Denbigh said to her. She refused to go out with him at any time, not from dislike or from caution, but because she had something so much better to do. She flew home to her baby as a white soul to heaven, and was divinely happy. She had no room for one thought of her dancing partner.

There used to be a proverb about the horse that was taken to the water and would not drink. Under modern conditions that horse would no doubt be forcibly watered and taught better. If Maisie refused to disgrace herself, then she must have disgrace forced upon her.

"See here, Maisie," Denbigh said one evening. "Let me come home with you and see this wonderful kid."

"Oh, I'd like you to!" she cried. "She'll be asleep, but sometimes I think she's prettier asleep than any other way. She gets a little paler, but that makes her lashes look so black!"

Mr. Denbigh was remarkably interested in her baby, but his entire behavior was remarkable that evening. He was terribly nervous, and seemed to be apprehensive about the time, consulting his wrist watch every few minutes.

VII

Lester Tracy was just leaving the house when he was called back to the telephone. He went petulantly. He wouldn't have gone at all if it had not been an anonymous call, and therefore faintly interesting. The past six months had not improved him; he was jaded, irritable, restless.

Maisie's quiet little voice had a singular effect upon him.

"Lester!" she said. "Will you please come? There's a man here, and he won't go away."

It was the first time he had ever been directly appealed to, had ever been asked to play a man's part. It steadied and fortified him miraculously.

"Of course I'll come," he answered. "What's the trouble?"

"I don't know. He said he wanted to see the baby, and when he got into the room he locked the door. He won't open it. Maybe he's been drinking. So I came here, to the telephone in the little dressing room—where I bathe the baby, you know," she explained in her careful, patient way. "It hasn't any door into the hall. I can't get out. And oh, I'm so afraid he might try to hurt the baby!"

Lester didn't think that. He wrote down the address and ran headlong down the stairs and into the waiting car.

VIII

It was by this absolutely unexpected action of Maisie's that Mrs. Tracy was defeated. Two detectives, who believed—because they had been so informed that they were employed by Mr. Lester Tracy to collect evidence against his wife, arrived precisely at the time when they had been told to arrive, and entered the flat. They found Maisie there, with a man who brazenly insisted that he was Mr. Lester Tracy. He didn't look it. He was disheveled, his coat was torn, he had a bad bruise on his cheek bone and a cut over one eyebrow, and he was incoherent with rage.

The detectives had reason to believe that the fellow was a Mr. Ainsworth Denbigh, and they said so. He told them that they would very likely find Mr. Denbigh in a hospital, although jail was where he belonged. He showed a marked inclination to make a row, which was not what they had been led to expect. In fact, he was so vigorous in his methods that the detectives were at a loss.

"Telephone to Mrs. Tracy," said he. "She'll come and identify me. Then you'll have the satisfaction of knowing who it is that kicks you out!"

They agreed to this, and sat down to wait. It was an odd enough group—the two detectives, both burly and severe, their hats on their knees, while up and down the room walked the disordered and vehement young man. All three were somehow overshadowed by the quiet and downcast Maisie, sitting with her feet crossed, her hands clasped, in that patient, meek attitude of hers. The light of a shaded lamp fell upon her shining dark hair, untidy as always. Just once she raised her clear, honest eyes to the young man's face, and he stopped short.

"Don't worry, Maisie!" he said. "I'll—I'll look after you!"

Mrs. Tracy had had to be fetched from a bridge party, and she was in no good humor. She was astounded, too, by the maladroitness of that man Denbigh in thus dragging her into an affair which she had strongly desired to avoid.

"I suppose something went wrong," she thought, "and he wants me to prove that he's not Lester. It's incredibly clumsy of him. Oh, I'll be so thankful when the wretched anxiety of this thing is over, and I have the poor little baby again! If it wasn't for the baby, I couldn't go through with it, but I'd do anything in the world to save the child from that outrageous girl!" She rang the bell of the apartment, and one of the detectives let her in. He was impressed by her frigid magnificence, her crown of white hair, her penetrating eye.

"Sorry to trouble you, ma'am," he said, "Won't take you a minute to clear this thing up. This fellow here claims he's Mr. Tracy, and—"

She smiled scornfully. The detective stood aside, and she preceded him down the hall to the living room.

"Where is this—" she began, but stopped short.

Her face blanched. She flung out her hand in a curiously helpless gesture, and it rested upon the detective's shoulder. She needed his support.

"Lester!" she said faintly. "Oh, Lester! It can't be—"

He had been filled with a terrible anger against his mother for this brutal and shameful ruse. He had thought he could never bear to see her face again, could never speak to her with common humanity; but when he did see her, in the anguish of her defeat, all that passed.

"Tell these men who I am," he said, "and send them away."

Her dry lips could scarcely frame the words.

"It's my son. Please go!"

With the resignation acquired in their profession, they went off, and the door closed behind them. Lester brought forward a chair, but Mrs. Tracy would not sit down. She had recovered something of her poise, and looked at him steadily.

"What does this mean?" she asked.

He did not find it easy to answer without reproaching her too cruelly.

"I'm glad it has happened," he said aloud. "I needed something like this to show me where I was drifting. If I hadn't known—if I hadn't come here—this—this crime would have been done, and very likely I'd have taken it all for granted. I've let this thing go on, I've let little Maisie be tormented and persecuted, and I've never lifted a finger to help her. It has been no one's fault but mine, because she's my responsibility. It's no use saying I didn't realize; it was my business to realize. But it's ended now. She's going to keep her baby!"

"Lester! My son! You don't know what you're saying! Simply because you've seen this girl again, and perhaps felt a little of your old, tragic infatuation—"

"I don't know whether it's that," he said slowly; "but whatever it was I felt for Maisie, there's never been anything else half so fine in all my life. I always knew that, but I hadn't the sense—or the manliness—to understand what it meant. I thought I'd get over it. I should have, in the course of time, and I should have been getting over the only thing in me that's good!"

He turned to Maisie.

"You're free, you know, Maisie," he said. "You can do exactly as you please. I give you my word you won't be disturbed again. You're to have the baby, and I'll see that there's a proper provision made."

"Lester!" cried his mother. "You cannot put me aside entirely—"

"I do put you aside," he said sternly. "It's Maisie's child, and she's going to have it. I wish to Heaven she'd take me, too!"

Maisie had not stirred or spoken a word. She got up now and went out of the room.

They looked after her with amazement. Mrs. Tracy came close to her son.

"Oh, try to realize!" she whispered. "It's your child, too. It's a Tracy. You can't abandon your own child to that ignorant, common girl!"

"Common!" said he. "I've never seen one like her!"

"She's—" Mrs. Tracy began.

Maisie reentered with the baby in her arms. It was asleep, lying limp and flushed against her frail shoulder. Over its dark, rough head, her eyes, misty with tears, met Mrs. Tracy's.

"I know it's my baby," she said in an unsteady voice. "My very own! It's wrong of any one to take her away from me, for one minute; but I know you love her. I wanted to say—" Maisie's voice broke entirely. "I couldn't be—cruel," she sobbed; "not now when I have her safe. I'll go to-morrow—I will indeed—to sign a paper—"

"What paper?" Lester demanded.

He came up beside her and put his arm about her. She looked up into his face with her old trust and candor.

"You don't need to sign any papers, Maisie, darling!"

"But I want to," she said. "I mean a paper to say that Mrs. Tracy is to have—" She paused for a moment, struggling with her tears. "I remember just how it goes. I want it to say that Mrs. Tracy is to have free access to the aforementioned infant at any reasonable hour. And *any* hour'll be reasonable—really it will. Even if the baby's in her bath, she'll be welcome to come in."

"Don't, Maisie!" cried Mrs. Tracy sharply.

"I mean it! I mean it with all my heart!" cried Maisie. "I know you love the baby. I know what it is to long to see her, and not be able to. I thought you'd like to hold her for a minute, now before you go home. It just makes the whole night different, when you've done that!"

On the way home in her car, Mrs. Tracy reflected upon the incredible thing that had happened. Of all wildly improbable things, the most improbable was that she should ever beseech and entreat Maisie to come home with her to live; yet she had done that.

Lester sat on one side of her, very silent, but she was not troubled by his silence. The sleeping baby lay against her heart, and one of her hands held Maisie's in a firm clasp.

Old Dog Tray

Murchison ascended the hill to the house that Saturday afternoon as usual, his pockets filled with presents for the children, and under his arm a box of Scotch kisses for Gina. His obstinate, lantern-jawed face showed all the satisfaction possible to it. This was always one of his happy moments, when he could almost fancy that he was coming home.

He had nothing else but Gina and Gina's children. It would not be true to say that he could not have lived without them, for he was not that sort. He would tenaciously have gone on living if he were translated among savages.

But the welcome he got at Gina's house was ineffably dear to him. From a distance he saw them all on the lawn. His face would have brightened, had that been possible to his dour visage, and he would have hastened his step, if he had not been already striding as fast as he could. Then one of the small boys saw him, and came rushing out of the gate.

"Here's Old Dog Tray!" he shouted joyously.

Gina called him back sharply, and came herself to welcome Murchison; but let her be ever so sweet and friendly, it was obvious by her overanxious manner and her flushed cheeks that she knew he had heard, and that she felt guilty.

Murchison was by no means delighted with the name. Quite the contrary—he was deeply affronted. He distributed the presents, but instead of handing the invariable box to one of the children, with the invariable joke— "Here are some Scotch kisses for your mother. You'd better give them to her"—he merely set down the box on the bench. He would have been glad to destroy the offensively arch object. He made up his mind never to bring another such box; and his mind, when made up, was an imposing thing.

"Old Dog Tray!" he thought. "That's how she sees it, eh?"

It rankled; it galled.

He conducted himself as usual. He played "red rover" with the children, dodging miraculously, lean, solemn, dignified even in his agility. He sat down to tea on the veranda, and when offered a slice of lemon he asked little Rose, according to precedent:

"Now do you think it would do more good to my complexion than harm to my disposition?"

There was his customary plate of buttered toast, and he ate three slices, as usual. No one but Gina, who knew him so well, would have suspected that he was hurt and angry.

She knew, though, that the only way to deal with Murchison was by rough outspokenness. He both dreaded and adored plain speaking. He was never happy until a thing was made clear and explicit, yet he shied away from any attempt at intimacy. He had, so to speak, to be seized by the neck and forced to listen.

She waited until the children were all in bed, and they had the sitting room to themselves, before she tackled him.

"Robert," she said, "I suppose you heard the silly thing Roddy said?"

"Aye!" said he, and at once began to sheer off. "Roddy's getting to be—"

"I'm sorry you heard it," she said gently. "It was just my own little name for you, and I wanted to keep it to myself."

There was magic in the woman, sewing in the lamplight. Even the few gray hairs in the shining flood of brown were dear to him, and so was the uncertain quality of her voice.

"Never mind it," he said.

"But I do mind it, Robert," she protested. "I'm sure you don't understand."

He looked nothing less than mulish, and she saw with despair that he intended not to understand. This must not be. The unclouded admiration of her faithful Robert was the breath of life to her. She looked long at him, but he smoked his pipe, refusing to raise his eyes, and at last she rose.

He glanced up quickly enough when he heard the piano. He liked nothing better than a song. Never did Gina touch his heart more surely than by her music. She was a slender, gracious little woman, still pretty. She often fancied that it was Robert who kept her young, that his sturdy refusal to admit any change in her arrested the course of time. She smiled over her shoulder at him, and began:

> "Old Dog Tray, he is faithful;
>   Grief cannot drive him away.
> He is gentle, he is kind,
> And you'll never, never find
>   A better friend than Old Dog Tray."

She sang it touchingly.

"Don't you see, Robert," she said, "that it's really a beautiful thing to think of you?"

"Yes, Gina, I've no doubt it's as you say," he answered, and she was satisfied.

She didn't know that she had made a terrible mistake, that she had done irrevocable harm. All the time she sang, he had endured torments. Suppose the children heard, or the servants? He was not Old Dog Tray! He would not be!

II

All the way over on the ferry Murchison deliberated the matter, and his slow wrath mounted high. He was not angry at Gina, for he could not be; what enraged him was his own position. He firmly believed that he possessed a fine Scotch sense of humor, but he was utterly incapable of laughing at himself. The idea of being sweetly sung to as Old Dog Tray had for him no comic appeal. On the contrary, he was obliged to admit that to some extent he was Old Dog Tray, and it was intolerable. "Kind" he was pleased to be, but "gentle" he was not, and "faithful" was no word to apply to a man.

He looked back over this affair. He had met Gina when she was a young girl, a lively, witty young thing. He had fallen in love with her, and had set to work in a decorous way to court her. He had come over to Staten Island twice a week. This had seemed to him sufficient evidence of devotion, but when he observed that other young men brought her presents, he did likewise. Books and music were what he preferred, and he was willing to go as far as candy, but he would rather have died than be seen carrying flowers.

Privately he thought this American lavishness very foolish. His idea was to save up to get married; but he realized that if he wished to marry Gina, he must please her. So he tried, but while he was engaged in the process, she married Wigmore.

It was then necessary for Murchison to show that he didn't mind that in the least, for he was horribly proud and sensitive. Obstinately he kept on coming twice a week with books and sweets, and Wigmore became attached to him. He was really more interested in Wigmore's conversation, and in the children, than he was in Gina, although he didn't know it.

Gina had changed astoundingly. She had ceased to be lively and witty, and had grown sweet and a little vague. Murchison was too obstinate to admit any change in her, however—or in himself, either. He refused to think at all.

When Wigmore died, and poor Gina had so much trouble about money, and was so ill and grief-stricken, she became real for Murchison again. He had felt a passionate tenderness for her. He had done everything in the world for her, though well knowing that such disinterested devotion might make him appear ridiculous.

After a seemly interval of three years he had suggested marriage. Gina asked for time to make up her mind. He thought that quite reasonable and proper, but it occurred to him this evening that five years was longer than necessary, even to the most cautious woman. It wasn't as if he were a stranger. She had seen him twice a week for nearly twelve years.

He was suddenly convinced that he was a fool. Other men came to see Gina when he wasn't there. He heard the children speak of Dr. Walters, for instance, as if he were a familiar friend. The same thing would happen again.

No, it wouldn't. Perhaps grief could not drive him away, but other things could.

When he returned to his boarding house, he wrote a grim letter to Gina, in which he said that she must make up her mind at once either to take him or leave him. At once, mind you; he refused to wait for an answer longer than six months.

He appeared again on his usual evening, and didn't mention the letter. Gina knew that he never would mention it until exactly six months had passed. He was quite as usual, and only one small incident perturbed her. After dinner, when they were alone, he said:

"Will you not sing 'Old Dog Tray' for me, Gina?"

"But—" she said.

"I'm thinking it does me good," said he.

While she sang, he sat there in wooden silence, smoking his pipe.

"Well!" he thought. "It's a queer world, to be sure! Who'd think that at my age I'd come courting, and the object of my affections a woman thirty-eight years of age? I'm forty-one, and here I come courting like a lad!"

This made him grin. It seemed to him a very humorous idea, and when, later in the evening, it recurred to him, he was obliged to grin again.

"Why do you smile, Robert?" asked Gina softly.

"Well—well, it's nothing, as you might say." But he could not banish the grin.

"Do tell me!" she implored. "It's so seldom you find anything funny. Please share it with me, Robert!"

"I'm thinking you might not like it," he said, with a chuckle.

"Oh, but I shall, Robert! Tell me!"

He burst into a shout of laughter, so that his lean face was creased with long lines.

"What will you say, Gina," he said, with difficulty, "to Old Dog Tray going courting, and you a woman of thirty-eight?"

She sprang to her feet.

"Robert!" she cried, quite pale with anger.

"It's the funniest thing—that's come to my mind—this long time," he said, almost helpless with laughter. "Think of it!"

"How dare you?" she said. "How dare you insult me like this?"

His jaw dropped.

"Insult you!" he repeated. "What's this, Gina? Insult you! Why, my dear—"

"You think—" she began, but sobs choked her. "You're laughing at me because I'm thirty-eight!"

"But I was not, Gina, my dear! Only it struck me comical for two old bodies like us to be courting."

"I'm not courting!" she cried. "Don't dare to say it! And I'm not old!"

"Of course, properly speaking, we're not old," said he. "But—"

"Every one else thinks I'm a young woman!" she sobbed.

"Don't you believe it, my dear," he said earnestly. "They may say so to your face, but behind your back no one would call a woman of thirty-eight—"

"Stop!" she cried hysterically. "Don't call me a woman of thirty-eight again!"

He was very much distressed.

"Don't be thinking I mean anything against your—your personal attractions," he said. "You're one of the neatest, best-looking women of your age—"

"I hate you!" said Gina.

"That's an ill-considered remark," replied Murchison, growing red, "to a man who's been your true friend for twelve years and ten months. I was only trying to tell you that I think as much of you to-day as I did when you were young and pretty."

"You needn't go on, Robert," she said, frigidly. "I appreciate your friendship, but I have never known a man so lacking in tact."

"I don't doubt you're right, Gina," he observed, also frigidly. "It didn't occur to me that a mature and sensible woman couldn't endure to hear her age mentioned."

"It's the way you did it—laughing like that."

"I wasn't laughing at you—only at myself, for courting you."

"Please say nothing more," she interrupted sharply. "There are other— other people who don't think it's so absurd to—to like me."

Now, well as Gina knew him, there were certain traits in her Robert which had eluded her. She never knew that by this simple remark she had mortally insulted him. She was comparing his twelve years and ten months of devotion to the false flattery of that Dr. Walters.

"Aye!" said he. "I've no doubt it's as you say."

And with that he took his leave.

III

On the last day of the six months Murchison presented himself before Gina, and without embarrassment, and also without fervor, requested to know his fate. He was greatly displeased with Gina's conduct on this occasion. She wished to be indefinite; she wished neither to take him nor to leave him, but to keep him in reserve.

"You know how fond I am of you, Robert," she said.

"No," he replied, "I don't. My question was just, as you might say, to determine that point."

"Sometimes I think that, on account of the children, I shouldn't marry again," she said tentatively.

"That's for you to say. You ought to know," he remarked.

"I suppose at my age, I ought!"

He bowed stiffly. There came to Gina the recollection of what Dr. Walters had said. He had assured her that she was like a young girl.

"You've never grown up," he had told her. "You never will."

"I'm afraid, Robert," she said, "that I never could make you happy."

He turned away, and was silent for some time.

"That's for you to say," he repeated. "You ought to know your own mind."

His chief purpose was to avoid showing how horribly wounded and bereft he was. So valiantly did he conceal his hurt that Gina herself was offended and angered by his high spirits.

"I believe he's glad!" she thought. "He's delighted to get out of it!"

She forgot entirely how she had lain awake at night, planning some way to tell Robert that she couldn't marry him. On that night she lay awake marveling at his treachery. She had decided that he didn't really care.

On the evening of his next visit she had Dr. Walters there. She had the doctor's superior devotion on exhibition, and encouraged him to be incredibly gallant and tender. He did his part admirably, but Murchison failed her. He was pleasant, unusually pleasant and talkative, and he gave no more sign of being a disappointed suitor than if he were her grandfather. He made a most favorable impression upon Dr. Walters.

Before he left, he did something which enraged Gina.

"Will you not sing 'Old Dog Tray'?" he asked blandly. "It is a great favorite with me."

She refused, but Dr. Walters joined his entreaties to Murchison's, and she had to yield. So she sang the simple old ballad with burning cheeks; and while she sang it, there sat Robert, smoking his pipe in wooden silence.

IV

He went home that night in a queer mood. He was hurt and he was angry, but depressed he was not. He went up to the room he had occupied for years and years—a room which, like his face, showed no trace of the spirit that possessed it. He sat down to unlace his boots and put on his slippers. When that was done, he filled another pipe.

"Perhaps it's just as well," he reflected, with a philosophy Gina would not have appreciated. "A wife's a very unsettling thing. Now I'll go on just the same!"

And, if you will believe it, the next Saturday afternoon he bought a box of blocks, and a doll's cradle, and the familiar package of Scotch kisses, and with perfect composure set off for Staten Island.

"There's no reason at all for a quarrel," he thought. "To be sure, I've nothing against the poor woman. I'm not one to change."

There was a heavy fog, and the boat was late. He stood downstairs, close to the gates. He was in no sort of hurry. Indeed, he rather enjoyed the little stir of excitement caused by the fog.

He heard people about him saying it was the worst they had seen in years, that a small boat had been run down a few hours before, that steamers were held up. He liked the din from the bay, the whistles low or shrill, the clamor of the bells, the blasting wail of a great foghorn.

There was, unfortunately, no way in which he could verbally express his scorn for this excitement, and his own miraculous coolness and detachment. He could look it, however, and more than ever he assumed the aspect of a wooden image. For some reason this inspired the confidence of a fellow traveler.

"Do you think there's any danger?" asked an anxious voice.

He turned, intending to answer somewhat loftily, but he was utterly disarmed at sight of the questioner. Indeed, he at once felt that there might well be danger. He removed his hat with ceremony.

"Nothing to worry about," he assured her gravely.

She was a tall and rather thin girl, very dark, with a wonderful rich color in her cheeks and great, serious eyes. That seriousness was the thing which first attracted him—that, with her sober dress. It took a second glance to reveal that her dress was shabby and her seriousness tinged with something forlorn; to say nothing of her being very young and very pretty.

Now Murchison was a cautious and practical fellow, by no means given to talking to strangers; and he decided that he would not look at the girl again. A boat had just come in, so that he really had something justifiable to stare at.

There came first the inexplicable persons who run and sometimes shout; then motor cars, and streams of people, and drays and trucks with vociferous teamsters. It was what happened every half hour or so, all day long, yet it had the thrill there always is at the end of a journey, no matter how short. And now, belated and fog-haunted, the incoming ferryboat might have returned from the Antipodes.

The traffic, the shouts, the procession of people, ended abruptly. Then the gates were pushed open, and the new swarm crowded forward, as eager to be carried south as the others had been to rush northward. Murchison was perfectly aware that the girl kept beside him, although he didn't turn his head. He could lose her easily enough by crossing over to the smoking cabin; but he had to let a truck go by before he could do so, and, without quite turning his head, he saw her, hesitant and dismayed, looking after him.

Long after he was settled with his pipe he remembered her dark face, her troubled eyes, something alien and tragic in her, and he felt uneasy, almost guilty. He knew it was nonsense, the particular sort of nonsense that he most disliked. He was sorry he had not bought a newspaper to distract his mind.

A bell clanged; the boat slowed down, and the throb and jar of the engines stopped. A great many people rushed to the windows, as always happens, and this gave Murchison the chance for being most notably Scotch, and not stirring. His sharp ears caught all the wild and confused rumors and surmises of those about him. He felt incipient panic in the atmosphere. He was grimly amused, until it suddenly occurred to him how silly women were—how very, very silly a young girl would be, with no Scotsman beside her!

He got up and crossed to the other cabin. That was not ridiculous; it committed him to nothing. He entered the cabin and sauntered through it, looking with an eye casual but very keen at the backs of the people crowded two deep at the windows.

That girl wasn't there. Perhaps she had rushed upstairs. If so, she might stay there, for he had gone quite far enough.

He pushed open the door, and stepped out upon the forward deck. No denying that the fog was unpleasantly thick, and that ominous and immense shapes appeared half hidden behind it. The bells and whistles on every side made a diabolic clamor. The boat was drifting silently, and the fog concealed even the water on which it floated; and yet, with nothing visible, he was in a crowded and noisy world, menacing, incomprehensible.

He saw her out there, one hand on the railing, her young face in profile. She had, he thought, such a forsaken air! She was so lovely and young! She put him in mind of the beloved and half forgotten creatures in the romances he had read in his young days—heroines brave, gentle, and beautiful, for whom a man could die gladly. She was shabby, she was frightened, she was alone, as a heroine should be. There was a halo of romance about her dark head.

But still Murchison was entirely Murchison. He could have leaped overboard and saved her from the sea more easily than he could address one single word to her. He was eager to speak to her, to reassure her, but it was not possible.

Her anxious glance, turning in his direction, fell full upon his face.

"Do you think anything's going to happen?" she asked, as promptly and simply as if he were an old friend.

"No, no!" said he. "But with these crowded ferries they're very cautious."

He came over to the rail and stood near her. He had an absurd desire to remove his hat and to stand bareheaded before her innocent youth; but he resisted this preposterous impulse, and spoke in his driest way. He gave her facts about the shipping in this stupendous harbor, quoting figures, reports. He had an uneasy feeling that he was tiresome, and probably making mistakes in his statistics, but he was so desperately occupied in not looking at her that it distracted his mind.

"I find it an agreeable trip," he ended abruptly.

He was obliged to look at her then, to see if his talk had wearied her, and he observed a strange expression upon her downcast face.

"I'm so afraid of the sea!" she said faintly.

"But this is only a bay—" he began.

She glanced up.

"My father was a captain," she said. "He was drowned when I was a baby; and my brother was drowned in the war. So—you see—"

"Yes," he answered gravely. "I see!"

He did not try to express sympathy, he did not speak one reassuring or consolatory word. He stood silently beside her, neither seeking nor evading her attention, simply being his own uncompromising self. Never in life had he tried, never in life would he try, to make a favorable impression upon any one. He took it for granted that she knew all the compassion, interest, and respect he felt; and she, on her part, accepted him without question.

"Do you think we'll be kept here long like this?" she asked.

"It's impossible to say; but there's nothing to be alarmed about."

"I'm late," she said anxiously. "You see, I've come all the way from Philadelphia this morning, and I got a little mixed up. I was expected for lunch, but it's much too late now."

"Won't the people—your friends—wait?" asked Robert indignantly.

"They're strangers," she said. "I've never seen them. I'm going as a governess. I was recommended to Mrs. Wigmore—"

"Mrs. Wigmore!"

"Oh, do you know her?" the girl asked.

"I am acquainted with the lady," said Robert, in so curt a manner that she was abashed.

She fancied that he regretted having been drawn into conversation with the governess of some one whom he knew. She flushed a little, and turned away her head. She expected him to make some excuse and to leave her; but he did not. He stood where he was, filled with the most unaccountable chagrin and disappointment.

She was going to Gina! She would see him there, see him as Old Dog Tray! He felt as if some ineffable happiness had been snatched from him. He felt suddenly middle-aged and preposterously unpleasing.

An instant ago he had really believed that this marvelous girl was interested in him, friendly toward him, even glad of his company. Well, only let her see him climbing the hill with his arms full of bundles, only let her see him playing with the children, being treated with slightly condescending affection by Gina, only let her see Old Dog Tray in his natural habitat, and he would never again be anything but that in her eyes!

"I'll not go," he decided. "I don't doubt they'll do well enough without me."

But, thought he, what good would that do? He knew so well Gina's fatal lack of discretion, her shocking habit of confiding in every one. It was impossible to believe that she could have a governess in the house twenty-four hours without telling—even boasting—about her Old Dog Tray.

"The devil!" he said, dismayed at the prospect.

Then he realized that he had spoken aloud, and he apologized earnestly to his companion. He was surprised and relieved to see her smile—not plaintively and sweetly, like Gina, but with a wide, youthful smile that was almost a grin. With a faint shock he realized that while she was undoubtedly an angel, she was also a delightful human being.

They were suddenly upon a new footing. They began to talk with miraculous ease. They exchanged names. She said she was Anne Kittridge, and instead of being, as he had half imagined, an isolated phenomenon, she had a mother and a home in Philadelphia.

"I've never been a governess before," she said. "I've never even been away from mother. I hope—do you think I'll get on with Mrs. Wigmore's children?"

"Aye," said he, "I've no doubt you will."

"But I'm not beginning very well," she said, "being late like this."

"And no lunch!" said he. "I'd forgotten that. It's—let's see—it's nearly three o'clock."

"I don't care," she said stoutly.

He did, though. He was greatly worried.

"Well," he said, after much thought, "I've a box of sweets here. Very poor things they are for the teeth and the digestion, but I dare say they're better than nothing."

He set to work to unwrap his neat package. As he did so, the box of blocks fell out upside down, and the contents scattered over the deck.

"Oh!" said she. "Were they for your little boy?"

He did not answer until he had picked all the blocks up. Then he straightened himself, with a slight frown.

"I'm a bachelor," he said. "They were for the child of an old friend." And he added resolutely: "A very respectable, middle-aged body."

The boat had started again, but they didn't notice it. Miss Kittridge was steadily and happily consuming Gina's Scotch kisses.

V

It would be impossible to any chronicler to describe all that took place in Murchison's soul during that brief trip. The easiest way is to say bluntly that he fell in love, and for most readers that will go a long way toward an explanation; but one must bear in mind the character of the man, his frightful obstinacy, his outrageous pride, and the matter-of-fact romanticism of his secret heart.

He was amazed, delighted, awed. He knew that he was in love; he knew that this was the real thing, for which he had always been waiting. Lack of self-confidence was not among his faults. He hoped, he believed, that if he could have a clear field, he would have a fair chance with this matchless girl. She liked him, she trusted him; she was amused by his jokes, interested in all the information he had to give. If he could keep her from seeing him as Old Dog Tray!

"I won't have it!" he thought fiercely. "I won't have this spoiled by such a thing!"

The boat bumped its way into the slip, and a lurching procession of people came up to the gates. Miss Kittridge wished to join them. She glanced anxiously at Murchison, but he didn't stir. The gates opened, and the crowd began to hurry off.

"Hadn't we better go?" she said.

"Very well," he answered absently, and off they went.

"Mrs. Wigmore told me to take the North Shore train," she began, but Murchison grasped her arm firmly and led her to the waiting room.

"Miss Kittridge," he said, in a peculiar voice, "you'd better not go there."

"But why?" cried the startled girl.

"Well," he replied, "well—mind you, I've nothing to say against Mrs. Wigmore. I've a very high opinion of her. She's a very pleasant, respectable woman; but I advise you not to go there."

"But I must! She's expecting me; and where else can I go?"

"Go back to your mother in Philadelphia," said he.

"I can't, Mr. Murchison. It was my own idea to go out and earn my own living, and I'm certainly not going home before I've even tried."

"There's a train every hour," said he. "I'll go with you, and I'll explain to your mother."

"Explain what?" she protested, overwhelmed with astonishment.

"It'll be better explained to your mother," he told her. "You're too young."

The doors were opened, and a new crowd was pressing through them. Murchison joined the stream of people, leading his reluctant and protesting companion back on board the ferryboat.

VI

Gina was shocked and hurt beyond measure. She had thought it very strange of Murchison to write to her from Philadelphia, to say, without explanation, that he would be there for a week or two on private business. How unfriendly of him to have private business after all these years!

After that he didn't come near her for three months. He telephoned now and then, and said he was very busy; apparently he did not notice how grieved was her manner,

And then, after all this, what happened? A thing incredible—he telephoned to her one afternoon and told her that he had been married that morning. She could never, never forgive such brutality. He might at least have given her a chance to marry Dr. Walters first!

"Where are you now, Robert?" she inquired sternly.

"We're in New York for—"

"Then you must come to dinner to-night with your—bride," she said.

"But—" he began.

"It seems to me that is the least you can do," said Gina, and he was defeated.

Naturally she had Dr. Walters there for dinner, and naturally she was charmingly gracious and kind. No denying that she was impressed by the youth and prettiness of Robert's wife. The fact that a well bred, lovely creature certainly not more than twenty-one or twenty-two had been willing to marry him forced her to admit that she had not appreciated him.

"You have a wonderful man in Robert," she gravely assured his wife.

"Isn't he?" said Anne. "There's no one like him!"

Then, of course, she had to look at him, to see if he was still there and still as wonderful. He was. He met her glance, and they smiled at each other with sublime confidence and understanding. Gina found it a little hard to go on talking.

"Do you know," she said brightly, "such a curious thing happened! A friend of mine wrote me about a girl in Philadelphia, and I sent for her to come as governess for the children. She told me that she'd arrive on a certain day, but she didn't come, and I never heard another word from her. I wonder if you know the name—Kittridge?"

"Philadelphia's quite a large place," said Anne hastily.

"Of course," Gina assented. "Now do tell me about yourself and Robert. Was it romantic?"

"Oh, very romantic!" said Anne, in no little confusion. "It was—I think it was —unique!"

There was a pause, and Robert came directly toward them.

"Will you not sing, Gina?" he asked blandly.

"No, thank you, Robert," said she.

But Dr. Walters came to entreat also.

"Please do, Gina!" he said, with all his honest admiration reflected in his beaming face.

"Sing 'Old—'"

"No!" said she, so vigorously that he was startled.

He turned to Anne.

"You should hear her sing 'Old—'"

"Please don't ask me!" she cried.

"Of course not, if you don't wish to," he said gently; "but upon my word, Mrs. Wigmore's rending of 'Old Black Joe' is—"

"It was 'Old Dog Tray' I had in mind," observed Robert.

"That's a hateful, silly song!" said Gina. "I can't endure it. It's—the whole sentiment is false. There are no Old Dog Trays!"

Robert's hand fell lightly on her shoulder, and she turned to look at him. Something that she saw in his face brought the tears to her eyes.

"There are old friends, though, Gina," he said, "and nothing drives them away!"

The Married Man

She had got used to Andrew's forgetting all sorts of important anniversaries. In fact, she rather liked him to do so. It gave her something to forgive, and fed her measureless indulgence. All his eccentricities, his absurdities, his brilliant and explosive energy, his terrible exactions, constituted "Andy's ways," which she loved with a deep and pitying love.

Even if he was clever and successful and attractive, he couldn't do the things she could do so easily and so well. He couldn't darn his own socks or cook a dinner or make a bed. She insisted that he was helpless—that all men were helpless. She was the sort of woman who would have pitied Julius Caesar because he couldn't make an omelet.

Something of this kindly indulgence was reflected upon her nice face as she sat in the library sewing and waiting for Andrew. She was a handsome, dignified, good-tempered woman of thirty-five, who was never to be taken by surprise. No matter what might happen, she would raise her eyebrows and smile and say, "Well?"— which was her nice, kind way of saying, "I told you so!"

And generally she had told you so, because, like so many other unimaginative people, she could almost always foresee ordinary consequences. Her prognostications were based, not upon probabilities, but upon experience.

It was the tenth anniversary of their wedding—an important day in a household. And yet, knowing Andrew as she did, Marian had made no preparations for festivity, because he was as likely as not to forget or to neglect even a special dinner. She would remind him when he came in, and smile at him, and he would be startled and contrite. She would not acknowledge the little wound that was there, even to herself.

Nor would she acknowledge what she really knew quite well—that Andy wasn't happy, as she was. Hadn't she provided him with all the materials for happiness—a lovely, peaceful home, three pretty, healthy children, and just the social background he required?

What is more, she knew that no just man could find a fault in her as a wife. She was thrifty, conscientious, sympathetic, a correct and popular hostess, an excellent mother. She was never irritable, never gloomy, never exacting. She was handsome, and understood how to dress. There was really nothing within the domestic cosmos to which a sane man could object.

That may have been the trouble. Andrew was a man who did not approve of happiness. He wanted and required to be forever struggling and rebelling and resenting. Marian had often, with amusement, noticed him trying to provoke a quarrel with her; but of course he never could, for she never quarreled.

The clock struck eleven. She sighed a little, laid down her sewing, and picked up a book. It had been a very trying day. Andrew had vanished, without the least regard for appointments he himself had made, or office hours, and she had had to placate all sorts of people without knowing at all the cause of his delinquency. It was simply another of "Andy's ways," and a very troublesome one in a doctor.

She recognized it as part of a wife's duties to smooth the path of her husband—above all, of a husband who was the next thing to a genius. She was accustomed to hearing him spoken of as "brilliant." She was proud of it, and secretly a little proud of his eccentricities. He was an extraordinary man, no doubt about it, and he required a wife of extraordinary tact.

He was a physician, but not satisfied with that. He liked to write articles and give lectures, and he had a reputation as a very daring if not very sound investigator along sociological lines. He had proclaimed and printed office hours; but if he were busy writing, he wouldn't see any one who came, and it was Marian, of course, who did have to see these people and get them away not too grossly offended.

At other times there would be some patient who interested him, and he would shut himself up with him or her; and again in this case Marian had to soothe and placate the other patients who had seen the favored one admitted, and who naturally resented being kept waiting so outrageously. There was not a trace of jealousy, or of curiosity, in Marian. She smiled at his interest in a pretty woman.

She wasn't too much interested in anything—certainly not in the book she had taken up, for she put it down again with a yawn within a very few minutes, to look at the clock and to give a small sigh. She couldn't help wishing that Andrew had remembered what day it was, at least to the extent of an extra kiss. Even the most sensible and placid woman might wish that.

Then, at last, he did come in, in a mood she knew well; and her faint hope that perhaps he had remembered, and would bring her flowers, fell stone dead. He flung himself into a chair, hot and tired and rather pale, with his red hair ruffled up, giving him the look of a sulky and earnest child.

"Well!" said Marian, with a nice smile. "Here you are! Such a day as I've had, Andy! People telephoning and insisting that they had appointments and refusing to be put off; and poor me without the least idea where you were or when you'd come back! There was that poor woman with the albino twins—"

He frowned impatiently.

"That doesn't matter. I don't want the case, anyway. No! See here, Marian. I want to talk to you."

She said "Yes?" inquiringly, with her kind and pleasant face turned toward him, but he didn't look at her. He sat staring at the ground, huddled down in his chair, rumpled, disheveled.

"What is there about him so attractive?" Marian reflected, not for the first time.

He was not handsome, he was very untidy, he was casual, rude, distrait; a slender, wiry red-haired fellow of thirty-five, with a sharp-featured, rather pale, freckled face and restless, bright brown eyes.

At last he looked up at his wife, still frowning.

"Don't be hurt!" he said. "And *try* to understand!"

"Of course I will, Andy."

"I've been walking," he went on, "for hours—almost all day—thinking it out. This lecture that I'm to give, you know, to-morrow—"

"Oh, yes—before the Moral Courage Club."

"I'd made fairly comprehensive notes of what I was going to say; but it's been growing on me, every day, how weak and cowardly it is—how evasive. I hadn't *dared* to be frank. I never have dared. I've compromised. I've lied. I've kept it up for ten years—ten years to-day, Marian!"

"Kept up what?" she asked, startled.

"This damnable hypocrisy!" he cried. "This wretched, revolting pretense! Do you know that it's the anniversary to-night of that horrible ceremony—that perjury—that mockery we called our marriage?"

Marian had grown quite white.

"Why, Andy!" she faltered. "I never thought—I thought—I always hoped you were—happy!"

He sprang up and began to pace the room.

"I can't *stand* it any longer!" he cried. "I'm at the end of my tether. Oh, this *marriage!*"

"Is it—me, Andy?" Marian asked rather pitifully.

"No! No! It's simply marriage—marriage with any one. It's this base, disgusting monotony, this abominable pettiness, this eternal talk about servants and children and coal-bills and neighbors and card-parties. It stifles me. It sickens me. I can't *live* any more unless I'm free!"

"Do you mean that you—want a divorce, Andy?" she asked, with a gallant effort to disguise her terror and distress.

"No," he answered, "not necessarily. I shouldn't like to lose you altogether, Marian—unless, of course, you'd like to form another connection. Would you?"

"No—no, Andy, I wouldn't!"

"I didn't think so. What I want, Marian, is simply to ignore our marriage. I want to be released from its petty restrictions and obligations. Will you do that, Marian? Will you absolve me from all these preposterous 'vows,' and so on?"

"Yes," she answered promptly. "I will—if you like."

"And you won't be hurt? You won't be petty? You won't think I'm not fond of you, Marian?"

She shook her head.

"You see, don't you, that we can be just as fond of each other, and yet go our separate ways?"

"Are we—does that mean—that we're to—part?" she asked.

He came over and laid a hand on her shoulder.

"My dear girl," he Said, "I can't live with you any longer."

She couldn't restrain a sob.

"Oh, Andy! Oh! Is there—some one else?"

"No! Can't you *see?* I want to be alone—to live alone—in freedom. I'll take a house for myself somewhere, and you'll go on here, just as usual; except that I'd like to have the children part of the time. I won't be unreasonable, though."

"I don't think I'd—like to—go on here, without you," she said in a trembling voice. "I'd be—lonely."

"Nonsense! Not after a day or so. You'd enjoy the freedom, too. I've got my eye on a little house that will suit me very well. And really, Marian, I'd very much prefer you and the children keeping on here in the same way. Of course, I should make you the same housekeeping allowance, and so on."

"I would like a little freedom, too," she said. "I—can't stop here—without you, Andrew."

"Well, of course," he answered, rather disconcerted, "I've no right to dictate to you."

"You can stay here," she said, "with the children, and I'll go and stop with mother for a few days, where I can think it over quietly. Then I'll send for the babies. I—you see, I want to—get used to this. It's—rather sudden."

It was no longer possible to conceal the fact that she was weeping. Her husband was really distressed. He patted her lovely, shining hair with a careless hand, while he scowled anxiously before him.

"My dear girl! Please! This isn't a tragedy, by any means. Simply let's be two sensible, modern people who refuse to be bound by certain conventions. Do be your own sensible self, won't you?"

"I—will—try!" she sobbed. "Only—you'll have to give me—a little time."

He looked at the clock; it was a little after midnight.

"Perhaps I'd better leave you alone," he said. "I'll be going now."

"Going? Where? At this hour?"

"Well, you see—that lecture to-morrow. It's to be 'Marriage from the

Man's Point of View.' I can't, with any dignity, any decency, say what I wish to say—be really honest—in the character of a domestic man. It would be a farce. I must be able to say that I'm a free man, do you see?"

"Yes," she said, wiping her eyes. "But—does that mean it's got to begin now?"

"What?"

"The—living apart?"

"I'm afraid so. I thought I'd go to a hotel for the night, and send after my things in the morning."

"Oh, no, Andy, please! I couldn't explain—to the servants. No! That's the only thing I ask you. Let me be the one to go. You can say it's a telegram from mother."

"Nonsense, my dear girl! I won't hear of it! Turning you out of the house at this hour of the night! Let *me* go!"

"No, Andrew, I'd rather; really I would! I'd *like* to go. I—need a change. If you'll call a taxi while I pack my bag—"

"You're quite sure?" he asked anxiously, and again she assured him that she really wished to go.

She went up to the big, lamp-lit bedroom, so immaculate, so charming, with its two brass beds, the dressing-table and bureau gleaming with silver, the soft gray rug on the floor, her dear little sewing-table, all the photographs

"Oh, *why?*" she cried. "Oh, why do I have to leave it?"

She went about in her brisk, sensible way, selecting things out of one drawer and another and packing them neatly into a bag; but long before she had finished a sudden spasm of pain overcame her. She sat down in her own particular wicker chair, and sobbed bitterly.

"I *don't* understand!" she cried. "I *don't! I don't!* Not a bit!"

II

She was her usual calm self when she came down-stairs again, and was able to give her husband a great many directions and suggestions as they rode to the station.

"I'll send a night letter to Miss Franklin to come and take care of the children till I send for them," she said. "I happen to know that she's free now. She's such a capable girl! You'll have nothing to worry about with her in the house."

Anxiously, but timidly, afraid that it was a reactionary and contemptible insistence, but resolute to save herself in the eyes of her world, contemptible or not, she added:

"And you'll be sure to say that I got a telegram from mother, won't you,

Andrew?"

She kissed him good-by kindly, pleasantly, and succeeded in getting into the train with her nice smile still on her lips. Andrew was reassured, and went home to spend what was left of the night in completing his lecture notes.

He fell asleep toward morning on the sofa in his office. He would no doubt have slept peacefully on till noon, as he had often done before, if it hadn't been for an unusual noise in the dining-room at breakfast-time. He was a little indignant, for he had never been disturbed before, and he was curious, too. His children—even the four-year-old Frank—were singing lustily, in unison, a jubilant sort of chant, led by a very fresh, clear, loud young female voice.

"Hail! Hail!" they shouted.

All ruffled and rumpled as he was, he entered the room, to find a strange spectacle. His three children were standing on the window-seat, with arms outspread and face upturned. Behind them stood a young woman in the same yearning attitude, while they all cried their invocation:

"To the glorious sun that gives us life, all hail!"

That must have been the end of it, for the children got down and made a rush at him.

"Oh, daddy! Mother's gone to grandma's!" the eldest little girl told him eagerly. "Miss Franklin's going to take care of us. *I'm* going to write to mother every single day, but not Jean and Frank. *They* only scribble. She couldn't *possibly* read it!"

He was not attending. He was looking at the young woman who stood beside him, smiling. She was a short, sturdy blonde with a very pretty and impudent face, a wide, jolly mouth, and queer gray eyes, which were at the same time immensely candid and quite mysterious.

"I'm Christine Franklin," said she. "I'm the originator of the Franklin method of child care. I dare say you've heard of me. Your wife sent me a night letter to come and take charge of your little family for a time. That's what I do, you know—go from house to house, and liberate."

"Liberate?"

"That's how I put it. I always insist that there shall be no interference from parents or relatives or servants. Then I begin to set the children free—to let them express themselves—to be natural."

"I see!" said Andrew. "Is breakfast over?"

It was not, and after a brief toilet he sat down to enjoy it with his family. He felt that he rather liked Miss Franklin.

"Nothing clinging and hyperfeminine about her!" he thought. "A man could make a friend of a girl like that."

He decided to study her. Now that he was free and couldn't be misunderstood, he had decided to make a comprehensive study of woman in general. He knew that there were points about them that he didn't understand. He couldn't really generalize upon the effects of marriage without a better knowledge of females—he admitted that. Why not, he asked himself, begin with this interesting specimen?

"What is the Franklin method?" he asked her.

"It's not really a method at all," she said. "It would be better to call it a theory. It's simply nature and art, hand in hand. I don't believe in directing or controlling a child. I simply help it along the road it indicates itself. My mission is solely to point out beauty to it."

"That's likely to make it very much more difficult for them to become accustomed to discipline and self-restraint when they're old enough to be held responsible."

"But, you see, I don't believe either in discipline or self-restraint, in children or in adults. The natural impulses are sufficient. No, Dr. Nature implants in us only right and beautiful desires. I look upon self-restraint as superfluous, if not absolutely wrong, in a wholesome person."

"Social interdependence requires—" Andrew began.

"We *shouldn't* interdepend. We should each be a law unto himself. Let us be healthy, in mind and in body; then let desire be the sole rule, the sole conscience. Personally, I know that if I want to do a thing, it is right to do it. If I want to have a thing, it is a right thing for me to have."

Andrew contested that, but she merely smiled at his arguments.

"Well!" she said. "As for *me*, when I want something, I go after it—and I generally get it."

Andrew met her clear, shameless glance, and an unaccountable shudder ran through him. What a girl! What an enemy she would make—or what a pursuer!

She was undoubtedly an interesting and convenient subject for his new study, but he didn't study her. On the contrary, he avoided her. He shut himself up in his study and tried to write, but the new freedom for his children entailed such a distressing amount of noise and quarreling that he accomplished very little.

He wished to write a long and careful letter to Marian. He was afraid that she hadn't fully understood, that she was a little hurt, in spite of what she had said; but he found it a remarkably difficult thing to explain to a woman that you are very fond of her and yet wish to be rid of her. He was not the first man who has essayed such a task.

The noise in the dining-room became intolerable. He tore up his third attempt at a letter and went in there, in a very bad temper.

"Why the devil do you stay in here?" he shouted to his young family. "Why aren't you out in the garden, or at school, or wherever it is your mother sends you? Don't you know that I'm trying to work?"

Miss Franklin had entered from the kitchen, eating a slice of bread and sugar.

"Ask the cook for some!" she suggested, and the children vanished. "What are you writing?" she inquired frankly.

He didn't care to mention the letter, so he said:

"My lecture. I'm giving one this afternoon, you know."

"What on?"

"'Marriage from the Man's Point of View.'"

She pricked up her ears.

"What is a man's point of view?" she asked.

"For a man," he said, "marriage is moral death. It is slavery—bondage of the worst sort. It is a handicap which prevents any effective progress. It is, of course, an invention of woman's, to safeguard herself and her off-spring. She has found it necessary to provide herself with a refuge, and she has ruthlessly taken advantage of her sinister influence over the more sensitive and conscientious man to impress him with a mass of false and pernicious ideas about the 'home.' Man has not one single advantage to gain from marriage, yet he has actually been taught, by mothers, by women teachers, by all the females who surround young children, to think of it as a privilege. He secures a home. What is a home? A nest for the woman, a cage for the man. What is a wife? The most unprincipled, exacting slave-driver ever yet developed. For her and her children he is required to give all the fruit of his labor, and, in addition, a fantastic and debasing reverence and flattery—"

"You poor thing!" said Miss Franklin.

He stopped short, in surprise.

"Why?" he asked. "What do you mean?"

"You must have been so wretched with your wife," said she.

His face turned crimson.

"I wasn't," he said, with an immense effort at self-control. "Quite the contrary. One doesn't apply general remarks to—specific cases."

"Oh, yes, one does indeed!" Miss Franklin insisted.

III

He went off quite in the wrong frame of mind to deliver his lecture. When he had taken a stealthy peep at his audience, he became actually nervous. The Moral Courage Club seemed to be made up almost entirely of women—rows and rows of earnest faces. It would be very unpleasant to wound and distress them, as his words were sure to do, especially as they had all contributed toward the fee he was to receive. For a minute he was almost tempted to soften some of his remarks, but his reformer's ardor flamed up again, and he went out upon the platform bravely.

The sight of their feathers and furs and earrings helped him. After all, they were nothing but barbarians, who must be enlightened at any cost. He began. He told them, as kindly as possible, how selfish, how greedy, how uncivilized they were, how unpleasant they looked in their skins of dead animals and feathers of dead birds, with all their savage and unesthetic finery; how brutally they preyed upon man.

"Marriage ruins a man," he said. "It stifles his ambitions; it coarsens him, it debases him. It outrages his manly self-respect. He is debarred from wholesome and essential experiences. He is shamefully exploited. He is forced into hypocrisy and deceit. Partly from his native kindliness, partly from his woman-directed training, he never dares to tell the truth to the opposite sex."

And so on, directly into those earnest faces, framed by all their barbaric plumes and furs and jewels. To his surprise and dismay, none of them changed, grew abashed or angry or stern. They were only *interested*, all of them.

They came up in a body when he had finished, and congratulated him.

"You are always so stimulating!" said one.

"You brush aside the non-essentials!" said another.

"It gives one a new outlook!"

"I hope to see it in print. It is so suggestive, dear doctor!"

Only one of the earnest horde made any sort of individual impression, and that was a slender, dark, elegant woman who approached him after every one else had gone.

"Doctor!" she said in a low, thrilling voice. "I feel that I *must* speak to you. Let me take you home in my car, won't you?"

She was interesting, distinguished, and, he fancied, intelligent; so he was quite willing to follow her to her waiting motor-car and to seat himself beside her.

"Your lecture," she began. "It's such a startling idea to me—that of man being the victim in marriage."

"Yes," he said. "It's not the conventional, romantic idea, of course."

"Nor the true one," she cried. "Oh, doctor, your brain may be right, but your heart is wrong! There is so much that you don't seem to know—to understand! You don't seem to realize how hideously *we* suffer—what *we* endure. I cannot pretend to be impersonal. I want to tell you the truth— a side of it that you don't know. I want to tell you of one case. Then you must tell me what you think."

She laid her hand on his arm and looked earnestly into his face.

"I want you to hear my story, and then tell me frankly whether or not *my* husband was a victim!"

It was a very long and very harrowing story. It obliged them to go to the lady's house and to have tea there, and to sit in her charming little sitting-room until dark, in order that it should all be told.

She was Mrs. Hamilton, she said, known to Marian, as to all other women of any social pretentions in that particular suburb, as the martyr wife of a fiendish husband. What she had suffered no one knew—except the twenty or thirty people whom she had told. She ended in tears.

Andrew comforted her with kindly words and complete exonerations. He said that she was blameless. The clock struck six, and he rose to take leave.

"Good-by!" said Mrs. Hamilton, giving him her slender hand. "Doctor, you've *helped* me. You've *understood*. Mayn't I see you again? You don't know what sympathy means to a lonely, heart-broken woman."

He assured her that he would be delighted to come again, as soon as he had a free moment.

IV

He had declined the use of Mrs. Hamilton's motor; he preferred to walk home and to reflect upon this new type. He was not altogether a fool. In spite of the fact that she was a very attractive woman, he had made up his mind that he would never go to her house again—not even to study her.

"No!" he was saying to himself. "She's morbid—irresponsible. They're really dangerous, that reckless sort!"

A hand clutched his sleeve and a breathless voice cried:

"Oh, doctor, I've been rushing after you for miles and miles!"

It was little Mavis Borrowby, daughter of an old patient. Always in the past Andrew had taken Mavis for granted as part of old Borrowby's background. He was quite disconcerted to see her, this spring evening, as a detached individuality, and a very vivid one.

She took his arm and hung on it, looking up into his face with babyish violet eyes.

"Oh, doctor!" she cried. "I went to your lecture. It was simply *wonderful!* But it depressed me awfully. Please let me walk along with you and ask you some questions!"

"Child, you shouldn't go to my lectures," said Andrew indulgently. "You're too young. They're not for you."

"Oh, but they *are*, doctor! Why, I'm engaged, you know—at least, I *was* engaged, but I sha'n't be any longer. I wouldn't for worlds do all that harm to a helpless man. I'm going to tell Edward so to-night."

Andrew was a little taken aback. He said something about thinking things out for oneself—not accepting another person's ideas.

"Oh, no!" said little Mavis confidently. "I know you can think ever so much better than me. I *like* to get my ideas from *wonderful* men like you!"

The innocent, naive, violet-eyed little thing touched him with pity. What, he thought, was there in life for her except marriage? He couldn't imagine her engaged in any work, any profession, any art. Would it not perhaps be better if some man were enslaved and sacrificed for the sake of this poor little baby-girl?

"Look here, Mavis," he said; "this won't do. You mustn't throw over this fellow, you know, without a great deal of serious reflection. You might ruin your life and his, too."

"But you said I'd ruin him by marrying him—"

"Never mind that. You—you're too young to grasp it. And there are always exceptions. If you care for this chap—"

"I don't really think I do, much," she said thoughtfully. "Anyway, I simply couldn't stand making a martyr of him, and having him be the one to do all the sacrificing. But, doctor, what *are* we to do, if men mustn't get married?"

He couldn't answer. To tell the truth, he had thought of marriage so exclusively from a man's point of view that he had quite overlooked the woman's. Freedom was all very well, but it wasn't for the little Mavises of this world. He began to deliberate whether there weren't certain men who should be set apart for marriage and martyrdom for the sake of the really nice young girls.

He was about to suggest this theory to Mavis, when he found himself before his own door.

"Hurry off home now, won't you?" he said. "It'll be dark soon. And see here, Mavis, don't say anything to your Edward just yet—don't do anything until we've talked it over. Come into the office some afternoon."

She said she would, and hurried off, in the sunset.

As he let himself in, he heard from the dining-room the uproar which seemed an inevitable accompaniment of the Franklin method. Because playing in the dining-room had formerly been an unimaginable thing rather than a forbidden joy, it was now the rule. The doctor didn't like it. He wanted his dinner in peace. It was not the sort of dinner he liked, either, and Miss Franklin distressed him by incessantly crunching lumps of sugar.

He retired to his study, where he swore furiously to himself; but for some reason which he didn't care to analyze, he dared not tell Miss Franklin to take away the children. Nor was he surprised when she knocked at the door, and, being told to enter, did so, and sat down opposite him, prepared to spend the evening.

Crashes, screams, and slaps from the dining-room disturbed her not at all. She said she didn't believe in supervising children; it hampered them.

She talked persistently about free love, which Andrew didn't like. When spoken of as the relation of the sexes, it was quite proper and scientific; but directly one introduced that idea of love, it was entirely changed. It became sensational and distinctly alarming.

He was thankful when an accident occurred in the dining-room which could not be ignored. Little Frank had climbed into a drawer of the sideboard and broken through, and in the course of his struggles he upset everything within reach.

Once he had got Miss Franklin out, Andrew took good care that she should not get in again.

V

He had forgotten all about Mavis, and he was pleasantly surprised when she came into his office the next afternoon.

"I pretended that I had a sore throat," she said, "so I could come and see you. You see, Edward came last night, and oh, doctor, he did seem so awfully *flat*, after *you!*"

"You mustn't be so extreme," he said. "There are some men who aren't at all unhappy in marriage."

"I know. Ordinary little men aren't. It's only the *wonderful* men like you. But, doctor clear, I couldn't be happy with an ordinary man. I—I want a man like *you!*"

It wouldn't do, of course, to tell her that there were mighty few men of this sort, and that they wouldn't care for naive little girls, anyway. Andrew wasn't even much flattered by her admiration; it was too indiscriminate.

"Suppose you don't marry," he said. "What will you do?"

"I thought you could tell me. I thought, of course, you had some perfectly wonderful sort of plan for women."

Well, he hadn't, and he saw that he must make one. It seemed that his first step toward the settlement of this specific case would be to make an analysis, and he at once began. Mavis answered all his questions readily and fully, but he had a suspicion that she told him what she thought he would like to hear, instead of keeping to facts. Still, even at that, he learned a great deal, for she was too ignorant and young to deceive a trained observer. Of course it took a very long time; his other office patients had to be sent away.

He went politely to the door with Mavis, and he was surprised to see Miss Franklin standing in the hall—the little private hall which was only for outgoing patients, and in which she had no possible business to be.

"What are you doing out here?" he asked.

"I was just wondering what you were doing," she retorted, "shut up in there with that girl all this long time!"

"I was writing an analysis of her."

"Let's see your analysis!"

"It's not finished. Besides—"

"Do let me see it! Perhaps I can help you."

"You don't know Miss Borrowby—"

"Oh, yes, I do know Miss Borrowby!" said Miss Franklin. "I know her better than you do!"

Andrew didn't like her tone, but he let it pass, with a meekness quite new to him. Miss Franklin smiled and went away.

He intended to spend the evening perfecting his analysis in peace; but scarcely had he got well started when Miss Franklin opened the door.

"A patient!" she said.

It was a lady. She sat down beside Andrew's desk, without raising her veil, and at once began to sob.

"Oh, doctor!" she cried. "I don't know what to do! Oh, my suffering! What shall I do?"

He felt quite sure that this was a drug addict, and his manner, though kind, was one of thorough sophistication.

"Now, now, my dear madam!" he said. "Don't excite yourself!"

"You don't even *know* me!" she cried, pushing up her veil.

"I do!" he protested guiltily. "It's Mrs. Hamilton. I knew your voice; but it's dark here in the corners of the room when there's only the lamp lighted."

She smiled bitterly.

"Yes," she said. "That's it. I'm lost in the darkness, outside the circle of lamplight!"

"This chair—"

"I'm speaking figuratively, doctor. I'm in such trouble. I wish I were dead!"

Reluctantly, but in duty bound, he said: "Tell me about it."

She began to weep again.

"You're the only one I can tell. You showed such an interest in me the other day. You cared, didn't you?"

"Yes, certainly I did; but please don't cry."

"Oh, dear doctor, it is your own great trouble that makes you so sympathetic to others, I am sure!"

"My own great trouble?"

"I heard of it indirectly—through Miss Franklin. She mentioned it to some one I know. She said that your wife"—Mrs. Hamilton dropped her voice, and ended with the greatest delicacy: "That your wife has left you.

I *am* so sorry!”

"Nothing of the sort!" Andrew began angrily.

Then it occurred to him that it would be difficult, if not impossible, to explain so modern a situation to so romantic a creature; so instead he encouraged her to tell him her own sad story.

He never learned what her trouble was, because she didn't tell him. "My husband" and "a woman's sensitive heart," and "disgusting intoxication," had something to do with it. She cried forlornly, and he tried to stop her. Common sense and all that he had learned from experience of her type warned him not to be too sympathetic, but it was difficult. She was exquisite. She had a sort of morbid charm about her—a sensibility at once dangerous and pitiful.

He rose, went over to her, and laid his hand on her shoulder.

"It's hard," he said. "Life is bound to be hard for people like you; but you must try to see it in a more robust way, with more humor, more indifference."

"I do! No one knows how I try!" she said, looking up into his face with her dark eyes, luminous with tears.

Suddenly the door opened, without warning. Miss Franklin looked in, and disappeared again. Mrs. Hamilton rose.

"Who was that?" she asked.

"That's Miss Franklin."

"Oh! I didn't know she was so young. Does she stay here as late as this?"

"She lives here."

"Lives here—with your wife away?"

Mrs. Hamilton was moving toward the door.

"Good night, doctor!" she said, and there was a decided coolness in her voice.

VI

Peculiarly disturbed, Andrew returned to his office, to find Miss Franklin there, waiting for him. He was about to reprove her sharply for her outrageous intrusion, but she spoke first.

"Who was that?"

"A patient; and you must never, under any circumstances, come into this room when I have a patient here."

"It's long after office hours. I didn't know it was a patient. She was 'a lady to see the doctor,' and I wondered what you were doing shut up here."

"You needn't constitute yourself my mentor!" he cried angrily.

"Why, doctor, I never thought of such a thing!"

"Then please don't do it again."

"But, if she wasn't a patient, what was she here for?"

He stared at her, astounded at her effrontery—and uneasy.

"As I told you once before, I am making a series of analyses. I was making a study of—that lady."

"You only analyze women, don't you?"

"Certainly not!" he answered with a frown. "Only they happen to be about—"

"Yes, they do!" Miss Franklin agreed warmly. "They certainly do happen to be about!" She sat down. "I've been analyzing *you*," she said.

Again instinct warned him, and he would have fled.

"Not worth it!" he said lightly.

"I can analyze you," she went on; "but I can't understand myself. I don't quite see why you should affect me so. I'm not at all inclined to sentimentality. I've never felt like this before."

He sat in frozen silence.

"And as a perfectly free woman," she went on, "I'm not ashamed to tell you that I want you."

"Want me to what?" he asked stupidly.

"I'd be even willing to marry you," she said, "as soon as you get a divorce. I can see that you're timid and conventional, like most men."

"Good God!" cried Andrew. "Please—"

"Why not? If you don't love me now, you will later. I'll make you. I've set my mind on you. I think you're a fascinating creature!"

"You don't know me!" he protested feebly.

"I do. I know that I'm in love with you, anyway, and that you're lonely and need me."

"Lonely!" thought the wretched man. "Not exactly!"

Aloud he said nothing, but sat silent, conscious of the steady gaze of her fierce, candid eyes.

"I hadn't intended to tell you to-night," she went on. "I know you're very shy, and I'd intended to win you over little by little. Not by any feminine trickery or illusion, you understand. I'd just reveal myself. I'm sure that if you knew me, you'd love me. We're so perfectly matched," she ended, a bit impatiently. "I wish there weren't all this fuss and trouble! I wish you'd make up your mind promptly!"

"But—" he began.

"Don't answer me now, when you're in this contrary, obstinate humor. I'll wait till to-morrow evening. Now let's talk about something else."

"No!" said Andrew. "I'm going to bed. Good night!"

He went off with a quick step and a frown; but his going was not effective. It was too much like flight, and it was spoiled by the grin on Miss Franklin's face.

Alone in his room he gave up the effort to hide his alarm.

"That woman's got to go!" he cried. "I'm not going to be hounded and bothered by her like this! How am I to do any work? How can I get rid of her?"

Reflection convinced him that he could not.

"Then I'll get myself called away, and I'll stay away until—"

Until what? What was to save him? Where could he find a refuge from feminine persecution?

He went to bed, but he could not sleep. He was quite worn and haggard in the morning, and Miss Franklin observed it at the breakfast-table.

"You look awfully tired," she said. "Why don't you take a rest to-day?"

"Never was busier!" he answered hastily. "I haven't a free moment all day. Please see that I'm not disturbed."

"How am I to know which women disturb you and which ones you're—studying?" Miss Franklin asked with outrageous impudence. "Better give me a list."

He strode into his office, closed the door, and tried to resume that unfinished letter to Marian. He hadn't got well started when the bell rang and the parlor-maid ushered in little Mavis Borrowby, flushed and out of breath.

"Oh, doctor!" she cried. "Such a row! Imagine! I've had to run away! Papa is in the most awful rage!" She sank into a chair. "You see," she said, "I told Edward last night that I wouldn't marry him—ever. I said I didn't believe in marriage. And he—nasty little sneak!—ran off to papa and told him. You can imagine how papa took it, with his old-fogy ideas. He roared and stamped and swore. He wanted to know where I got such ideas from; and I said, very calmly, from you. Then he said I must never speak to you again, and all sorts of nonsense. Of course I said I *would* speak to you, and I would never, never renounce you for any one—"

"Renounce me! Really, Mavis, isn't that a bit—"

"I told him that you were the most wonderful man I'd ever seen, and that I would not give you up. But, doctor dear, where are you going to hide me? He'll be here after me any minute!"

"I'm not going to hide you at all!" cried Andrew. "It's all nonsense!"

"Oh, but you must!" she cried. "You can't be so horrible, when I've been so loyal to you."

"There's no reason for hiding, you silly child! You've done nothing wrong."

"Oh, but papa thinks so! He told me not to *dare* to see you again. He says it's all your fault that I won't marry Edward. He says you've put all sorts of awful ideas in my head. Oh, doctor! There's the door-bell now! I know it's father! Oh, don't let him get me! He says he'll send me to a convent!"

She had clutched his arm frantically and was looking into his face with brimming eyes.

"Oh, please, please hide me!" she cried. "Just till I can think of some sort of plan!"

He faltered and weakened. At last he opened the door of a clothes-closet.

"Lock the door and keep quiet," he said. "I'll see if I can get him away."

After an earnest look around to see that she had not left any trace of herself—hat, gloves, or other incriminating articles—the doctor opened his office door, and there stood Mrs. Hamilton. She looked very pale and ill.

"Just an instant!" she said, with an odd smile. "I won't keep you a minute. I only came to say good-by."

"Where are you going?" he asked kindly.

She smiled again.

"It doesn't matter. I thought if I came early, before your office hours, I might catch you alone for a few minutes; but it doesn't matter."

"But you have caught me alone," he answered cheerfully. "Sit down, Mrs. Hamilton. I'm in no hurry."

"Please don't try to deceive me," she said coldly. "I know all about that girl who came in here. That nursery governess—that Franklin person—told me in the hall. I have no claim on you, doctor. There's no reason for deceiving me. You're quite, quite free to do as you please. You won't be troubled with me again. I'm going away."

"Where?" he asked, wretchedly scenting some new and obscure trouble.

"It doesn't matter," she said again. "Nothing matters. My husband insists upon my going out to Wyoming with him at once. Of course I refused; so here I am penniless, alone in the world—"

"Your children?"

"He's going to take them. They're better without me, anyway. I'm a weak and indulgent mother. I love too intensely. That's my nature—to be intense. I give—I ask nothing, I expect nothing, I simply give and give. I'm not complaining. I only wish," she ended, with a pitiful little break in her voice, "that there were some one—just one person in the world—who cared! I'm not strong enough to stand alone. I'm not complaining. I know one can't command the heart; but for a little while I did think—"

He felt like a brute.

"Good-by!" she said, holding out her slender hand and smiling pitifully. "Good-by, my dear!"

He grasped her hand.

"Where are you going?" he demanded.

She looked at him steadily.

"Good-by!"

"No—look here! You won't do anything reckless?"

"I shall have to carry out my plans. Good-by!"

"I sha'n't let you go like this!"

"Please let go of my hand! There's some one coming!"

VII

As Mrs. Hamilton went out, there came brushing by her, bursting into the room, a stout, middle-aged man. It was Mr. Borrowby, in a terrible fury. He resembled a heavy, solid little dog. One could imagine the impact of his body against the furniture, how he might hurl himself about and always rebound unhurt. His talk was like barking, growling, and snapping, and his bloodshot eyes were fixed unwaveringly upon his enemy. He was terrific.

"Where's my girl?" he bellowed.

"Don't shout like that!" said Andrew. "I can't stand it. I'm worn out."

"I'll wear you out! Where's my girl?"

"I don't know."

"Don't lie to me, you dirty, low-lived, degenerate hound! You vile, treacherous Bolshevist!"

"You're going too far!" cried Andrew. "You'll behave yourself, or I'll put you out!"

"No, you won't! I'll have my daughter, or I'll call in the police. Don't you dare!" he shouted, shaking his fist in Andrew's face. "Don't you dare deny it! That young woman who opened the door for me told me Mavis was in here."

It occurred to the desperate Andrew that the only possible course was that of complete candor.

"What if she is?" he replied. "I'm not—"

"I know what *you* are! Didn't the girl herself tell me that since she'd known you, she could never marry? Good God! I could kill you, you scoundrel! Where is she?"

"In there," said Andrew. "I sha'n't deny it. There's nothing to be ashamed of—absolutely nothing wrong."

He was really afraid, for an instant, that the angry little dog was about to launch itself upon him. Instead, to his relief, Borrowby began to pound upon the closet door.

"Open the door!" he roared.

"No, I sha'n't!" came Mavis's calm response.

"I'll break in the door!"

"All right! Begin! There's a window in here, and I'll jump out of it and run away; and every one will see me from the street!"

In the midst of this pounding and shouting the telephone rang.

"*Keep quiet!*" Andrew roared. "Stop your infernal noise! It may be something important!"

Mr. Borrowby desisted for an instant. Andrew took up the receiver, to hear the voice of Mrs. Hamilton.

"I want to say good-by to you," she said in a calm and bitter voice. "It's the last word you will ever hear from me. This is really good-by, to you and to all the world. I have something here that will end it all, all my sufferings—"

"No!" he cried. "No! What are you thinking of?"

"Don't worry!" she said. "It is the best way, my dear!"

The doctor gave vent to such a strange and terrible howl that even Mr. Borrowby was startled.

"What is it?" asked a quiet voice beside him.

He was not surprised to see Marian there. He was past surprise.

"Mrs. Hamilton!" he explained. "Going to take poison!"

"Speak to her," whispered Marian. "Tell her you're coming at once."

He did so, and hung up the receiver.

"Now, go up-stairs and lie down, dear," said Marian. "You're worn out. I'll send your lunch up to you. Don't worry about anything. I'll manage."

"There's Mavis Borrowby shut up in the closet," he told her wearily; "and Mrs. Hamilton—and something worrying about Miss Franklin—I've forgotten just what."

"Poor boy!" she murmured. "I'm so sorry! Go on, dear, and lie down. Try not to worry."

He went up-stairs to his room and lay down on the bed, quite exhausted, trying to think, but unable to do so. A long time passed. He watched the trees moving in the April wind, and the clouds slipping across the gay blue sky.

VIII

At last Marian came, bringing a lunch-tray well laden with the proper things. She set it down on a table at the bedside, and drew up two chairs.

"Now, Andy dear!" she said in her old pleasant way. "Come on! You need food, you know. It's after three o'clock!"

He was really very hungry. He began to eat without delay, while Marian watched him indulgently.

"I telephoned to Dr. Gryce. He'll take your patients to-day," she said. "You need a rest, don't you? Miss Franklin's gone home. Mr. Borrowby took Mavis home, and left a note, apologizing for his mistake. I explained to him about your theories, you know. I sent for Mr. Hamilton,

and I stayed with his wife until he came. They had a perfectly beautiful reconciliation. They're going out to Wyoming with the children, to start a new
life; so there's nothing to trouble you, is there?"

"Marian," he said gravely, "I'll tell you all about it later on. Just now I
can't think of anything but the relief—"

The parlor-maid knocked at the door.

"There's a young gentleman from the *Daily Review*, sir," she said. "He
says the doctor promised him an interview."

"The doctor is resting—" Marian began.

Andrew sat up.

"No!" he said. "I'll see him. Bring him up, Sarah!"

"I'll go," said Marian.

"I'd rather you stayed," said Andrew. "I'd like you to hear what I'm going to say."

He was sitting up in bed, more rumpled and excited than ever, when the
young man entered. The interviewer was surprised and a little embarrassed
by the presence of a wife, because the opinions which the doctor was reputed to hold on marriage were not the sort of views that most wives like.
However—

"We thought it would be of great interest to our readers if you would give
us a few words on 'Marriage from a Man's Point of View,'" he began;
"along the lines of the address you gave before the Moral Courage Club
one afternoon last week, you know."

"I said that marriage hampered and degraded a man, didn't I? I said that
marriage was slavery for my sex—don't take that down, that's only what
I said last week. *Now*, please get this properly. I offer, as my earnest conviction, based upon experiment, that marriage is man's only safeguard.
Without its protection man could not survive. This is a woman's world,
dominated and developed by women. Every man imperatively requires the
protection of a wife. Without it, he—he would be hounded to death."

"Andrew!" murmured Marian, rather shocked.

The young man wrote it all down as faithfully as he could.

"That's all. You can enlarge on that. I suppose you would, anyway. You
might head it 'Marriage—Man's Only Hope.'"

The young man thanked the doctor, took up his hat, and left.

Andrew looked at Marian, and she smiled affectionately at him.

"I shall never know," said he, "whether you had any hand in all this, or
whether it just happened; but I'm beaten, absolutely, and you are supremely
vindicated. That's what women always do. They're able to prove a man
wrong and make him see it himself, in spite of the fact that he's right!"

THE END

Elisabeth Sanxay Holding Bibliography
(1889-1955)

NOVELS

Invincible Minnie (1920)
Rosaleen Among the Artists (1921)
Angelica (1921)
The Unlit Lamp (1922)
The Shoals of Honour (1926)
The Silk Purse (1928)
Miasma (1929)
Dark Power (1930)
The Death Wish (1934)
The Unfinished Crime (1935)
The Strange Crime in Bermuda (1937)
The Obstinate Murderer (1938; reprinted as No Harm Intended, 1939)
Who's Afraid? (1940; reprinted as Trial by Murder, 1940)
The Girl Who Had to Die (1940)
Speak of the Devil (1941; reprinted as Hostess to Murder, 1943)
Kill Joy (1942; reprinted as Murder is a Kill-Joy, 1946)
Lady Killer (1942)
The Old Battle-Ax (1943)
Net of Cobwebs (1945)
The Innocent Mrs. Duff (1946)
The Blank Wall (1947)
Miss Kelly (1947)
Too Many Bottles (1951; reprinted as The Party Was the Pay-Off, 1951)
The Virgin Huntress (1951)
Widow's Mite (1953)

STORIES/NOVELETTES

Patrick on the Mountain (*The Smart Set*, July 1920)
The Problem that Perplexed Nicholson (*The Smart Set*, Aug 1920)
Marie's View of It (*The Century Magazine*, Dec 1920)
Mollie: The Ideal Nurse (*The Century Magazine*, Jan 1921)
Angelica (*Munsey's*, May-Oct 1921)
The Married Man (*Munsey's*, Dec 1921)
The Foreign Woman (*Munsey's*, July 1922)
Hanging's Too Good for Him (*Munsey's*, Sept 1922)
Like a Leopard (*Munsey's*, Nov 1922)
Lost Luck (*The Bookman*, Dec 1922)
The Girl He Picked Up at Coney (*Metropolitan Magazine*, Feb/Mar 1923)
The Aforementioned Infant (*Munsey's*, Mar 1923)
It Seemed Reasonable (*Munsey's*, Apr 1923)
Unless Experience Be a Jewel (*The Sovereign Magazine*, Apr 1923)
Horseshoe Over the Door: Stories (*Woman's Home Companion*, May, June, July, Aug 1923)
Old Dog Tray (*Munsey's*, May 1923)
The Matador (*Munsey's*, June 1923)

A Hesitating Cinderella
   (*Munsey's*, July 1923)
The Postponed Wedding
   (*Munsey's*, Aug 1923)
With Unbowed Head (*The
   Century Magazine*, Aug 1923)
This is Life (*The Nation*, Aug 15
   1923)
The Marquis of Carabas
   (*Munsey's,* Sept 1923)
Out of the Woods (*Munsey's*, Oct
   1923)
Miss Flotsam and Mr. Jetsann
   (*The Dial*, Nov 1923)
Benedicta (*Munsey's*, Dec 1923)
Keeping the Boy at Home
   (*Woman's Home Companion*,
   Dec 1923)
Nickie and Pem (*Munsey's*, Feb
   1924)
His Remarkable Future
   (*Munsey's*, Apr 1924)
His Own People (*Munsey's*, July
   1924)
Who Is This Impossible Person?
   (*Munsey's,* Aug 1924)
Ye Gods and Little Fishes (*The
   American Magazine*, Aug 1924)
Mr. Martin Swallows the Anchor
   (*Munsey's*, Sept 1924)
Too French (*Munsey's*, Jan 1925)
The Good Little Pal (*Munsey's*,
   Apr 1925)
Flowers for Miss Riordan
   (*Munsey's*, May 1925)
Mrs. Prunes (*Woman's Home
   Companion*, May 1925)
Marionette (*The Century
   Magazine*, June 1925)
Sometimes Things Do Happen
   (*Munsey's*, June 1925)

Miss What's-Her-Name
   (*Munsey's*, July 1925)
The Long Night (*Ladies Home
   Journal*, Sept 1925)
The Wonderful Little Woman
   (*Munsey's,* Sept 1925)
As Patrick Henry Said (*Munsey's,*
   Oct 1925)
The Worst Joke in the World
   (*Munsey's*, Nov 1925)
As Is (*Munsey's*, Dec 1925)
That's Not Love (*Munsey's*, Jan
   1926)
Rosalie Gets Out of the Cage (*The
   American Magazine*, Feb 1926)
The Thing Beyond Reason
   (*Munsey's*, Feb 1926)
Dogs Always Know (*Munsey's,*
   Mar 1926)
Highfalutin' (*Munsey's*, Apr 1926)
Bonnie Wee Thing (*Munsey's,*
   May 1926)
Memory of a May Night
   (*Pictorial Review*, May 1926)
Vanity (*Munsey's*, Jun 1926)
The Compromising Letter
   (*Munsey's*, July 1926)
Miss Cigale (*Munsey's*, Aug 1926)
Blotted Out (*Munsey's,* Sept 1926)
Pale Pink Crime (*Woman's Home
   Companion*, Sept 1926)
Human Nature Unmasked
   (*Munsey's*, Oct 1926)
Chris Had Gone (*Ladies' Home
   Journal*, Nov 1926)
Home Fires (*Munsey's*, Dec 1926)
Totally Broken Reed (*Woman's
   Home Companion*, Mar 1927)
The Grateful Lunella (*The
   American Magazine*, May 1927)
The Old Ways (*Munsey's*, July
   1927)

By the Light of Day (*Munsey's*, Aug 1927)

Out for a Good Time (*Woman's Home Companion*, Oct 1927)

For Granted (*Munsey's*, Nov 1927)

Incompatibility (*Munsey's*, Dec 1927)

In Chains (*McCall's*, Dec 1927)

One Misty Night, (*The American Magazine*, Feb 1928)

Derelict (*Munsey's*, Mar 1928)

Half an Hour Late (*Woman's Home Companion*, Mar 1928)

This Road Is Closed (*The American Magazine*, Apr 1928)

Inches and Ells (*Munsey's*, June 1928)

It Is a Two-Edged Sword (*McCall's*, June 1928)

Too Late (*Liberty*, July 21 1928)

Proud and Pig-Headed (*Pictorial Review*, July 1928)

Outside the Door (*The Elks Magazine*, Oct 1928)

Hard as Nails (*Liberty*, Oct 20 1928)

Important Things (*Liberty*, Nov 17 1928)

A Dinner Date (*The American Magazine*, Jan 1929)

Vera's Superior Smile (*Pictorial Review*, Jan 1929)

Saving Up (*Liberty*, Jan 5 1929)

Flow and Ebb (*Liberty*, Jan 26 1929)

Without Benefit of Police (*Complete Stories*, Feb 1929)

The Sin of Angels (*The American Magazine*, Apr 1929; *The Grand Magazine*, Jan 1939)

Dare-Devil (*The American Magazine*, June 1929)

Little Deeds of Kindness (*Liberty*, July 6 1929)

Broken Faith (*The American Magazine*, Oct 1929; *Cassell's Magazine of Fiction*, July 1930)

Prelude (*The Delineator*, Sept 1929)

Carline (*Liberty*, Oct 12, 1929)

Rose-Leaves (*Liberty*, Jan 18 1930)

The Chain of Death (*Liberty*, May 24, May 31, Jun 7, Jun 14, Jun 21 1930)

On Condition (*The Elks Magazine*, Sept 1930)

Mrs. Herbert's Notion (*The Delineator*, Nov 1930)

The Girl in Armor (*Street & Smith's Detective Story Magazine*, Aug 8, Aug 15, Aug 22, Aug 29 1931)

Porthos (*Maclean's*, Sept 15 1931)

It's All Right for Men (*Liberty*, Oct 10 1931)

Humility (*Maclean's*, Nov 15 1931)

Brides of Crime (*Street & Smith's Detective Story Magazine*, Nov 7, Nov 14, Nov 21, Nov 28, Dec 5 1931)

The Preposterous Mrs. Manders (*Woman's Home Companion*, Mar 1932)

Hound's Bay (*Street & Smith's Detective Story Magazine*, Mar 5, Mar 12, Mar 19, Mar 26, Apr 2 1932)

Wonderful Day (*Good Housekeeping*, Jan 1933)

If It Hadn't Been for Laurel (*Liberty*, Jan 28 1933)

No Personal Calls (*Maclean's*, July 15 1933)

That Woman (*The Delineator*, Oct 1933)

Like Father, Like Son (*The Novel Magazine*, Jan 1934)

A Man Can Take It (*Collier's Weekly*, May 12 1934)

The Green Bathtub (*Collier's Weekly*, June 16 1934)

Vital Interlude (*Redbook Magazine*, July 1934)

The Last Night (*The Passing Show*, July 14 1934)

All She Could Get (*Collier's Weekly*, Sept 15 1934)

The Unfinished Crime (*Street & Smith's Detective Story Magazine*, Nov 10 1934)

"I Could Brighten Your Life!" (*The American Magazine*, Jan 1935)

The Bride Comes Home (*Cosmopolitan*, Feb 1935)

Dawn Smile (*The Strand Magazine*, Apr 1935)

The Root of Evil (*Collier's Weekly*, Apr 27 1935)

Nobody Would Listen (*Mystery*, Aug 1935)

Somebody's Cynthia (*Collier's Weekly*, Aug 3 1935; *The Passing Show*, Nov 2 1935)

It's Time Life Began! (*Redbook Magazine*, Dec 1935)

You Never Can Tell (*Collier's Weekly*, Dec 14 1935; *Grit*, June 1936)

Bermuda Murder (*Street & Smith's Detective Story Magazine*, July 1936)

Unscathed (*Ladies Home Journal*, Jan 1936)

Lost (*Redbook*, Feb 1936)

Cross Purposes (*Collier's Weekly*, May 30, 1936)

Can Do! (*Pictorial Review*, July 1936)

Scandal (*Woman's Home Companion*, July 1936)

Background (*Redbook Magazine*, Aug 1936)

Intent to Kill (*Street & Smith's Detective Story Magazine*, Sept 1936)

Night Life (*Redbook*, Sept 1936)

Murder Solicited (*Street & Smith's Detective Story Magazine*, Nov 1936)

Third Act (*Pictorial Review*, Apr 1937)

Drifting (*McCall's*, May 1937)

Wedding Day (*Cosmopolitan*, Sept 1937)

The Nicest Little Lunch (*Cosmopolitan*, Nov 1937)

Echo of a Careless Voice (*McCall's*, Jan 1938)

Illusion (*Good Housekeeping*, Aug 1938)

They Take It So Lightly! (*Cosmopolitan*, Oct 1938)

Two Passes for the Show (*Liberty*, Nov 5 1938)

So Sort of Proud (*Good Housekeeping*, Mar 1939)

Money Can't Buy It (*Liberty*, Aug 5 1939)

Open That Door (*Liberty*, Aug 26 1939)

Blonde on a Boat (*The American Magazine*, Dec 1939)

Late Date (*Cosmopolitan*, May 1940)

Proposal (*McCall's,* May 1940)

On Yonder Lea (*Good Housekeeping*, Aug 1940)

Tropical Secretary (*The American Magazine*, Feb 1941)

Tomorrow's Not Soon Enough (*McCall's*, Mar 1941)

What It Takes (*Grit*, Mar 9 1941)

Loved I Not Honor More (*Liberty*, Apr 12 1941)

The Fearful Night (*The American Magazine*, June 1941; expanded to *The Obstinate Murderer*)

Another Baby (*Woman's Home Companion*, Nov 1941)

I'll Never Forgive You (*The American Magazine*, May 1942)

Not Goodbye But Au Revoir (*McCall's,* Oct 1942)

The Kiskadee Bird (*Cosmopolitan*, 1944)

The Old Battle-Ax (1943; abridged, *Liberty,* Mar 18 1944)

Mrs. Henry Gibson (*Cosmopolitan,* Aug 1944)

Bait for a Killer (*Collier's Weekly,* Sep 30 1944, as "The Blue Envelope"; *The Saint Mystery Magazine,* Mar 1959; *The Saint Detective Magazine* [Australia], Nov 1959; *The Saint Mystery Magazine* [UK], Oct 1960)

The Unbelievable Baroness (*The American Magazine*, 1945)

The Net of Cobwebs (*Collier's Weekly,* Jan 6, 13 & 20, 1945)

Ten-Cent Wedding Ring (*Cosmopolitan,* Feb 1945)

Funny Kind of Love (as by Elizabeth Saxanay Holding, *Boston Sunday Globe Magazine*, Nov 11 1945)

Farewell to a Corpse (*Mystery Book Magazine*, Oct 1946)

The Other Mrs. Minor (*Cosmopolitan*, Sept, Oct, Nov 1946)

"Be Careful, Mrs. Williams" (*Cosmopolitan*, July 1947)

Second Marriage (*Cosmopolitan*, Apr 1948)

The Bird of Time (*Cosmopolitan*, May 1948)

The Stranger in the Car (*American Magazine*, July 1949)

People Do Fall Downstairs (*Ellery Queen's Mystery Magazine*, Aug 1947; *Ellery Queen's Mystery Magazine* [Australia], Aug 1949)

Friday, the Nineteenth (*The Magazine of Fantasy and Science Fiction*, Summer 1950)

The Legacy (*Liberty*, Dec 1950)

La Signora from Brooklyn (*Cosmopolitan*, Dec 1951)

Farewell, Big Sister (*Ellery Queen's Mystery Magazine*, July 1952; hardboiled satire)

The Death Wish (*Cosmopolitan*, Feb 1953)

Most Audacious Crime (*Nero Wolfe Mystery Magazine*, Jan 1954)

Shadow of Wings (*The Magazine of Fantasy and Science Fiction*, July 1954)

Glitter of Diamonds (*Ellery Queen's Mystery Magazine*, Mar 1955; *Ellery Queen's Mystery Magazine* [Australia], May 1955)

The Strange Children (*The Magazine of Fantasy and Science Fiction*, Aug 1955)

Very, Very Dark Mink (*The Saint Detective Magazine*, Dec 1956; *The Saint Detective Magazine* [UK], Oct 1957)

The Darling Doctor (*Alfred Hitchcock's Mystery Magazine*, Mar 1957)

Game for Four Players (*Alfred Hitchcock's Mystery Magazine*, June 1958)

The Blank Wall (*Alfred Hitchcock Presents: My Favorites in Suspense*, 1959)

www.ingramcontent.com/pod-product-compliance
Lightning Source LLC
Chambersburg PA
CBHW071729190726
48292CB00003B/674